Wendy Robertson has lived and worked in the north-east of England for most of her life. Before moving to full-time writing she worked in teaching and in Teacher Education, whilst publishing some short fiction and, in the 1970s, writing a regular column for the *Northern Echo*. Wendy has two grown-up children and lives in Bishop Auckland, County Durham, with her husband.

Praise for Wendy Robertson's novels:
'A lovely book' *Woman's Realm*
'An intense and moving story' *Today*
'A rich fruitcake of well-drawn characters'
Northern Echo

Children of the Storm

Wendy Robertson

HEADLINE

First published in hardback in 1997 by
HEADLINE BOOK PUBLISHING

First published in paperback in 1998 by
HEADLINE BOOK PUBLISHING

10 9 8 7 6 5 4 3

'Warning to Children' by Robert Graves
is taken from *The Centenary Selected Poems*,
edited by Patrick Quinn, published by
Carcanet Press, 1995. Reprinted with
permission of Carcanet Press.

ISBN 0 7472 5184 3

Typeset by Palimpsest Book Production Limited,
Polmont, Stirlingshire
Printed and bound in Great Britain by
Clays Ltd, St Ives plc

HEADLINE BOOK PUBLISHING
A division of Hodder Headline PLC
338 Euston Road
London NW1 3BH

For Virginia H, who also likes the music hall

The Priorton Novels

Livesay Woods
Susanah & Jonty camp here

beck

river

stream

Old Morven
(ancient pit village)
Shona works at the pit

Swanby
(hamlet with old mill)
Kitty Rainbow works here

Purley Hall
William Scorton works here

New Morven
(ironworking village)
Farrells live here
Montagues live here

Ishmael finds Kitty Rainbow here

Banville Hall
Michael, Jonty & Tom make their attack here

railway

Shotwell
(new township serving the railway industry)
The McNaughtons are kingpins here

To Darlington

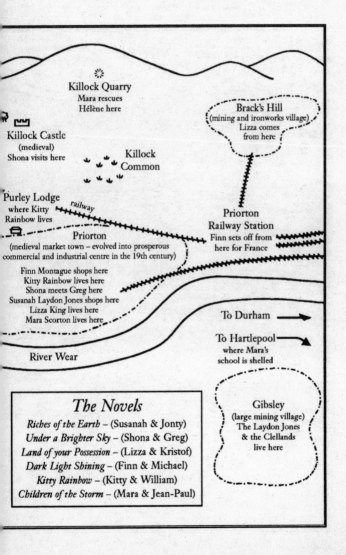

Killock Quarry
Mara rescues
Hélène here

Brack's Hill
(mining and ironworks village)
Lizza comes
from here

Killock Castle
(medieval)
Shona visits here

Killock
Common

Purley Lodge
where Kitty
Rainbow lives

railway

Priorton
Railway Station
Finn sets off from
here for France

Priorton
(medieval market town – evolved into prosperous
commercial and industrial centre in the 19th century)

Finn Montague shops here
Kitty Rainbow lives here
Shona meets Greg here
Susanah Laydon Jones shops here
Lizza King lives here
Mara Scorton lives here

To Durham ➡

To Hartlepool ➡
where Mara's
school is shelled

River Wear

Gibsley
(large mining village)
The Laydon Jones
& the Clellands
live here

The Novels

Riches of the Earth – (Susanah & Jonty)
Under a Brighter Sky – (Shona & Greg)
Land of your Possession – (Lizza & Kristof)
Dark Light Shining – (Finn & Michael)
Kitty Rainbow – (Kitty & William)
Children of the Storm – (Mara & Jean-Paul)

PART ONE

Distinguished Conduct

1914

And, if he then should dare to think
Of the fewness, muchness, rareness,
Greatness of this endless only
Precious world in which he says
He lives – he then unties the string.

Robert Graves, 'Warning to Children'

PART FOUR

Distinguished Conduct

1914

1

A Bombardment and an Initiation

Turning the corner, Mara Scorton was nearly swept off her feet by the forward rush of people and the clanking bustle which dominated the old harbour street. Mara had been in Hartlepool for three months now, and had still not quite accustomed herself to the dense activity of the port, and the press of busy people and unlikely objects. And she still caught her breath with excitement at the clatter of a hundred hooves, the slap of water on wood and steel, the click of the rigging poking up from scores of jostling boats, and the guttural shouts of an army of workmen – the cacophony of noises tearing holes in the dawn blanket of the gloomy December day.

Mara rummaged in her satchel and brought out a handkerchief to filter the stink of the rank detritus of a thousand catches, mingling with the fresher salt-laden savour of today's fish and the sooty tang of a thousand chimneys. She wrinkled her nose as, with some delicacy, she picked her way along the cobbled street.

She flinched as a sharp gust of easterly wind cut through the grown-up bun which graced her neck these days. Her brother Tommy had roared with laughter at the sight of her with the heavy lump of hair stuck on the back of her head, instead of her usual mane of hair flowing wild and free.

The teasing about the bun was stopped with unaccustomed severity by their mother, Kitty. 'It's time the child looked grown-up, Tommy.' Kitty Rainbow had stroked an escaping curl behind Mara's ear. 'Else how can she stand in front of a class of children and be Teacher – at her age?'

'She's too young anyway,' said Tommy sulkily. 'Fifteen's ridiculous for a teacher.'

'Pupil-teacher,' corrected Mara, turning this way and that, surveying her strange mirror-self. 'An apprentice. I'm to learn how to do it. Mr Clelland says I'll take to it like a duck to water.'

'He said she was very clever,' nodded Kitty.

'It's stupid. You could have stayed at school yourself, Mara, gone to Priorton High School, even Bracks Hill Higher Elementary. I hear they do French there.'

'You know they wouldn't have had me, Tommy. Never learned to sit still long enough.' Rheumatic fever at the age of seven had left Mara with St Vitus' Dance, which had caused her dismissal, in the midst of anarchic laughter, from several classrooms.

In the end, her education had been an almost random patchwork of opportunity and insight. Her mother Kitty had taught her herself, guiding her reading with books of all kinds, ranging from manufacturers' catalogues left over from her shop, to biographies and novels bought cheap from the stock of a travelling library. Mara's father had taught her ancient history, geography and Latin, replicating his own long-ago boarding-school curriculum. A teacher from the town, Mr Clelland, was brought in one evening a week to teach her modern history and mathematics.

In this way, Mara had been educated at home, reading voraciously and writing at length in her spiky script. However, her brief experience of school had left an indelible mark; her favourite game had always been playing Teacher with a class consisting of her dogs and cats, her dolls and pet rabbits.

'Anyway, Tommy,' Mara had thumped his shoulder, energetically refuting his criticism, 'there's this war. Think of our Leonora out in Russia. She's doing *her* war effort there – I'm

4

doing mine here.' For despite her lack of experience, Mr Clelland had pulled some very powerful strings to get young Mara placed as a pupil-teacher.

Now, in Hartlepool, on her way to that very school, Mara smiled grimly as she hurried along. She had not known then about the ill-lit, crowded classrooms, the smell of unwashed bodies and the way unshod feet shone purplish-blue in the cold winter light. And, unschooled herself, Mara was astonished at the way the Head Master, Mr Clonmel, ruled his little world like an emperor, with powers just short of death and imprisonment over his subjects.

Minutes later, she arrived at the school. Mr Clonmel was already there in the central hall, fussing like a prancing cockerel around Joseph Bly, the handyman. Mr Clonmel was reminding Joseph, in precise tones, not to be too profligate with the coal in the classroom stoves. Money, after all, did not grow on trees. Mr Bly surely was aware of that?

Standing discreetly behind an elaborate cast-iron column, Mara watched as Joe Bly put down his coal hod, took off his battered cap, and ran his hands through his greasy, greyish-red hair. 'Why, Mr Clonmel,' he said with grave respect, 'it's true money doesn't grow on trees, I know that well enough. But isn't it true that coal itself grows on trees, in a manner of speaking, like? Isn't there a chart on young Miss Scorton's wall showing how coal comes from trees? Isn't the ground beneath our feet, from here to Carlisle, fathoms deep in coal? And, with respect, Mr Clonmel, this being the case, there seems little call to begrudge the bairns a bit of warmth on a cold December morning, does there?'

Mr Clonmel's cheeks, normally yellow, as yellow as old apples, flushed with high colour. He folded his arms. 'It is gratifying, Mr Bly, that you yourself are learning, as you pursue your labour about the school. However, I must remind you that the justly earned wages and emoluments of the miners and managers, coal merchants and coal-men, preclude us from a free access to the bounty you describe. In addition, may I remind you that the country is at war? The coal is needed so that the finest craftsmen in the world may reverse the classical legend and hammer ploughshares back into swords.' He smiled thinly. 'There will be shortages, you may be sure. So I would adjure you, Mr Bly, to husband our resources with great care, else these *bairns*, as you call them, will be shivering in the March winds. I should tell you also that when I require a lecture on the petrified forest I will attend one at Durham University.'

Joe replaced his cap and touched the peak. Then, with an insolent lift of the elbow, he threw the rest of the hod of coal into the gaping mouth of the iron stove in the main hall. With an excessive show of care, he replaced the tall guard. 'Right you are, Mr Clonmel,' he said meekly.

Mara remained lurking behind her column, as the head teacher strode across the floor of the central hall and upstairs to his eyrie in the rafters of the building. Mr Clonmel stayed on Mara's mind as she made her way to her classroom. She hung up her coat and hat on the peg beside the door and, taking up her chalk, started setting out the first exercise of the day up on the board.

She found him a good enough man, Mr Clonmel. He took her training as a pupil-teacher very seriously. His early doubts about her extreme youth had been resolved by her evident quick intelligence. He tutted only slightly at her lack of formal schooling, saying if she 'stuck in . . . stuck in', she would make up those years when she was forced to lie abed after rheumatic fever, when schools sent her home, blaming her fidgeting and choreic jumping for the destruction of the calm of their classrooms.

Mr Clonmel observed that Miss Scorton was obviously very intelligent. One could discern that from her talk. So they would set about repairing the damage, at the same time as initiating her into the mysteries of the teacher's craft and the arcane habits of the classroom. So long as she was prepared *to stick in*, he said firmly, all was not lost. 'If you stick in, Miss

Scorton, you may well matriculate properly in the end then, given that you show the aptitude, you can go to Training College and enter this sacred profession . . .'

Once, he had enquired about her recovery from the debilitating and anti-social effects of St Vitus' Dance. She had shaken her head then, and said, 'It's a mystery to the doctors, Mr Clonmel. A complete mystery.'

She did not feel able to tell him that it had coincided with the onset of her monthly show. Mara had more than one reason to welcome the fact of becoming a woman. But for now, 'being a woman' meant toiling over grammar exercises and algebra, preparing for her own examinations, as well as teaching the children in her charge.

She was grateful to Mr Clonmel for all his support, but at the same time she condemned him for being severe to the point of cruelty with the pupils. His heavy stick would be taken from a very public hook in the large hall for the slightest misdemeanour. Wriggling during hands-on-head time and whispering during arithmetic were elevated in this school to the status of major crimes. 'We are holding back tigers, Miss Scorton, seated astride a volcano,' he would say, his tone disconcertingly mild.

The frightened awe which he imposed on the children sometimes made Mara resentful on their behalf, even though she had to admit that this was the reason the forty-five seven-year-olds in her class were usually quiet and obedient. The children kept one eye, as they worked, on the rattling glass partition, through which the keen wind of Mr Clonmel's displeasure could so easily blow.

Mara was very aware that she herself was under surveillance through that same partition. Mr Clonmel had intimated early on that he did not expect his teachers to be sitting on their platforms at their high desks. They were to be down with the children, supervising, helping, discovering just where the mistakes were being made and what was required for each individual child in terms of learning and teaching.

Mara, only a degree less terrified of him than were the children, worked assiduously at her own lessons, and her own preparation and marking, all of which were scored by Mr Clonmel as if they were a Standard Three exercise.

She smiled ruefully to herself. Being a teacher – certainly being a pupil-teacher – in no way resembled those games she had played in her sickroom, with her dolls and toy animals all in compliant rows. Being a teacher then had been more the pleasing experience of sitting at the front, being the boss, and ordering other creatures' lives.

Now she knew different. Teaching was all about standing beside and bending over small children and their desks for hours on end during the day. Then, with tired legs and a stiff back, working long hours over her own and the children's books every night. It was about falling into her narrow bed, exhausted, ready to get up again at six-thirty, tumbling out of the house on the cliff by seven-thirty, then trudging along to school to get her classroom ready for the day's onslaught.

'Ah! Miss Scorton!'

She jumped as Clonmel's brisk voice belled out to her from the classroom doorway. He must have returned down the stairs on his quiet feet.

'Mr Clonmel?' She stood defensively with her back to the blackboard. 'Good morning.'

'It is pleasing to see you getting into school in such good time, Miss Scorton. And I note that your blackboard work is so much improved during these weeks. Good preparation is all.'

She smiled nervously. 'So you always say, Mr Clonmel.'

The most difficult thing about this man was that he never stopped teaching. She had a sudden vision of him over the supper table, lecturing his wife on the properties of cocoa.

'You find your lodgings good, at the Misses Clarence house on the cliff, Miss Scorton?'

'Yes, thank you, Mr Clonmel. They're most welcoming.' In fact, the Misses Clarence, one fat, one thin, were like a pair of genteel mice. The food they gave her was shop-bought and unsustaining; the house was freezing.

Clonmel rubbed his narrow hands. 'Good, good. The Misses Clarence have always taken excellent care of those of our pupil-teachers who travel a distance. Miss Heliotrope Clarence in particular is a great benefactress to the town. You will know that?'

Mara stayed silent. She did not like fat, complacent Heliotrope Clarence, who sat on her skinny sister like a fluffy mother hen. The silence, which Mr Clonmel frequently used as a teaching tool, lay heavily on Mara. She bore it for as long as she could and then burst into speech. 'It's so dramatic up there on the cliff, Mr Clonmel. Waking up to the rush of the waves and the cry of the seagulls. And there are the ships, great and small, to watch coming in and out of the port. Though, to be honest, with all the mist this morning it was impossible to see anything.'

'Ah! *Cumulus congests*, or more properly *stratocumulus*,' he said. 'And a gathering of *low stratus* cloud in the east, I think. Very portentous.' He paused. 'So, having been with us for three months, Miss Scorton, do you miss your home ground?'

She flushed. The eleven weeks since she had come here to the coast had seemed very long. It was the first time she had been away from home, after a life spent half in a sickbed and half running wild in the hills and woods of County Durham. Her heart ached for it all. The letters from her mother there at home, and sister Leonora away now in Russia, were no substitute for their cheerful voices, their warm scented presence. The chilly house on the cliff was no substitute for the sunny house in Weardale, with its wide corridors and high windows.

'The Misses Clarence make me very welcome, Mr Clonmel. But I miss my family, my sister particularly.'

'And is your sister at school, still?'

'No. No, Mr Clonmel. Leonora's much older than me. At

first she helped our mother with the shop. Did you know she has a shop? Rainbow and Daughter, it's called. But then our Leonora went off to Russia to teach a girl to speak English, so there's no daughter in the shops now. Leonora writes me wonderful letters. Now she's training for their Red Cross and will nurse on the Front there . . .'

He put up a hand, stemming the flow of embarrassing confidence. 'That is very laudable. I have to say this.'

'Anyway I must admit that I miss the hills,' Mara said wistfully.

'Ah yes. It is very different there, is it not? The lift in the land. *The water running by,* as the great hymn says. Even with the pit heads grinding away in the midst of all the green, and the coke ovens smoking away, South Durham can be very beautiful.'

She looked at him in surprise. 'You know South Durham, Mr Clonmel?'

He laughed hoarsely and pulled down his snowy cuffs. 'Born and bred in those parts, Miss Scorton. It is my old stamping ground, as you might say. My own father delved for coal in many of those mines.' The head teacher watched her through narrow eyes. 'Mr Clelland, who is your sponsor in this post, was a young comrade of mine. A man of great conscience. Is it not through him that you come to be in my school? Certainly his recommendations weighed against your . . . unconventional . . . educational experience.'

Mara nodded, her cheeks flushed with the honour of his confidence. The conscientious Mr Clelland had taught her at home, had built up her confidence and had invited her to his classroom to get the feeling of being a teacher, to see if she liked it.

'Yes, he was always very kind to me, Mr Clelland,' she said softly. 'I didn't know this, though, about you coming from over there, Mr Clonmel. About your father and the pits and all that.'

'You are surprised my father was a humble pitman? I take

pride in that fact, Miss Scorton, as did he. His endeavours gave me my chance in life, a fact which I honour each night in my prayers. Thus I stand before my pupils, Miss Scorton, however indigent they may be, I stand before them as a living example of the benefits of education. It will be different for you. I know that you yourself are from a prominent family . . .'

She was aware that somehow this was a criticism. She interrupted him. 'I'm not certain what you mean, Mr Clonmel. I too take pride in my parentage. My mother has a shop now, but she started with nothing, sewing sleeves and selling them for pennies. And my father is a clockmaker, whose father was a clockmaker before him. My other grandfather was a fighter. A pugilist in the boxing ring . . .'

Mara hesitated. She couldn't tell him that her parents were defined by another thing, in narrow Priorton society. In all their long relationship, which spanned twenty-five years, her parents had not troubled themselves to marry in any church or chapel. Perhaps Mr Clonmel would not take that as a further qualification for ordinariness.

He was nodding now, a slight smile on his face. 'Then you too are an example to our children, Miss Scorton.'

She struggled to think well of all this, but was uncomfortable again about how he turned even this fascinating idea into a boring lecture. She was relieved of the responsibility of answering by a heavy rumble in the direction of the harbour.

Mr Clonmel turned his head. 'Guns,' he said. 'The soldiers in the battery must be practising.'

She was just glancing past him, looking for some means of escape, when the earth beneath her seemed to ripple like thrown silk and the whole building shuddered like a restive horse. For a second, everything, even the dust in the air, seemed to be suspended. Then there was a great creaking and groaning of wood; every pane of glass in the partition cracked like a rifle.

11

Then everything went black.

When she came to, Mara found she had been flung into Mr Clonmel's arms. She could smell his tobacco, the cheesy scent of his tweed jacket. Embarrassed, she fought to loosen his grasping hands. 'Mr Clonmel!'

There was no reply. Desperately she pulled herself out of his frozen clasp and he fell away from her, insensate. The shriek of bursting shells pierced the fabric of her brain. She struggled to her feet and looked at the crumpled figure on the floor. She leaned over, then recoiled from the mass of blood and brain matter spilling from the back of his head.

'Let's at him, Miss Scorton. Give us a see.'

She looked up as the soot-covered figure of Joe Bly moved towards her, crunching over broken glass. He knelt down opposite her and put a blackened hand on Mr Clonmel's scrawny white neck. 'Is he dead, Mr Bly?'

Joe shook his head slowly. 'Nothing so sure, Miss Scorton. Dead as a doornail. Seen a few like that in Africa, fighting them Boers.'

Mara's skin felt bone dry, as though it had been scoured. She was conscious now of a great booming noise which beat into her ears and cut for a second through the creaks and crashes of the collapsing school. She peered into the dusty space around her. Her classroom no longer existed. It was open to the sky, spars of the roof timbers sticking up like ribs. Grey slabs of cut stone were scattered on the desks, a large piece of coping stone crouched on the top of a cupboard like an animal.

Joe leaned across Mr Clonmel's body and pulled a great shard of glass from her hair. 'An' you've had a close shave yersel', lassie.' He shook his head. 'Not old enough to be away from yer Mammy yersel', bairn that you are.'

Mara hauled herself to her feet and clambered across a fallen desk to the place where the window had been. She peered at the turmoil outside. 'What is it, Mr Bly? Bombs?'

He came to stand beside her and shouted into her ear

over the noise. 'Must be them bliddy Germans, beg your pardon, miss. Can you hear our batteries, rattling out between the booms? They are firing out to sea. They'll have a job missing the lighthouse. The devils're bombarding us, if I'm not mistaken.'

'German ships?'

'Well, lassie, I sincerely hope they're not our own ships. Can't think what the British Navy has against poor old Hartlepool.'

'The Germans here? On our beaches?' She could hear her own voice, high-pitched against the noise, sounding more like that of a child than a young woman of fifteen years, who yesterday had been teaching forty-five seven-year-olds.

'What d'yer think the batteries're for, miss? To watch out for the Hun, that's what. Let's just hope our lads're giving those buggers Old Harry and managing to miss the lighthouse.'

As suddenly as it had started, the clamour ceased. All Mara could hear was the heavy ticking of the old school clock, still clinging for dear life to a fragment of wall. As they watched, the fog rolled in towards the shore on the tips of the waves and joined with the dense clouds of rising dust thrown up by the collapsing buildings. In her head she could hear Mr Clonmel sounding off about *cumulus nimbus*. She turned her head quickly, but the Head Master's body was still slumped, the blood still red. She began to thread her way through the debris towards him, Joe picking his way behind her.

'We'll have to get him out of here,' said Mara, reaching for Mr Clonmel's ankles. 'Could you take his shoulders, Mr Bly? The building'll fall down on us any minute.'

'Nothing can help him now, lassie,' said Joe. ''Cept a prayer, mebbe, him being a big Christian.'

'Come on, Mr Bly. Come on!' Suddenly the voice in her own ears no longer sounded child-like, but brisk. She sounded like her sister Leonora. 'We can say the 23rd Psalm as we carry him out, if you like. There'll be not a shred of him left if you leave him here. Not a shred.'

The jewelled icons seemed to glow from within, reaching out to the flickering candles, whose translucent flames danced with their reflection in two elaborately designed silver bowls, one of which held holy water; the other was heaped with small crosses the colour of blood.

Leonora Rainbow flexed her toes inside her boots and concentrated on keeping her hands lying together like doves in their prayer-like attitude. She resisted the temptation to smooth down her grey dress and white apron, or to tuck a wandering curl under the white veil. The other fifteen nurses, all much younger than Leonora, stood as still and rapt as the icons around the walls, their eyes glued to the back of the gold-clad priest as he made his way to the altar.

The perfume of incense wafted across and made Leonora's nose itch. The breath of the priest iced on the air as he made the Signs of the Cross. Leonora was used to these elaborate rituals, having quite regularly attended services with the Poliakovs. In fact, her young friend Lucette Poliakova was here, first in the line of young nurses waiting for the priest's benediction.

Suddenly, the dark jewel light and the heavy incense began to pick away at an old sore of guilt in Leonora, making her think of Mr Vaux, the lay preacher back at home. Mr Vaux had always interpreted any use of the 'base senses' in the service of God as the subtle and seductive work of the devil. What would he have made of the seductive brilliance of the icons and the sultry scents hanging in the air?

Now the priest was turning to face them, causing a ripple of indrawn breath, a rustling of feet from the congregation as he held out his jewelled crucifix to full view. Then very slowly he nodded to Lucette Poliakova, standing with uncharacteristic patience at the end of the line. In a rustle and flutter of long skirt and veil, she and the three young women beside her

14

paced forward and knelt at the altar. The priest blessed the heap of red crosses on the silver salver, then, having asked the name of each girl, blessed her, presented her with a red cross and offered her his crucifix to kiss.

After that four more nurses went forward, then four more. Leonora was part of the last group, relieved that, apart from transforming her name instantly to *Leonya*, the priest commented neither on her foreign accent nor her foreign demeanour. She bent her head to the rich elaboration of his benediction. 'To thee *Leonya*, child of God, servant of the Most High, is given this token of faith, of hope, of charity.'

She swayed forward slightly, drunk with feeling, as his voice whirled up with the incense to the high decorated ceiling. The actual words became meaningless, even more foreign, as she thought of her own home half a world away, and the bare little chapel where she had knelt as a child; where she had put her hands together for the first time and felt intoxicated with the mysterious torrent of alien adult words.

Now she shook her head and took a deep breath, forcing herself to concentrate.

'. . . thou shalt tend the sick, the wounded, the needy; with words of comfort shalt thou cheer them.'

She moved back to her place, exchanging delighted smiles with Lucette as she passed her. It was right to do this thing. She felt it in her bones.

By August this year, when war had been declared, Leonora had been in Russia for more than a year, working as a language governess for Lucette Poliakova.

Unlike her non-existent English, young Lucette's French was immaculate. It was the second language of her father, who was half-Polish; his first wife, Lucette's mother, had been French. This first Madame Poliakova had died when Lucette was seven. Monsieur Poliakov had mourned her with operatic bitterness for two years then took to himself a much more robust lady from Kiev. Within five years this wife had borne him five equally robust sons. These she ruled with an

15

iron rod and the help of a *babushka* who had travelled with her from the Ukraine.

The new Madame Poliakova – for Monsieur Poliakov preferred to retain the French style of address – was rather nervous of the fine-bred coltishness of her stepdaughter Lucette, and left her to the varied ministrations of maids and governesses. Lucette had used up several English governesses before the arrival of Leonora. These admirable creatures all failed to teach the girl English for one simple reason: being cultivated women, although they spoke no Russian, they all spoke more or less fluent French. With them, Lucette simply insisted on speaking French or Russian. She also put rats in their beds and salt in their jellies.

These stubborn ploys did not work with Leonora Scorton. Although clever and very articulate, she had been educated at home, and (the mere daughter of a shopkeeper and the granddaughter of a boxer) she spoke neither French nor Russian. However, she could match Lucette blow for blow in terms of stubbornness. After a few hard battles, some of them bruisingly physical, Leonora got Lucette to teach her some Russian in exchange for some of the boxing moves she had learned from her grandfather. In the end, Lucette had to learn some English phrases to get Russian into what she called the Englishwoman's 'thick skull'.

Monsieur Poliakov, no mean negotiator himself in the world of international trade and commerce, stood back observing this, then gave Leonora a rise in pay.

In the process, despite being Lucette's senior by eighteen years, Leonora and her pupil had become close friends. When war broke out, they had trained at Princess Golitzin's hospital, then qualified as Red Cross nurses. To Leonora's regret they were about to part company soon; M. Poliakov drew the line at allowing his beloved Lucette to witness the depredations of nursing at the Front. She was to stay in Moscow and work on at Princess Golitzin's hospital, where wounded soldiers home from the Front were cared for. This would be sufficient. Work

16

like this was just as necessary, declared M. Poliakov, for the great campaign of beating the Kaiser and his battalions.

Lucette, furious at being deprived of the glamour of a posting to the Front, had thrown chairs and smashed priceless china, but her father had remained adamant. He put a hand on her shoulder.

'We cannot prevent Leonora, our English daughter, from helping her poor Russian brothers. That is her decision. But you, my darling Lucette, are all I have left of your blessed mother. Not even for Mother Russia will I throw you into that furnace.'

Now, here in the cathedral, M. Poliakov was weeping with the rest of the congregation as the graceful line of nurses, the proud insignia of the Red Cross pinned to their breasts, were making their way through the murmuring crowd to the great arched door.

Standing in the shadow of that door, a tall man in high boots and a shaggy hat was carefully scrutinising each veiled face. Suddenly Leonora's hands were grabbed and she was pulled against a great chest in a bear-hug which brought with it the smells of snow and tallow candles, of pine forests and tobacco. She struggled to free herself and stood back to identify her assailant.

'Leonora! Leonora! Leo!' The voice that clipped its way through the massive beard was English and she knew it as well as she knew her own reflection in the mirror.

She drew closer to peer into the man's face in the pearly half-light which strayed into the cathedral from the snowy square outside. Now she could make out, in the gap between the straggling silver fox of his hat, and his bushy black beard, two glitteringly pale blue eyes, and eyebrows which were raised in an achingly familiar fashion.

'Samuel!' She finally got the word out. 'What in heaven's name are you doing here?'

2

Rescue

Mara teased out the fragments of plaster which had snagged themselves in Miss Pansy Clarence's once crisp lace curtains. Their former curd-cream perfection was now filmed with a grey slime of dust soaked in the water still dripping from a burst water-pipe. Miss Pansy, the younger Clarence sister, had been in charge of the fabric and function of the house on the cliff, which was kept as clean and coldly elegant as a first-class clinic.

The older sister, Heliotrope, was deeply involved in the affairs of the town, being on a chapel committee, a boot committee and the board of an orphanage. It seemed to Mara that the senior Miss Clarence, so very busy in the outside world, did not trouble herself with the affairs of the house, apart from appearing to keep a tight rein on the finances, and indulging her charitable instinct for waifs and strays by thrusting them into the apparently nervous care of her younger sister.

The Clarence sisters had been truly devoted to each other: a chill passion only occasionally expressed by a slightly warmer word, or the thin hand of the younger Miss Clarence pressed on her sister's plump shoulder. To Mara the sisters were like a married couple, in unspoken communion, complete in themselves and excluding outsiders. Unlike spinster ladies of Mara's acquaintance back in Priorton, who wore their single state like a wound, the Misses Clarence were entirely self-sufficient.

It had taken these importunate German battleships to break

19

that self-sufficiency. Here in the middle of the muttering crowd crouched Miss Pansy, on her narrow knees beside the inert bulky shape of the elder Miss Clarence. Her fluttering fingers dabbed and patted her sister's shrouded shoulder; she was muttering wildly. 'Now lettest Thou Thy servant depart in peace, Lord . . . Allow only this, Dear Lord . . . Don't forget now, Lord, her name was Heliotrope Clarence. Beautiful when young, Lord, truly beautiful. Much sought after. And good, too. A virtuous woman. She helped the poor, ask anyone round here. Now lettest Thou . . .'

Miss Pansy's voice, mumbling, murmuring on and on, began to enlarge itself and boom its way into Mara's ears, violating them just as painfully as the German cannon two hours earlier. She clapped her hands over her ears and began to run along the cliff road, passing clusters of worried people who hovered around houses, churches and shops: the buildings were still occasionally belching dust, their roofs open to the sky, their walls still creaking and falling.

She turned a corner by one of the shipyards and nearly tripped over a man in working clothes. He was kneeling by another man who was lying white and still in the road, bleeding from the mouth. Behind him stood a much younger man nervously clutching and unclutching his cap.

The man on the ground croaked something, but the man tending him shook his head. 'Ah canna mak out a word he's sayin', Tadger,' he said.

'The gadgie's a Frenchie,' said the younger man. 'Ah seen him down the dock, unloadin', working like fury. The lads telt us he wus a Frenchie, like.'

'That's what he's talking,' said Mara. 'French.'

'D'yer ken that crack, hinney?' said the old man. 'A bairn like you?'

'I'm nearly sixteen,' said Mara. 'And my brother Samuel learned me some French from when I was ten. He lived in France once.' She bent down and put an ear to the painfully moving, bloody mouth.

'*Mes enfants,*' the man was mouthing, his throat gargling. '*Dîtes à mes enfants, Mademoiselle . . .*' With an enormous effort he flapped one hand up towards his breast pocket. Then he fell back. A gleam of winter light pierced the dusty gloom and reflected dully on the rolled-up whites of his eyes.

Mara glanced up at the other men, then awkwardly put her hand into the Frenchman's pocket. She pulled out a bulky creased package, sealed but unposted. She peered at it. 'It's addressed to Bridge Street, Priorton. I know Priorton – I come from there. It's made out to J.P. and H. Derancourt. French names. *Mes enfants*. That's what he said. To tell his children.'

'Can yer dee that, hinney? Tell the poor feller's children?' said the man called Tadger. 'It's like Bedlam here, no tellin' if owt'll get done at all in this hullabaloo.'

'I can . . . I could.' She glanced out to sea, where the fog had rolled down once more and the water had returned to its sullen grey neutral state. She thought of Mr Clonmel and her lip trembled. 'They wouldn't want me here, in the middle of all this, would they? The children are safe, even though the school's in ruins.'

'Who's they, hinney?' said the older man.

'My mother and my father.'

'Nivver in the world,' said Tadger. 'I'd not want no bairn of mine on this coast in these times.'

'Aye,' said the other. 'No tellin' when them German wolves'll be prowling down this coast again.'

'Our Navy lads will have got 'em,' asserted Tadger.

'Ah dinnet knaa about that, son. They stealed away like thieves in the night, them Huns. Firin' on churches and women and children then stealin' off like thieves in the night.' The older man paused. 'No sayin' when they'll be back like.' He bent down again and closed the Frenchman's eyes. 'We'll look after this one, hinney. You get that package ter the feller's kin. Give him his last wish, eh? An' get outta here yersel'.'

Mara turned and trudged slowly back up the cliff road,

clutching the package to her chest and concentrating on the thought of home, her little, lively mother and her sweet, grave father.

Outside the house stood the undertaker's wagon, a neat boy in a black cap holding the head of a horse. Miss Pansy was shouting, 'No! No! The hospital! She should go to the hospital! The doctors there know her. They'll make her better. She worked for their charity.' She was wrestling for possession of her sister's body with two undertaker's men in dusty bowler hats, who were trying to load it into the wagon, which already contained three anonymous lumpy shrouded shapes.

'No, miss,' said the taller undertaker firmly. 'She has to come with us.'

Mara took Miss Pansy's shoulder and pulled her back. Miss Pansy clutched at the man's sleeve. 'Then I'll come with her. She's my sister, you know,' she gabbled. 'Miss Heliotrope Clarence.'

With a final heave the man finally got the shrouded form straight in his wagon. 'The minister's there at the mortuary chapel, Miss Clarence, waiting for these poor souls. Why don't you make your way down there afterwards?' He was weary with his business, but there was still a thread of kindness in his voice. He glanced at Mara. 'Can you get Miss Clarence a coat or sommat, miss? She'll get a death o' cold, out here on a cold winter morning.'

That was a strange turn of phrase on this particular morning. Mara glanced at him sharply, but there was no irony in his gaze. She looked back at the house. The parlour had been excavated from the house like a wrenched tooth. The ceiling was hanging down, the plaster laths hanging like a ragged fringe from the roof guttering. A corner of the parlour, still in one piece, protected the massive bureau where Miss Clarence senior wrote her many letters, and her committee minutes, in her immaculate copperplate hand.

The rest of the house was intact.

Mara hung onto Miss Pansy's elbow. 'Come on, Miss

Pansy. We'll make a cup of tea, then we can get our coats on and go down to the mortuary chapel to see the minister.'

The kitchen, though covered to the last hanging pan with dust, was eerily ordinary. The fire in the range still flared merrily and the kettle steamed lazily to one side of it. Mara settled Miss Pansy in the windsor chair and went through the scullery to scrounge in the pantry for tea. She paused a second to stare at the heavily-laden pantry shelves. Row upon row of jars and pots, tins and packages met her eye. She smiled briefly, thinking of the meagreness of her own meals at the sisters' table. Somebody had been fed from this bounty, and it certainly wasn't her.

On the corner of the nearest shelf was a small book bound in marbled paper. Inside the front, in Miss Pansy's spidery writing, was laid out an exact record of the bounty on these shelves. On the back page was recorded, to the last ounce, the precise daily withdrawals from these shelves. These, in turn, were ticked off in the firm hand of the senior Miss Clarence; it was this hand, too, which occasionally accorded Miss Pansy a flamboyant *Excellent!* or *Bravo!* in a flourishing copperplate script.

Mara grabbed the tea caddy and fled, wondering briefly at the nature of the closeness between the Misses Clarence.

When she returned to the kitchen, her landlady was sitting in the wooden chair, her eyes half-closed. Mara moved about quietly making the tea and pouring it into the best white china. She thrust a cup and saucer into Miss Pansy's hands. 'Here, Miss Pansy, drink this. It'll warm you.'

Pansy looked at the tea as though it were rat poison. 'I can't drink this, dear,' she said dully. 'I have to go to Heliotrope at the chapel.'

'It'll be no good doing that yet,' said Mara quietly. 'The undertaker's man told us he had more calls to make, don't you remember? Now drink the tea, Miss Pansy. It'll steady you.'

She forced the cup towards the woman's mouth. Miss Pansy gulped some tea then grasped the cup and drank the rest very quickly. She put down the cup and sighed.

'I am about to ask you something strange, my dear. I wonder if you would be so kind as to call me "Pansy"? I've not a soul in the world to call me Pansy. Not a soul. And in a day I'll not have the courage to ask. And I'll never hear my Heliotrope say my name again. Not ever.' And she started to shake and weep.

Mara blinked at the unusual request, but she put her arms round Miss Pansy's shoulders and stroked the thin dark hair which was straggling down onto her neat collar. 'Now Miss . . . now Miss Pansy, shshsh. You go upstairs and get yourself dressed and tidied. Then by the time we get down to the chapel Miss Clarence will be there. You will be able to speak to the minister. Then you'll feel better.'

She half-carried Miss Pansy up to her narrow cell-like bedroom and pushed her inside, closing the door firmly behind her. Moving on, she paused beside the elder Miss Clarence's open door. Before, this door had always been closed as she crept past on her way down to breakfast or up to bed. She stepped inside.

'Well!' A frisson of shock rippled through her at the contrast between this sprawling, untidy room and that of the sister across the landing. The great untidy bed was tumbled with plump heaped pillows and embroidered eiderdowns. The triple-mirrored dressing-table was cluttered with bottles and quilted sprays, and draped with gauzy scarfs and glittering beads. The cavernous wardrobe stood open, and hanging from the carved door was the elegant draped crêpe dress which was obviously Miss Clarence's redundant choice for today's round of committees and good works.

A heavy sigh at her shoulder made Mara jump.

'Heliotrope liked such pretty things,' Miss Pansy said. She must have dressed at lightning speed. Her hair was neat, her face was calm. She adjusted her hat. 'Now, my dear, I am ready to go to the chapel.'

'I'm sorry, Miss . . . Pansy. I shouldn't be here. The door was open. I . . .'

Pansy took a step further into the room. 'No harm in it now, dear, is there? Heliotrope was very particular about her things. Would not let anyone touch them. Do you know, she never even let me across this threshold?' She picked up a fox-fur which was lying over the end of the bed and put it to her cheek. 'Not once.'

Mara frowned. That was a lie. She had heard the sisters talking in that room more than once. As her mind wrestled to understand why Pansy should tell a lie at a time like this, she started to shake. 'I – I – need to do something,' she said. 'You stay here for a minute and I'll be back. And then we can go to the chapel.'

She raced up the narrow staircase to her own room and sat for a minute at the table under the window taking very deep breaths. She longed for the hard strong arms of her mother; she wanted them tight, tight around her. The trembling slowed down. Then she pulled the Frenchman's package from her belt, smoothed it out and peered at the address once more, after which she took out her own writing paper and pen and scribbled a letter to her parents, telling them what had happened, assuring them she was still safe. Somehow in writing the letter she was tapping into their calmness, their strength. The trembling finally stopped.

She stuffed the letter in an envelope and stamped it. Then she put on her only remaining coat, pushed the letter in her pocket and raced back downstairs to find Miss Pansy standing by her sister's dressing-table running some heavy pearl beads through her fingers.

'Come on, Miss Pansy, let's go.'

Miss Pansy looped the pearls over her head and tucked them inside her plain navy coat. 'Very well, my dear. Very well.'

In the days following the raid, the town hummed and bubbled with the drama and its aftermath. The ruined buildings, the full mortuary, the shattered railway yard, the busy hospitals and surgeries were all reminders that the savage raid of the sixteenth of December had been no bad dream.

Two days after the raid, a rumour whipped up that the Germans were back and another raid was imminent. Mara had physically to restrain Miss Pansy from going to rescue Heliotrope from the mortuary. The streets hummed again with panic and fear, which melted as soon as everyone realised it was a false alarm. Then, finally, the people of the town got back down to their lives with the dogged determination not to be put off their stroke by these treacherous Huns. Their town might have endured the first assault on British soil since the Normans, but it would be letting the side down to seem unduly disturbed. Men and women from all walks of life went back to work. The schools and churches reopened as soon as humanly possible, and where practicable, people re-occupied their own shattered buildings, determined not to be put out by the enemy.

Mara was not so brave. She set out several times to go back to school, but reached no further than the end of the cliff road, racing back in tears into the waiting arms of Miss Pansy, who welcomed her back because she hated being left in the house with the suddenly oppressive scents and echoes of her dead sister Heliotrope.

Miss Pansy was so keen to keep Mara by her that she wrote a letter to the chairman of the school board, a close acquaintance of her sister, who had shared membership of several committees with him. Miss Pansy acquainted him with the sad news of her own bereavement, although she imagined he would have heard the dreadful news. She then went on to include a note on the nervous state of Miss Mara Scorton. The pupil-teacher, she said – a mere child herself – had witnessed the savage death of her Head Master in the raid and was laid very low by this and found it impossible to return to school. The chairman, a public-spirited soul much in demand in these days of crisis, paid a hurried call to the house on the cliff, then left them both in peace.

'There now, dear,' said Pansy to Mara. 'You have no need to worry. Now then, shall I make you a nice plum pie for tea? I have bottled plums in the pantry.'

These days Mara was being treated to the kind of food that Pansy had obviously prepared for her sister Heliotrope. Mara, who had no appetite at all, found herself stuffing herself with the food so that she did not hurt Miss Pansy's feelings.

One day the school caretaker, Joseph Bly, turned up at the house. He brought Mara the remains of her school coat and the dusty bowl of Christmas hyacinths which had been growing on the windowsill in her classroom. He refused a cup of tea but said he was glad to see her much better and she was not to worry about the children, as Miss Goldthorpe and Miss Smith had come out of retirement to repair the breach, so to speak. Their little bit for the war effort, he said. Then he said that Mr Clonmel had been the best Head Master a man could wish for, and the town was much the worse for his loss. Mara remembered the battles he'd had with Mr Clonmel, whom he had seen as a cold pedant. But she understood that he couldn't bring himself to speak ill of the dead.

Mara did not tell Joe Bly, or anyone else, how most nights she woke up silently screaming, in flight from vivid dreams of Mr Clonmel with his head blown away, and rows and rows of children lying in shrouds on the desks in her classroom. In one dream she leaned over to pull the shroud away, only to reveal a child's head in the same state as that of Mr Clonmel.

Mara was visited by a bizarre sense of completion at the finality of the newspaper reports, to actually read the sad litany of names – men, women, boys, girls – of those who were surely dead. They, like Miss Heliotrope Clarence, were declared to have been 'killed by enemy action'. Somehow this statement lent to their dying an aura of heroism. Mara welcomed the implication that, by sacrificing their lives, they had made a positive contribution to the cause of peace.

Then as each day passed, as though to prevent people from imagining that things would ever be the same again, the paper carried lists of those who had died since the raid; they, too, were declared to have been 'killed by enemy action'.

Mara listened as Miss Pansy read the lists out loud, and watched as she cut the notices out of the paper and underlined those known to herself and Heliotrope. She made it quite clear to Mara that these unfortunate people and their families were mere acquaintances, that the Clarence sisters were only truly intimate with each other.

On the day of Heliotrope's funeral, Mara and Miss Pansy returned to the house from the chapel, removed their hats, and sat side by side on a hard sofa in the darkened room.

Pansy clasped her hands tightly together. 'It's truly hard to think that I'll never see her again.'

'She's there in Heaven, Miss Pansy.' Mara's words were automatic. She believed there was a Heaven just as she knew the River Gaunt finally flowed into the North Sea. She went on: 'Miss Clarence is at peace now.' Mara, trying to cling to something herself in the middle of all this carnage, had a sudden image of Mr Clonmel and Miss Heliotrope Clarence cavorting in a place called Heaven. She fought down a ludicrous desire to laugh.

Pansy wrinkled her nose. 'At peace? Do you really think so?' she said dryly. 'I never thought much of all that Heaven stuff myself, dear. That was the one thing upon which dear Heliotrope and I disagreed. And sitting there, listening to the pious things being said over those poor souls today, I feel more than ever that this is all we have.'

Shocked to the core, Mara started to tremble. She grasped at Pansy's thin hand, tears coming into her eyes. It was too terrible to hear a grown-up say such things. 'No, Pansy, you can't say that. You *must* be wrong. I—'

She was interrupted by bangs and crashes from outside. The two women jumped up and raced to the window.

'It's started again,' wailed Pansy. 'Those devils are firing at us again.'

Mara pulled back the heavy curtain, peered through the

28

glass and then laughed. Her trembling faded. There, crouched at the narrow gate, still settling on its springs, was a shining, long-nosed motor car. A man in goggles sat at the wheel, a woman swathed in heavy scarves beside him.

'It's not devils, Pansy!' Mara said. 'It's angels. Angels from a little town called Priorton.' She pulled Pansy by the hand along the passage towards the door. 'Come on!'

She opened the door to see the driver stepping down. He removed his goggles and instantly seemed ten years younger. He grinned at them and moved round the car to hand down the woman who threw back her heavy veil and limped towards Mara.

Mara flung herself into her arms. 'Mama! Dearest Ma!'

She was head and shoulders higher than her diminutive mother, but as she felt herself enclosed in the familiar strong arms, it was as though she were three again and she had scraped her knee. She was comforted.

Another heavier arm came round her shoulder. 'You're fit then, old girl?'

'Tommy!' She turned to her brother, loving everything about him: his squat chunky stature, the very red rim where the goggles had pressed into his smooth young brow.

Kitty Rainbow held her daughter away from herself so that she could take a better look. 'No letter after that first one, child. And all that dreadful stuff in the *Echo*. I needed to come to see for myself. This poor town! This poor house. What a hole that is.' She reached up to push Mara's black hair away from her cheek. 'And what are those dark shadows! You look as though you haven't slept for a week.'

'Well, you're right on that. I haven't slept for a—' Mara turned to look back into the doorway of the house. 'Pansy . . .'

But her landlady had shrunk into the wall, further back in the shadowy vestibule.

She took her mother's hand and led her forward. 'You must come and talk to Miss Pansy. She's grieving so terribly for her sister.'

29

Pansy, faced by the bold sparkling face of Kitty Rainbow, shrank even further into the house. By the time they caught up with her she was at bay in the kitchen.

'Don't run away, Miss Pansy. Let me introduce my mother, Miss Kitty Rainbow.' There was the familiar awkwardness of the moment – introducing a mother with a different name – even in these special times. 'Miss Pansy Clarence, Mother, who's taken care of me all these months. And here is my dear brother Tommy, Miss Pansy. They've motored here all the way from Priorton, to see us.'

Pansy, her hand crunched in Kitty's strong grasp, turned petrified eyes on Mara. 'You're going away, child?' She turned from Mara's young, open face to that of the girl's mother, which though equally bright and vivid was undeniably that of a woman well into her fifties. This was an old mother for such a young girl.

'I'll have to . . . I want . . .' Heart sinking, Mara turned to Kitty. 'I can't leave her, Mama. She has no one.'

'The shell that took our . . . my parlour made the hole you saw, Mrs Rainbow.'

'Kitty, please,' said Kitty.

Pansy blushed at the unlooked-for intimacy. '. . . Er . . . Kitty? That shell also took my . . . took Heliotrope, my sister. There is no one else. We are just returned from Heliotrope's funeral. There is nothing left of her except that which the worms may take for their honest use. Other poor souls were buried just near her. The crowds in the chapel flowed right out of the doors.' She folded her hands together very tightly. 'There have been so many callers these last days. So much appreciation of a life well-led.'

Mara looked at her, startled. Apart from the chairman of the school board, there had been no one.

'Your sister must have been a remarkable woman,' said Kitty gently. 'You must have close friends on whom you can now rely, Miss Pansy?'

Pansy shook her head. 'Heliotrope and I were all we had,

30

and all we needed. Of course, there were those who thought they were her friends . . . she was well-known in the town, a figure of great respect, loved by so many people.'

Kitty nodded slowly. 'And none of these would . . . ?'

Mara touched her mother's arm. 'Miss Pansy has not strayed more than six feet from my elbow since it happened. She knows no one, Mother. These people were all the other Miss Clarence's acquaintances. Miss Pansy knows none of them. I'll have to stay here, or she'll be on her own.'

Kitty looked from one to the other. 'You two look like a pair of graveyard ghosts.'

'Drowned rats,' volunteered Tommy.

'There's only one thing for it,' said Kitty. 'You can both come home to Priorton. Home with me.'

'Home?' Pansy looked round the dusty hall. 'Here is my home, Mrs . . . Kitty. I've had no other. This was our dear father's house and his father's before that.'

'The house will still be here, Miss Pansy, in a month, in a year. We can lock it up tight. Put boards over the holes. Then, come the right time, we will bring you back here and help you sort it. I promise you,' said Kitty. 'You can see, can't you, that I couldn't leave my little daughter here? She'll be coming back with me whether you come or no.'

Mara could feel the relief flowing into her. 'Just for two weeks or so, Pansy. Till you feel better. Till you know what you want to do. And it'll be safe. There'll be no war cruisers in the country.'

'What about German fliers?' said Tommy helpfully.

'Shut up, Tommy,' said Mara. Her automatic reproof was belied by the sheer love she felt as she looked at him, with his wide grin, his open, confident face.

But Pansy Clarence was not to be so easily won. In the end the process of persuading her to come back with them took some hours, by which time it was well after dark. This meant that Kitty and Tommy had to stay for the night. Kitty slept with Mara in Heliotrope's great bed and Tommy slept in Mara's narrow bed up in the attic room.

It was ten o'clock at night before Mara got Pansy settled, and had locked the front and the back doors with their great keys. She came into the bedroom to find Kitty sitting up in bed, her curly hair done up in a rough plait. 'Well, little Mara, this room's a bit of a surprise when you see the skinniness of the rest of the house and the mouselady called Pansy.' She chuckled. 'This could just be your Auntie Esme's bedroom, don't you think? Did I tell you she's coming out of retirement in that Blackpool eyrie of hers, to do some war-benefit concerts?'

Mara nodded, agreeing with her on the similarity of the bedrooms. She smiled at the thought. Aunt Esme, Kitty's oldest and dearest friend, had once been quite a famous artiste on the music halls. Once or twice a year, Esme swooped in to visit them with her handsome, silent husband Thomas in tow. Mara's second name was Esme, and Tommy was named after Thomas, who spent most of his visits showing her brother how to play the concertina. They had been christened together when she was five and he was seven, both called Rainbow after their mother. But at their father's insistence, also called Scorton after him. He might not be allowed to marry their mother, but he would insist on giving his children his own name.

'I think the Clarence sisters were very different from each other, Mama,' Mara said now. 'Different as chalk and cheese. It's all a mystery to me – except, somehow I think things weren't quite what they seemed. It seemed as though Heliotrope was in charge and Pansy was her little slavey. But I'm not so sure now.'

She blew out the lamp and slid down in the bed. She heard Kitty slither down beside her, and snuggled into her. Then she felt Kitty's arm round her waist, Kitty's voice in her ear. 'Sleep, little Tuppence. Get some sleep!'

Sleep she did; dreamlessly for the first time since the raid. She did not wake till early the next morning. She stretched and surveyed the empty bed beside her. Through the window came the sound of Tommy tuning up the engine of the motor car, the air pumping from the exhaust in the cold winter air.

'And are you from Siberia, *sesistra*?'

They were in a dark shop by a narrow alley up from the river. The old man had been listening as Leonora bartered with his son for a black leather jacket lined with fur. Samuel, whose Russian was near-perfect, had left her to it. Now he was laughing at her openly for her efforts.

'No, sir,' she stumbled on, telling the old man she came from *Anglia* – 'a country which is Russia's friend . . .'

The old man scratched his head under his felt cap.

She tried again. Just as the glorious army of his *batyushka* Tsar now had the fiendish Germans in retreat in Poland, even as far as Galicia, so her own King Emperor was fighting them off in France.

The old man nodded, still puzzled but too polite to pursue it. 'Just so, *sesistra*.'

After waiting for the jacket to be wrapped, Leonora and Samuel strolled on, arm in arm. She glowered at him with a false scowl. 'You should have helped me, Sam Scorton,' she protested.

'I have to admit, *sesistra moya*, your Russian is execrable.'

'We're not all not born linguists, you know.'

'You had your chance!' She had haughtily turned down his offer to teach her French alongside Mara, when their little sister was ten.

'Well, I can manage kitchen Russian and the vocabulary to do with basic nursing care. Even so I only managed to pass my Red Cross exams by learning the whole lot by heart, like a baby learning a nursery rhyme, not knowing one word in ten. I speak only English with the Poliakovs. That's what they pay me for, after all.'

'But they love you, these Russians. All of them. Strangers in the street call you "sister", even "little sister". *Sesistra*. I love the sound of that!'

'Oh, I'll grant you they're keen to web you into their family. Mr Poliakov calls me his English daughter and Lucette calls me her sister. They swamp you with feeling. Then there's the Tsar who is *batyushka*, their Little Father; even God gets called *batyushka*. Do you know I saw the Imperial Family on their way to the Cathedral of the Assumption in August, to pray for the soldiers going to war. The people were in ecstasy. It was hard to see who they were praying to, their Little Father-Emperor, or their Little Father-God!'

'Rather different from England and its sailor-king, but don't make the mistake of believing all Russians think like that.' Samuel smiled thinly. 'I agree with you. Sometimes it *does* seem as though His Imperial Highness rules over an empire of infants. Even so, some of them are growing up to be rather troublesome young adults. There's unrest at home, unrest out there at the Front. There are changes afoot, you mark my words.'

'But right in the middle of this war? I've never known such patriotism, such fervour.'

'My letters have it that the streets of England ring with just such a patriotic chime these days. Recruiting in hundreds of thousands, they say. Still, just to be on the safe side they're planning compulsory call-up, even if Asquith does deny it.'

'You've heard from home?' she said eagerly.

'I had a hasty note from Kit, saying young Mara was caught up in that bombardment on the coast. Hartlepool or somewhere.' Samuel, like his brother Michael, always called his stepmother Kit.

Leonora stumbled a little on the uneven stone pavement. 'From Mother? Did she say Mara was hurt?'

'No. No. She's fine, apparently. But dear Kit was just setting out on her white stallion to rescue her little ewe lamb. She wired me, then wrote to me specially to seek you out and tell you about it. Feared a letter would be too much of a shock.'

'Shock? What does she think I am? Here I am, about to tend the wounded in a bloody war and she's afraid I might faint away at the sight of a letter.' Leonora sighed. 'I suppose that is why I came here in the first place. To prove I could plough my own furrow, without her sharpening my ploughshare all the time in her own benevolent fashion. She's a wonderful woman, but . . .'

'It took you long enough to do it,' he said thoughtfully. 'You must have been all of thirty-six when you got out here.'

'Still a child compared with you, you old greybeard,' she retorted. It was true. There were threads of silver in his thick black hair. 'Anyway, she needed help with the shops. I'm a time-served draper, don't forget. And Kitty's such fun to be around. That can be a trap in itself. And remember, there was young Mara to watch out for.'

'Ah, the child.' Samuel laughed. 'So young in this elderly family of ours, is our little Tuppence.'

She smiled faintly at his use of Mara's baby pet-name.

He went on: 'Well, Leo, you did a good job there. Just about brought her up, Kit being so busy. No easy task with Mara so ill in the early years. But she's sturdy now. And sweet. And has a conscience, I'm pleased to note. Teaching should suit her, even though she can hardly know what a school is.'

Leonora glanced sideways at Samuel. 'Anyway,' she said. 'My brain's too tired for Russian now. At the next shop I require you to take charge of the negotiations. I wish to buy a sheepskin waistcoat, to keep me warm in my tent on these cold nights. I checked the word for it. *Dushegreychka*. It means "soul-warmer".'

He laughed and tucked her arm more securely under his elbow. 'Lead on, Macduff. I'm yours to command.'

On the journey back to their South Durham home, notwithstanding the jolting of the car on the less-than-perfect roads, and the discomfort of being wedged in the back between Miss Pansy and their joint piled-up luggage, Mara went fast asleep.

Miss Pansy finally woke her with a gentle mouse-like pulling on her coat. 'We're here, my dear. We're here!'

The jolting and bumping had stopped, but it seemed to Mara that they were in the wrong place. 'We're not here, Pansy,' she said sleepily. 'We've got to go up the drive first.'

'Miss Pansy is right,' said Kitty, taking off her scarves. 'We're here.'

'This is the Lodge,' yawned Mara. 'Mr and Mrs MacOnichie live here.'

'Well,' said Tommy cheerfully, 'Mr Mac's volunteered for the Army, lucky duke, and Missis and the children have gone off to Cumberland to stay on her family's farm. So this is where we're staying – the Lodge. Nestling close like peas in a pod, if you ask me. But Kit keeps telling us it's a palace compared to where she grew up, so . . .'

'What's happened to the big house? To Purley Hall?' said Mara blankly.

Kitty tugged at her arm to get her out of the car. 'There was talk of it before you went, Mara, you must remember. And I wrote to you. We've turned it into an auxiliary hospital till the war's done. There are beds for a hundred and twenty soldiers. We've handed it over for a resting centre for soldiers just out of surgery,' said Kitty. 'It's the least we could do.'

'Pa paid for the work and Mama had it redone and ready to hand in four weeks,' said Tommy. 'Those Army medical fellows were very impressed.'

'Of course the shop has been terribly neglected,' said Kitty ruefully. 'Thank the Lord they have no more use for me here now. It's full of whiskerly orderlies and dimity nurses now. And a few patients, of course. *And* a fierce Commandant who fought the Zulus in the Zulu wars.'

The door opened. 'Mara! Dearest little girl.' Her father was standing at the door, his arms open wide. Mara scrambled over the piled-up luggage and flung herself into his arms. 'Pa!'

He kissed her on both cheeks. 'Tuppence! So you really are all in one piece. I couldn't keep Kitty here a moment longer.

She just had to come for you. Now, perhaps we'll get some peace.' William Scorton, upright and still handsome despite his seventy years, glanced fondly at Kitty. 'Welcome home. I have missed you for a long time, Mara, and Kitty for a short time.'

'And I suppose you ain't missed me at all?' said Tommy, heaving the bags out of the car.

'Not at all, dear boy. Not at all.' He paused, his eye alighting on Miss Pansy as she fell out of the car before Tommy could get to her. He managed to catch her by the shoulders just in time to prevent her falling full-length on the gravel.

'Ah, I see we have a guest,' said William.

Mara grinned. 'Pa, this is Miss Pansy Clarence, who was my landlady in Hartlepool.'

Pansy pulled down the wide skirts of her navy coat and smoothed them with a trembling hand. 'I h-hope I do not intrude, Mr Scorton. I did say to Mrs . . . to Mrs . . . Kitty that it might not be the most convenient . . .'

He shook her vigorously by the hand. 'Welcome, Miss Clarence, to Purley Lodge. The more the merrier. I like to think, with the King himself, that these worst of times bring out the best of times in all of us.'

3

At the Waterman's Cottage

Early the next morning, William Scorton announced to Mara that he would show her his new workshop. 'You must come and see my great work,' he said, pulling her hand through his arm. As he led her along familiar riverside pathways she could feel his child-like delight in his secret. He led her to a small cottage situated somewhat precariously on a promontory overlooking a bend in the River Gaunt.

'Workshop? But this is the Waterman's Cottage!'

'So it is.' He laughed, and rang the bell which dangled beside the door.

She touched the damp grey wall with some affection. The Waterman's Cottage was her mother's special place. Kitty had lived here with Leonora and old Ishmael in the early days of her relationship with William. Then when Ishmael died she had moved up to the Hall to be with William, refusing yet again to marry him. It was at the Hall that Tommy and then Mara had been born. But still Kitty had kept the simple cottage warm and aired; she had her mail delivered there and walked down to collect it every day. Mara and Tommy had spent happy hours here beside the river, tumbling about on the grass, while their mother raced through with characteristic efficiency, cleaning and dusting the cottage. Mara had supposed that holding onto the cottage was some kind of sop to notions of respectability in Priorton, but knew it must be more than that. Kitty was not a hypocrite. Keeping the cottage was some kind of gesture

39

to her own childhood and the old man who had brought her up.

The door was answered by Luke, her father's ancient Egyptian friend and aide who at one time had presided over the gardens of Purley Hall. In the tiny vestibule Luke greeted them both with a mannerly bow.

'Since our ejection from the Hall in the furtherance of the war, Luke takes care of the workshop upstairs and lives downstairs,' said William. 'Waterman's Cottage is now his home.'

Mara smiled at Luke and returned his bow. She would have loved to have hugged this grave old man, whose hand had held hers on many a childhood walk, who had made her many a delicious spicy nursery tea, who had planted bulbs and seeds with her and joined in her delight as the little plants grew. But he would have been insulted by anything so informal as a hug, so she had to confine herself to a warm handshake and a delighted smile.

He disentangled his hand. 'You are well, Mara, I see,' he said.

'As always, Luke. Bouncing back even under the shells of the Kaiser.' The words sounded melodramatic, childish.

'It was not your time, Mara.' He said the words with calm certainty.

'No, thank God,' said William. 'And now, Luke, we should show her our secret.' He took Mara's hand and pulled her towards the narrow staircase and up the steep stairs. 'Kitty and Luke spent half the summer plotting, Mara.'

To everyone except total strangers, William always referred to Mara's mother as Kitty. Tommy and Mara, the youngest members of this stretched-out family, and their only shared offspring, usually called her 'Mama'. To her stepsons Michael and Samuel she was known as 'Kit'. Even her own daughter Leonora often called her 'Kitty'. Mara only realised how eccentric this was when, as a child, she had ventured into other households where even the man and his wife called each other Mister and Missis Something.

Now Mara turned round the top banister and exclaimed as a great flood of white winter light hit her eyes. 'Good heavens!' she said. Great skylights had been built into the sloping ceilings which were supported by weathered oak beams cut from the ancient Priorton Forest. Beneath the skylights were two large square work-tables. A brightly flickering fire warmed the room and the low walls were lined with sturdy shelves from which spilled books, many with titles familiar from Mara's childhood.

'It's wonderful,' she said. 'Perfect for your work, Pa.'

William smiled his satisfaction. 'Luke and Kitty plotted together. They had all this done as a surprise.'

Mara sensed his satisfaction also that Kitty had at last given up her special retreat; the final signal of her independence from him.

'My workroom and study at the Hall are now the domain of the Commandant, some retired Colonel who's been in Africa half his life. He has the head of a stuffed lion over his desk. Well, my desk, really. Revolting thing. Kitty knew I'd miss my books and . . .'

'What about the factory – your workshop there in the town?'

'Michael's taken that over; made it another area for manu-facturing.' William had retired from the factory years ago, but had still retained a workshop, where he made mechanical things and worked on his inventions. 'I was a bit disappointed about that, though I knew it was necessary. Then one day Kitty and Luke brought me here blindfolded. The fire was blazing, my books were here, and my instruments were on the table.'

His small vices and tools, his eyeglasses and his tiny screw-drivers, were placed on the tables, arranged on their linen cloths with a surgeon's precision.

Eager to get on now, he removed his hat and his jacket and gave them to Luke, who shook them out and hung them on a stand in the corner. Then the old man bowed and left them. 'You will excuse me. I have tasks,' he said.

41

William settled down at a table and removed the cloth which was covering a half-made watch.

Mara sat beside him. 'So you're not at the works at all now, Pa?'

He shook his head. 'Michael's completely in charge there now. Quite right too. More than capable of running the whole affair. I decided to stop treading on his heels. He's complaining at the moment at them doubling income tax, of course. Won't have it that it's coming back into the company's coffers in terms of profits.'

She touched the finely worked mechanism of the watch under his hand. The edge of the striker was finely etched with an acorn design.

'This is for Kitty – a Christmas-cum-birthday present for Christmas Day. She doesn't know, of course. Thinks I'm making model engines. I made her another one, many years ago. But I thought this . . . well, a second one will do no harm.'

'Christmas! I'd forgotten all about it. How can there be a Christmas in wartime?'

'That's a mystery to me, my dear. A mystery. There's little to celebrate with all these deaths. All these young men sacrificed to war.'

'You must miss the works?'

He shook his head. 'Not once they turned the whole caboodle over to armaments. I was heartsick, oppressed by the sight of the rows of bullets and shells. In some way they look so beautiful, do you know? A terrible beauty. Apparently the word is that our little town makes a great contribution to the war. Scorton's is a major player in the war effort in the region. But while those around me celebrated enormous production figures, I had bad dreams every night. Arrows of death. All the young men slain. One by one, ten by ten, and hundred by hundred. Boys like Tommy. Men like Michael. Mown down in the smoke by shells made here in this peaceful little town.'

'Germans!' Mara said scornfully. 'Who cares about mowing

them down? Did those Germans care about lobbing their shells at me from their ships?' She shivered for a second. 'You're not the only one who has bad dreams, Pa.'

He leaned across and put an arm around her. 'I forgot! How could I do that, my dear? You must have been terrified. Just think, for a few moments you must have shared the perpetual terror of those poor boys at the Front.'

'I wish them none of that,' she said soberly. Images of the bloody head of Mr Clonmel, and the blank eyes of the Frenchman flashed before her eyes. 'I was not terrified. "Horrified" might be a better word. But even worse – I was relieved, relieved because what happened to Mr Clonmel and old Heliotrope didn't happen to me.'

'As our boys must feel when their comrades are killed.' William nodded thoughtfully. 'But you shouldn't feel guilty about that, Tuppence. Anyway, as for working at the factory, I thought there were thousands enough pairs of hands making bullets and shells. They even use watchmakers to develop the trigger mechanisms, you know. Not so many just making watches now.' He poked at the watch before him with a small screwdriver.

She smiled, so full of love for him she wanted to cry. 'You're right, Pa. Not so many making watches.'

'There'll be watchmakers in Germany, you know, just like me. Desperate to make watches and not triggers for guns and shells. We met some wonderful men, skilful men. You remember Kitty and I travelled there in 1910?'

Mara nodded. That was the summer her stepbrother Samuel was home, when he taught her some French.

William continued. 'I met many German watchmakers then, who'll be feeling just like I do at this minute. How wonderful is a watch or a clock, compared with a gun.'

'There you go again. What do we care about German watchmakers?' He was making her uneasy. In the papers, in the streets, they were comparing Germans to unthinking beasts.

'Those watchmakers are human beings, just like you and

43

me. Like Tommy and Michael and Sam.' He fixed his glass into his eye. 'Don't you forget that.' He picked up a tiny tool.

She stood up. 'Well, Pa, I'll get back to Mother. She was battling to extract a few words out of Miss Pansy when I left.'

'Kitty'll be quite content, my dear. She's a great one for waifs and strays. After all, she was one herself.'

Mara nodded. It was a well-rehearsed tale in their family that Kitty had been found under Priorton viaduct by the prizefighter, Ishmael Slaughter, and brought up as his own. The tales of Ishmael's life were as familiar to Mara as those of the Brothers Grimm, which Leonora had read to her when she was little.

'Miss Pansy needs a bit of nurturing,' she said. 'She and her sister Miss Heliotrope were closer than sisters, even though they were so different. Like Jack Spratt and his wife.'

'An old-fashioned creature for her age, I think, Miss Pansy,' said William.

'Age?' Mara had not thought of Miss Pansy as having an age. It was like thinking of a worm dancing or a bird giving a lecture on mice. 'How old do you think she is?'

He took out his eyeglass and pursed his lips. 'Thirty-eight? Thirty-nine? No older than Leonora, I would think.'

Mara raised her brows. She thought of the vivid, powerful presence of Leonora, who just a year ago was tumbling around with her like another child in Livesay Woods, and racing her in Purley Park for pennies. 'Never!'

'You think so?' He smiled. 'Oh. Perhaps you think Leonora's like Kitty. Of all ages and no age at all.'

'What – have you heard from Leonie?' she said eagerly. 'I should have asked. But so much seemed to be happening last night, what with finding bedspaces and all that. So she's well, Leonie, is she?'

He snorted. 'Well, you know that the latest is this hare-brained scheme about nursing Russian soldiers? It seems to me that women now are "half in love with not-so-easeful death", to paraphrase poor old Keats. As though staunching the blood can be patriotic in equal measure as spilling it.' He cleared his throat. 'She'll have a long trek to get to those wounded fellows. Apparently the Russians are halfway through Poland now.'

'You think she's in real danger?'

'In danger – why not? She longs for it! Danger, adventure – she relishes it! Otherwise she'd have stayed here and run Kitty's shop as agreed, and not gone off to that Godforsaken freezing country.'

Mara laughed. 'She always was a restless one, hemmed in here at home. Wanting to go here, wanting to go there . . .' Mara had witnessed her older sister many times pacing the bedrooms and the corridors. She would pad around in bare feet like a caged lioness, bemoaning the prim safety of the shops and the comically narrow views of the people who bought the gowns and hats, the ribbons and silks from her mother's well-laden shelves. More than once she swore that she would steal out and obliterate the *And Daughter* from the shop signs. Somehow the privilege and responsibility of being her mother's partner had lost its attraction through the years.

It was Mara, longing for some kind of adventure for herself, who had finally urged Leonora to leave, to get away. 'Get off and do something, Leonie, or you'll blame Mama and say it's her fault. Lots of women are going off now. I read of them . . .'

It was Mara, too, who found the advertisement in *The Times*, which led to Leonie's employment by the Poliakovs.

'Would you not miss me then?' Leonora had challenged her.

'Miss you?' Mara had scoffed. 'Might as well miss an alligator.'

'Then I'll go.' At that Leonora had given her an enormous hug and raced up to the attic to look for her stepfather's old travelling trunks.

Now, William was fiddling with his eyeglass, blowing away an imaginary mote of dust. 'What is it, Mara? Daydreaming again?'

'I was just wondering why Leonie waited till she was thirty-six to do what she always wanted.'

He smiled at her gently. 'Oh, there was a reason, Mara. A very good reason.' He coughed. 'Now. The bicycles are in the sheds behind here. Why don't you leave Kitty and Miss Pansy to their conversation and take a ride up to the house? There are changes there. You might be interested. Poor old Purley Hall's now turned into a cross between an Army camp and a hospital. And perhaps you'll see some of the men who marched off so jauntily in August. The state they're in now.'

Old Luke helped Mara haul her bicycle from the depths of a large barn in the lane beside the cottage, and brought out an immaculate white cloth to dust it. She hitched up her skirts and set off to pedal between trees which had been dark sentinels in her childhood games, across pastures where she and Tommy, exhausted with their play, had lain on summer afternoons watching clouds race across bright blue skies. The familiar line of elms that led towards the house dripped on her, relieving themselves of their night-time's rain.

She stopped at the last wide gate and looked back across the valley towards Priorton. The bustling little town sat beside its great viaduct, tangled in the pall of smoke from its many coal fires, pierced by pointing chimneys and blocked with gaunt warehouses of the burgeoning Co-operative Society, which was a little city on its own beside the railyards. The viaduct, important in her own family's story, loomed over the sturdy mediaeval bridge which had opened the way to the dale for wheeled traffic since Roman times.

Mara frowned then, suddenly remembering the package in her suitcase from the Frenchman who had died on the streets of Hartlepool. That had a Bridge Street address. She would cycle across and deliver it this afternoon. She shivered and tucked her scarf inside her coat. Then she mounted the bicycle to make her way towards the Hall, which revealed itself bit by bit through the trees as she rode towards it.

At the bottom of the shallow steps, drab wagons attended

by patient horses were drawn up in order, flanked by two sleek motor cars. As she watched, a taxi drew up and disgorged three men in uniform, one on crutches and two with heavy bandaging on their arms.

A movement beside her made her jump. 'A spy in our midst, by Jove!' a voice trilled to her left.

She turned to face two men. One was tall, even willowy, the other shorter and much more square. The taller one put his walking stick under his arm, stood still a second to establish his balance, clicked his heels and bowed. 'You must be some *Fraulein* come to spy on Britain's finest warriors at rest?' he drawled.

'Nothing of the sort,' she said crisply. 'I've come to see my home. I grew up here, in this house.'

The broad face of the smaller man split into a grin. 'Your house, is it?' he said. One of his arms was in a sling and his greatcoat was draped awkwardly across his shoulder. He hissed slightly on his 's', reminding Mara of a Welsh minister they had once had at the chapel. 'So it's we, not you, who intrude.' He saluted. 'Name's Dewi Wilson, ma'am. Late of some muddy hole in France. Shot in left side. Arm broken, can you believe it, falling down some bally French hospital stairs. Fractured, if you please, not even a clean break. We're presently in residence in your handsome home yonder, being patched up ready to return to said muddy hole. And this long string of lard beside me with the shotup leg is Alexander Hacket-Barrington. Even the *Honourable* Alexander whatsit.'

The Honourable Alexander flourished a bow. 'At your service, ma'am.'

'My name's Mara Scorton.' She bobbed a curtsey, expressing more irony than respect. She smiled from one to the other. Even with the dark rings under their eyes these were boys only a few years older than Tommy. 'You look too fit to be patients,' she said.

'That, fair maid, is the pity. Still *hors de combat* but stitched up, patched up, talked to nicely, will soon be ready for off.

47

They have an urgent need for bodies over there, doncha know? Too damn fit for our own good,' drawled the Honourable Alex.

'Too damn fit,' agreed Dewi. 'Too soon mended and ready for service.'

'You'll be going back?'

A shadow moved across the Welshman's broad face. 'Oh yes, we're going back. Our country needs us. Haven't you seen the posters?'

She stood back against her bicycle. 'Is it terrible over there?' she asked earnestly.

They exchanged glances. 'It's a muddy war,' said Dewi gruffly. 'It's not quite rearing steeds and slashing sabres.'

Alex grasped her elbow. 'Here, Dewi *mi bhoy*, you take the lady's bicycle and she can show us around her wonderful home. We cannot have the Lady of the Manor in our grasp and allow her to escape.'

She pulled her arm away from his hand. 'I'm not the Lady of the Manor. It's not like that, here at Purley.'

'So what is it like?'

'It is my father's house . . . and my mother's,' she took a breath, 'though she is not his wife.' She relished saying this, feeling the need to prick the bubble of their certainties.

Dewi whistled.

'So there's none of that Lady of the Manor nonsense here. Just a family and a wonderful place to be a child. Or it was, when I was a child.'

Dewi looked her up and down with an analytical eye. 'A child still, if I'm not mistaken.'

'That's not true!' she protested.

'So how old are you, then?' he challenged.

'Nearly sixteen,' she said. 'But I'm a teacher. I've just come from—'

'A teacher?' scoffed Alex. 'I was just into my second school as pupil when I was fifteen!'

Mara stood astride her bicycle and hitched herself onto the

saddle. 'It's a wonder they let you out and into that uniform at all,' she said scornfully. 'You're not old enough to be let out of the nursery.'

At that she set off pedalling, hurtling away, almost sweeping Dewi off the path in her forward push. The boys careered after her, calling their apologies, but she soon lost them and made her way out of the park and down back towards the Lodge, her mind buzzing with cleverer things she might have said in response to their teasing.

She was just parking the bicycle beside the back door when it occurred to her that she had thought almost nothing today about the collapsing school and the bloody head of Mr Clonmel. She leaned against the wall and closed her eyes, guilt sweeping through her for daring to be carefree, for forgetting the terror.

'What's this, Tuppence? Asleep at your post? Men have been shot for less.'

She opened her eyes to look into her brother Tommy's beaming face. She shook her head. 'No. No. Just thinking.'

'Well, I was sent to get you. Luncheon is ready. The strange little Miss Pansy turned out to be the most wonderful cook.'

In the crowded parlour which was doubling as a dining room, Mara was just in time for her startled eye to rest on Pansy spooning out the most delicious-looking beef pudding onto eagerly waiting plates.

Pansy smiled secretly at her. 'Heliotrope loved my steamed puddings,' she murmured. 'Just loved them.'

This was obviously the reason why the elder Miss Clarence used to eat in her room, declaring exhaustion from her immersion in the day's affairs. No wonder she had been as fat as an egg.

A tall man stood up at the far end of the table. 'Now, Mara, it is good to see you well.'

She flew round to hug her oldest stepbrother but found herself shaking his hand rather formally instead. 'Michael! Why are you not at the works?'

Michael took after their father in looks, but lacked the sparkle, the childlike enthusiasm of William; in many ways Michael seemed the older of the two men, always avuncular rather than brotherly to Mara. 'I came with some papers for Father to sign.'

'He's down at the Waterman's Cottage,' said Mara. 'I was just with him.'

'I called in here to check just when young Tom was getting back to his workbench . . .'

'. . . and the smell of Miss Pansy's pudding persuaded him to dine with us!' said Kitty, beaming.

Mara slipped into her place and watched as Miss Pansy Clarence, unrecognisably pink-cheeked and lively, gave Mara's eldest stepbrother Michael an enormous helping of her very special beef pudding.

In the afternoon, Mara turned down Michael's offer of a ride into Priorton with him and Tommy, who now looked much more familiar in his work clothes. She shook her head. 'No, I'll cycle down. I've errands down there.' The package for the French children was burning a hole in her satchel.

Michael pulled on his gauntleted gloves. 'You're well, then, Mara? The shelling was very heavy according to the reports.' It was the first time in a long lunchtime that he had mentioned her ordeal.

'It was very bad. Buildings were smashed. The railway . . .' The words were meaningless as they streamed from her mouth. She had repeated them so many times now.

'I've sent a man down there to pick up the leavings – shell-cases et cetera. See what they're made of.' His tone was brisk, scientific, not horrified or even sympathetic as the others had been.

'How is it, down at the works?' said Mara.

'Never busier. The government man is delighted with our expansion.'

The heavy wheels of the car ground in the deep mud before

it got away. Mara guided the wheels of her cycle into the hardening tyre tracks, reflecting on how little she knew of Michael. He had never lived at the Hall in her time there, although he was on cordial terms with his father and Kitty, and turned up for dinner on high days and holidays. He lived in a big house in Priorton Market Place, was a member of the Gentleman's Club, and played the French horn in the town orchestra. He played cricket for Priorton, and golf on the newly-laid golf course in the Priory grounds. He had a circle of hearty acquaintances who respected him as a sportsman and businessman and were not challenged by his solid views on life. Indeed, his steady ways went a good way to compensate for the unease generated by William and Kitty's unconventional manner of going about things.

Being practical as well as pragmatic, solid Priorton citizens could not deny that Mr Scorton senior was a successful manufacturer, and Kitty Rainbow a successful businesswoman. But they were somewhat confounded by the rather liberal set-up at Purley Hall, which was staffed by ancient Egyptians and where Mr Scorton, respectable enough himself, was partnered, without ecclesiastical benefit, by the admittedly vivacious Kitty Rainbow. The two children of the union, Mara and Tommy, were virtually unschooled, running wild apart from that time the boy was sent away.

At least, though, William Scorton had done the decent thing and given them his name. Then there was Michael's brother . . . Samuel, was it? Harum scarum from the start and even now, in his forties, he was gallivanting round the world. He was in the papers sometimes, reporting from the four corners of the earth.

In contrast to all this, the sturdy, hardworking Michael was something of a relief. He even went to church every Sunday. Very reassuring.

It took Mara twenty minutes to get to Bridge Street. She pushed the bicycle the last hundred yards as the road was too steep to pedal and she was gasping as she knocked hard on the door of number nineteen.

The door creaked open and a woman's face, white and frightened, stared back out at her.

'Are there some children here? I seek the children of a Monsieur Derancourt.'

The woman's hand came to her mouth and she screamed. A tall thin man came behind the woman and thrust her to one side, saying aggressively, 'What is it? What is it? We have had enough of this bullying, I tell you. Enough!'

Mara took in his angry eyes, his pale, distinctively marked face, the great cloud of black springy hair, tied back with string. She took a breath. 'I have come to see the children,' she said. 'The children of Monsieur Derancourt.' She faced the man steadily, wondering just what would come next.

4

Christmas Preparations

'There are no children here.' The man's voice, despite being soft-toned, was threaded with steel, compounded by the foreign accent. 'What do you want, miss?'

Bewildered by the man's belligerence, Mara dropped her gaze and rooted in her satchel. 'I've a package here for J.P. and H. Derancourt. They are the children of a man with whom I spoke . . .'

He reached out, grasped her arm, glanced into the empty street behind her and pulled her into a plainly furnished kitchen. The frightened woman was at the far side of the room, pressing her back to the wall, her hands spread against it as though she would feel her way through its solid mass. She was sobbing, her eyes wide open, tears pouring unchecked down her cheeks.

'There are no children here,' the man repeated. 'I am Jean-Paul and this is Hélène Derancourt. It seems you have spoken to our father . . . You know where he is?'

Mara shook her head. 'I spoke with him . . .' To her dismay she found tears coming to her own eyes. 'But he . . . he said to give this to . . . he said *"mes enfants"*, and I thought he meant little children.' She held out the package as though it were a shield.

The man called Jean-Paul snatched it from her but didn't open it. 'And our father? Where did you speak with him?'

'I was in Hartlepool, out on the coast. I think he'd been

working at one of the shipyards. Do you know the Germans bombarded it on the sixteenth of this month? Your father was there . . .'

He was shaking his head. 'I did not know this. He is gone from here a month now . . .' He looked at her squarely. 'Where is he now?'

'He was on the pavement,' she gulped. 'I'm sorry, but he died, only a minute after telling me of the package.'

His ruddy face paled and he breathed out very slowly, and the girl against the wall started to sob again. 'Mademoiselle, we have been impolite.' He indicated a seat by the small fire. 'Will you take a seat? We must speak.'

He took his sister's hand, unclamped her from the wall and led her to sit on the bench opposite Mara. 'Who are you, Mademoiselle, that you would do us this kindness?'

'My name is Mara Scorton. I live just outside this town, but I have been teaching in Hartlepool. I told them I would bring the package to you, the men who were helping him. But he talked about his children. He said *mes enfants* . . .' She was sobbing herself now, her head aching again with the great booming sound of the guns, her throat choking with the memory of the dust.

Hélène Derancourt stood up and came to kneel at her feet. She stroked the tears from Mara's face with her apron, murmuring words in French which Mara did not understand.

Mara looked at Jean-Paul. 'What does she say?'

'She says that you are only a baby yourself and we should cry for you too.'

'Doesn't she speak English?' Her tears dried. Hélène Derancourt stood up and returned to the bench beside her brother.

'Oh yes, she speaks English, but she seems to have forgotten it. Our mother was English from a place near here called New Morven. She came to France many years ago, to work for the doctor in our village in France.'

'Is that why you came here?'

54

'Yes, that is why. It was a mistake, but . . .' He paused, then shrugged. 'We will look at the package.' He took a knife from his pocket, slit the string and opened the package. Inside was a leather bag which chinked with coins, two small photographs, and some official-looking documents. 'Ha!' he said. 'All his papers. The farm and the land.'

'Your father did not live here with you?'

He shook his head. 'No. At first he did, but not now for one month. There was a disagreement.'

She looked steadily at him, waiting for the explanation.

He shrugged. 'Some *jollee chaps* from this town of yours took us for Germans. They called us Huns, tormented Hélène and beat me. My father stood and watched them, shaking with fear. Then he slunk off in the night, full of shame.'

'You should have got the policemen,' she protested.

He shrugged again. 'It is the second time. It is best to leave things.'

'Here in Priorton? I can't believe . . .'

He shook his head. 'The last time was in France. Our village was just near the front line. Our father brought soldiers home, and they all drank wine and played cards. Too much wine. Then the soldiers held me and my father while they . . . violated . . . my mother and my sister.' He drew a deep shuddering breath. 'They threw money on the floor as they left. My mother had a seizure and died the next day.' He pushed his hand over his face and through his hair, his eyes bleak. Then he said, 'And you see how Hélène is affected.'

Mara exploded. 'Those beastly Germans, those beastly Germans,' she raged.

He looked at her coolly. 'Oh no, *Mees* Mara Scorton. The soldiers were not German. They were English.'

She hated him then. He had been playing her, like a fisherman plays a fish. She stood up. 'You must hate all English people then, M. Derancourt. I can't think why you came here to live at all,' she said stiffly.

55

'The soldiers were arrested and their officer – a decent-enough chap – was full of shame and apology. He ensured us free passage. So we came here so that my mother's people could mourn their daughter, their sister, their cousin. But all these English do here is say that if my mother had not married my father, if she had stayed here in Durham, she would have been safe. They hate us,' he said bitterly. 'And when the men follow us and beat us in the streets, it seems as if history repeats itself; once more, my father runs away in shame.'

'I can see that you have good reason to hate us. I can see that,' said Mara. 'I should go home now.'

He nodded gravely, his eye straying back to the contents of the packet.

She picked up her satchel and made for the door. The woman called Hélène stood up and grasped her, kissing her on both cheeks. 'Thank you, *ma petite*,' she said.

'Yes, we thank you for this,' said Jean-Paul gruffly.

Mara fled. She jumped on her bicycle and careered back down Bridge Street. She was so preoccupied with keeping her balance that she did not notice that Hélène Derancourt, fleet-footed as a gazelle, had set off in pursuit. And only an old man, down on his haunches on a street corner, noticed when Hélène finally lost touch with the speeding bicycle, and turned back again, her head sunk down between her shoulders, to trudge back to Bridge Street.

'Are you sure the invitation included me?' Leonora scurried to keep up with Samuel's long stride. Since they had met in the doorway of the Cathedral they had spent all their spare time together. He had dined at the Poliakovs' and been subjected to young Lucette's most dazzling and seductive flirtation technique. They had ridden in a *troika* to the Poliakovs' *dacha* for a weekend of skating and sleigh-rides.

All the time they talked of Priorton, of the games they had played when Leonora and her mother had come to stay with Samuel's father; when Samuel and his brother Michael had incorporated Leonora as Guinevere into their games of King Arthur.

In their adult years, with Samuel away on his travels, they had drifted into a kind of warm distance, occasionally writing to each other, catching up, revisiting their childhood affection on the rare occasions Samuel made his way back to Priorton.

But now during these cold Moscow days, they were rediscovering each other anew, reflecting on a cosy past, haunted by an unseen future. The days raced by too quickly. Leonora thought about Samuel when he was not there and was conscious of a certain uncharitable sourness as she watched Lucette flirt with him.

'Are you sure the invitation included me?' she repeated, tugging the cuff of his great furry coat. Tonight was the last night before Samuel went off again, and before Leonora reached the final stage of her commitment to the Red Cross.

They had had to leave the Poliakovs' carriage and driver out on the broad street, at the narrow entrance to a square which opened up into further squares like an architectural Chinese puzzle. The archways and entrances to the squares were narrow, having been built with horses rather than carriages in mind. Samuel strode along with the appearance of someone knowing exactly where he was going. Looking round, Leonora wondered how he knew. The squares seemed identical: there was the odd single tree black against the snow and the winter grey stone; old *babushkas* dragging a child here, carrying a child there.

'Samuel!' she said, exasperated.

'They will welcome you as my sister. Among these people you will need no personal invitation. This is Moscow, not Harrogate. There is great, grand warmth here, not narrow judgmental chill.'

He turned then and drew her into a wide arched courtyard. It was like the interior of a great well, with a square of white light at the top and exquisitely wrought balcony railings looped around like lace. Samuel led her up steep stone steps to the

57

first floor and took off a fur glove to bang hard on the door. They stood there stamping in the cold for several minutes. He knocked again and called his name. Now they could hear whispering and rustling before the door opened.

Leonora flinched back as a man with a great red beard threaded with silver loomed before them. The man grinned at the sight of Samuel, pulled the door open wide, then grabbed him and gave him a resounding kiss before shouting and chattering to him in heavily guttural Russian. The man then turned to Leonora and she was treated to a similarly hearty kiss on the hand before being pulled right into a narrow corridor. The heavy door thudded shut behind her. They were drawn along the corridor past several closed doors to the open door at the end.

The room was full of light; many candles and lamps had been lit against the dark afternoon. In the corner was a large four-poster bed, and in the centre, a table, around which seven or eight people were gathered. Before them were bottles and the aromatic detritus of a large meal.

Everyone leapt to their feet at the sight of Samuel, greeting him in a similar fashion to that of the man at the door. Samuel made a general introduction. 'And here is my sister, Leonora Rainbow.' He translated the name and there were smiles all round. 'Leonora, this is my friend Valodya and his friends.'

Now she counted eight people in the room: two of them women younger than Leonora, one of whom had plaits wound twice round her head. The rest were men around Samuel's age. They all looked at her with curiosity laced with a certain abstract kindness. A large glass of wine was put into her hands and they resumed what had obviously been a serious discussion, this time throwing out remarks to Samuel like lassos, bringing him into their company.

They rattled away to each other and Leonora was lost almost immediately, only recognising the odd isolated word. She did understand the word for *police*, and from their gestures and uneasy, slightly hysterical laughter she grasped that they had been shocked at Samuel's authoritarian knock at the door; they thought he was someone from the Tsar's police. The relieved laughter rippled from person to person and Leonora smiled, feeling as though she were watching them from a great distance, as they drank and chattered away their recent fright.

As the talk went on she felt more and more excluded, like a clockwork fairy her stepfather William had once made for her, a doll which bounced away on a spring, untouchable inside a glass bubble.

After an hour she decided she had sat there long enough for the demands of good manners, and stood up. Heads swivelled towards her, and Samuel stopped mid-sentence. 'What is it, Leonie?' he said.

'We're invited to the Poliakovs' for supper, Samuel. Monsieur Poliakov said he particularly wished me to be there tonight. And I've a busy day tomorrow. We've the final check on supplies and will be assigned to our unit.'

He laughed easily and translated her intentions to the company. They all laughed then, and Valodya made a comment which brought more laughter. Leonora sensed derision. 'What did he say?' she said sharply to Samuel.

'He said you're a heroine of the Russian people, doing such great work.' He stood up and started to button his jacket. 'He also said that you must save no plutocrats and that you're to convert your grateful patients, make them support the revolution.' He was watching her carefully.

She adjusted her hat and tied her thick scarf round her neck. 'Did he, now?' She smiled at him. 'Will you tell your friend Valodya that without arms or legs, with his chest blown out, it is very hard to tell a soldier's rank.'

'Bravo!' said the girl with plaits, and the others followed suit, the recent brief tension dissolved in laughter.

Before she was allowed to leave she was kissed on the lips by the girls, and on the hand by all the men. At the door, Valodya bent over her hand. 'My friend Samuel's indeed lucky to have such a fine sister,' he said in heavily-accented English. 'One

59

would not know that you are brother and sister, you are so very unalike.'

Outside, Samuel tucked her arm in his and kept his hand on hers. 'Are we really expected at the Poliakovs' for supper or was that just a ruse to escape the Tower of Babel in there?'

'Well, not supper. And not you. But he did say he wanted to see me for a special reason tonight. And yes, I did want to escape that Tower of Babel. My Russian is not up to it and it was making my head whirl.'

'It was thoughtless of me. You don't like my friends?'

'Are they anarchists? Revolutionaries?'

'They are political. Committed to righting iniquities and not frightened of change.'

'Revolutionaries, then.'

'You might say that. Natasha, the young woman with the plaits, sends packages to her friends in the Army full of leaflets telling soldiers to abandon the fight and come home. She takes great risks.'

'And why do you run with her, with them? Are you a revolutionary?'

'Me? My dear girl, I'm a true-blue Englishman. No revolutionary.'

'So why do you associate with them?'

They finally came out onto the broad street to find their driver patiently waiting for them in the snow. 'Look,' said Samuel, 'there's no time left for explanations. I've a supper arranged for us in an interesting spot – a special goodbye feast. I'll explain to you there what I think I'm doing, consorting with these revolutionaries.'

She did not challenge this and they sat in silence as the fiacre picked its way through the streets and finally stopped outside what looked like a narrow house with all the lights at the windows blazing. A small boy dressed in eighteenth-century dress showed them into a great foyer. On her left she could hear the music and laughter of some kind of music hall. As the boy led them up a plush-lined staircase, Leonora

60

felt a tension arising in her, an unthinkable thought dawning.

In an elegantly furnished small room a single table was set with candles, silver and crystal, plates of food and a great silver bucket groaning under its burden of ice and a ridiculously large bottle of champagne.

She sat opposite Samuel and looked at him in the candlelight. His face was heavier than that of either Michael or their handsome father, his brows more beetling, his hair wilder. But with his large bright eyes and his face ready creased for laughter, Samuel had always been the more attractive brother. She had had fun through the years, teasing him about all the hearts he had broken; all those women, some with wonderful combinations of looks, personality and rank, who had wished him for their husband.

Samuel had been near to marriage just once; to a charming if minor Spanish opera singer he had come across in Milan. That marriage was abandoned when it was discovered that the singer was already married in a Roman Catholic, undissolvable fashion, to a Spanish wine exporter who turned up on the wedding day and swept the singer away, wedding dress and all.

Now Leonora found herself looking at Samuel frankly as a man, not just her brother. She remembered how each man to whom she'd been attracted had always come off very badly in comparison with Samuel or with her stepfather William: even men with whom she'd enjoyed satisfyingly close relationships. There was that very early disaster where she was promised marriage by a man who turned out to be married to someone else and left her pregnant. Apart from that, the closest she herself had come to marriage had been a long, occasionally exquisitely consummated relationship with a clergyman whose wife was perpetually ill. The wife had finally died, and instead of marrying Leonora as she had firmly expected, the clergyman was consumed in a miasma of remorse, and had finally been dragged off to Africa by his pious sister-in-law, there to save some souls in the Upper Sudan.

Leonora had just been contemplating this devastating gap in her life when young Mara had taunted her into applying for the job in Moscow, and she had at last broken the ties that kept her so close to home.

'Well, dearest Leonie? Do I survive such close inspection?' Samuel pulled down his cuffs and shook out a napkin onto his knee.

She blushed. 'Well, I suppose you'll do,' she said brightly. 'Now tell me about this motley crew we met tonight. Are they really your friends?'

He glanced at the boy, who poured champagne till both glasses brimmed. Then Samuel lifted a glass and toasted her. 'Your health, dearest Leonie. Valodya? Natasha? They're very intelligent people. People of principle. I admire them.'

'So they *are* your friends?'

He shrugged. 'That's much harder to say. I'm a trader. A businessman. A commentator. An observer. I love this country. It's mysterious, and yet bruisingly open, over-religious and at the same time paganish and lewd, rich in so much and yet heartbreakingly poor. It is stuck in the past, yet it had been on the brink of great change for many years. In this country, they all live somewhere near that edge; it is a country absolutely bursting with all kinds of possibilities, good and bad. We need to know the detail of what's happening in such a place.'

'"We"?' she echoed.

'I am a patriot,' he said carefully. 'I trade here. I write articles to show the nature of this wonderful country to the world. As well as this I make deals between people here and people in England. I have helped to set up factories and workshops here, establish modern processes. This is a great market. Now in this war it is a great ally. I work for England.'

She leaned forward. 'You are a spy,' she whispered.

He shook his head.

'Are you spying on Valodya and the others? If that's so, how can you call yourself their friend?'

'It is not so simple. It's well-known that I know a great deal about the whole of this region. I have travelled here. I have traded here. I have written my views on this region for the newspapers. So when my own government wishes to avail themselves of my insight, as a patriot I can only proffer it.'

They ate in silence for a while.

Then she put down her fork. 'So does Valodya know you report on his meetings?'

He shrugged. 'He gives me messages for the British government, which I pass on to the Consulate here. He offers commitment, if and when . . .'

'Why does the British government bother about them? They're so—'

'Ordinary? Down at heel?' He shook his head. 'Valodya and his friends are not the only group I'm in touch with, but amongst them are people who could be very powerful in the next generation – more powerful than princes and potentates.'

'I can't believe that our government would have truck with a rabble of revolutionaries.'

'They don't have truck with them. *I* have truck with them. But through people like me, they know who's who in the half-world of revolutionaries and anarchists, whom to have truck with, who, if the time arrives, to—'

'Assassinate?' she interposed.

'I was going to say who to deal with.'

'You get paid for this service?'

He shook his head. 'My business dealings furnish me with more than enough for this wandering life. What I do, I do for Britain, and for the future of Russia – whatever that may be. The key is always to know the people at the centre.' He signalled to the boy, who replaced the champagne and placed the used dishes on a silver salver. Then he withdrew and the great door clicked behind him.

Leonora looked again at the rich tapestries on the walls which showed scenes of courtship, stags and does, and birds of paradise: erotic scenes, for all the orderly stitching. 'So where have you brought me, Sam Scorton? Is this some kind of bordello?'

He laughed. 'Always so very direct, Leonie.' He looked at her levelly across the cleared table. 'It's not quite a bordello, but it's a place of assignation. In these rooms, Grand Dukes and Princes entertain . . . friends and intimates. There is a story that two Grand Dukes were here, unbeknownst to each other, entertaining each other's wives. There's another that that animal Rasputin entertains various dimensions of low life here.'

'Am I to be thankful you're not a Duke? Or a long-haired monk?'

'I had thought you would be entertained by this place, a side of Moscow life as yet unfamiliar to you. Part of your education. To compensate for the stifling bourgeois virtues of the Poliakov ménâge.' He walked round the table and pulled her to her feet so she was facing him. 'Would you say we were grown-up, Leonie?' The hands holding hers felt familiar, unthreatening.

'Sometimes over-grown-up, if you ask me.'

'And here you are going off tomorrow to risk your life and save others under enemy guns. And here am I off to Switzerland to talk to watchmakers and gunmakers and a few more revolutionaries, some very bad men among them.'

'So?'

'Who knows if either of us will be here next week?'

'I understand that, but . . .'

'Old Valodya put his finger on it earlier. Trust him.'

'Valodya?' She knew in her heart what was coming. Her hands clutched more tightly onto his.

'When he said how unalike we were, for brother and sister. But then we're not, are we? Brother and sister? When Valodya said that, I was struck by this great bolt of lightning which has been nudging at the edge of my poor slow mind for years. My feelings were very unbrotherly, when I saw you standing like some madonna in your veil that day at the Cathedral.'

64

'Samuel . . .'

He opened his arms. 'What I really want to do, Leo, is finish once and for all with the fiction of being your "brother" and kiss you properly.'

Then she put her arms around his neck and drew his mouth to hers.

It was like coming home.

Kitty Rainbow decided that, with William's permission, the family should have their Christmas dinner in his workshop at the Waterman's Cottage. They would dine on the great tables in his room. 'Then there will be room for us all!' she beamed.

'All' for Kitty was an amorphous group which changed each year. She cast a wide net at Christmastime when she celebrated not just the birth of the Babe in Bethlehem, but her own birth, some unknown day around Christmas, to Maria Tipton, the mother she had never known. This year, as well as the family, there would be old Luke, William's Egyptian servant; Luke's even more ancient brother Matthew, who lived in a little mediaeval hospital in Priorton, with six other frail old men. Of course there would be Miss Pansy, who had settled into the Lodge with an ease which surprised Mara. Miss Pansy watched and adapted, fitting in like some fragile animal, taking the colour of new country.

Some days before Christmas, Kitty and Tommy were sitting with Mara in the parlour of the Lodge, watching the firelight and listening to the mouse-like clicks and clatters in the kitchen as Miss Pansy made her special Christmas cake.

Kitty ticked her notebook. 'Mrs Grayling the cleaner from the Priorton shop is coming. Her husband has just died, and her two sons are off training somewhere with the DLI. And Miss Aunger, of course.' Miss Aunger, a graceful old spinster who managed the lingerie department, always came to Christmas dinner. 'And I've told the Commandant at the hospital that any soldier who could not get home would be welcome.'

'That could be dozens.' Mara moved to sit on a windowsill. She lifted the curtain to peer at the sleet outside, giving half an ear to Kitty as she went through her list

'He said just two of them. Apparently those boys have had lots of offers in the district. They've had to share them out rather thinly.'

'Can I invite two more, Mama?' The words were on her lips as the thought came to her mind.

'There's always room. You know that.' Kitty sucked the end of her pencil. 'Who've you in mind?'

'You remember the brother and sister, those French people? I brought them a letter from their father, the man who died . . .'

'Oh yes, poor scraps!'

'Scraps!' Mara sighed impatiently. She loved her mother dearly, but it had always been a problem trying to get her total attention. She had tried to tell her mother about the French people, and had to give up in the end as Kitty had been distracted with some crisis in the shops, and with trying to make Miss Pansy feel at home. 'Mama, you didn't listen. You never listen. This 'scrap' is a grown man, at least twenty-five and as sour as a bunch of lemons. The sister's younger and as mad as a hatter.'

'They sound delicious, but do you know them? Do you really want them here?'

Mara paused, wondering why she was asking this. The fact was that the two strangers on Bridge Street had been on her mind, burrowing away like a pair of moles. 'They were a funny pair, but they were sad, Ma. They're having a bad time. Do you know their mother came from round here? But in spite of that, they've been attacked in Priorton market and accused of being the dreaded Hun. The woman's hair was pulled. Think of that.'

'But they're French!' said Tommy indignantly.

'So they are. I tried to tell you about it. In France they were attacked in their own village by English soldiers'. She paused, then said painfully, 'Their mother and the girl Hélène were

66

raped. Oh Mama, the mother died soon afterwards and her daughter's mind has never recovered. So, for shame, they were given safe passage back to their mother's home.'

Kitty frowned fiercely. 'And their father was killed in the bombardment, did you say? How terrible.' Her face cleared. 'One of our Christmas dinners might make a small difference. Luke's cooking some of his spicy things, and I've ordered a big goose at Gregg's. And Miss Pansy has promised us her special herb puddings and Durham Salad, as well as this Christmas cake. Then your French friends'll know they're welcome here, with that inside them. 'She looked at Mara over her silver-framed spectacles. 'And there'll be entertainment. Did I tell you your Aunt Esme and her Thomas are coming? They'll perform for the boys in the hospital on Christmas Eve. And for us at home on Christmas Day.'

Tommy groaned. 'You won't let her sing that awful song, will you? What is it? 'A Little of What You Fancy'?'

Kitty chortled. 'Oh, aren't we all pompous, little Tuppence? I'll have you know, Tommy, Esme's sung for the Old King many times and *he* didn't mind "a little of what you fancy".'

Mara stood up, away from the window. 'Oh, Mother! You're too bad!'

'Aren't I?' said Kitty. 'I've told you many times you have to do your damnedest at whatever you do and be yourself, whatever happens. And that's what Esme does. No pretence. Tuck in your chin and set square to it all, as Ishmael would say.'

Ishmael, who had brought Kitty up after she was abandoned by Maria Tipton, had taught her to box, a skill which, one way or another, had stood her in good stead all her life.

'That's what Esme's done and I'm proud of her. So don't you turn your nose up at her, lady!'

Mara blushed. She'd had the 'boxing lecture' from Kitty several times in her life; the last when, having read some rather jolly novels on boarding schools, she had taken it into her head that she wanted to 'go away' to school. Kitty had refused point blank, saying Mara's childhood illnesses would be bound to return, in such prisons of places.

'I'm not turning up my nose, Ma. Esme's one of my favourite people.'

'And Thomas is fine,' said Tommy from his corner. 'I'll get my squeeze box out and we'll play you music to dance the year out.'

Kitty took Mara's hand and looked up at her. 'Well, invite your French people for their dinner, child. It would be nice to think we would be able to celebrate with them the end of the war. How many people said it would all be over before Christmas!'

'No chance of that,' said Tommy from his corner. 'Things are only warming up over there.'

'Wishful thinking,' said Mara. 'You're just waiting to go! Don't want to miss it.'

'Wouldn't any man?' said Tommy fiercely. 'Wouldn't anyone worth their salt?'

'Well, Tom,' Kitty nodded, 'that's facing up to it. Ishmael would have approved.'

'Then you must let me go, Mama.'

She shook her head. 'You're too young, Tommy. Bide your time. It says in the paper the Prime Minister has promised there will be no conscription, but everyone else says it's bound to happen. Bound to . . .'

'I'm not waiting to be forced,' he said vehemently. 'I'll enlist like any man should.'

'As I said, Tommy, you're too young.' Kitty stood up and tucked her notebook into her pocket. 'I'll just go through there and see what havoc Miss Pansy's making with her inspired cooking.'

The door clashed behind her. Mara looked at Tommy. 'I wish she wouldn't do that.'

'What?'

'Call me child!'

★   ★   ★

Jean-Paul stayed at the door and kept Mara standing on the pavement. 'For our Christmas dinner?' he said, frowning.

'At twelve o'clock on Christmas Day.'

'I do have Christmas Day off work,' he said cautiously.

'Where do you work?' Somehow she had not thought of him as working.

'I work in the mine. Black Owl Pit it is called.'

'You're a pitman – a miner?'

He shook his head. 'I do not dig for coal. I am a joiner, I work with wood in the mine.'

'Well, if you have Christmas Day off, you can come for your dinner.'

'I would not know where to go.'

'Don't worry, I'll come and guide you.'

On Christmas Day Mara persuaded Tommy to drive William's motor car down to Priorton to collect the Derancourts. Mara was impressed that Jean-Paul did not comment on the strange gleaming monster that sat before his narrow door, even though it was surrounded in seconds by wide-eyed barefoot children who considered the sight of the motor car an unexpected Christmas treat.

Jean-Paul looked neat and surprisingly young in his collar and tie and his short jacket. His ruddy skin gleamed with recent scrubbing and his unruly black hair had been imprisoned inside some shining pomade. Hélène looked breathtaking in a narrow black dress simply decorated by a fine organdy collar edged with lace. She drew on a heavy shawl with a long silk fringe and smiled at Mara. 'Now I am ready, little one.' Her voice stumbled over the English. 'It is kind for you to say come to dinner.'

Tommy, with another man in the car, could not resist showing off and driving fast, and they all had to clutch onto their hats on the way back. As they drew up in the dirt lane beside the rough gates Mara felt pleased that it was the Waterman's Cottage to which she was bringing them, not the imposing portico of Purley Hall itself. Through the years she had escorted various waifs and strays through that great portico, only to have the poor souls run away in terror. Some braver souls, once inside the house, were so stiff that they were unrecognisable as the delightful harum-scarum companions of hedgerow adventures.

Mara was old enough now to realise what a dilemma her unconventional family placed on the people who swam in their direction. The Scorton-Rainbow ménâge did not – could not – 'move in society' as Miss Pansy Clarence might put it. After all, the head of the household was not married to his lady, was he? In fact, there was no proper 'household', as the whole *shebang* was run by three Egyptians, whom William Scorton had brought back from an early archaeological trip to Egypt. Not a butler, housekeeper, or gardener to be seen. Now, of course, there was only Luke with John dead and Matthew in his old man's retreat.

The people who comprised 'society' in Priorton were at a loss to know how to deal with this strange family at all. So, in the way of such things, they closed their eyes to the problem altogether, and dealt with William Scorton as a successful and important manufacturer, and with Miss Kitty Rainbow as a clever woman of business who owned and ran that wonderful drapery shop called Rainbow and Daughter.

And that was that. Mara and Tommy suffered the occasional abusive cry of 'bastard' in school and street; this was eventually avoided by Mara not going to school at all, and Tommy going away till he was sixteen to a school in Knaresborough.

As Mara walked with Jean-Paul and Hélène into the work-room, white winter light was flooding down from the great skylight, spilling onto the centre of the table, which was laden with fruit and fine crystal. The room seemed full of people sitting, standing and lounging around it. In a corner stood Thomas Druce, playing something from Handel on a magnificent piano accordion. Mara's Aunt Esme, magnificent in feathers and a velvet dress with a high collar studded with semi-precious stones, was holding court at one end of the table. Two young soldiers in blue hospital uniforms were hanging onto her every word.

Mara blinked, recognising them as the two soldiers she had talked to in Purley Wood: Dewi and Alexander they were called, weren't they? Tommy moved across to sit beside them, lining up questions in his head to ask about the excitements of fighting the war in France.

Hélène Derancourt took a step back. Mara grasped her arm and pulled her forward. Kitty walked towards them, beaming. 'So these are your French friends, Mara?' She shook them both by the hand, and put an arm through Hélène's.

William, at the head of the table, tinkled a little crystal bell and everyone took their seats in a random fashion: no set places, another informal custom of the house bewildering to outsiders. Mara smiled her delight across at old Matthew, Luke's brother, a figure of ancient dignity sitting to William's right hand. There was an empty seat beside Matthew, reserved for Luke, still busy in the kitchen below. Mara noted that Michael seemed to have ensured there was an empty seat beside him, obviously for the absent Pansy, also still busy downstairs alongside Luke.

Kitty led Hélène to the table. 'You sit with me, dear. I've been longing to talk to you.' They sat down and Kitty introduced Hélène to Mrs Grayling.

'We're old sparring partners, aren't we, Mrs Grayling?'

'I worked for Kitty here since she was a lass,' said Mrs Grayling, her face folding into a smile which involved the reorganisation of a thousand wrinkles. She cackled. 'A grand lass, Kitty. Allus was.'

Jean-Paul followed Mara and sat beside her. Opposite them were Dewi and Alexander, who grinned at her cheerfully. She introduced them to the French brother and sister and they all leaned across the table to shake hands. Alexander held onto Hélène's hand too long and she snatched it away.

William tinkled the crystal bell again. The door opened and they all clapped as Luke staggered in carrying a great silver tray

71

laden with an elaborately garnished goose, which till a few days ago had been swimming contentedly on a pond on the farm belonging to Mr Gregg the butcher. Pansy followed Luke, with another tray laden with dishes of steaming vegetables.

Pansy and Luke vanished and returned again. This time Luke had a tray of small silver bowls which exuded exotic aromas, and Pansy brought her herb pudding on a Wedgwood dish.

William glanced at Tommy, who filled their slender wineglasses from two bottles of Madeira. Then William stood and held up his glass. 'First I give you the King!' he said. 'Long may he reign over us.'

They all held up their glasses and took a sip.

'Now,' he said, 'I give you ourselves. And may we all be where we wish to be this time next year.'

Mara caught the anguished look which passed between Dewi Wilson and his fellow soldier before they drank this toast. Almost immediately they were cheering with the others and making their toast. Mara nodded and smiled at Dewi and drank hers all off.

'Mara, my dear!' Pansy's plaintive voice came from the other end of the table. 'It is not ladylike to quaff off your wine like that, is it, Kitty?'

Kitty stood up and smiled at her old friend Esme, sitting opposite her. 'I don't know whether any round this table could call themselves a lady,' she said, then drowned out Pansy's protest and raised her glass. 'I would like to toast my daughter, Leonora, my first precious offspring, adventuring now in the cold wastes. We must all pray with all our hearts that she's not taken for a spy. They say it is happening. And my dear borrowed son, Samuel, scamp that he is . . . .' Her voice faltered a little. 'But we have been sent another brother and sister to our table this year, to warm their place. And for this we thank Jean-Paul here, and Hélène, for gracing our table. But for our own two, who are not here, both absent from us now . . . I give you their health.'

Mara stood and lifted her refilled glass with the others, wishing in the depths of her spirit that Leonora were here to share the fine food and the good company, to meet Dewi and Alex, and Hélène and Jean-Paul, even Pansy. Then she would know that, even here in little Priorton, even this little world was expanding in the wake of this terrible war, which everyone had said would all be over by Christmas.

5

'Let the poetry arise from the dead'

'My dearest daughter.' Monsieur Poliakov eased the chain over Leonora's head then kissed her brow. 'This will render you protected in the trials to come.'

'I shall treasure them, Monsieur Poliakov, I promise you. All my life.' The words sounded theatrical and false, but they were pulled out of her in this elaborate situation by the rapt faces of the household looking on under the rheumy, benign gaze of the scruffy old priest who had just blessed both cross and icon to the tune of the slow scrape of violins of the trio in the corner.

Monsieur Poliakov shook his head. 'You must call me Papa, as does Lucette. You are my daughter now.'

She stood up and shook her head slowly. 'I am sorry, dear Monsieur Poliakov. I cannot do that. My own father died before I was born, in a coal mine where he was crushed by a wagon . . . I can call no one else Father. Even my dear stepfather I call by his given name.'

He frowned. 'It would not be appropriate for you to call me by my given name. Madame . . .' he glanced across at his wife sitting on a chaise longue like a collapsed balloon '. . . would not care for it.' Then his brow cleared. 'I have it! You will call me Uncle! Uncle Clément. Thus Russia claims you for her own.' He kissed her on the brow again and his lips felt dry and full.

Lucette clapped her hands. 'Ha! Now we'll be cousins as well as sisters, Leonora.'

Madame signalled a servant by the door, who picked up a tray of tiny glasses filled with a sweet blackberry liqueur and started to offer it to everyone, servants and all. Lucette moved in close behind Leonora and whispered in her ear: 'And where is the handsome Monsieur Samuel tonight? If I had a brother like that, I would never leave home.'

'Lucette!' said Leonora.

Lucette shrugged. 'I'd have thought that he would be here. Papa did invite him, he sent a note. I sealed the envelope myself.'

Leonora shook her head. 'I do know that he's not returned to his lodgings since dawn,' she said carefully. 'I saw him today briefly, but there was no mention of an invitation to this house.'

The time at the 'place of assignation' had been all too short. The carriage had bumped over the road on the way home. Samuel held her hand tightly but he was silent, stunned as was she by the enormity of the step they had just taken. He held her and kissed her before she drew the curtain and alighted from the carriage.

'No going back now, *Leonya*,' he murmured. 'You must take great care of yourself out there under those guns. But if there is a God, He will watch over you. He could not give us this great gift and take it away. When I return from Switzerland I'll call here and find just where you are. And I'll write.'

'Will you?' she had whispered.

'I swear I will.'

Standing now in the Poliakovs' drawing room she felt again his strong body above her, the smooth skin of his shoulders.

Now her elbow was being tugged. 'Leonora, you're blushing! Just what is going on in that secret little head of yours?' said Lucette. 'You are to take a glass and drink the health of Mother Russia.'

Monsieur Poliakov was ringing a little brass bell. Silence

dropped on the room like a veil. He raised his glass. 'I give you Mother Russia and the children who fight to preserve her honour.'

Every member of the company, even the musicians, roared a kind of *huzzah!* and drank off their liqueur before throwing their glasses into the broad hearth, where they were smashed to smithereens on the stones and the great wooden logs, the residue of the alcohol flaring up in blue flames.

Leonora joined in reluctantly, wondering what Kitty would have thought of the waste. More glasses were handed around and Monsieur Poliakov rang his bell again. 'And I give you these two little angels, whose healing hands will bring succour to the bleeding bodies of Russia's children. I give you my daughter Lucette and her English sister, my other daughter Leonora.'

There was an even greater roar this time; the glasses were raised, the liqueur quaffed, and the glasses smashed. The little trio struck up again and Leonora sat on a convenient chair and settled down to enjoy herself among people whom she had come to like, if not love, in this alien city.

It was three in the morning before she got to bed. At four o'clock she found herself fighting off a great body which was attempting to get into bed with her. 'Stop. Stop, will you?' she raged.

'Ah, my little Leonora must have a kiss from her old Uncle Clément, who will miss her so much when she is away.' Monsieur Poliakov's voice was slurred and he smelled of brandy.

She heaved him off her; he fell heavily to the floor and stayed there. She leapt out of bed and snatched up a poker from her hearth. She kicked his side. 'Now get out, you foolish man! Get out!'

He muttered and moaned and raised himself on all fours. She kicked him again. 'Out, I say! Or I'll have Madame in here in a trice.'

He started to moan. 'No, no, sweet girl. *Je suis désolé* – sorry,

77

so sorry . . .' He started to crawl towards the door. She kicked him in the rear to help him on his way, then secured the door behind him.

The poker still in her hands, Leonora leaned against the door and started to laugh. It was not the first time she'd had to resist the very resistible charms of her employer. Normally Monsieur Poliakov was very abstemious; he drank little. However, on occasions which he judged merited it, he could drink as deep as any full-blooded Russian. On these his desire to bed everything in sight – not excluding his own daughter or her companions – was an open secret.

All had their own strategies for resisting him. Leonora had given him a black eye more than once. The next morning in a ritual fashion he would go round and apologise to every woman in the house, for what he might have done. This was a necessary ploy as, after his third drink, a powerful, some would say convenient, amnesia descended upon him. He was genuinely mortified by these lapses and for this was usually forgiven.

Leonora chuckled now at the contrast between the comical battle with Poliakov and the earlier swooning consummation of her relationship with Samuel who, up till this week, she had considered her brother.

She wished she were already at the Front. Things would be simpler there. Perhaps there this powerful pulse inside her which was still beating to the rhythm of Samuel's name, of the swooping endeavours of his body, would cease.

'Mara, my dear, I wonder if you would tell that young woman to either come in or go home?'

Pansy was lifting the lace curtain at the little window. Mara squeezed beside her to see Hélène Derancourt, coatless in the evening gloom, her hair streaming about her shoulders, moving and dancing among the trees along the lane from the Lodge. She was swinging round one tree and then another, talking and singing away to herself.

Mara grabbed a cloak from a peg and raced outside. 'Hélène!' she called.

Hélène flinched away from her, then relaxed. 'Come and see, little Mara, come and see the shining ones.'

Mara approached her and threw the cloak over her, fastening the toggles as though Hélène were a child.

Hélène's hand grasped her chin and forced her to look upwards at the sky. 'See the shining ones! And see – Sister Moon.'

Mara looked up through the tangled lattice of winter trees and saw the bright stars of early evening, coldly brilliant in the winter sky. Hélène's soft, slightly accented voice whispered on in her ear. 'There they shine, little one, there they shine. We fumble and we fall and they still shine, up there for us. Vile creatures oppress us and thrust their way into us, and still the stars shine and Sister Moon rides high. She has no care for them, no care for us. But she shines on us just as true. She shines down on my village at home, my cousins and my friends . . .'

'. . . and she shines on Leonora, my sister,' said Mara, struggling against the hand which was still clutching her chin.

Hélène's voice went on: '. . . And Mama deep in the earth across there, and Papa here in England in the earth beside the sea . . .'

Mara pulled her chin free and brought Hélène's glazed, wide-eyed face towards hers. 'They *are* amazing, Hélène, yes – they are wonderful. But you must come inside now. Look, your hands are blue with the cold.'

She took the cold hands and pulled the babbling Hélène towards the house. Once inside, she sat her beside the parlour fire. Pansy stood in the doorway, her arms folded. 'She is not fit company for you, my dear,' she murmured. 'I have mentioned the fact to your mother a number of times.'

Since Christmas dinner at the Waterman's Cottage, Hélène had turned up at the Lodge every two or three days. One time she brought a jar of face cream for Mara. A velvet hair ribbon.

A string of glass beads. She would thrust them through the door, then run away. This was the first time she had been inside the Lodge.

Mara started to remove the cloak and realised the shoulder under her hand was shuddering. Hélène's smooth brow was burning. 'Hélène! You're not well. Pansy, will you get her a rug?'

Pansy hesitated for a second longer than necessary, then went off and brought a blanket from Mara's own bed. Hélène was still muttering under her breath about the moon, her beloved Sister Moon.

'She's raving mad,' said Pansy. 'You could see that from the first.'

'She's very ill,' said Mara. 'You would be raving if you were boiling up like this.'

Pansy sniffed. 'I hardly think so, my dear.'

Mara longed for Kitty to be there to bring her own brand of common sense to the problem. But these days her mother was immersed again in some quandary about the shop. She was losing all her assistants to the Army and the better paying munitions factories, and was having to appoint and train older women who had never been out of the house before. She clicked her tongue about this, saying it ate up such a lot of time, but Mara knew her mother was never happier than when getting her teeth into a big problem, and also that the fluttering Pansy was getting on even the charitable Kitty's nerves, as she was getting on the nerves of everyone in the house. Tommy kept asking in sepulchral tones when the dear lady was going back to Hartlepool?

'Miss Derancourt should go home,' Pansy was saying with whispery determination. 'If that young woman is ill she should be in her own home.'

'Jean-Paul will be at work, so we can't take her home,' said Mara, equally firmly.

'He's a workman, I believe?' said Pansy.

'Yes. He's a joiner at Black Owl Pit. He says there's lots

80

of work down there, with all the men volunteering and them recruiting miners to the army to dig their trenches and tunnels for them.'

Pansy sniffed.

'There's nought wrong with being a workman, Pansy!' protested Mara. 'My own father was just such when he was young.'

'My dear, I did not say there was. It is just that your poor dear mother, such an energetic and dedicated person, does not go into society and does not truly understand—'

'My mother, Pansy, understands perfectly well about things.' She brushed past Pansy and made her way towards the kitchen. 'Now, where can I get a cloth and bowl, to cool poor Hélène's fever?'

That evening, with the French woman ensconced in Mara's bed and the house safely in her mother's, rather than Pansy's, hands, Mara cycled down to Priorton and knocked on the door of the house on Bridge Street. It was wrenched open instantly by a wild-looking Jean-Paul.

He peered into the darkness behind her. 'Where is she? Where is my sister?' he asked roughly. 'I have combed these streets.'

'She's in my house, in my bed,' said Mara. 'She wandered down there. She has some kind of fever. She needs taking care of.'

'I will take care of her. I take care of her always.'

Mara almost flinched at the resentment, the pain in his handsome face. She stifled a longing to reach out and touch him, to ease his mounting despair.

'My mother says she is too ill to move, so she must stay there. She'll be better in a day or so, and I'll bring her home then.'

He groaned, and opened the door a little wider. 'I am sorry, Mees Mara, always so . . . Come in.' She followed him into the square kitchen. The fire was roaring and the table was set for two. 'I thought she had fallen into danger. Some . . . people had got hold of her and knocked her about again.'

81

'It still happens?'

'They still shout at us. At the pit today there were two dead rats nailed to my workbench.'

'They are still calling you Germans?'

He shrugged. 'War is being pumped into them at every hour. Their brothers are killed and maimed. They need an enemy. They wear the khaki arm band which says they would go to war if the pit would let them go. I don't do this, so now they say I am the cowardly Frenchie who runs away from the fight when their cousins and brothers die for France.' He leaned against the high mantel and looked into the fire. 'In some ways they have justice. If it weren't for Hélène I'd be there fighting with my countrymen, and yours.'

'Our Tommy's burning to fight, desperate to get over there.'

'The soldiers at your dinner table were not so very eager to talk about how wonderful it is there.'

She nodded. It was true; all through the Christmas dinner Tommy had plied Alex and Dewi with keen and probing questions, but the soldiers had fobbed him off, making a joke of his eagerness.

Jean-Paul pursed his lips. 'They know all too well it is purgatory, not glory. They say it brings out the best in men. Per'aps it does. Me, I have seen that it brings out the devilish worst.'

Timidly she put a hand on his arm. 'Don't blame us all, Jean-Paul. Those men . . . they're not all of us.'

He looked at the hand then turned and took her by the shoulders and kissed her broad brow. 'You are too young to be so wise,' he said. She stood very still, not wanting to make any move which would spoil the moment. She could feel his strong hands through her coat. Her pulse raced and she knew her face had blushed bright crimson. Then, finally, he put her away from him. 'Now what will we do about my poor sister?'

She took a breath. 'Let her stay with us a few days. Then I'll bring her back when she's better. She likes it there. I think she thinks she's my friend.'

*　　*　　*

Leonora sat with a letter-pad on her knee in the doorway of the house, drinking in the sight of the endless line of mountains which undulated in the distance, stretched out like the contours of a great cat sleeping under the moon; she peered at the swathes of trees glowing six shades of inky purple in the evening light. She had asked Pavel Demchenkov about the howling that came intermittently out of the forest. He had puffed on his great cigar and assured her it was wolves. 'And there are bears also here in the Carpathians, sister. Lynx too. Your Mr Browning writes of him. *A black lynx snarled and pricked a tufted ear.* A fine poet, Mr Browning.'

Pavel Demchenkov was the fat surgeon, one of two surgeons attached to their unit, their 'flying column'. Pavel was forceful to the point of bullying, but had never been less than polite with Leonora. He had reduced another nurse, Larissa, to tears more than once in the month it had taken them to get to this, their first stopping place. But he talked to Leonora.

He had just been telling her about reports he had heard that the English and German soldiers on the French Front had drunk and danced together, played football and exchanged gifts on Christmas Day. 'They say it put the English generals in a great rage.'

'What do you think about it?'

'I think the ordinary man dares to see the truth, the sane truth – that they are merely pawns in a great game. And it being a game, they can make a truce and recognise their own humanity.'

'And what do the generals think?'

'They think it is treason.'

The clean scrubbed house which was to do service as their clinic seemed rather ordinary, bleached of personality or the mark of human occupation. Nevertheless the guns which boomed in her ears told Leonora that all this would not seem ordinary for long.

She took up her pen and wrote again. *So, dearest Mara, it has taken us a month to get here. A whole month! We came through Przhevorsk, Lantsut, Rzheshchuv, Shchani, Rhopchytse, Dembitsa, Yaslo, Krosno and now Gorlitse. Such names! But Gorlitse is a sad town, five months under gunfire, its people starving, begging food off our soldiers . . .*

She could hear a stirring behind her, smell acrid cigar smoke spiced with a lavender scent. 'You should be asleep, sister. You will need all your strength tomorrow if you are to help our poor brothers in arms.'

She was about to protest that she was a grown woman, then sighed, snapped her notebook shut and stood up. 'Perhaps you're right, sir. There will be time enough to write letters.'

Pavel Demchenkov shook his head. 'I don't know about time, sister.' He leaned back and she had to squeeze past him. She felt his plump hand on her forearm. 'Prepare yourself, sister. The territory we inhabit between life and death is like one of the Circles of Hell. Prepare yourself.'

The next day she thought of his words, felt again his plump hand on her arm, as the neat house was shaken to its foundations, the very hinges on the door rattling. In their corner she and Larissa dealt with one battered lump of flesh and muscle after another. Some of these lumps had voices, limpid pleading eyes. Some had clutching hands which grabbed her arm, reducing the glamorous snowy linen to a kind of ginger muddy colour, the colour that children make when they are left with the paint box too long.

And still they came, crawling and hobbling in their impossible hundreds. With only eight nurses and two doctors they could only deal with one soldier, then another one, then another one, becoming machines of careful, skilful response to what were impossible demands.

Some of the walking wounded were sent stumbling straight on to find their way to units further back. Some were patched and heaved onto ambulance wagons to be sent off to hospital. At about the fifteenth hour, Leonora closed her eyes just once and could see, crystal clear in every detail, the production line at Scorton's Works, with girls head down over their delicate war machines, their shells and bullets, just as she and Larissa bent over the bodies of these poor boys. She blinked her eyes and started again. 'And now, little brother, let me help you. Your arm must hurt you really badly.'

After twenty hours she and Larissa were ordered to bed by Pavel Demchenkov. They crawled onto their cots in their filthy uniforms and slept instantly. Leonora dreamed of the other time of blood, when she was twenty-three and had just lost the baby which was the consequence of her first failed affair. She and the bed were covered in blood. It seemed as if her mother Kitty, too, was up to her elbows in gore.

'Oh, Leonora,' Kitty was saying in a bubbling underwater voice. 'Oh, my poor dear Leonora. How could you?' And then Kitty seemed to turn into Pavel Demchenkov, whose voice was booming out, reciting the cantos from Dante's *Inferno*, then bellowing loudly in her ear, 'But remember Purgatorio, sister. The great Dante tells us, *But here let poetry rise again from the dead*. From the dead, sister. I say from the dead.'

Then Leonora was looking down between her legs and there was a young boy with blood on his face and very blue eyes. And he was saying, 'Tell them my name is Yevgeni Teresov, *sestra*. Tell them!' His bloody hand came towards her.

She screamed. 'It is a boy. A boy!'

'*Leonya!*' Her arm was being shaken, her face slapped. 'Come on, dear friend. There is more work to do.' Larissa's anxious, frightened face loomed close to hers. 'More of them are coming. We are needed!'

6

Picnics

'Aye, Tommy, how's tha' gannin'?'

'Aye, bonny lad, whay moves ye?'

Tommy winked and grinned at the two women on the assembly line. 'Now, Maisie, Ethel, what or who it is that moves me's too dangerous for sweet innocents like you to know.'

Maisie hooted with laughter and Ethel winked back at him. The women, who had both passed the first bloom of youth, still glowed with present promise. The fact that they glowed a vivid yellow was not their fault – rather that of the deadly materials which they daily handled with such skill and careful ease.

He paused a second to count the raw materials at the end of their line, and carefully noted the numbers in his book. As he passed the gleaming rows of shells nestling in carefully contrived tiers of cases made of bright undressed wood, he put his shoulders back with a certain pride. The town of Priorton, and the people at Scorton's Works, could hold their heads up with pride, he thought gravely. England had not found them lacking when the call was made. These commonplace axioms came to him naturally, readymade for him from his close reading of the press since the day war was declared. He was consciously proud that Scorton's were upping production every week, and in the town men were pouring out of the shops, the pits and the ironworks to volunteer for the Army, to be heroes for their homeland.

Tommy marched along the walkway, disconsolate again at being denied his right to to play his part. By the time he was old enough, the whole show would be over! Lads from the works who were younger than him had already gone off and joined up. True, they must have puffed out their chests and stood up on their heels and claimed to be eighteen. But that wasn't a hanging offence, at least not in these times.

Tommy had cornered his brother Michael in his office yesterday on just this matter of volunteering. Michael had heard him out, then left a silence which lasted too long. 'Don't be silly, Tommy, dear boy.' Michael had coughed then, and adjusted his immaculate necktie, a rather brightly coloured item which had been a Christmas present from Pansy. 'Time enough for you to go to war, old boy. Scorton's needs you here. We've slimmed down too much here, with all these fools rushing off to war. Skilled men, too. There are too many women around here as it is. The place is like a hen coop. And now the government's agreed to subscription, even the unwilling fellows will go. Not that you should worry about that – there's grounds now to keep you here at Scorton's as essential labour. No tribunal would turn us down, believe me.'

Tommy had groaned, then stuck out his chin. 'I'll tell you this, Michael. The minute I'm eighteen, I'm off. This place can run without me. Easy. Bring in someone – anyone, Miss Pansy – in my place. I don't care.'

'There was the slightest flicker in Michael's eye at the mention of Miss Pansy, before he glanced down at the seductive figures in his ledger. Tommy knew he had been dismissed.

'Daydreaming again, Tommy lad?' Maisie, gently laying her lethal shell to rest, called across to him.

Tommy put down his notebook at the end of her bench, removed his brown work coat, folded it and placed it on top of the notebook. Then he turned on his heel.

Ethel's voice followed him. 'Where to now, bonny lad?'

'The Army,' he said. 'I'm sick of this.'

A ripple of cheering followed him as he strode towards the

big doors. His shoulders went back again. His step lightened. This was more like it!

He turned many heads with his bold fresh face and his handsome head of hair as he marched through the bustling Market Day crowd. In his imagination he was already wearing his khaki battledress and his smart DLI cap. As he turned into Neal Street, the door of the billiard hall stood drunkenly ajar, exhaling a seductive draught of fuggy heat, beer, and tobacco smoke. Almost without thinking, he turned and walked through it.

The long low room was dark; sooty lamps hung over two of the eight tables. Four elderly men were leaning over the green baize, their cues clicking drowsily against the balls.

'Now, Tommy,' said Titus Lawler, an ancient Scorton hand. 'In for a game?'

'Might as well,' said Tommy. 'It'll be my last.'

'Why's that, son?'

'I'm volunteering today.'

'The regimental band was marched down the High Street yesterday, flags flying,' said Titus, rubbing his chin. 'Recruitin' by the dozen, they were. They think it'll be a bliddy picnic.'

'Aye,' said another old man at the table. 'It's mebbe all right, now, marrah, with them pipes skirling and those bright buttons. But wait till all that steel cuts a feller's flesh, that's what I say.'

Titus fingered his nose and peered at Tommy. 'Aye, lad, Old Volley here knaas what's what, son. Saw it all against the Turkeyman, and at Mafeking.' He coughed and spat into a convenient spittoon. 'Now what about this game?'

Tommy shrugged out of his jacket and hitched his sleeves up inside his arm bands. 'All right then, one last game,' he said. 'Before I go.'

After a few days at the Lodge, Hélène Derancourt's fever abated and she started to wander downstairs. Pansy was most affected, tutting over her undressed hair, her wild singing and in French too! The others barely noticed her. William was always at the Waterman's Cottage working away with old Luke on some project or other, and Kitty and Tommy were off each day at the crack of dawn for their work in Priorton. Tommy in any case was full of talk about the young flier who had bombed a Zeppelin over London, asking anyone who would listen whether he should opt for the Royal Flying Corps rather than the Army.

One day Mara, nerves jangling with Pansy's delicate complaints, suggested she and Hélène go off together for a picnic. Hélène clapped her hands at this, and Pansy stifled her automatic protestations, rather engaged by the thought of having the run of the house for most of the day.

She did make a token protest. 'It's too cold to go wandering off,' she grumbled. 'Even for April.'

'If we put on thick coats and wear boots,' said Mara, 'we'll be fine. We'll go down through the Livesay Woods, to the Bird Hide.'

Pansy frowned at her. 'The Bird Hide? A shooting lodge?'

'No, not for shooting. It's a kind of stone shelter. William and Matthew built it years ago, so Tommy and I could watch the birds.'

The day was bright and cold. Mara slung a canvas bag on her back and they set out. Before long she had to shorten her stride to match Hélène's, who was half a head smaller than she, and had much shorter legs.

They paused on the high plains above Purley Hall for a while, watching the comings and goings at the hospital. A creaking wagon crunched across the gravel and drew up before the portico. A nurse came out and assisted the orderly in lifting the injured men down to the ground. Some set off painfully on their own, on crutches; others had to wait for basket chairs. Some were still in battledress, not the innocuous pale hospital uniform.

Hélène clutched Mara's arm. She spat. 'Look at them in

their dirt-coloured coats!' she said. 'Bad men, little Mara, very bad.'

Mara frowned, then realised that Hélène had fixed her attention on the men in battledress. Crossly she shook off Hélène's hand. 'First of all I'm not little, Hélène. I'm twice as big as you. And no, those men down there are *not* bad. See? They're crippled and hurt – poor ordinary men just like Tommy and Jean-Paul. They've gone out there under the guns and been mown down like so much grass.' Then she realised that she was shouting and stopped. Hélène was standing there with tears rolling down her face.

Mara took out her handkerchief and wiped the tears from the other girl's face. 'Oh, Hélène. Those men that did that thing to you were bad men. Wicked men. But . . .' She paused. It was hard for her to find an explanation. If the men had been German it would have been easier. The newspapers were full of reports about Germans doing similar things to Belgian women and children. Oh, those terrible details . . . But to think they had been English soldiers, who were supposed to be the heroes of the hour!

'Those horrible men are not fit to be in any army,' she said weakly. She took Hélène's arm and they turned their backs on Purley Hall. 'Those men are not fit to fight for England.'

It took them a good half-hour's walking to get to the woods and the Bird Hide, a stone shed with a vast unglazed window on one side. Mara busied herself at the hearth and got a small fire going with dusty coal and sticks which were always kept in a great box beside the fireplace.

She handed Hélène an old tin kettle. 'There's a beck – a river – just down the bank at the back of the house. You fill the kettle and I'll get this fire roaring.' She smiled with remembered delight. 'Then we can have the picnic. Me and Tommy used to do just this when we were little.' Wonderful times. Tommy used to love being out in the open, tramping through the woods, digging dens and lighting fires.

Hélène made off with the kettle and Mara concentrated on

the fire. In ten minutes it was blazing and Mara had laid out the picnic on the stone bench under the window. She peered at the chill world outside. There was no sign of the Frenchwoman. She sighed. Hélène was not fit to be out. Now she'd even lost herself on a twenty-yard errand.

Mara strolled down in the direction of the river, to be pulled up short by the sound of laughter. Working her way round a clump of trees she saw Hélène clutching the kettle to her breast. She was laughing in a coquettish fashion up into the eyes of Alexander Hacket-Barrington. The Welshman, Dewi Wilson, was leaning on a tree trunk throwing a small black ball from hand to hand, joining in the laughter. There was something very grown-up about the scene, with something in the air that Mara could not quite fathom.

Dewi looked up, saw Mara and raised an arm. 'Morning, Miss Mara Scorton! Isn't it a fine spring day?'

Hélène, Alex and Dewi were smiling directly at her now, grown-up smiles which seemed to exclude her from their play.

Mara marched up to Hélène and snatched the kettle from her, spilling water down her own long woollen skirt. 'Where on earth have you been? I've been waiting forever for this water.'

'*Doucement*, Mara!' Hélène smiled indulgently at her. 'There is no need for such concern.'

Mara could not believe that just an hour ago she had been wiping childish tears from this woman's face. Hélène put a friendly arm through hers. '*Ma petite*, I've just invited Alex and Dewi here to join us in our *pique-nique*! Isn't that wonderful?'

Mara shrugged. 'I'll go and put the kettle on the fire,' she said, and stalked off, resenting their laughter as they strolled along behind her.

Dewi ran to catch up and wrested the kettle from her. 'There's lucky you are, Miss Mara, to have such a fine place as Purley Hall for a home,' he said. 'Quite the county grandees, your family.'

She glanced at him, sensing a faint note of sarcasm. 'We're lucky, Mr Dewi,' she said. 'But we're no grandees. We don't hunt or shoot or fish, or hold balls or *soirées* or go to concerts. My brother Michael does a bit of that down in Priorton, but then he's made his own life now, away from us.'

'So you're the odd fish out, are you?' Dewi threw his hand out in a gesture which encompassed the whole of the landscape. 'I've always thought it strange, people owning great tracts of land, being in possession of rivers and hills. Like rivalling the gods themselves, you might say.'

She frowned. 'Nothing wrong with it as far as I can see.'

'You can't think it's fair, living like that, when you go down those back streets in Priorton and out to the villages, New Morven, Brack's Hill, say. There's children there tumbling round in the mud with black hungry eyes and no shoes. And here's you with your rosy cheeks living in that great Hall.'

'We don't live in the great Hall,' she said crossly. 'We live in Purley Lodge. It might be better than the cabins, but it only has two bedrooms and there's five of us living there. I've to share a room with Hélène now, and with Pansy who snores, and our poor Tommy sleeps on a dess-bed in the parlour.'

'Ah, very cosy! But that's the war. You're playing at it, like little girls playing with their dolly's houses.'

Alex and Hélène were right behind them. Alex's light fine voice floated towards her. 'Take no notice of the Welshman, Miss Scorton. Calls himself a Liberal but he's really a Bolshevik with a very black heart.'

They all laughed at this, Mara with them. She relaxed then, at one with them again, included with the grown-ups.

As they ate their plump cheese sandwiches and drank smoky tea, they put their elbows on the stone sill and looked out of the wide window. Before them bushes and trees were disclosing their bright spring green. They watched as two red squirrels made scratching, scattering progress up a large oak. On the far bank a hundred darting rabbits played like children.

Alex and Hélène had their heads together, murmuring and laughing almost inaudibly.

Dewi put a hand on Mara's shoulder. 'Look, a hawk!'

The bird hovered in the air above the bank before plummeting like a lead-weight and scattering the rabbits, then rising again in the air. In its clawed feet its victim struggled only slightly. 'Ugh!' said Mara.

Dewi's hand tightened on her shoulder. 'Law of nature, isn't it? Kill or be killed. It's happening in France and Belgium at this very minute.'

She turned to him. 'But we're not animals, are we?'

He grimaced. 'No, we're not animals. That bird there kills because he has a nest high on that crag, with a mate to feed, who'll give him fine offspring. He kills one at a time. He doesn't pile up the dead in charnel-houses and watch them rot. He—' The door clashed behind them. Dewi's hand dropped from her shoulder. He peered through the window to see Hélène and Alex running back down towards the river. He leaned out across the stone sill. 'Where are you off to?' he yelled.

Alex put up a hand and waved. 'A kingfisher! I saw a kingfisher!'

Mara turned. 'A kingfisher! It's ages since I saw one here. Come on! We'll go and see.'

Dewi shook his head and looked at her with great seriousness. 'I think not, dear child. We'll let them look at the kingfisher on their own, shall we?'

She went bright red then, but kept her peace. She had wanted them to treat her like a grown-up and this was obviously the price. 'Hélène,' she said: 'She's not been very well. Something bad happened to her in France.'

He touched the back of her hand. 'Did you see them skipping down the hill? She looked as happy as a bird herself.'

Mara could not deny that. She reached into her canvas sack. 'I have binoculars,' she said. 'You can see further with those.'

They watched the birds for half an hour and then Dewi proposed another cup of sooty tea, which he made himself. She peered at him over the rim of her cup. 'Those two have been a long time,' she said.

He glanced down the bank. 'They'll be here soon,' he said easily. 'Perhaps there were many kingfishers.'

'I'm responsible for her.'

'Responsible? She must be twice . . . she's much older than you.'

'She's been ill,' Mara repeated. 'Her head . . .'

'Oh, you mean she's a bit cracked? She doesn't look it.' He rubbed his own head. 'Perhaps we're all a bit cracked, these days.'

'She's not like that. But she gets agitated. And she talks to the moon.'

'Well then,' he said. 'A lunatic.'

'No, no!' She pushed him away from her playfully, just as she would have pushed Tommy when he had teased her too far.

Dewi caught her hand and pulled her to him and laid his lips on hers. She let them lie there a second, one part of her enjoying their alien smoothness, which made her own lips itch. Then she wriggled away.

He took a step back. 'I say, I'm sorry. I shouldn't have done that.'

She put up her chin. 'Why not?' she asked.

'Because you're too—'

'Young? Oh, I'm not young, Dewi. I can't be young. I've seen things . . . I was there when they bombarded Hartlepool. I saw things that day – dead and broken bodies, torn houses. My own Head Master with his head . . .' Her voice faltered.

He struck his own forehead with his fist. 'I'm sorry, sorry, sorry,' he said. 'I didn't mean that you were young in that way. Just that you were innocent. A blind man could see you're the most sensible person here today. The rest of us are all lunatics. It's just, being down there at Purley Hall seems to have taken the brakes off a man somehow.'

She leaned back against the stone bench and looked at him. 'You have someone, Dewi? A sweetheart of your own?'

He shrugged. 'I did. But she went off with the local butcher and now I'm very lovelorn.' He put on a hangdog expression and they were both laughing at this when they saw Hélène and Alex walking across the field hand in hand. Hélène's hair was half down and her cheeks were rosy. A section of her long dress was hoist up somehow, and they could clearly see her ankles.

'Uh-oh,' said Dewi. 'Brakes off all right.'

Michael made his way purposefully through the shop and sought out Kitty in her little mahogany-lined cubicle. She came out to meet him, pulling off her black linen half-sleeves. She smiled. 'Michael! Not often we see you here. Come, let's take a walk round the shop.'

He glanced at the gleaming shop. 'Business good?' he asked, genuinely interested. In many ways, as he got older, it seemed to him that Kitty became more and more eccentric. What had once seemed charming now seemed more and more perverse. However, on matters of business he retained great respect for her.

'Hard times.' She shook her head. 'My customers are the ordinary folks, wives of miners and clerks. There are so many breadwinners away at the war now, and those who're left are stockpiling with essentials. There's not much money to spare for the silks and cottons and fancy goods which are my staples. Nothing coming in from Germany. Little from France to tempt those with money. Hard to get stock in at all anyway. Yes, these are hard times for all of us.'

Michael shook his head. 'Hard to believe that, Kit. Little gold mine, your shop.'

She smiled ruefully. 'Times change, Michael. Now if we were turning out Army uniforms, or guns . . .' They stopped just inside the glazed mahogany door of the shop. Kitty looked directly at him. 'Now, Michael, to what do I owe the rare pleasure of your company?'

'Tommy. Did he come over here?'

She shook her head. 'Tommy? Why, what's the matter?'

He frowned. 'The lad downed tools and left the works just

after dinner. Not seen hide nor hair of him since. Really, Kit, that boy's a liability. If he was anybody else he'd have had his notice months ago. He's losing me time as we speak – time I can ill afford. Mooning about the place, sounding off about going in the Army. He'd be better over there in France.'

She put a small hand on his sleeve. 'No, Michael. I want him here as long as possible. I keep thinking the war might be over before it's time for him to go.'

'Not very patriotic, Kit! Mothers all over the place are proud that their sons are taking up the challenge, giving white feathers to those who don't. There was a fight in the High Street over it on Market Day.'

'More fool them,' growled Kitty. 'More fool them. That boy, as you call him, is your little brother, Michael. You saw those soldier boys down at the hospital at Christmas. Not much older than Tommy and so much bloody pulp.' She shuddered.

Michael winced at her language but did not comment on it. 'That's war, Kit. You're saying you don't believe in this war?'

She frowned. 'I don't like it invading my front parlour, engulfing my youngest children. Poor Mara's been going around in a glaze since that horrible business at West Hartlepool.'

He shrugged. 'She's a spoiled, wild child, is Mara. Pansy had a much worse deal, losing her sister like that. But see what a brave soul she is.'

Kitty cocked her head to one side like a bird and looked up at him. 'I do believe you like our Miss Pansy quite a lot, Michael.'

His veiny cheeks blushed an even brighter red. 'Miss Pansy's a sensible woman. Charming. Knows how things should be.'

'Easy to see she's taken with you as well.'

He stroked his chin. 'Sometimes you're so vulgar, Kit. Can't imagine where you get these ideas. Now! What'll we do with Tommy? I always said he was short of a good strapping, that boy.'

She drew herself to her full height, which still left her lower than his shoulder. 'William never strapped you, or Samuel. And he'd have had me to contend with if he'd tried to hurt Tommy or Mara.'

'You've ruined the pair of them, Kit, let them run wild. The girl's unschooled; Tommy's barely literate. And now Mara's running around with those foreigners. Pansy says—'

'Oh, "Pansy" is it!' she said, putting her hands on her hips. 'I'll tell you this, Michael: I'd rather have my children know themselves, and know what it is to be free, than serve their time as a lickspittle if-it-please-you-sir kind of person, greedy for money and making others into lickspittles in their turn.'

He scowled. 'You're making savage insinuations, Kit. Pansy . . .'

The tension went out of Kitty then, and she laughed heartily. 'Oh, haven't I let you get under my skin today, Michael Scorton! Listen, if you and Pansy Clarence want to get your heads together over me and my ways, get on with it. I'm sure it'll amuse you, just as it's amused Priorton folk for half a century.'

'Kitty – about Tommy . . .'

'I will chastise him roundly and send him back to work at the crack of dawn, you can depend on that.' She pulled on her black sleeve-guards, an action which signalled his dismissal. 'But however much you try, I don't think you'll make a lickspittle of our Tommy. Now, I've work to do, as I'm sure you have.'

Michael watched her walk the length of the shop in her tripping gait which only half-disguised a limp she had acquired as a child. He rubbed his chin. You had to admire her, whatever Pansy said. You had to admire Kitty Rainbow. This was how she'd got away with her unusual life all these years: a potent combination of intelligent charm and very hard work.

'Hurrah! Hurrah!' Lucette Poliakova leaned on Samuel's arm

to jump up to get a better view, past the soldier in front of them, of the Royal party as it made its steady way through the crowd towards the Cathedral. 'See, Samuel, the Tsarevitch, poor thing! But he is so beautiful.'

The boy was cradled in the arms of a seven-foot Cossack, his pale face and lambent eyes displaying, as Lucette asserted, an innocent beauty. 'And see the Princesses, and Her Royal Highness,' she chattered on.

'Moths,' grunted Samuel. 'White moths buzzing round the flame which will burn them to a crisp before long.'

Lucette stopped jumping, and looked uneasily at the back of the soldier before them. 'Shshsh, Samuel! You'll be arrested. You'll get *me* arrested.' She pulled his arm and dragged him off through the crowd.

Samuel followed her bidding easily enough. She was right, of course. The Tsar's secret police were everywhere; he'd known them drag people off with even less excuse than some foreigner talking about moths.

They went to a small restaurant where he ordered iced coffee and spiced cake. The place smelled of dust and nutmeg and there were flies buzzing round the lamps, but the cloths were clean and the waiter attentive.

'Didn't you think they were beautiful?' challenged Lucette.

He shrugged. 'If you think corpses dressed and prinked by the undertaker are beautiful.'

'Ugh. You have no sensibility, Samuel. No sensitivity.' The revulsion in her words was belied by the purring warmth of her tone.

Samuel looked at her over the rim of his glass. Lucette was beautiful herself, like a figurine in spun-glass, delicate but somehow exaggerated. Her clothes were fashionable but pulled a little too tight here and there; her hat was tilted just a little too far for good taste; one fragile silk-shod ankle was too much in evidence beneath her slender gown.

He smiled easily at her. 'You're a minx,' he said.

She pouted. 'Is that what you call me?'

'Yes. And an idle puss, to boot. Throwing in your good work at the hospital like that.'

She shrugged. 'I was so exhausted lifting those poor men, and doing all those dressings. The doctor insisted I go home.'

'I could just picture the scene,' said Samuel.

So he could. The fatherly doctor succumbing, as they all did, to Lucette's wistful childish ways, fighting, as they all did, for a place under her exquisitely manicured thumb. The technique she had practised and perfected with her father all these years she put into practice with every man, and some women, she met. She had even inveigled the sympathetic admiration of that crusty old revolutionary Valodya.

Her combination of guileful helplessness, ruthless charm and effective bullying continued to get her just what she wanted in life.

And now, Samuel knew, she wanted him. He was certain, however, that he was proof against her charms. In the meantime she was an amusing-enough companion for these stopovers in Moscow which comprised a combination of the driving excitement of being at the hub of intrigue and change, and neutral stretches of time waiting to see some significant person, or to receive a crucial telegraphic message from London.

He had been glad to accept an invitation to late supper and cards at the Poliakovs' tonight, and would most certainly accept Clément Poliakov's invitation to stay over, and avoid another night in his dreary lodgings. London was always very grateful for his ideas and information, but expected him, like a good patriot, to fund it out of his own pocket. His business deals were drying up in these wartime conditions. There were strikes in factories he dealt with; warehouses were being burned, and he was strapped for cash yet again. He stirred his coffee. 'So why did you really finish working at the hospital, Lucette?'

She shrugged again. 'The uniform lost its charm. The work was unpleasant. Without Leonora it was not such fun.'

He lit a cigar. 'You liked it, working with Leonora?' he said, pleased to talk about his . . . sister. His instinct was still to call her that in his mind.

'But yes, Samuel. Playing with her too. She is a good playmate – hard, giving no quarter. I like that. You also? You liked to play with Leonora?' She put her head on one side.

He laughed easily at that. 'Leonora and I have played with each other since we were children. I used to save her from dragons.'

'Ah. You are sister and brother. I forget. It is easy to forget, no?' She half-closed her eyes and looked at him through her thick lashes.

He drew on his cigar and looked at her through the smoke. 'There's no blood connection between us, of course. When my father and her mother met we were children.' He paused. 'However, we are effectively brother and sister.'

'Effectively? What a very English word!' From her bag Lucette took a silver case and removed a slender cigarette. She closed the case with a snap and held up the cigarette for him to light. 'Are you in love with her?' she said.

He blew out the match. 'Don't be ridiculous,' he said.

'Because it is unnatural, to be in love with your sister?'

'No, not that. As I said, she is not really my sister. Our parents are not even married.'

'Ah! The English. So unconventional!' She drew on her cigarette. 'But why is it ridiculous, to be in love with Leonora? Is it because she is so old?' Complacently she pulled at a small curl that just dropped casually by her ear.

'Old? She is not old. If she's old, I'm antediluvian.'

'Ah, but it is different for men. Everyone knows that.' She spoke with certainty.

'Nonsense. Leonora is . . . ageless.'

'How kind of you to say that. But you're not in love with her?'

'No.'

'You are! You're in love with her.'

He threw down his cigar and the waiter hurried to pick it up. 'No, I am not, I tell you.'

She sat up straight and put one hand dramatically to her ear.

'Now what is it, you minx?' Entertained despite himself, he could not keep the indulgence from his tone.

'I'm waiting to hear the cock's crow. Three times have you denied—'

He stood up, and the attentive waiter caught his napkin as it flew to the floor. 'That's it! Come on – time for home, little lady, before I spank your bottom for you.'

She stood up and pulled her furs to her chin. 'Even that, Samuel, if I deserve it,' she said provocatively.

Later that night he joined Lucette and her father for a substantial meal and several bottles of wine. He played cards with Clément Poliakov and lost all the money on his person. Clément waved off his offer of IOUs for the rest. 'Merely a game, dear boy, merely a game.'

He had been in bed for five minutes, just waiting for the click in his body which would let him sleep, when his bedroom door swung open. He lifted himself up on his elbow. 'What is it?' he said fuzzily. Then he sat up fully. 'What is it?'

Lucette stood before him a second, then leaned to turn his lamp up. His breath caught at the sight of her small round breasts under her fine lawn nightgown. The bed creaked as she sat on it. 'I have a present for you, Samuel.'

'Present?' he said foggily.

She drew a hand from behind her back and held out a small riding crop in fine leather. The handle was slightly darkened with use.

'What's this?' Involuntarily he took hold of it.

'For you to give me a good spanking. That was what you said, wasn't it?'

Sweat started to pour from his brow, in his armpits. 'Lucette! You stupid child! I was—'

'Like this?' she said in a sweet child's voice. She turned

her back on him, leaned over a dresser and hitched up her nightdress. He had an agonising glimpse of round perfect buttocks and slender legs, then he was out of bed, shouting, 'Stop! Stop that, you stupid child!'

He had pulled down her skirts and was shaking her and she flopped around like a senseless doll. She was smiling, her light eyes gleaming up at him. 'Do you want me to do it to you? It that what you want?'

'Stop this! You're turning your father's house into a brothel.'

She sparkled up at him. 'No need to do that. He did it many years ago.'

Samuel dragged her to the door and flung her out in the corridor. He threw her riding crop after her and slammed the door.

Lucette sat where she had fallen for a second, then wiped the blood from her mouth where she had bitten it. She leapt to her feet and battered on the door. 'Perhaps I should be your sister, Samuel – perhaps then you'd let me stay.'

She was sobbing as she walked along the corridor. Seeing her father's door half-open, she went inside. 'Oh, Papa!' she wailed. 'Did you hear?'

Monsieur Poliakov was sitting in bed, waiting. He pulled the eiderdown to one side. 'Close the door, dearest child, and come here to your Papa.'

Back in his bedroom Samuel poured water into his bowl and splashed his face. He patted it dry then walked over to the door and turned the heavy key. Climbing into bed again he smiled slightly to himself. He'd never thought he would see the day when he would throw out a beautiful, if predatory, young woman from his bedchamber and lock the door behind her. He must be getting old.

He took out his last, much-read letter from Leonora. The paper was dirty and stained, as it had been when he received it. Leonora was going through hell out there. She had a brave soul as well as a beautiful one. It seemed such a long time since he was saving her from dragons in Livesay Woods and on the plains above Purley Hall, eating makeshift picnics and drinking water from bottles.

The thought of this made Samuel suddenly very hungry, and he found himself unlocking the door again and creeping along the corridor in search of food. From Poliakov's room came the distinct sound of riding crop on flesh, accompanied by rhythmical groans of pain and delight from the mouth of Clément Poliakov.

He passed the firmly closed door of Madame Poliakova and reflected on something he had known for some years, that there were really no secrets inside families, rather facts which, by some kind of numb consensus, were designated secret to keep the lid on the status quo. It was a secret known to many that those Imperial moths were fluttering far too close to the flame. He and other, much more illustrious, people had said it, time and time again. But it had to be kept a secret, as though keeping it a secret would make it vanish from the universe altogether.

That was as unlikely as a man walking on the moon, in his view.

7

Games

'Mara! Mara!'

The glass in the window was rattling.

She paused a little to ensure that Miss Pansy was still snuffling and snoring, then crept over Hélène's unconscious body to open the window. In doing so she nearly knocked Tommy off the narrow section of roof outside.

'Whoa,' he whispered hoarsely. 'Move away from the window, will you, old girl?' Then very gingerly he climbed over the sill and into the room, his boots in his hand. He crept to the door and Mara followed him along the landing and down to the kitchen. She pulled him round to face her.

'Ugh. You smell of tobacco and old beer,' she said, wrinkling her nose.

He giggled. 'Bin down Neal Street billiards all day,' he said. 'Fine set of gen'lemen down there. All day long. Played fifty games of billiards, must'a drunk twenty pints of beer.'

'You haven't!'

'I have. Insisted on it, they did. Played me for beer as I was going off to beat the Kaiser. An' . . .', he flopped down on the bench, '. . . I won and won and won. Can you believe it? Just wait till I get over there, Mara. Those Huns'll go down like ninepins.'

She shook his shoulders. 'You idiot, Tommy. Mama's had everyone out looking for you. We've been trawling through

Priorton. Mama even sent someone to the recruiting offices in Durham and Darlington.'

She told him how Kitty had started off by being irritated, then had become angry, and then very worried. Finally she became frantic, convinced that Tommy had been set upon and murdered.

He giggled again. 'And all the time I was potting balls down there in Neal Street.'

'Oh, go to bed. You're drunk and you're stupid.' She hauled her brother to his feet and pushed him through to the parlour, propping him against the wall while she pulled down the dess-bed and threw on the blankets. Then she pushed him sideways onto the bed and lifted his feet onto it. 'Now go to sleep, you idiot. Pity the army that depended on *you* for fighting.'

'Mara, don't say . . .'

'Go to sleep.'

When she got back upstairs, Kitty was waiting for her on the tiny landing, with William standing behind her, and Pansy standing behind him. 'I suppose that was Tommy?' said Kitty.

'Yes.'

'Is he all right?'

'Yes. He's been playing billiards and has drunk a bucket of beer, as far as I can see. He's in bed asleep already.'

Kitty shook her head. 'I won't see him now, or I'll give him a punch that Ishmael would have been proud of.'

'He'll be there in the morning,' William yawned. 'You can tear a strip off him then, Kitty.'

The next day Tommy cowered at the breakfast table while Kitty delivered her ultimatum. 'Your father and I've discussed this, Tommy. You go straight down to Scorton's and you do your shift, and two hours extra for the time you missed yesterday.'

He kept his aching head down. 'Yes'm.'

'Before that, you go to Michael and tell him that you

will work on Saturday afternoon to make up for the inconvenience.'

'Yes'm.'

'Then on the seventeenth of next month, when you will have been eighteen for a whole day, I'll take you down to the recruiting office myself.'

He looked up, beaming. 'Yes, ma'am!'

Mara suspended her fork. 'I wish I were a boy so I could fight,' she said suddenly. 'I'd show those Germans what for.'

Kitty frowned. 'I'd have thought you'd had enough of all that across in Hartlepool,' she said.

'Yes, quite enough, my dear,' murmured Pansy.

Mara looked from one to the other. 'I'd like to take a gun and shoot every German I see, for what they did to those boys down in the hospital at the Hall, and to Mr Clonmel, and to Hélène's father and Miss Heliotrope. *And* me and Miss Pansy. I'd kill every one of them!'

'Mara!' William sounded troubled. 'Don't say that.'

'There's enough with the boys having to do it, love,' said Kitty uncertainly, 'without you doing it. Or Leonora, come to that.'

The pursuance of this war seemed right and proper to Kitty, whatever the difficulties, but the violence of Mara's feeling worried her, despite the fact that many mothers would be delighted at such intense patriotism in their offspring.

'You were so affected by the raid, child,' she went on. 'And you have too much time on your hands. Perhaps you should find something to do, dear. You could work in the shop, perhaps?'

Mara scraped back her chair and stood up. 'I don't want to work in your dratted shop, Ma. And I wish you'd stop, for once and for all, calling me "child". I'm sick of it. Sick of it!' She raced out of the room and they could hear the back door clashing.

Hélène leaned across, picked up Mara's toast and put it on her own plate. Pansy clicked her teeth in disapproval. Tommy chewed a mouthful of bacon. 'Seems like we're all running away, Ma. Must be the season.'

Kitty opened her mouth to chastise him, then gave up. 'Michael keeps telling me what mistakes I'm always making with you two, and I'm beginning to believe he might be right.' But there was the faintest of smiles on her face.

'Oh yes,' said Pansy earnestly. 'Michael is so wise. You would do well to take notice of h—'

She stopped in confusion, confronted by mother and son breaking out into laughter, with William looking on. Pansy stood up and placed her napkin, with enormous care, to the side of her plate. 'This family!' she said. 'This family.' Then she flounced out, pursued by the laughter.

Mara clambered higher and higher until she was in Purley Woods high above the Hall. Once there, she climbed up through the branches of an ancient oak tree until she could see the countryside rolling away beneath her. She clung on, clasping the trunk and laying her face to its rough surface. Behind her in the tree the birdsong seemed to be stilled, and in her ear, under her cheek she could feel and hear a distant hum and for a second she wondered whether she felt the whirling hum of the earth itself.

'Hey! Mara!'

She sat back and peered down at the figure of Dewi Wilson, which looked comfortingly small beneath her. 'What?' she shouted crossly.

'What are you doing there?'

'I'm gathering peascods!' she bawled.

'I'm coming up.'

The tree swayed with his moving weight as he ascended.

'Not here!' she said. 'Sit on that branch. This one'll break with both of us on it. I must weigh as much as you.'

Putting his arm back into its sling and gasping to regain his breath, he looked her up and down. 'Well, you are a fine figure of a woman, but I think I could easily give you a stone.'

She was mollified by his use of the term 'woman'. 'Well, anyway, sit there. I don't want you on my branch.'

'What's brought you all the way up here, like Patience on a monument?'

'I wanted to get away from the Lodge.'

'So what's happened now?'

'I was just saying how I'd like to fight the war like Tommy and they . . . my mother . . . you'd think I'd said I wanted to change into a fish.'

He was staring at her soberly. 'Really, Mara, how could you say that? About fighting?'

'Oh, Dewi, it must be wonderful, fighting them, fighting for what's right. Doing so much good.'

'Good!' he yelped. He stared at her. 'I'll tell you what it's like, little girl. You get orders to go up, over the top. The mortars boom overhead and your heart booms inside you, wanting to break out. A whistle blows and that's it. You do it, because everyone else does it. Your boots slither and squelch a bit in the mud. You crunch over skulls. But still you walk forward, nice and steady. That's the way to do it. Their machine guns crackle and spit. The man who you just enjoyed a cigarette with, *he* falls screaming to your left.'

Mara put a hand to her mouth. 'Dewi.'

'And the boy who's just shown you a photo of his little brother, *he* keels over on your right. You stumble over an obstacle and your nose tells you that it is a comrade, bloated and stinking, unretrieved from two days before. You played football with him behind the lines three weeks ago. He scored a goal. What a right foot!'

He was staring away from her, out over the tops of the trees to the horizon now.

'Then there is this great bang and you're flung to the ground. You feel yourself all over. No damage. Nothing. No reason to stay there. So you haul yourself to your feet again. On. On. Now you get the order and raise your rifle and start to shoot away at them. It's a relief, I tell you, to pull the trigger, but it has no more effect than spitting in the wind.'

For a second Dewi sat quietly on the branch then pulled out a cigarette packet. Absently he offered her one and she took it. He waved his unlit cigarette at her. 'Then you get into a Hun trench and your insides melt with the slightest thrill of success. Our forward bombardment took care of these Huns all right! Here are two bodies. One grey-haired man, arched back, snarling in death. The other just a boy, mousy-haired and muddy-faced, his skin still fresh and full. He could have been my friend the footballer, or the boy with the picture of his little brother.'

Dewi lit his cigarette and leaned across to light Mara's. 'Then I feel this great thump in the arm. I've been shot. Funnily enough the shot came from our side. One of ours, I think, though I don't say so. I tell you, Mara, when I saw my own blood pumping out though the khaki, all I felt was relief. Yes – I was relieved. Now I knew I wouldn't have to march forward in that walk of death any more. My head was dancing with this thought. *No more.* No more of that carnage. It seemed so then. But now, here at the hospital it seems they're very pleased with my progress. Seems I'll be back with my regiment in a week or so.'

Mara suddenly choked on her cigarette and Dewi was full of consternatior... He clambered onto her branch and clapped her heartily on the back. 'Oh, I'm sorry. I never thought. Of course you don't smoke.'

She reached out and put her arms round him then, and kissed him with all her strength. After a second, very gently, he pushed her away to make a safe space between them. 'Now what was that about, young Mara?'

She tossed her head. 'Nothing,' she said, and slipped down the tree and raced down the hill towards the distant Lodge. He stayed there watching her, thoughtfully pulling on his cigarette, then he threw it away half-smoked and followed her down the hill.

★   ★   ★

Pansy Clarence caught sight of herself in the window of Herbert Read's furniture emporium. She nodded her approval of the neat narrow outline, the curled brim of her plain hat as she trotted along with her neat basket towards Michael Scorton's tall neat house.

Mrs Malloran, Michael's housekeeper, let her into the hall and stood with her hands on her hips as Pansy struggled to unfasten her cloak. Finally Pansy handed her the basket and smiled her slight smile. 'Perhaps you could relieve me of this, Mrs Malloran. Would you put the chutneys in a cool pantry and the herb pudding ready to warm over for Mr Scorton's supper?'

Mrs Malloran nodded without smiling. 'I've kedgeree on, Miss Clarence. It'll not go . . .'

'He'll still want it, I'm quite sure,' said Pansy, sailing past, ignoring Mrs Malloran's scowl.

The housekeeper called, 'I should tell Mr Scorton . . .'

'No need, Mrs Malloran, no need. I know my way.' Pansy knocked gently on the study door, put her nose through and, her voice changing entirely from its earlier confident tones, said timidly, 'Michael? I hope I do not disturb you.'

He leapt up from his desk where he was ploughing through a pile of government papers. 'My dear Miss Pansy, it is always a pleasure to see you.' He looked round at the cluttered study. 'We'll go into the parlour.' He swept her before him, back in the hall and into the parlour where a low fire burned. Michael liked his comforts.

He settled her in the deep chair by the fire and turned back to the door. 'Tea, Mrs Malloran, tea!' he bellowed, before closing it behind him and coming to sit opposite Pansy. 'Now, Miss Pansy, to what do I owe this great pleasure?'

Her cheeks were bright pink and she pulled at her sleeves with an affecting nervousness. She had been in this house twice before with Kitty, each time bringing some little thing she had cooked as a tribute to the one person in this wild family whom

111

she recognised as a human being. 'I brought herb puddings,' she said hesitantly. 'I gave them to Mrs Malloran.'

'Splendid. How kind. I'll have them tonight for my supper.'

'I am not sure that Mrs Malloran welcomed them,' she said uncertainly.

'Nonsense. That's just her manner.'

Pansy nodded wisely. 'So difficult to train staff, and you, a man on your own . . .'

He looked at her blankly. 'Anyway, it is good to see you, Miss Pansy.'

She sighed. 'I am aware that this may be indelicate, my calling.'

He sat back complacently. It was odd about this mimsy little woman. From the first time he met her, there had been a 'fit' between them. Like a well-oiled key in a lock. He had been down to the Lodge at Purley more in the previous two months than he had been in the whole of last year. When she had first come into his house he had felt a rush of joy only matched by the time Scorton's had got its first government contract.

He met her nervous, earnest gaze with a firm nod. 'We're mature people, Miss Pansy.'

She touched her cheek, now bright red. 'I wished to talk to you about my concerns.'

He smiled expansively. 'And what concerns might they be, Miss Pansy?'

'Mr Scorton, my sister Heliotrope and I lived the perfect life. We were all in all to each other.'

He nodded gravely; the epitome of sympathy.

'With her passing it was as though my own life was over. But then your little sister Mara took me under her wing and I am in the bosom of your family. A strange family, it cannot be denied. I am at a loss to understand its moral base – that Frenchwoman! – yet you welcome me.' She took a deep breath and sat up very straight. 'Perhaps it is that which makes me so bold. And in that welcome is hope. When I first spoke with you, I felt . . .' Her cheeks were fiery red.

He was on his feet standing before her, his own veiny cheeks flushed in their turn. 'Stop now, Miss Pansy. Let me speak.' He sat beside her on the sofa and took her hand in his. 'Miss Pansy, I am a man who enjoys the things of a man's world. But in you I see a woman . . .' He paused, then laughed shortly. 'We are grown people, yet it's hard to go about this. Let me try again. If your sister were here perhaps I would talk to her about my growing affection for you. And my wish to . . .'

'To . . . ?' asked Pansy innocently.

'To call on you, to give you my earnest affection. To . . . dammit . . . to ask . . .'

'Ask?' she echoed, her eyes bright with excitement, staring into his.

'Ask you to be my wife,' he spluttered. 'There. It's out.'

There was a rattle at the door and Mrs Malloran came in with a very heavy tray. Michael withdrew discreetly to the other end of the sofa and the housekeeper plonked the tray on a small table. She looked from one to the other.

Pansy smiled up at her sweetly. 'Thank you, Mrs Malloran. That will be all.'

They watched as the housekeeper stomped out of the room. Pansy hitched herself to the edge of the sofa. 'I imagine you would like me to pour, dear Michael.'

She poured steadily, one hand placed on the teapot lid, her little finger delicately raised. 'And my answer to your question is in the affirmative. It will be my pleasure, my delight, to take care of you.'

She handed him his teacup and looked him deep in his eyes, and in his breast his heart beat faster than it had on the immortal day when he scored a hundred runs for Priorton against an Oxford Colleges team which fielded three internationals.

When Mara got back to the Lodge from her escape to the woods she found Hélène sitting on their bed wearing her coat and her neat cloche hat. She told Mara very seriously that the tree by the gate had told her that it was time that she returned to Jean-Paul.

'The tree?' said Mara.

Hélène nodded. 'On the first day it told me to stay near you. And now it tells me to go home.'

'Do . . . er . . . things often talk to you?' asked Mara curiously.

The other young woman shrugged. 'Sometimes the tree, sometimes the stone wall. Always the same voices.'

'What do the voices say?'

'They tell me what to do. Where to go. They warn me of the great catastrophe. I heard them in the village when I was a little girl. They told me of the war and the rain of death and said we must come here, to my mother's home. But my mother did not believe my voices and so she died.' There was detachment as well as sorrow in her voice.

'Well, then,' said Mara cheerfully, bouncing onto the bed beside her, 'if they say you must go home, you must go home. I'll come with you. I need a walk.'

Mara went to find her own hat. She was just a little distracted, still smiling inside at Dewi Wilson's surprise when she kissed him. The kiss had been a gesture of pure defiance against all these people who called her 'child', and 'young Mara'. Her action had certainly surprised him. She had even surprised herself. The feeling that rippled down to her very toes was vastly different from the generalised warmth and pleasure she felt when her mother or father kissed her, or when her beloved Leonora gave her a warm hug. She knew that with that playful kiss on Dewi Wilson's lips she had taken a step, almost accidentally, on the longed-for road from child to woman.

'Yes,' she said. 'I could do with a walk.'

The day was fine and they pulled off their hats as they walked along the winding road by the river, swinging them from their ribbons. As they strolled side by side Mara thought how little she knew of Hélène. She knew that she liked the Frenchwoman, that she was comfortable in her presence, somehow more, not less, at ease because of her winsome ways. She knew she felt hot with rage and shame at what Hélène had endured in France . . . responsible for her, in some oblique way. But these voices! She knew Hélène thought that the moon spoke to her, but it seemed now these voices were an ordinary everyday occurrence in Hélène's life.

There was another thing. She was puzzled that Hélène had spent these weeks at the Lodge and not troubled herself once about Jean-Paul, who had taken such care of her most of her life. There was a coolness, a detachment about Hélène in this respect which was bewildering.

At the place where the road forked, one road going down to Priorton, the other bending off to Durham, they came upon Alex and Dewi sitting on a gate. The two boys jumped down and walked towards them.

'Well, well, look who's here. The woodland nymphs,' said Dewi.

'Where to, my ladies, with your heavy bag?' drawled Alex. 'Are you running away?'

'Alex, my dear boy!' Hélène handed him her bag, smiling up at him. 'You must carry this. It is so very heavy.'

Alex grinned his delight, took her bag and offered his arm; the two of them set off walking. This coquettish display made Mara scowl. She turned her cross expression on Dewi.

He tipped his cap. 'Morning again, Mara,' he said, grinning widely. 'Not up a tree this time, I see.'

'You,' she said, 'you . . . man!' And she marched on with her long loping steps.

He let her go on a little, then ran to catch up with her. 'Now, steady Mara. You were not such an off-put this morning, were you?' he said, gasping slightly.

She slowed down and glanced across at him 'That? Oh, that was an experiment.'

'So kissing me was an experiment, was it?'

'Yes, it was. I wanted to know what it felt like.'

'And was it successful, this experiment?'

'I'd say so. It was very nice. Different. I was surprised.'

He looked at her thoughtfully. 'If I didn't know you better, Mara, I'd say you were playing the *coquette*, like your French friend down there.'

'But you do know me better, don't you?'

'And do you see your way to repeating the experiment, then?'

She shook her head. 'No,' she said. 'Not in the foreseeable future.'

They both relaxed then, and walked along in a companionable fashion. On the edge of Priorton, where the straggling streets started, he stopped and pulled her to a halt with a hand on her arm. 'Mara, I've a favour to ask.'

She cocked her head.

'When I got back to the Hall, there was a note from the Commandant, saying I'm due a week's home leave, and then must go on to Wrexham to retrain for the Front.'

'So you're leaving?' she said dully.

'Will you write to me?'

'If you write to me,' she said.

'And can I come back here after all this, if I'm still in one piece? If there is an "after"?'

'Why would you want to do that?'

He grinned then, his broad face smooth and full of light. 'Just to see whether you think it might be worth proceeding with the experiment,' he said.

The town of Priorton was out of bounds for Alex and Dewi so they left Hélène and Mara to make their way through the streets alone. Hélène was chattering feverishly about Alex and how much he loved her, and how he was going to his home in Hampshire, and how he said she was to visit to meet his parents . . .

As they were walking down Bridge Street a voice behind them called them to a halt. They both turned to see Jean-Paul hurtling down the hill after them. Mara felt her heart lift at the sight of him. He was in his work clothes and his face was set in with coal dust. The whites of his eyes shone against the black flesh as he hugged Hélène and kissed her many times on both cheeks.

She put him from her. 'Jean-Paul! I will be covered with coal!'

He grinned, unoffended. 'You are well, Hélène. You look so well!' He turned to Mara. 'Thank you, Miss Mara, for taking such good care of my little sister.' He took her hand and bent over to kiss it, then looked up at her, his black-visaged face full of warmth, his strong black hair standing out like a halo. Mara's heart turned over. She left her hand in his, not wanting to pull it away. Then his expression softened and he clasped her hand tighter for a second before relinquishing it.

He coughed. 'Now, Hélène, Miss Mara, let us drink Home and Colonial tea to celebrate my sister's good health and,' he met Mara's unblinking gaze, 'three friends here in this strange land.'

As Mara followed him into the tiny immaculate house she knew her experiment earlier in the day had backfired. Kissing Dewi Wilson had indeed been a prank, a self-indulgent experiment, but it had awoken something in her, something which meant that a single deep look from Jean-Paul Derancourt could make her blood boil in her veins, and her body, under its girlish garments, curl up in a tight uncomfortable fashion. And somehow it gave her the knowledge that Jean-Paul felt like that too, and that it was only a matter of time before that feeling would be expressed between them in one way or another.

In the weeks she spent in the field of war, Leonora Scorton learned from the surgeon Pavel Demchenkov a harder, more detached attitude to their shared task of dealing with the victims of mass slaughter. She became aware that this unsentimental attitude helped her to remain sane, and thus rendered her more useful to her patients.

In many ways Pavel reminded her of Samuel's friend, Valodya. In the very rare quiet moments, late at night or early in the mornings, Pavel would talk to her in English, sharing his radical view that the weakness and the vanity of the Tsar had exacerbated the sufferings of his people, that he was too ignorant or innocent to realise he was on borrowed time since the 1905 uprising. 'There are strikes in the cities now, unrest in the Army. It is only a matter of time for the soldiers to go on strike.'

'If that's how you feel, why are you here, risking your own life with the Army?'

'That is very simple, sister. These are my people. My loyalty is to them.'

Leonora's fellow nurse Larissa, overhearing these conversations and half-understanding them, was worried and shocked. For her the Tsar had the clear and unambiguous status of a god. What Pavel Demchenkov was speaking was treason. Leonora would shake her head when Larissa said this. Was not brother Pavel risking his own life for all the Tsar's subjects, from the mightiest to the most humble?

Sometimes these discussions made Leonora remember what Samuel had said about the English King, that bluff creature, cousin to Nicholas II yet altogether a more domestic creature: 'Like a farmyard hen beside a peacock.' She stretched, thinking Pavel might be amused by that analogy. Even in the muddy, blood-infested houses they inhabited during the headlong retreat, the thought of Samuel could make her pause for a second and smile. She had written many letters to him and dispatched them back behind the line. She'd received none in return – but after all, where would they go to be delivered? The temporary stations of the unit changed every day as they followed their own wounded, ever backward in the retreat through the cold and the mud of the Russian spring. It would be a vanity to suppose that post would reach anyone here.

Leonora was by far the oldest woman in the unit and found herself being cast by Larissa and the others, in the Russian fashion, in the role of 'mother' or 'aunt'. Like herself, these girls had set out on this black odyssey with naive and holy ideals which came crashing down around them with the passing of each despairing and death-ridden day. But it was to her that they turned for succour and wisdom in equal parts, and she was happy to give whatever she could, though she thought it very little.

But it was when the young soldiers called her 'Mother' that her heart ached most in her breast. One night she knelt beside a young soldier who had been muttering and twisting, his anguish permeating the air around him. The boy had the dark curly hair of the South and his narrow eyes were set in an upwards slant. He could be eighteen, but looked much younger.

'Mama, Mama,' he muttered, coughing and choking. She put an arm under his head and lifted him slightly, smoothing his brow with her other none-too-clean hand. 'Sshh. Shsh,' she said. 'Quiet now, my son.'

His eyes opened and he stared into hers. 'I am frightened, Mama. So afraid.'

She held him to her. 'Do not be afraid, little one. I am here. God is with you.' The boy shuddered and became very still, and then she started to cry, her tears falling on his greasy black hair. 'I feel for you, little one,' she whispered. 'You could be mine, but I wouldn't let you live, would I? So here on this field you're dying again and again, and again and again.'

But for the accident, she would have had her own child. He would have been the age of this boy. The pregnancy was a consequence of a passionate interlude which she had not regretted, but which had no future. At that time her mother Kitty was carrying Mara, bouncing around like a ship in full sail, intensely delighted that even at that late date she could provide a brother or sister for baby Tommy. Leonora's own condition only became evident when she had fallen down steps at Purley Hall and had miscarried mid-term. Even amid the despair and astonishment around her, she had insisted that they show her the bloody parcel and had known he was a boy.

After the first shock Kitty had taken Leonora into her arms and said they would survive this together. She had kept Leonora at her side every minute of the day. She had banished poor William to his dressing room, and brought Leonora's bed into her own bedroom, right up till her own baby's birth. Leonora had been there when Mara was born, and Kitty had put her into Leonora's arms and said she was hers.

Leonora loved Mara. She poured into Mara all the maternal feeling dammed up inside her since she had lost her own baby. It was for Mara that she'd stayed home so long. She closed the eyes of the Russian boy and thought of her own family. What a mixed-up lot they were. She had a sister whom she cared for like a daughter, a 'brother' with whom she was passionately in love . . .

Now, caring for these boys, and with her own life in danger, she recognised again the mother in herself. She felt increasingly that all these boys were her own children. Every one of them. She clutched the dead boy to her.

'*Leonya*, my dear.' Pavel's podgy hands were on her shoulders.

At his side, Larissa gently disengaged Leonora's hand and arm from the dead boy. She closed the half-open eyes. 'Let him go, *sesistra*, let him go.'

8

Strategic Retreats

After their encounter on the branches of the tree in the woods, the friendship between Dewi and Mara, now carrying shades of unspoken affection, moved on from mere acquaintance. Dewi had been touched by Mara's gesture in kissing him; at the same time he was moved by her innocence. His merry assignations in *estaminets* behind the lines in France had been with heartier and rather more experienced girls.

Mara, aware of the honour of Dewi's confidences in recounting the terror he felt at the Front, felt closer to him than before. Even so, the warmth of their friendship was unmarred by passion.

She felt differently about Jean-Paul Derancourt. There were times when she could close her eyes and see him, even feel his touch on her hand. His pale face and strong features appeared unbidden in her dreams. She visited the Bridge Street house most days now, to see Hélène, or to call for her and take her off on some jaunt with Alex and Dewi. When she and Jean-Paul met, Mara was restrained and pleasant and he was always polite. But she felt certain that something was ticking away between them and, looking into his bland dark eyes, wondered if he realised it, too.

According to Tommy, Michael was 'not speaking' to him at the factory. 'Pansy gets down there, taking his lunch, whispering in his ear.' Mara could just hear her, adding fuel to the fire of Michael's annoyance with the boy, twittering her apparently innocent concern into Michael's ear.

'I wish she'd never come here,' said Mara with sudden vehemence. 'She should get herself back to Hartlepool.'

'That shouldn't be too difficult,' said Tommy.

'Not too difficult? It's impossible if you ask me!'

'Nothing's impossible, my dear girl, to a man of great resource.' Tommy slapped her on the back and swept off to work.

Mara saw Pansy and Michael in the street together that same afternoon. She was returning through the town, after a weird morning spent reading Lord Byron's poetry to Hélène, who wished to find lines to write to accompany a small gift she was making for Alex.

Mara stood in the street and watched the scene with amazement. Pansy was walking alongside her bicycle, whose baskets, fore and aft, were weighed down with groceries. Beside her, pushing the bicycle, his head bent attentively towards her, was Michael. So intent was he that he ignored several acquaintances who hailed him.

Mara did not bother to greet them herself, but dashed home on her own bicycle. Purley Lodge was empty, so she hurried along to the Waterman's Cottage and, after exchanging a few inconsequential pleasantries with her father, mentioned seeing Pansy and Michael in very close conference in Priorton High Street.

William smiled up at Mara. 'Now is there a law, sweetheart, against speaking to an acquaintance in the High Street?'

'But he was wheeling her bicycle, Pa! And you should have seen the way he was looking at her. He was blind to aught else.'

William smoothed the bit of beard on the point of his chin. 'Well, you might have something there, Tuppence. It was like that with myself and my dear Kitty. Still is, I'm pleased to say. So perhaps you're right.'

'So what will you do about it?'

He frowned. 'What should I do about it? It is not my affair. Michael's forty-six years old, and Pansy's . . . well, the lady must have obtained her majority many moons ago.'

Mara stared at him and flushed, wondering why it all bothered her so much. Perhaps it was something to do with the way she was feeling about Jean-Paul. She had not been so churned up about things since she had kissed Leonora goodbye as she set out for Russia. She stared at her father's slightly amused expression and shook her head. 'There's something about Pansy,' she said. 'Something very strange.'

She went on to tell William about a theory she was evolving. Pansy had paid very little attention to Mara since their journey to Priorton. Sensing who was in charge, Pansy had focused all her attention on Kitty. She insisted on doing the shopping, although Kitty usually had her groceries delivered. She pampered Kitty when she came in from the shop, insisting that she rested, that she should not lift a finger. Kitty took all this in good part, her only comment a raised eyebrow in the direction of Mara or William.

'Look how she sucks round Mama,' said Mara uncertainly now to William.

'It does make Kitty uncomfortable. After all, she has fended for herself all of her life. She would not . . . will not let me cluck after her. Never has. But . . .'

'But?' said Mara, frowning.

'She says she allows it because Pansy has lost her sister. She's used to having someone to cluck after. So Kitty says just to leave her for the time being. It'll wear off.'

'It's ridiculous. And now it looks as if she's got her refined little claws into Michael.'

William picked up his hammer. 'Well, then, perhaps it will take the pressure off Kitty, so you should be happy.'

Mara gulped back her annoyance, clumped down the stairs then strode off in search of Tommy.

Pansy and Michael had actually spoken with each other of their matrimonial plans, but Pansy was very keen at the moment to keep them confidential. 'I am so recently bereaved, dear Michael – what would people think?' She sniffed and dabbed her eyes. 'I know that dear Kitty and William's own

. . . er . . . situation is somewhat unconventional. So hard to understand when one is brought up in an entirely proper fashion. My heart bleeds for those poor children, blighted for life by what must only be a whim, a whim.' Her voice dropped in obvious sorrow. 'The fact of Tommy and Mara's illegitimacy must weigh heavily on poor you, dear Michael. You have to hold up your head in the wider community of Priorton, after all.'

He smiled, touched by her concern, and helped himself to more food from his dinner-table, where they were sharing the midday meal. 'Don't concern your head, Pansy. Your sensibilities do you credit, my dear. But my father and Kit have always ploughed their own furrow. And Kit – well, she has always been a good stepmother to me and Samuel, if very . . . er, *individual*. The way they are is accepted, oddly enough, even in the wider society of Priorton. You must not trouble yourself over this, Pansy. I may regret it but I must accept it. If we are to commit ourselves to each other, my dearest . . . so must you accept it.' He speared a feather-light dumpling and ate it with relish. 'Mrs Malloran's cooking is improving by the second, my dear.'

Pansy blushed and wriggled in her seat. 'She's a very good woman, Michael, but rather crude in her approach to things.' She lowered her gaze, omitting to tell Michael of Mrs Malloran's recent disgraceful show of temper. There would be time enough to deal with that.

That evening young Tommy waylaid Pansy on her way into the Lodge. He asked how she was, and she said she was very well indeed, thank you.

'Thing is, Miss Pansy, I have to take a trip in the old motor car to West Hartlepool, to . . . er . . . collect some special fine steel for my father. I wondered whether you might like a trip across to see that your house is all right. Perhaps you . . .'

Her bony face was bright red and her eyes sparkled as she looked up at him. 'How very kind of you, my dear.' She turned to Kitty, who was coming up the pathway. 'Tommy is offering to take me home, Kitty. Isn't that kind? Of course, I would go if you wished me to. I'm sure it would be better for you all if I were to leave.' Tears were dripping off her chin now. 'I am so grateful to have been taken into your home and your heart.'

Kitty opened her arms and Pansy walked into them. 'Don't talk such nonsense, Pansy. You can't go home to an empty house. And they could bomb Hartlepool again at any time. No question of it. You must stay here until all this business is over.'

Pansy raised a piteous, tear-drenched face to hers. 'Dearest Kitty, are you sure?'

'Sure as shot.' Kitty patted her shoulder. 'We all have to help each other in these terrible times. I'd not forgive you if you left us.'

Tommy made his way into the house and found Mara, who was watching the affecting scene from the window. 'Sorry, old girl. Seem to have made things worse. Ma's invited her here till the war's ended now, and she looks like saying yes.'

Mara threw a cushion at him.

'Hey! Hey! Stop that! I did my best. Made up the phoney story about going to Hartlepool. But all that Pansy did was bleed over Ma, and . . .' He paused. 'You're right about her, Mara. Half the time she seems like a wet dishrag, but she knows exactly what she's up to.'

Late that night, Mara was called up to her mother's bedroom to help her turn out her linen cupboard.

Kitty pulled her in and shut the door behind her, and then stood with her back to it. 'Now then, Miss, how did Tommy come to offer Pansy a lift back to Hartlepool?'

'Well, he and I—'

'How dare you?' said Kitty in a hissing whisper. 'How dare you plot behind my back to drive a guest from my doors?'

Mara put a hand to her mouth, afraid of her mother's rare disapproval. 'Mama, I just thought . . . It was because of me she's here, and I—'

'Just thought!' said Kitty witheringly.

'Michael was wheeling her bicycle in the town and I—'

Kitty held up her hand. 'I forbid you to say any more.' She put her hand on the worn wooden knob. 'Now I'll go down and help Pansy with the cocoa, and try to make her feel welcome once again in *my* house.'

The door rattled shut behind her and Mara stared blankly at it, her lip trembling. Her body started to shake in its old fashion. The more she tried to stop it, the more she shook. Her mother had never ever spoken to her like that before. Even Mr Clonmel at his most severe had never made Mara feel so bad. She sat down on Kitty's bed and covered her face with her shaking hands, feeling cold and lonely, wishing with all her heart for Leonora's hearty presence, the unambiguous warmth of her embrace.

Leonora had been working three days almost without stop, sleeping odd minutes in her sodden clothes, then rising with Pavel and Larissa and other members of the unit, to attempt to dress wounds and staunch the river of Russian blood which was flowing through their station.

They kept the very unfit wounded with them, and sent the walking wounded back to safer stations behind the line. Sometimes, with guns booming over their heads, they had to load their supplies and their soldier patients into primitive wheeled carts, cradling them against the bumps and jolts of the rutted track. Then, at a spot which seemed safe, they would set up yet another dressing station.

By now the rough cleaning-up of wounds and the hasty application of dressings had fallen to the level of numb automatic routine. Leonora's eyes were dry and bleary, her arms crusted down to the wrists with tide marks of blood and mud. She had to use water and alcohol to keep her palms and fingers clean in a travesty of clinical habit.

The soldiers who were coming to them now had had to resort to fighting with sticks in the absence of ammunition for their guns. Pavel Demchenkov had commandeered the house of a cowman as a clinic. Each narrow room was packed with wounded men lying on straw on the floor. Only the occasional whimper or stifled groan gave voice to the pain which the men were suffering. One man kept up an endless stream of chanting which Larissa told Leonora was the Orthodox liturgy. Leonora thought blankly that there could not be a God who would let this suffering go unabated. The high-mindedness and the glorious blessing implicit in the Cathedral ceremony, where they had all received their red crosses, now seemed to her a complete sham.

One dark morning Pavel came in scowling after consulting with a mud-encrusted Captain riding a once-fine horse. He called the nurses into the narrow scullery area of the commandeered house. Very carefully, Pavel removed his cigar from his mouth and examined its glowing tip.

'You might have guessed it, dear colleagues, but our glorious Russian Army is now in full, official, *in*glorious retreat. The enemy is within whistling distance. There is, as you know, very limited transport.' He paused. 'We are to quit this place now. And we have been ordered to leave our wounded comrades behind. They will delay us and the enemy is almost upon us.'

They all stood for a second in stunned, exhausted silence.

'Come on,' said Pavel roughly, 'they're on our heels. The time for thinking, the time for feeling is over. We are animals, like all the rest.'

'No, we can't do that,' said Leonora.

'I will not go,' said Larissa. 'We can't leave those poor men to their mercy.'

'It is an order,' said Pavel briefly. 'Just make them comfortable and then we must go.'

Some of the men were up on their elbows. 'What is it, *sesistra*, what is it?' said one young man, his eyes wide, his nostrils flaring.

Leonora packed more straw under his bloody head. 'We must go, little brother. I am so sorry, but we must go.'

His hand clutched at her long skirt. 'No, *sesistra*, don't leave me! They will feed us to their dogs!'

Other men took up the pleading chant, clutching at the nurses as they moved among them to make them a bit more comfortable. Then, as they withdrew to the doorway, the pleading voices took on a new, uglier note and they were cursed as whores of God and accomplices of the Hun, as travesties of true womanhood.

Leonora lingered last and Pavel hauled her away through the narrow door. He yelled at her in English. 'Harden your heart, stupid woman, if you wish to survive to be useful to this Tsar-ridden, priest-infested rabble another day.' He threw her into the crowded cart, ignoring the outraged look of Larissa, who had caught the treasonous drift of what he had said.

'Look, there's Dewi!' Hélène shouted in delight, scrambling up the bank. He was sitting there in the window on his own. His arm was out of its sling now, and he looked broad and handsome. Anxiously Hélène peered behind him. 'Alexander?'

Dewi smiled blandly. 'Colonel Black has the Honourable Hacket-Barrington in his office, writing reports. He has a fine hand, old Alex. The Colonel's making the most of him before we go away.'

'Away? Alexander will go away?' Hélène's voice squeaked.

'We're both going, Hélène. You know that. We have always said we must go back. Now we've been told it's tomorrow. We'll go back to Wrexham to learn again how to put our caps on straight, then on to the Front, I should think.'

Mara noted the tremor in his voice. 'No more playmates?' she said mournfully.

'No more playmates.' Dewi nodded.

'So what today?' said Mara.

'I thought a good walk up along the valley onto Killock Crag. That might blow away the cobwebs and stop us all thinking of tomorrow.'

'I'm game,' said Mara. 'Come on, Hélène.'

The Frenchwoman's hands hung slackly at her sides, her eyes were almost vacant. 'Hélène!' repeated Mara commandingly.

Hélène had her head on one side, staring at the wall. 'Yes. Yes,' she said, 'that is true.' She turned to Mara. 'They say I have to go home to Jean-Paul. Or Jean-Paul will die.' She turned and started to walk steadily down the bank.

'What's happening?' said Dewi.

Mara grimaced. 'She hears voices in the walls, and the acorns, the barks of trees.' The scornful words were out before she knew it. She burned inside at her betrayal of her friend. Perhaps she really was a bad person, as her mother had implied.

Dewi was putting out a hand. 'Come on, Mara, let's go.'

Mara glanced back at Hélène.

'Leave her!' said Dewi urgently. 'This is the last time I can be here, Mara. She'll just wander back to Bridge Street. You'll see.'

She nodded slowly, put her hand in his, and walked with him towards the stone bridge which would take them across the river and up towards the fell path. For a few minutes she continued to think about Hélène, but then she was caught up with Dewi's game, chasing down the meadow, balancing across the stepping stones over a swirling beck, then racing up the bank, scrambling towards Killock Crag. Mara, as tall as Dewi, kept up very easily, and it was he who dropped gasping against the high escarpment called The Edge. 'Aren't you tired yet?'

'No, I'm not tired. Just look at all this.' She raised her arms and spread them to encompass the whole landscape then turned round and round, her skirts billowing around her. High above, patches of pale blue sky were fighting a battle for territory with silver-edged clouds. Below them the heather was sprouting the rusty fringe of its first bloom; the feathery surface of the rough moorland grass was rippling in the wind. She felt full of simple life.

'Stop, stop, you're making me dizzy.' Dewi folded his arms. 'As for me, you sprightly mountain goat, I'm tired, and am not moving from here for ten minutes. So you may as well sit down.'

She sat down against the rock. He shuffled until he was right beside her and took her hand, which lay easily enough in his.

'What about Alex?' she said. 'Why did he stay away today? Did the Colonel really get him to write his letters for him?'

He squeezed her hand. 'You don't miss anything, do you, young Mara?' He leaned back against the rock and closed his eyes. 'Old Alex knew that this would be the last time seeing Hélène and he was scared.'

'Scared of Hélène?'

He nodded. 'Well, she takes all this very seriously. She is very . . . dramatic, and that scares him. Plus she's very attached to Alex, as you know.'

'Looks to me like he's very taken with her, too. He's always touching her hand or her arm, dragging her off into the woods.'

'Ah, that's different.'

'Different?' She removed her hand from his and stood up. 'Is it?'

He stood beside her, retrieved her hand and held it tight. 'We're different from them, you and me, Mara. We're good friends.' He paused. 'To be perfectly honest, old Alex is a bit of a light-minded loafer. Never takes anything too seriously. He likes Hélène, truly he does. But in a way, he's seen her as part of his "rest cure", and is girding himself up now for the inevitable return to France. It fills his mind. It does fill your mind, Mara, all that, for good or ill. He's already forgotten her.'

'The rogue,' said Mara fiercely, bringing up an arm to thump Dewi. He caught her wrist and held it from him.

'Hey! Hey! I'm not Alex. I'm Dewi Wilson! You must see the difference.'

He pulled her to him and kissed her. For a moment she

kissed him back, enjoying the experience. Then she pulled away. 'No,' she said.

He took a step back. 'I'm going away tomorrow,' he said anxiously, a certain entreaty in his voice.

She shook her head. 'We're friends, Dewi, you and me. But I don't feel . . . all that stuff. To pretend I did would spoil it.'

He laughed, an edge of bitterness in his voice. 'Such a very honest friend! So, dear Mara, shall I come up here to Durham to see you when it's all over? That is, of course, if I'm not in a dozen pieces in a stinking fox-hole somewhere.'

She winced, allowing the familiar ghastly image of Mr Clonmel's corpse to flow through her. 'Dewi!' Then she forced herself to laugh. 'I'll haunt you if you don't.'

'And will you write to me? Can I write to you?'

She nodded. 'Of course I'll write to you. Isn't that what friends do?' Then she lifted her skirts a little and set off slowly down the crag. He waited a second then followed her. They climbed down in silence. At long last there seemed nothing to say.

In the event Mara received two letters from Dewi – one from his home on the Welsh coast, laced with comic tales of being welcomed as a hero in his small village, the other, more sober, from Wrexham, with tales of training optimistic new recruits before their entrainment to France.

She did not show the letters to Hélène, who came to Purley Lodge every day now, and often insisted on dragging Mara up to the Bird Hide or to the places they had been with Alex and Dewi. One day she brought a soft bag to the Lodge with her. She promptly sat down on the couch, pulled out some cloth, threaded a needle and started to sew.

Mara looked up, then continued to read a piece in the *Northern Echo* about the loss of key Russian strongholds to the Germans. She paused halfway through to think about Leonora, and how long it had been since she had written. After a few industrious minutes, Hélène held up her sewing to the light and Mara glanced across. 'What on earth's that?' she enquired.

Hélène was stroking a tiny collar. 'A small coat for the baby. I embroider it myself.'

Mara's blood ran cold. 'Baby? Whose baby is it for?'

Hélène's laughter tinkled through the room. '*Eh bien, ma chère amie*, it is a great secret. But my husband and I—'

'Husband?' The word shot from Mara's mouth like a bullet.

'You know him, dear little Mara. Alexander, my brave, brave boy.'

'But Alexander's not your husband, Hélène!' said Mara. 'You don't understand.'

'I have told you, Mara, it is a secret.'

Mara left it at that, saying nothing as, in the following weeks the cloth bag of clothes became larger and larger. She even found small scraps of fancy cloth from her mother's cupboards to keep Hélène busy. Her strange friend appeared to be happy about this mythical baby and that seemed, for a while, reason enough to go along with this fiction. But as time went on, she began to contemplate the ghastly suspicion that there might be some truth in what Hélène was saying.

One day she walked back to Bridge Street with Hélène and encountered Jean-Paul in the back yard, his canvas toolbag over his shoulder. They watched Hélène run into the house.

'Do you know what she's making, Jean-Paul? Clothes for a baby.' She watched him closely, pleased as always for the excuse to be near him.

He shrugged. 'She is happy. Leave her with her happy thoughts.'

Mara flushed bright red. 'But what if she . . . if they . . . They were alone together, and—'

He let her sputter to a helpless silence, then put down his bag, his face grim now. 'It is no matter where they were, whether they were alone or not, or even what they did.' He paused. 'I am content that she had a brief time of happiness with the Englishman. But there is no worry. I told you another

132

time about the attack on her and our mother in our village. The doctor say no baby, no children ever for Hélène.' He shrugged. 'So if she dreams a little now we can grant her a dream, can we not?'

'I'm sorry,' Mara whispered. 'I didn't understand.' She put a timid hand on his muscular arm.

He pulled his arm away stubbornly. 'She seemed happy for a time while the English soldier was here. With that I was content,' he muttered. 'But there will be no child. Do not worry – there are poor women in this street who will take the clothes. They will not be wasted.' His glance fall back onto her and softened just a little. 'You're too young to understand. Wait – wait, Mara!'

But Mara was walking away, plodding back up the hill, feeling stupid and young. It was as though she were looking at the world through glass. She could see everything that was happening, but could not hear a thing being said.

Leonora could not fathom the reason for the break in hostilities, nor why their headlong retreat had converted itself to a more leisurely progress. Suddenly there was a little time for them to wash their hair and to boil and starch their uniforms. She and Larissa went out in the meadows and gathered glorious armfuls of summer flowers and placed them in great stone bread jars in the corner of their billet. In the evenings they would sit round a clapboard table to eat improvised albeit substantial and surprisingly dignified meals.

There was some desultory discussion about the progress of the war and the state of the returning soldiers. Larissa told Leonora about her own father, a doctor, who had a new young wife who had swept Larissa and her three sisters out of the house and was proceeding to give the doctor a very satisfying stream of male progeny.

Their postal packet finally caught up with them. Larissa had a letter from her sister bewailing the evils of their terrible young stepmother. Leonora had one from Lucette, who said she had given up the hospital, but: *Your dear brother Samuel and I are getting along famously. He has introduced me to such fascinating people and Papa is loving him more and more by the second.* There was one from Samuel: *I am on and off the train from Zürich with little time to do anything else. Things are at a crucial stage here. But even in the midst of all this you are never far from my mind . . .*' He did not mention Lucette at all.

Then there was a letter from Mara telling of her escape from the bombardment at West Hartlepool, of some French refugees in Priorton, and the curious presence at the Lodge of an odd woman called Pansy. *But in all this, Leonie, you're much on my mind. I'm so proud of my brave sister and tell everyone I meet of your wonderful work.*

The grave, formal tone of her young sister's letter made Leonora's heart ache. Face to face Mara was such a joker, so lively, such a beauty in her own way. She looked up from her letter, blinking in the smoky lamplight.

Larissa was smiling down at her, her slightly slanted eyes gleaming. 'Everyone wishes to write to you!'

Leonora smiled back. 'My brother and my sister and my friend,' she said.

Larissa settled down in the chair beside her. 'Now you must tell me about them, Leonora. The little father God only knows when there will be time again to speak together of our other selves. The selves who live back there in the real world. Come on, dear sister, tell! Who knows when the guns will crack out above us once more?'

9

The Revolt

Kitty looked up at Mara over her half-glasses. 'Would you race up to the Waterman's Cottage, Mara, and get your father? Pansy has the supper almost on the table.'

Unwillingly, Mara put down her letter from Dewi Wilson, describing how they had captured some German trenches and found Belgian civilians there, including women, who had been consorting with the Germans. *Even worse*, he wrote, *we found coffee and cigars, even wine and cheese. Unheard of in our trenches. It vanished very quickly, I can tell you.*

Mara scowled her protest at her mother, whose head was already back down over her account book. Since the *contretemps* over Pansy, relations between her and Kitty had been just a little bit cool.

As she picked her way along the pathway to the Waterman's Cottage, Mara reflected on this new preoccupation with food in the house. In the old days, they had always had such an informal régime. Kitty and William were often late from work, if they turned up at all for a meal. The food was always there, of course, usually prepared and left by Kitty or old Luke. Those who wished to eat had to help themselves. On high days and holidays there were celebratory meals, but by and large people got on with their lives and fitted food around them.

But now large, elaborate and admittedly delicious meals were being prepared every day by Pansy. Even worse, Kitty was now insisting they show good manners and be punctual. She even brought her order books to work on at home, so that she was on time for supper herself. The tasty vegetable concoctions prepared by Luke had been put aside by Pansy with a delicate shudder. She favoured puddings and pies, stews, rice puddings and blancmange. One strange consequence of this was the fact that Kitty was thickening up around the middle, fattening up in her face, as was William. Before Mara's eyes, her parents were changing.

Mara only picked at the food and was rewarded by long-suffering sighs from Pansy and glances of embarrassed annoyance from her mother. Mara remembered the meagre meals meted out to her in the Clarence sisters' house on the headland at Hartlepool: herrings and broth for the most part, supplemented by porridge and cheese sandwiches.

It had taken the bombardment for Mara to realise that upstairs Pansy's beloved Heliotrope had been fed on the fat of the land, being plumped up like a Strasbourg goose. Mara had come to understand that Pansy used food like a message, to secure the affection of those important to her, to bind her chosen ones tightly to her. Now Pansy was practising this food magic on Kitty and William and, indeed, on Michael in his house in Priorton. Mara could finally see that her own meagre meals in Hartlepool had also been a message: a message that she was unwelcome.

Mara quickened her pace. That was it! That sly cat Pansy was currying favour, making all their coats sleek and herself indispensable. And worst of all she was trying to cut Luke from their affections, dealing with Kitty and William just as she had with her sister, cutting out all friends and reducing them to acquaintances. Mara heard the echo of the tremulous voice: 'Heliotrope and I were all we had, and all we wanted.'

'Huh! Sly cat!' she said now, halting by the cottage door. She was met by a worried-looking Luke. She peered behind him. 'Where's my father?'

He shook his head. 'Your father is not well, Mara, not well at all.' He led her through to the small back room which served as his own bedroom. William lay in Luke's narrow cot beside the plain white wall. His eyes were closed, blue veins showing on his lids.

Mara opened her mouth to speak, but Luke's small hand on her arm pulled her out of the room. He closed the door softly. 'He has had some kind of attack. He was violently sick. You must hurry to get your mother. Hurry!'

Her mother listened to her tale, sent Tommy for the doctor, and herself ran the quarter-mile back to the cottage, keeping up with Mara all the way.

When they arrived, they found William conscious, but his face still a dreadful grey. He lifted his head and winced. 'Kitty,' he said, one hand lifting in her direction.

His wife knelt by the bed and took his hand in hers. 'Now, my dear boy, what's up? Been in the wars, have we?'

Mara backed out of the room, and moved into the little kitchen where Luke was standing by the window, firmly rooted as an ancient tree. 'Is my father very ill, Luke?' she asked.

His large brown eyes rested on her a moment. Then he nodded. 'There is a great tumult inside him.' He touched his own stomach. 'Very serious. Perhaps too rich food.'

There was a knock on the door and Pansy pushed her head round. 'How is he?' she said timidly. 'How is poor William? Can I see him?'

Mara moved towards Pansy to stop her getting further into the room. She felt a great surge of hatred for the little dithering woman, but spoke to her in sweet, gentle tones. Two could play at that game. 'He's poorly, Pansy. Mother's with him now. She said she knew that she could rely on you to hold the fort at the Lodge.' She bustled Pansy out of the doorway and back onto the beaten-earth path.

'But who'll take care of him?'

'Mother will. And Luke. He's in the best hands.'

'That foreigner!' A waspish note spiked Pansy's tones. 'Poisoning him with that foreign rubbish.'

Mara pushed her then, on her way. 'Go back to the Lodge, you silly woman,' she said. As she closed the door again she wondered why Pansy had mentioned poisoning. For all she knew, William might have had an accident or some other kind of seizure. And if, as Luke said, rich food had caused the 'tumult' inside, then Pansy herself would be the cause.

The doctor eventually decided that it was indeed a serious stomach upset, some food poisoning, perhaps. Fish that was 'off', meat that was 'off' – they could all be killers, he said airily. He gave William an emetic and they all had to stand in the kitchen and hear him being violently sick. Kitty sent Mara and Tommy upstairs to the workroom, out of the way.

'Poor old boy,' said Tommy, his broad face softened with real concern. 'Never does a thing wrong to anyone, and this happens.'

Absently Mara started to put William's instruments in neat rows. 'Poor old boy,' she echoed soberly.

'Old's the word, when you think of it,' said Tommy gloomily. 'He must have been more than fifty when I was born, and even older when you were born. What if he never even sees me in my uniform, Mara?'

'He'll be all right,' said Mara fiercely. She wrapped the tools up in their velvet roll. 'Tommy,' she said slowly, 'what do you think of Pansy?'

He touched his upper lip, where he was trying in vain to grow a moustache. 'Her? Mad old coot. Irritating, like a fly buzzing on fly paper. Makes good dumplings though. I did try to get her back to Hartlepool, remember.'

'Do you think she's doing all this deliberately?'

'What?'

'Currying favour with Ma and Pa, and Michael. I told you I saw him wheeling her bicycle for her, didn't I?'

He frowned. 'What do you mean, deliberately? They certainly seem to like her. Nought wrong with that, even if we do think she's a bit of an old biddy.'

'Well, on the one hand she seems all simpering sweetness, helping with the cooking, running around after everyone. On the other hand, since she's been here, everything has changed. People are not what they were. They're fatter than they were, for a start!'

'Nobody's what they were, Mara. There's a war on. Everybody changes in a war. And no, I'm not going to offer to take her back to Hartlepool again. There was enough trouble last time.'

'But . . .'

'Mara! Tommy! Where are you?' It was Kitty calling from downstairs.

They raced down the narrow stairs. Kitty was smiling very slightly. 'He's all right, I think. The doctor says we must keep a close eye on him, but the worst is over now. He says it was a good thing dear old Luke was here when it happened.'

'Phew!' said Tommy.

'I wanted to take him back to Purley Lodge but the doctor said he was best here, it's so clean and quiet – good as any hospital ward. Luke was pleased at that.'

William, slightly less pale now, had a weak smile for them. Mara put her hand on his. 'You gave us a fright, Pa.'

He turned his hand and clasped hers. 'Nothing to worry about, Tuppence. I'm in good hands.'

William was in bed for a week, but after two days insisted that Kitty went back to the shop and left him and Luke in peace. Kitty stopped Pansy sending baskets of food along to the Waterman's Cottage, saying Luke's cooking had suited him for forty years, so could not do him any harm now.

William had rather a stormy visit from Michael, who tried to get him to go to the Infirmary, or at least to his house in Priorton where the doctor was to hand. William, supported by Kitty, refused to do this. 'I'll get nothing more there than I get here,' he said wearily.

Back at Purley Lodge, Michael stormed at Kitty. 'This is irresponsible, Kit! From what the doctor says we could have lost him for good, down there in that hovel.'

'It is not a hovel,' said Mara swiftly. 'Luke keeps it like a little palace.'

'And that's another thing. I'm fond of Luke myself. I know he's been a game old boy in his time, but how can he take care of Pa now? He must be eighty if he's a day. More.'

'I have been trying to tell Kitty,' began Pansy timidly.

'Please, Pansy, keep out of this,' said Kitty very crisply. 'As I have said to you before, this is a private family matter.'

Pansy's eyes were full of unshed tears. She staggered a little and Michael put his arm round her. 'My dear,' he said. Then he turned to Kitty. 'The thing is, Kit, Pansy here is just about family. We're to be married as soon as she feels capable. Although with mourning her sister, that may be some time.'

Kitty looked from one to the other, her eyes narrowing slightly. 'Well, Mara did suggest . . .' Then she beamed. 'Well, heartiest congratulations, the pair of you! That is good news at rather a grey time.' She shook hands with Michael and gave Pansy a chaste kiss on the cheek. 'Congratulations, indeed.'

They all looked at Mara, who murmured her congratulations.

Kitty walked to the hearth and then turned to smile at them easily. 'But you'll both do me the kindness of allowing me to care for William in the way I choose. He wishes to stay down at Waterman's Cottage with Luke and I will, I assure you, make sure he gets his wish.'

Mara, sitting quietly at the table, almost applauded, noting with satisfaction the slight tightening of Pansy's loose lips. Pansy was not pleased to be routed. Not pleased at all.

Kitty's covert pugnacity, however, spilled out the next day onto Mara herself. Kitty had returned from a long evening spent sitting with William to find Mara in the parlour lying on the floor before the blazing fire, reading an article in the newspaper about American dismay at the Germans torpedoing the passenger ship *Lusitania*. Kitty removed her hat and leaned towards the mirror, tidying back her curly hair. 'I think you've lain around here quite long enough, Mara. You must find something to do. Pansy was saying about the devil making use of idle hands.'

'Pansy!' said Mara bitterly.

Pansy had not spoken directly to Mara since being thrust bodily out of the Waterman's Cottage, her offer to nurse 'dear William' roughly rejected. Kitty put up a hand. 'She might be a bit of a twitterer, but sometimes she talks a deal of common sense. She just said you were energetic, clever. You should have some work to do.'

'I bet she'd have me go into service and be a housemaid scrubbing floors, given half the chance.'

'Don't be ridiculous. All you have to do is make up your mind to do something. Would you like to teach again? You could matriculate, go to college and learn properly.'

Mara shook her head, shuddering at the remembered dreams of shrouded children.

'Well, if not that, then the shop! You must come and help me. You can be an apprentice draper, just like me and Leonora. Now *she* was a very good draper.'

'Leonora couldn't wait to get away from the shop,' said Mara quickly, then nearly bit her tongue.

Kitty looked at her thoughtfully. 'Leonora was eager enough in the beginning. She enjoyed it at first, until she wanted to go off, to do things for herself. I think she stayed for you.'

Mara's head went up. 'Me?'

'She was specially attached to you, right from when you were born. More of a mother than I ever was to you, when you were little.' Kitty laughed. 'I think she didn't want to leave you to my tender mercies.'

Mara hauled herself up from the carpet. 'Oh, Ma, I don't mean . . . I miss her, you know. Really miss her.'

'Me too, love.' Kitty put a hand on Mara's. 'Don't think I don't know it was hard for you in the bombardment. What happened. What you saw. You've faced it out well. Many a girl would have taken to her bed after that. You'd have had an excuse, the way you were so poorly when you were little. But you've pulled through. You've had your rest. Now's the time to "face up", as Ishmael would say – to get to work. We're working people in this family, Mara, not fancy ladies who sit around sewing fine seams. Think of our Leonora out there, toiling day after day for those poor broken men. And she risks capture by the Germans. They could take her for a spy.'

Mara nodded slowly. Kitty was hard to quarrel with, in any serious fashion. In the end, she was so very often right. Which was how Mara came, neat in a black skirt and jacket, to travel in the motor car with Tommy and Kitty, to play the part of the daughter at the large store in Priorton High Street called Rainbow and Daughter.

The week whirled by in a bustle of belts and sleeves, ribbons and silks, gowns and dolmens, and it was a weary Mara who made her way the following Saturday evening straight to the Derancourts' house on Bridge Street. Working from dawn till well after dusk, there had been no time to tell Hélène that she could not 'come out to play' any more.

She was obstructed on one street corner by a crowd around a tall dark man with unruly hair who was pinning up a notice. Two old men were peering over his shoulder. One man spat at his feet. 'Thoo should be ashamed o'thesel'. Bliddy coward.' The crowd murmured in agreement and started to drift away.

'Traitor, more like,' said the other old man, bumping deliberately into the dark man before he stalked away with his friend. The man regained his balance, then called after them, his voice mild: 'It's a matter of proper conscience, brothers.

We're men with free will, not beasts of the field.' He looked back and smiled cheerily at Mara. 'Ah, Mara Scorton! I see I have an audience,' he said.

'Mr Clelland!' she exclaimed. Her mother had engaged Jonty Clelland to teach Mara in his spare time, to show her the ropes so that she could have a stab at teaching. It was he who had found her the school in Hartlepool, run by his old friend Herbert Clonmel, where her obvious cleverness would be seen as proper compensation for her lack of certification.

He shook her hand in a crushing, enthusiastic grip. 'How are you, young lady? I heard you'd been in that horrible business across in Hartlepool. Poor old Clonmel. Bad news. Scarborough and Whitby too! I should have got in touch with you straight away, or your Ma. But these affairs here are running on so fast.' He nodded at the notice, which announced a meeting to discuss the importance of resisting conscription. 'I've felt guilty at sending you there under the guns. And when I read that my old comrade . . .' A shadow fell across his earnest face.

'Mr Clonmel,' she said soberly.

'It's a waste. It's all such a devilish waste.' There was true desolation in his voice. Then he coughed. 'Now, young Mara. Are you coming to my meeting?'

She read his notice more carefully. It was for the following evening. 'Tomorrow night? Well . . .'

'You may not agree with our arguments, but at least you'll hear about our view of things, even if you disagree with it. Ignorance, not knowledge, is the problem in all things. You were always a good learner, Mara Scorton.'

She shrugged. 'All right, Mr Clelland, I'll come to your meeting. An' I'll bring our Tommy if I may. He might learn something. He's not waiting to be called up. He's enlisting in two weeks' time, on his eighteenth birthday. It's my birthday too, but I'll just be sixteen years old on that day. I wish I could enlist, to do my bit.'

Mr Clelland's serious face lit up, reminding her, for a

minute, of her father. William, too, was a good man in whom goodness was not a tedious peculiarity. 'Then you must both come. You are obviously in need of some rational argument.' He rubbed his hands together. 'The more the merrier, Mara Scorton. The more the merrier.'

She finally arrived at the house in Bridge Street, only to find it empty and all the doors open. She walked through the rooms, looking for Hélène, but she was nowhere to be seen. She did not admit that she was also looking for Jean-Paul. The empty house made her feel suddenly desolate. She had to take a very deep breath to force herself to face the long walk home.

At first Tommy was very unwilling to go to Mr Clelland's meeting with her, saying that he had much better ways of spending his time than sitting listening to a lot of traitorous, prattling idiots.

'Come on, Tommy. Be a sport,' she wheedled. 'What alternative faces you? Are you so very desperate to listen to Pansy quoting "dear Michael" to Ma? Take your choice.'

'I can't think why you're always moaning about Pansy Prim, Mara. It's you brought her here in the first place.'

'Huh! Don't remind me of that. And don't change the subject! Are you afraid that they'll change your mind, these traitorous idiots?'

'What? The King himself couldn't change my mind! And yes, I suppose you're right, anything's better than hearing old Michael pontificating second-hand.'

When they arrived at the hall, it was so full that they had to squeeze in to get a squashed seat on one of the back benches. The noise and shouting of the people reverberated off the bare stone walls. On the platform were three men, including Mr Clelland, who now stood up and raised his hands high above his head like a conductor. He waited until, very gradually, the cacophony stilled to a subdued muttering and a rattling of chairs.

'Gentlemen! And ladies!' He bowed to a group of women

in the front row. 'Thank you kindly for your attention. All we ask is that you listen! We're here to put a certain point of view. If you disagree with it, fair enough. But at least you'll have given us a hearing, which is the way of civilised men. Now, may I introduce Colonel Albert Black, who will be too modest to tell you of his medals for great bravery in defence of what he saw, then, as Britain's interests.'

This first speaker, elderly and upright, spoke of his experience as a decorated soldier in the South African war, how the terrible things he saw there made him vow never more to raise his hand against another man; how he was eventually drawn into the company of Quakers who by their faith do not harm any living thing.

The second speaker was a man with a black moustache who had the shoulders of a coal-hewer straining the seams of his black serge suit. He spoke in a soft Durham voice about men being born free and equal, and how wars were simply the instruments of kings and emperors to ensure the continued slavery of the plain man all over the world. There were mutters of approval at this, but more shouts of 'Treason!' Still, he went on to say that in an ideal world where all were equal, there would be no orphaned children, no husbandless wives, no mothers sitting by their hearths mourning their dead sons. In a world where equality ruled, the greed and envy which bred great conflict, forced one man's hand against another, would be as much part of ancient history as the wars between the Greeks and the Trojans.

As he sat down there were shouts from all parts of the hall, and Mara had to put a hand on Tommy's arm to stop him from leaping up and joining in the yells.

In the end Mr Clelland rose and held up his arms again for silence. He looked round carefully. 'Unlike these gentlemen, I come from this town, and see faces here of people who I've gone to school with, people whose children I now teach in my school . . .'

There were shouts of 'Shame!' at this.

'. . . but I sit on this platform with these gentlemen, and I sit here because I agree with what they say. My particular desire this evening is to speak of conscription. This forcing of a man to fight in spite of his conscience is now a certainty – have no doubt about that. Believe me, every man who is able will be called to the colours. Then willingly or unwillingly, he will have to kill, mutilate and maim another human being; be party to the killing of thousands of brothers in Christ. Whole families of men will be wrested from their hearth and home, to succour the great monster that is war. And aye, I tell you, they'll be swallowed up in its great maw, never again to see their hearth and home, the light in their children's eyes.'

A voice emerged from the front row. 'Gerraway, man. Ye're nowt but a bliddy Hun in sheep's clothing yerself.'

The word 'Hun' fluttered up and down the rows of men like a frantic moth.

Mr Clelland's voice deepened and strengthened. 'I am no Hun, sir, no more are these Englishmen, these gentlemen here on this platform. I'm a patriot, I love my country and my fellow countrymen and I do not wish to be an approving witness to their being scythed down, or being so brutalised that they celebrate their own dreadful actions with the victory howl of animals. And when the ordinary soldier, in his wisdom, chose to celebrate Christ's birthday on that first Christmas of the war, declaring their and their enemy's humanity, what happens? This is seen as a matter of shame. Shame, gentlemen? I say to you that that was the most honourable action in the whole of the war. Would that all plain soldiers laid down their arms and at a stroke ended this slaughter.'

The rumble grew again.

'One final thing. Friends! Have you talked with anyone who has been there in the trenches and come back, missing a leg or a hand? Have you seen the look in their eyes? If you have, then you'll know they don't talk of it, won't tell you what it is that's happened, what they've seen. Why not? Because it's so terrible, friends, so appalling, that it's beyond your imaginings. Once home, these men pretend that our fond thoughts of nobility and heroism are the truth. I tell you, it is all a lie! An insane lie. And if we wish to reject this insanity we will refuse the monster of conscription. And, friends, if we all do this in concert, then our masters'll have to think again before sending us all like herds of swine to the slaughter.'

One man called out: 'You're the traitor pigs, yeh lot. Huns and cowards all.' A rotten egg landed on Jonty Clelland's face and suddenly the place was in chaos. Vegetable, eggs, rotting refuse, all plopped on the stage. One man picked up his chair and started brandishing it above his head.

Tommy jumped to his feet. 'Traitor!' he shouted. 'Traitor!'

'Come on!' Mara grabbed Tommy's arm. 'Let's get out of here.' She pulled him out of the hall and along the street and sat him on a low wall by the Wesleyan chapel.

'I should've stayed,' he said sullenly. 'I wanted to punch that Clelland feller on the nose. I'd've punched all three of them on the nose.'

'They've a right to their opinion.'

'No, they don't. There's a war on. No space for opinions in the war.' He peered up at her. 'What's the matter with you? You don't agree with all that rubbish, do you? You've told me before that if you were a man you'd fight yourself.'

She sat down beside him and thought about what they had just heard. So much that had been said sounded right, rang true. And Mr Clelland! She wished suddenly she had been in his class at school, listening with others who were swayed by his teaching. This must be what it is like to really teach, she thought, inspired. How wonderful to teach like that.

'No,' she said uncertainly. 'I don't really agree with it. We've to fight, I feel that – no doubt about it. I've seen what those Germans do to us, remember? But what Mr Clelland said about those who come back – it's true. Dewi told me something of it, once, and I had just a glimpse of it. Dewi, he's not keen on it at all, even though he's going back, and thinks he should really go. And he's been there. Not like you or any of those other men in the hall. Anyway, what about the man who said about us being born equal. Don't you think that's true?'

Tommy jumped down from the wall, smiling suddenly; his anger leaving him like water seeping from a leaking tank. 'Of course it's true, Mara dear, unless, like you and me, you're . . .' he pinched her cheek '. . . bas— sorry, lovebegots! In which case you're a lot less equal, as we both know.' He set off again, walking jauntily, whistling a tune which she recognised as 'A Little of What You Fancy Does You Good'.

'Where are you going, you foolish boy?' she called after him.

'To the billiard hall. You get a better class of patriotism down there.'

She walked home slowly, her brain buzzing with what she had heard. She was for the war. She was definitely for the war. If she were a boy she'd have enlisted the minute she was able, just like Tommy. But things were not straightforward, not straightforward at all.

When she got back to the Lodge, Michael's motor car was standing outside. Not able to face the twittering of those two lovebirds she walked steadily on, not stopping till she reached the Waterman's Cottage.

She lifted the sneck and went in, but the orderly, sparse kitchen was deserted. She knocked on the little bedroom door and walked in. 'Father, I . . .' She blushed. 'Oh, I'm sorry.'

He mother and father were sitting up in Luke's little bed side by side, like a pair of grizzled dolls. Kitty's laugh chimed through the cottage. 'Come in, Tuppence!' She patted the bed beside her. 'Squeeze on if you can.'

Mara did as she was told, and Kitty put an arm round her. 'Do we look guilty?'

Mara hesitated. 'Well, yes, you do, seeing as you ask.'

'So we should. Or so I should! You see before you the failing hostess. When Michael's motor car drew up yet again, my poor old heart sank at the thought of him and Pansy dancing more mediaeval minuets round each other. So I invented another errand up here to see your father.' She chuckled. 'In fact, I'd just returned from here. My supper was cold and Pansy was distraught at the thought of cool food passing my sacred lips.'

'And,' said William, squeezing his wife's hand, 'your poor mother raced back so agitated about those two that I had to hold her close to calm her down.'

'Mmm, scared off, were you?' said Mara, looking from one to the other, smiling faintly. Her parents had never made any secret of their closeness, their affection for each other. They needed little excuse to show it. 'Me too. I took one look at Michael's motor car and came straight up here.' She looked round. 'Where's Luke?'

William glanced at the ceiling. 'He's bedded down in the corner of the workshop while I'm here.'

'When are you coming home, Pa? You look better now. Thinner but better.' That was not quite true. There were shadows under his eyes and his cheekbones showed sharp in the candlelight.

'That's Luke and his vegetable concoctions. According to him, the "Lady Pansy", as he calls her, fed me too much dead animal and that made me sick.'

'Wise man,' said Kitty. 'Can I live here too?'

'And me?' said Mara.

He looked around the tiny bedroom, and drew a hand over the narrow bed. 'Bit of a squash, don't you think?' he said.

They all laughed uproariously at that and within a second Luke popped his head round the door and asked if anything was required. Perhaps a nice soothing drink?

The next night Kitty had to stay at the shop to see a supplier and Mara walked back from work. By the time she turned the lane towards the Lodge she was footsore and tired. She had just taken off her hat to shake her hair free, and cool her head, when she came upon the tall figure of Jean-Paul Derancourt waiting for her at the broad field gate which led down to the Lodge.

'Hello, Jean-Paul.' She smiled easily, her mind still on her sore feet. She peered behind him. 'Is Hélène with you? I've not seen her for days and days. I came to visit you the other day but you were both out. I thought she might come into the shop to see me.'

He shook his head. 'My sister, she is back in some strange world of her own. She wanders the streets. I've had to return two stolen babies to their mothers just this week. I give them money not to go to the Constable about Hélène.' He shook his head. 'She gets no better.'

'Poor girl,' she said sympathetically. 'She means no harm, they should see that.'

He shrugged. 'They say next time she kill a baby. One person spat at me that she was a witch. Someone broke our window with a stone.'

Mara stood uneasily before him. There seemed nothing useful to say about Hélène, and yet she was pleased Jean-Paul was here on her territory and she didn't want him to go.

He coughed. 'You look very pretty tonight, Mara.'

She froze. 'Jean-Paul, I—'

She longed to say that he looked so handsome tonight himself, his face scrubbed so clean and his thick hair brushed back so neatly into its string tie.

From behind his back he brought out a wrapped parcel and put it carefully on the fence. 'I make you this because you, only you, are kind to Hélène. And because there is a big space in our house when you do not come. Now I go.' He turned on his heel.

'Wait, wait till I open it.' She was scrabbling with the brown-paper wrapping. Inside was a finely made, brass-hinged box. On the top in the centre was a brass disc etched with her initials. It smelt of wood shavings and new oil, and she knew Jean-Paul had made it himself.

She peered down the pathway. His figure now was small, anonymous in the distance. Still she put the box down, cupped her hands to her mouth and bawled, 'It's lovely! Thank you, Jean-Paul. Thank you!'

As she went into the house she raised her head and sniffed and realised again that the house smelled like the one on the headland in Hartlepool; like the house of the Misses Heliotrope and Pansy Clarence. It did not smell like her mother's house at all. She could hear Pansy's mouse-like rustle in the parlour.

For a second the joy of Jean-Paul's gift was dimmed. Then she leapt up the stairs two at a time and placed the box on her wide bedroom windowsill, examining its smooth finish inside and out. She reached into her dresser drawer and took out her letters from Leonora and Dewi, placed them in the box and closed it.

'Now that's a very nice box, dear.' She swung round. Pansy had come into the bedroom on her silent feet.

Mara left the box on the windowsill and stood with her back to it, defending it from Pansy's wandering gaze. 'It's just an old box, Pansy.'

'And a present from the Frenchman, I see. I don't know whether . . .' Her voice faded at the fierceness of Mara's gaze. 'And I'm sure you shouldn't go bawling down the lane like that, my dear. Not ladylike at all. You have to be so careful, a young woman in your position, lacking legitimate status.'

Suddenly Mara exploded. 'Out! Get out, you interfering old cow.' She took Pansy by her fragile arm and thrust her out of the room, bolting it behind her. 'And stay out! I'm sick of you and your slimy, conniving ways. Sick of you.'

One part of her knew she would regret it later, but as Mara stood there with her back to the bedroom door she felt good. Time someone told the old harridan. Absolutely. She guessed even the elephantine Heliotrope had never plucked up the courage to do that.

Leonora pulls her foot out of the mud but with the next step it is sucked back noisily into the greedy earth. Her eyes cast round in vain for a dry place to walk. She can feel the anxiety of the man beside her, the urgency to find the place where they make love. Her own body participates in the urgency. She frowns. She can't quite make out whether the man is Samuel or the other one, the one from before. Now what was his name? She mutters in the effort to concentrate, to try to remember, to bring the name and the face to mind. She can recall the clerical collar, with the engaging fall of sallow flesh above it. But the face is blank.

Her companion's voice, hollow and distant but much beloved, is insisting that the special place is near here, near here. They will be snug and dry there and he will take her in his arms and the world will be shut out. There will be no more thump-thump, throck-throck; there will be no bleating, agonised pleading of souls in purgatory. He will take her in his arms and gently, as gently as he has before, he will make her happy. They will bathe together in soft clean water. He will love her and pat her dry with the great soft robe draped across his shoulders. He will make her calm and whole again. And then they will come together as only man and woman can, and in their coming together the world will be made afresh and there will be no more screaming.

But every corner, every space is filled with mud. And when they try to lie down on the grassy earth, flat water is lurking beneath the waving grasses. They are sinking now, both of them; the water is entering her mouth, her eyes.

She shouts, then screams – a gurgling scream. Her eyes snap open and her body tenses like a hunted hare.

The dream persists as Leonora plummets into wakefulness. The scream is coming from a dying soldier whom she has been tending. He is drowning in his own blood; she has dropped off to sleep standing up in the corner of the ram-shackle shed.

'Wake up, sister.' Pavel was shaking her by the shoulders. 'You must go to lie down.'

'I have to stay. They need to be watched. There is so much . . .' She was mumbling; her lips felt swollen, thick as sausages, as she forced the words out. Tonight she'd had to cope without the support of Larissa, who was lying in a little lean-to beside the kitchen, sweating and turning in the depths of a fever.

Pavel pushed her roughly towards the door. 'Go, sleep, sister. I will call you in an hour. You are no use to me or to them, like this. No use at all.'

'What on earth did you say to her?' Kitty's voice came crossly to Mara in the gloom of her bedroom.

'Some horrible things,' whispered Mara. 'But she's a snake.'

'Nonsense. She's just a poor little woman.'

'Poor little woman? Look at us, Mama! Father's turned out of his own house. Tommy's spending all his time in the billiard hall and anyway is off to war next week. Pansy's installed in your bedroom, in your bed. And we have to whisper in case she hears us. She's not a woman, she's a stringy cuckoo!'

There was a hastily suppressed giggle from the other bed. 'Oh, go to sleep, Tuppence,' said Kitty. 'To be honest I'm beginning to think you're right. I'll sort it all out in the morning.'

The next day Kitty went along as usual to the Waterman's Cottage to have her breakfast with William, but Pansy was sweetness itself to Mara. Her face was neutral as she asked the girl if she wanted another helping of porridge. And later she was very businesslike. Notebook in hand, she waited for Kitty's return, to ask if she wanted anything from the shops, as she was in Priorton shopping for dear Michael and it would be no trouble, no trouble at all to pick up something for dear Kitty.

'Don't worry about me any more, Pansy. I'll send a note along from the shop and Mr Wilson will deliver, as he always has.'

'Oh, do you think that's wise, Kitty? You know I said the quality of that other bacon he sent was less than satisfactory.'

Kitty looked at her for a second without speaking. 'To be honest, I didn't see that bacon which was so bad. And I do know that Mr Wilson was mortified when you returned it to him. Quite upset.'

Tommy was stuffing his mouth full of the last of the thick white bread. 'And Mr Crissop,' he said.

'As was Mr Crissop over the bread,' agreed Kitty.

'Well, they would be, wouldn't they?' Pansy put her head on one side and smiled her sweet smile. 'They are tradesmen. No one likes to be caught out.'

Kitty put the cutlery on the tray, ready for the sink. 'Nevertheless we'll return to Mr Wilson's deliveries. And Mr Crissop's.'

Pansy held her gaze a split second longer than was polite. Then shrugged her shoulders and sighed. 'Very well, dear Kitty, you know best. Obviously, it is your household.'

Kitty beamed. 'So it is, Pansy. Now, can we give you a lift into Priorton?'

Pansy shook her head. 'There are the dishes to clear and I have some cakes to bake. I will cycle into Priorton.'

There was merriment in the motor car as it purred and rattled down the hill to Priorton. 'Round one to you, Ma,' chortled Tommy.

'There'll be a few more rounds after this one,' said Kitty with a wry smile. 'The next one is to get my bed back. And after that, to get your father back into it.'

Tommy raised his eyebrows at Mara. 'This separation business is certainly making you say your piece, Ma!' he said. 'I think we'd all like Father back.'

'It won't be a day too soon,' agreed Mara fiercely.

As they walked into the shop Mara asked Kitty if she could take extra time at lunchtime. 'I have to go and see Hélène. According to Jean-Paul, she's been stealing babies down at Bridge Street. She thinks she's going to have a baby, though she's not.'

Kitty paused with her hand on the office door. 'Yes, I suppose you could,' she said. 'But you must ask permission. If Miss Aunger says you must do more time to make up, you must do it.'

They both knew the permission was a matter of form. Miss Aunger, this week teaching Mara her particular tricks of the trade, was in charge of the hosiery department. Kitty knew quite well that permission would be given. Miss Aunger worshipped Kitty, and if Kitty said her daughter should have an extra hour off, she might 'hum and ha' a bit, but there would be no problem.

It was two o'clock when Mara finally got away, and as she was walking down Bridge Street, she caught up with Jean-Paul. His face lit up when he saw her, then reddened under its layer of coal dirt. He put a hand to his face. 'I am black,' he said.

'I've come to see Hélène,' she said.

'Yes. Yes. She will be pleased to see you.' He paused. '*I* am pleased to see you.'

She held his gaze. 'I love the box, Jean-Paul,' she said simply. 'It's beautiful.'

He put one hand on her sleeve, then pulled it away, groaning. 'Oh, I'm so black from the pit. Come! I will wash myself and you can talk some sense to my crazy sister.'

She walked steadily beside him, smiling inside. The door was wide open but Hélène was not in the house. Jean-Paul's mouth tightened. 'I will have to go and search for her again.'

'*We* will have to search for her,' said Mara firmly. 'You go and wash yourself and then we will find her.'

When he came back out of the scullery in a snowy white shirt and his hair slicked to one side he looked like an entirely different man.

Their gazes met.

'Come here,' ordered Mara.

He came and stood before her, one corner of his mouth twitching with amusement. She leaned forward and kissed him lightly. 'Thank you for the box, dear Jean-Paul.'

He grasped her shoulders and kissed her hard in return, a clumsy, fumbling experience which left them both trembling. He moved to kiss her again, but she drew back, shaking her head. 'That was so we know now what we're about. That there's no pretence between us.'

'But you're so . . .'

'If you're going to say young, I'll punch you. I'm sixteen next week, and old enough to call myself grown-up.'

He grinned at her, and for the first time in their acquaintance it was a warm, relaxed smile. She saw the boy he had once been.

'Are you now?' he teased.

She punched him on the arm. 'Stop that!' she said fiercely. 'Now we've got to look for Hélène.'

They searched as far as Livesay Woods for Hélène, but she was nowhere to be found. Then they trudged back wearily to Bridge Street.

'She will arrive. She always does.' Jean-Paul pulled Mara's arm through his and bent his head towards her. 'So what about us, *chérie*? What are we to be now?'

'Best friends?' she said, her head on one side.

He shook his head. 'Not enough. You are best friends with my sister.'

'I was best friends with Dewi,' she teased.

'Huh! That Welshman.'

'I like him. He is a best friend.'

'So what are we?'

'Well, then, what *are* we?'

'What is the English word? We're sweethearts. That's it. Sweethearts.'

He glanced up and down the deserted street, then pulled her to him and kissed her, and she kissed him back, enjoying the feel of his skin against hers, the sense of power that buzzed between them. Somewhere far away she heard the noise of a motor car as it drew to a halt, and then was jolted out of Jean-Paul's arms.

'Mara!' Michael held tightly onto her upper arm. 'What on earth do you think you're doing, making an exhibition of yourself like this? Get into the motor this minute!'

She hung onto the door.

He turned to Jean-Paul. 'As for you, I should knock your block off and horsewhip you, you French swine!'

Jean-Paul lunged towards Michael but Mara put a hand up to stop him. 'Don't worry, Jean-Paul. I'll go with him. But I'll see you later. Go home, go home! Hélène might be back.'

She watched him turn and stride away, then went and sat in the car. 'Now, Michael. Just what do you think you're going to do with me?'

10

A Time for Heroes

In the headlong rush backwards, Leonora's unit had hauled itself to a stop and set up clinic in a little deserted church. There was another strange lull. For days they had had no new wounded. Again they could take precious time to wash their clothes and clear their bedding by burning the bugs. The nursing brothers had even built woodland houses in preference to tents. For dining they constructed a three-walled arbour composed entirely of pine branches. Here the unit ate and, astonishingly, lolled around for want of something to do.

Larissa was only slowly recovering from her fever and Pavel was very concerned about her. He said they must nurse her a few days more, and then she should be passed back behind the lines to a hospital at the first opportunity. He pushed aside Larissa's weak protests, saying curtly that they had enough work ahead with the wounded, without having a sick nurse to care for.

The high road which ran alongside their clinic rumbled with sound all day long. Provision carts and munition wagons lurched and creaked along the rutted track. Foot soldiers, uninjured by anything except pure despair, straggled and stumbled by. Cavalry contingents made greater haste, cantering proudly westwards, then perhaps a day later, plodding resignedly back towards the east. Threading among the soldiers, trekking along in weary clusters, with mountainous packs, or old people on their backs and children on their hips,

159

was the endless army of homeless, dispossessed by alien armies ebbing and flowing over them in conflict with each other.

Leonora had grown to recognise the style of the regiments, and understand their different characters. A company of horsemen passed and she noted the red hoods of the Third Caucasian Corps who had such a brave reputation. One of the brothers told her the Caucasians had, more than once, flung themselves and their horses between the advancing enemy and the retreating infantry.

Only the Cossacks made Leonora uneasy. They would come riding through the trees, eye Leonora and her colleagues with curiosity, and pass surly remarks among themselves. The presence of women, even uniformed nurses, among the soldiers seemed to be offensive to them.

One day Leonora decided to take advantage of the lull, telling Pavel and the others she would go and look for wild strawberries. She left the church and the busy road and made her way up through pine trees and stands of silver birch. Above her the cooing and chirruping of birds took her back for a moment to Livesay Woods in Priorton, an altogether cooler and more temperate place. The ground was thickly covered with small dark green bushes laden with strawberries which were almost as small as cranberries. They were very sweet.

As she gathered them in her stuff apron she ate some, ignoring the juice as it dripped from her chin. Larissa would enjoy these; perhaps they would cheer her out of the last stages of her fever. As she picked, Leonora lost track of time, focusing on the cleansingly simple task, her mind still in Livesay Woods, where she had walked many a mile with Mara on her back, handing up blackberries for the toddler to push into her pouting mouth.

Leonora was hauled back to the present by the sound of shouts and screams, the bark of dogs and the honking of geese through the trees. Cautious, as she had now learned to be, she approached the top of a ridge, tied the ends of her apron tight round her waist to secure the strawberries, and peered through the trees to a village in a clearing below.

Cossacks, mounted and on foot, were commandeering geese and chickens, and two squealing pigs, tying them to their saddles. In an open space they were corralling village men, the youngest and the strongest, pushing them with bayonets, making them cluster together.

Before one of the larger cabins a woman was screaming as two soldiers hauled a kicking, struggling lad from her house. 'My son, my little boy! He is the only one left. Highness, he is the only one.' The woman launched herself towards the Cossack leader, only to be held back by the hairy hands of a beefy soldier.

The leader spoke sharply to the woman and she looked up at him for a long moment before she went into the dark interior of the cabin and brought forth a jumble of heavy rope. The Cossack used his boot to kick the rope towards his men, who tied the boy's hands, then looped the rope around his neck. The terrified mumbling of the village men and the screaming of the women ceased. They watched the Cossack leader with sullen, terrified care.

Finally he nodded at a soldier, who entered one of the cabins and emerged with a flaming torch. Other soldiers produced straw torches and Mara watched as the flame was passed between them in a kind of rippling dance. They eyed their Commander, who nodded. Then they set fire, one by one, to every single building in the village, then moved to nearby fields and started firing those as well.

The woman whose young son had been the last to be taken let out a yodelling wail. 'And these are our own soldiers! Our own Russians.' She quietened down, and looked the leader in the eye. 'How can you, Highness? How can you do this to us?'

He reined up his horse and cantered gently over to her, then, raising his dusty boot, he heeled her hard in the shoulder, sending her sprawling back towards her burning house.

Her son darted forward in protest, only to be hauled back on his rope like a disobedient dog. The fires crackled, and everyone – the men, the women, the children and the waiting soldiers – watched the leader, who suddenly wheeled his horse and surveyed the surrounding trees. Leonora pulled back quickly, certain that he could feel her burning, indignant gaze.

Then the Cossack shouted orders to his men, who herded their captives before them and began to move out of the village towards the road. She watched as the women attempted in vain to beat out the flames in their houses, wailing their despair to the dry June skies.

Leonora turned and ran, not stopping for an hour, until she reached the clinic, where she sought out Pavel. Gasping, she rattled out a short report of what she had seen, and demanded he do something about it.

He listened respectfully, then took her elbow and steered her into a camp chair. 'Calm, sister, calm,' he murmured.

'Something must be done!' She glared at him.

He shook his head. 'It is a task of war,' he said. 'There are those who enjoy that kind of thing too much, but it is still a task of war. The land must be taken, razed, so it does not give succour to the enemy. And the battle needs more "volunteers" from the land to fill its hungry mouth. This war has a very heavy appetite for conscripts.'

'But those women they are burning out, they're our people. They are Russians.'

He shrugged. 'There is no certainty of their loyalty, faced with a German bayonet.'

'So they must starve, even die?'

'Casualties, *Leonya*, casualties like the boys who come through our hands.' He stroked his beard. 'And I am afraid I have news of another casualty, our dear sister Larissa.'

Leonora leapt up and pushed past him. 'She is in the church, *sesistra*,' Demchenkov called.

They had set Larissa beside the ruined altar on one of

the little trestles which they carried with them on the carts. Someone had dressed her in her nurse's veil and placed an elaborate crucifix in one crossed hand, an icon in the other. Her face was beautiful and so very young.

Leonora kissed her friend's brow, which was as cold as woodland mushrooms. 'You should have waited, *sesistra*. I brought you strawberries – the first of the season. At home in County Durham we put fruit in pastry pies and eat them with cream. You should have waited.' She tried then to pray, but no thought, no true blessing, would come to her mind.

She looked up to find Pavel watching her from the doorway. 'Yes, sister,' he said. 'I agree. It is all useless waste. There must be a better way. And there will be, you'll see. I swear to you there will be changes.' He clicked his heels and she heard his boots stomping away on the old stone paving.

She was still there in the following dark dawn when she felt his hand on her stiff shoulder. 'Can you hear it again, sister?'

She cocked her head to the dread familiarity of the boom of shells. 'Another offensive,' she said.

He nodded. 'Another harvest of broken bodies for our care and, I feel certain, another retreat for us very soon.'

She looked down at Larissa's face, gleaming palely in the opalescent light of dawn.

Pavel shook her shoulder as though to bring her into this world from the half-world of the dead. 'Our brothers have made Larissa a nice little space in the shelter of the church wall, and I have some very fine prayers for the rest of her immortal soul.' His voice became brisker. 'We must do it now.'

'Yes, we must do it now,' she said, standing up stiffly. 'And then back to work. There's nothing else, is there, Pavel?'

When Michael's car pulled up at the shop, Mara refused to get out and go inside, forcing him to go inside himself and harangue Kitty about her daughter's disreputable behaviour. 'She refuses to get out of the dratted car,' he fumed.

Kitty shrugged. 'Well, I'm not coming out to shout at her in the street. Most undignified.'

Michael glared at his stepmother, suspecting her of laughing at him, then stormed out of the shop and peered through the car window. 'Right!' he growled furiously. 'Get out. According to your mother you must go in there on your own and face the consequences.'

He wrenched open the door and almost pulled Mara out, to the entertainment of passers-by. She scrambled out onto the pavement and went straight through to the hosiery department where an anxious Miss Aunger was standing beside Kitty, whose face, usually so lively, was impassive. 'You're late,' said Kitty quietly. 'You said you'd be an hour.'

'I'm sorry, Mother . . . Miss Aunger. Really sorry. Hélène had run off again, and Jean-Paul was worried. She's been strange lately, really strange. We searched everywhere, but she was nowhere to be found.' She blushed. 'Then Michael—'

'We don't want to hear about Michael,' said Kitty briskly. 'You can tell me about that at home.' She turned to Miss Aunger. 'What do you say, Miss Aunger? Will the apology do?'

'Well, if you think, Miss Rainbow—'

Mara butted in. 'I'll stay late tonight and tomorrow to make up the time,' she said meekly. 'There's the stock-count to do. I'll stay till it's finished.'

This agreed, Kitty marched off to greet a supplier who was bustling through the etched double doors, removing his cape and setting his face with the broad beam that worked so well with most shopkeepers, although he knew from experience that this Kitty Rainbow was a tough nut to crack. No pleas of wartime shortages worked with her, even if they were true.

Mara worked on after the shop closed at eight o'clock, counting the various categories of hose and entering them into the ledger, her head whirling with images of Jean-Paul's face, the feeling of his lips on hers. She had a hard job stopping the smile rising to her face.

Later that evening, as she walked into Purley Lodge, she was informed by the slightly aggrieved Pansy that they, including Michael, were all along at the Waterman's Cottage. That was, all of them except Tommy, who'd had tea then rushed out again to watch some foot races. 'Gambling, no doubt!' Pansy's bruised presence seemed to fill the house now, and Mara was rather pleased to know that, in facing the truculent Michael, she would have both her mother and her father by her side.

'You are to go along there directly,' said Pansy, folding her lips. 'Michael says you deserve the severest of reprimands.'

At the Waterman's Cottage Mara was met by Luke. 'They are all upstairs in the workroom, Mara,' he whispered. 'Mr Scorton has abandoned my bedroom down here. He does not like Michael to see him in bed.'

Despite the warm evening William, looking pale, was sitting on a small couch beside the blazing fire. He had a blanket over his shoulders, and still seemed very frail. Kitty sat on a hard chair beside him, and Michael was hovering by the work table, turning over some tools.

Mara hesitated beside the door. Her father put out his hand. 'Come in, Tuppence. And for heaven's sake don't look as though we were the Inquisition.' She went to sit beside him and he took her hand. 'Now, love. What have you been playing at?'

She took a breath. 'I went to see Hélène, Pa, but she was missing. Jean-Paul and I looked everywhere but she was nowhere to be found. We were just coming back when Michael grabbed me, thrust me in his car and transported me to the shop.'

'She was lying in the arms of that man in the middle of the road,' growled Michael.

'What?' said William, eyebrows raised

Mara flushed. 'We were not . . . doing what he said. That's not true.'

'Then what were you doing?' said Kitty.

She turned and faced her mother, excluding Michael from

165

her line of vision. 'He kissed me. Or rather we kissed each other.'

'In the street?'

'Yes. It just happened. Anyway, I like him. We like each other.'

'Couldn't be less suitable,' spluttered Michael. 'He's a Frenchman – and a pitman to boot.'

'I wasn't aware that we were at war with France,' retorted Mara. 'And there's nothing wrong with men who work down the pit.' She turned to Kitty. 'Leonora's father worked in the pit, Mother, didn't he? And Leonora's turned out all right.'

Michael's tone softened a fraction. 'It's different with Leonora,' he said sharply.

Kitty smiled slightly, remembering Michael as a stolid, kindly boy who had been so protective of his new stepsister. Then she shook her head. 'No, you're right. It's not different. Leonora's father was a pitman and,' her voice went up a pitch, 'a brave and honourable man – well, boy, really. There's no reason why the Frenchman should not be the same.'

Michael placed his bulky frame before the fire and folded his arms. 'But it *is* different, Kit. Pa! You must agree with me. We've a certain position in the town, now. We've gained respect here, even though, to be brutally frank, you and Kit have never troubled yourself with the matrimonial knot. That's all very well, but Mara and Tommy are left with a status which is not of their own making but which blights them in the eyes of others. Pansy says—'

'Ah, Pansy,' said Kitty gently.

'Kitty!' warned William.

Michael flashed at his stepmother: 'You have little need to mock, Kit. You've let your daughter run wild to the point where she thinks there is nothing wrong with kissing and fondling on the high road.'

'Mara doesn't run wild. She's had a little rest after being nearly blown to smithereens on the coast, and now she's a draper's apprentice. Hardly running wild.'

Michael flushed. 'Well, she was out . . .'

'She was looking for her friend who was lost and in distress.' She paused and glanced at William. 'And as for places for fondling, Leonora herself was started from a little bit of true love shown on a gravestone in Priorton graveyard.'

'Kitty!' warned William, his lip twitching nevertheless on the point of a smile. Even Mara had now gone a little pink at her mother's indiscretion.

Kitty took William's hand. 'Oh, I'm sick, dear boy, sick of all this hypocrisy about things. I've tried to live my life true and straight, like Ishmael taught me. And I'm not going to let any pompous, false virtue despoil that truth and make me hide it. And I will not accept by insinuation the notion that my daughter is, and by some kind of implication *I* am, some kind of harlot.' They were all astonished to see tears in Kitty's eyes.

'Kit! I didn't mean . . . I've always respected . . .' Michael was his old self, gentle, bumbling and full of concern.

She waved a hand, got out her handkerchief. 'Oh, Michael, forgive me for going on.' Then she scrabbled around in her capacious bag. 'I've had a letter from her, from Leonora . . . Such dreadful experiences. They're retreating again, you see. They had to leave wounded men to . . . those animals.' She blew her nose very efficiently. 'This,' she said, 'should be our priority, not some tittle-tattle about a boy-girl romance. Or even –' turning to Mara – 'being indiscreet enough to arouse that tittle-tattle.'

She handed the letter to Michael, who took it closer to the lamp to read it. Then he gave it back to her, shaking his head. 'She shouldn't be there. So foolish of her to go.' His tone was affectionate, concerned.

'Somehow,' Kitty said, 'you've got to contact Samuel, Michael! He's still somewhere there, isn't he? There must be a way. Make him go and pluck Leonora, willing or unwilling, away from this horror. Just think, if William had not recovered, she . . . she . . .' The rare tears began to flow again and this time William had to offer her his handkerchief.

Mara looked at them all in astonishment. She had resigned herself to being a whipping girl, to enduring Michael's pompous condemnation and, even worse, her dear parents' understanding sorrow. But somehow her misdemeanour had been swallowed up by other, more important things. And she now had the wondrous thought to contemplate, of her dear Leonora being . . . what was the phrase, now? . . . conceived *on a gravestone in Priorton cemetery*. At every turn she learned new things about this strange family of hers.

'Well, *sesistra*, thank you for your interest. The mutton is marinaded in the sun with onions, pepper and salt. Then after three days it is skewered and roasted over the red ashes of a hot fire.'

The Caucasian cook was proud of his culinary skill. Leonora's Red Cross unit had set up yet another clinic at the edge of yet another village. Their cottage overlooked a brigade of the Caucasian Infantry who were encamped nearby among old and stately pines. The soldiers had stacked their rifles like sheaves of corn, bayonets pointing upwards, and were themselves mostly asleep in odd positions, or busy with their fires. Their thirty-six-inch guns, two hundred yards from the village, were seldom fired but when they were, the whole village vibrated, including the Red Cross clinic. Its ceiling, already cracked, would shed bits of mud plaster into the nurses' tea and coffee.

On the day of their arrival, the Caucasian cook had come upon the nurses, kneeling on flat stones, scrubbing and rinsing their clothes, washerwoman style. He had talked with them as he washed his pans, and promised them *shashlick*.

Leonora, politely asking how it was made, was treated to the long and elaborate explanation. Now three days later she was eating it with relish, trying not to wonder too hard about which poor farmer the mutton had come from. In the event they were eating their *shashlick* as guests of the Caucasian officers, some of whom they had met before, nearer the Front, at a dressing station, patching them up before they returned again to the heat of the fighting.

The officers and their guests sat around a flat square of grass which had had deep narrow trenches cut all round it. They were shown how to drop their legs into the narrow trench and sit up to the square of grass as though it really were a table. Lances, hung with torches lit against the growing dusk, had been set up at each corner. Leonora blinked at the incongruous sight of a silver wine jug surrounded by crystal glasses placed carefully at the centre of the grass table.

The fare was simple – the *shashlick* and potatoes, followed by a kind of fruit compôte. Even so, the ceremony with which it was served was a reminder for all of them of another world beyond the thump of guns.

'Now then!' The Colonel, a florid man with dark rings under his eyes, stood up and gestured with his knife towards the woods. 'Who have we here?'

An officer was riding towards them, becoming visible, then invisible, as he moved in and out of the pines. He was wearing a long, dark red tightly fitting coat, with buckles and cartridge cases of Caucasian silver, and he carried a long curved silver scimitar at his side. A black felt coat hung loosely over his shoulder; he wore the red hood twisted round his neck and falling onto the coat, and a high fur cap on his head.

As he approached, his pristine image was spoiled by the sight of his dusty boots and mud-splashed coat. At last he came within the range of the firelight and torches, and a cheer went up round the grass table. The Colonel and several officers greeted the newcomer, leaping up to slap him on his back, while Pavel and the other nurses looked on with interest.

Leonora stood up. The rider brought his horse to a halt in front of her, removed his hat in the English style, flourished it and bowed from where he was sitting on his high horse. 'Is there a Sister Rainbow anywhere here?' he called.

'Samuel!' She was racing towards him. He reached down and pulled her half onto his horse and gave her a resounding kiss. The soldiers cheered and clapped.

She struggled. 'Let me down,' she said.

He placed her neatly on the turf and she adjusted her skirts and veil. 'You're thinner,' he announced.

'And you look like something out of the Music Hall,' she retorted. 'What are you doing here?'

'I've business in the Army and was allowed to be an honorary Caucasian for a while. They are decimated up there at the Front, d'you know that?' His voice was rough, raw for a minute as he spoke swiftly in English. 'The whole thing is set for disaster, Leonie. Idiots are running the show. Hundreds of thousands of cartridges have been sent there, none of which fit a Russian rifle. Two hundred usable shells out of thirty thousand! Some soldiers are just walking away, declaring their allegiance to the revolutionaries, while others are hewing clubs from the forest for weapons. Out of the Fifth Caucasian Infantry, just two thousand men are left out of twenty-five thousand. Some of those are old friends and comrades of mine.'

'I know,' she said soberly. 'Some of them I have nursed, and sent back. Others I've held while they died.'

'So many heroes.' Then he shrugged his great shoulders. 'Anyway, I wanted to see you.' He paused. 'I have missed you, darling girl,' he said.

There was a cough behind her. 'Oh, Pavel. I must introduce my—'

Samuel jumped down from his horse as lightly as a much younger man. 'I am Miss Rainbow's fiancé,' he said. 'And you are Pavel Demchenkov? I have friends in Moscow who have great respect for you.'

Pavel stroked his beard. 'I can't think who they might be, Mr . . .'

'Samuel Scorton, sir.' He wrung Pavel's hand as though it might come off.

The Caucasian Colonel stepped forward then to embrace

Samuel, and pulled him to the table to share in their feast. Samuel insisted on sitting beside Leonora. Under cover of the loud talk she whispered to him, 'Why are you really here?'

'For the reason I said. And as well, I have telegrams, four of them, sent by Michael to different places, with orders from Kit to take you home. It's not very often she makes a command, old Kit, but when she does, a fellow steps to, I can tell you.'

She shook her head. 'I'm staying here. This work's not done. You can't just pick it up and drop it as you choose.'

'We'll see,' he said. 'We'll see.'

After supper, Pavel and the nurses returned to the clinic, while Leonora and Samuel went for a walk deep into the pine wood and, in the darkness, enfolded each other, hungry for closeness and tearful with passion. But despite their isolation among the scented pines, they could not make love, both holding back for reasons which neither could fathom.

'Perhaps it is inappropriate,' said Samuel, with uncharacteristic, despairing sadness.

Leonora went to bed cross and unsatisfied. Samuel sat round a fire with some soldiers talking well into the night. After a while Pavel strolled over and offered Samuel one of his cigars and began to enquire after his friends in Moscow.

The night Leonora dreamed again of the child she had lost in the bath of blood. Then Kitty was there, handing her her own baby, Mara, whose small mouth was puckering to a smile, chubby arms reaching out. 'Take her, Leonora, take her. She'll make you better. Surely she will.' Then as she looked, Mara's face dissolved and became that of Larissa, childlike in her final sleep. Leonora blinked herself awake and sat up, wrapping her arms around herself and rocking to and fro on her cot, thinking of all those at home; her mother and father, Tommy with his cheery grin, and Mara who was so very nearly her own child.

The thought came to her that even if she died here, like Larissa, Mara would somehow be her heir: someone she had nurtured, had a hand in forming. Mara was there. She would

171

pass onto the next generation. Somehow she would live on in her younger sister's place . . .

She jumped, her ears invaded now by the familiar thud of guns and a sudden noisy tumult outside their tent. She stood up, pulled on her skirt over her shift and started to shake the other nurses awake. The rough voice of Pavel Demchenkov penetrated the canvas. 'Wake, sisters, wake! We are to move back again. Full retreat they say, full retreat again!'

Leonora rushed from the tent and raced across to the clinic to start to throw things into packing cases. She looked across at the soldiers' encampment. There was no sign of Samuel's bulky figure in its Music Hall uniform. Pavel looked up briefly from his task. 'Your fiancé, sister, has gone forward. A messenger came, and he rode on last night as we retired to bed. He says he will find you again.'

'Forward? I thought we were in retreat.'

'He has business at the Front, news of a meeting which will happen in Switzerland. Important people will be there. They will make a manifesto.'

She packed the dressings tightly in their wooden box. 'A revolutionary manifesto?'

Pavel continued packing; his neat surgeon's hands worked swiftly, placing every instrument with great care into its correct slot. 'You and I are lucky in him, *sesistra*. He is a great friend of Russia.'

Leonora found herself blushing. 'To be honest, he was always a bit of a black sheep in our . . . in his family,' she puffed, rolling and tying thin mattresses with bailing twine.

Pavel frowned. 'Black sheep? Ah, I see! Well, perhaps black sheep make good friends. And perhaps it is his time to be a hero.'

Leonora worked on, wondering at her own selfishness, in the middle of this great conflict, in wishing Samuel had waited to say goodbye to her.

11

Recovery and Retreat

Kitty was throwing Pansy out of the main bedroom of the Lodge; her modest possessions were moved onto the landing. 'I must have my bedroom back. You'll have to share with Mara, like it or not, Pansy. William's not getting any better down there, and I want him here in his own home.'

William's condition had suddenly deteriorated. He was slipping in and out of consciousness and could barely breathe. Old Luke, who had taken such good care of him, was dropping with exhaustion himself.

'Perhaps you could put him in Purley Hall?' Pansy suggested, her wavering voice threaded with the finest filament of steel. 'It is a hospital, after all.'

'He'll have nothing of hospitals, Pansy. He will come here. I will take care of him.'

'We will *all* take care of him,' said Mara firmly.

'Perhaps you will harm him by moving him,' ventured Pansy.

'Oh, for goodness' sake, woman, shut up!' said Kitty, heaving the feather mattress off the bed.

Mara swallowed a smile as Pansy's eyes widened and her small paw of a hand went to her mouth. 'My dear Kitty, there is no need to—'

Kitty took her by the shoulders and pushed her through the narrow bedroom doorway. 'Will you let me get on? Tommy and Michael and I are going to fetch William any minute. And that's it.'

'Well!' Pansy's voice was cracking, ugly with anger. She turned and flounced out and they could hear her clattering down the stairs.

'Now!' said Kitty. She and Mara stripped the bed and made it again with snowy linen. They worked together in silence. Kitty swept all Pansy's clutter from the top of the dressing-table into a drawer. Mara opened the window wide for a few minutes to clear the air of the wistful scents of its former occupant. Then she set about lighting a fire in the small fireplace to warm the room while Kitty went off with Tommy and the pacing Michael to collect William from the Waterman's Cottage.

Half an hour later they were back and Tommy was carrying his father, bundled and wrapped like a chrysalis, up the twisting stairs.

Kitty shooed them all out, telling Mara to make cups of tea for everyone. When Mara got downstairs Michael and Pansy looked across at her like conspirators. Pansy was in her outdoor clothes and had a small travelling bag beside her. Old Luke was sitting very upright in a hard chair beside the scullery door, his eyes closed.

Michael was quite red about the face. He coughed. 'We, that is Pansy and I, have decided that perhaps she should stay in Priorton.' He looked meaningfully at Mara. 'She has felt for some time that her presence is unwelcome here. Now, with illness in the house . . .'

Mara pushed her hair back wearily. 'No, no, Michael. It's just that she can't have the big bedroom any longer because Pa needs it. She will have to share with me again.'

'In any case, my dear, at times like these a family needs to be together.' Pansy pulled on her lace gloves. 'I am an intruder.'

'Times like these? Times like what?' Mara glanced from one to the other. 'You think Pa's gonna die, don't you?' She was suddenly very angry. 'Well, you'll be sorry to hear that he's not. Because me and my mother are going to take great care of him.'

'Me too,' said Tommy belligerently.

'I also.' Luke's voice from the scullery corner was the slenderest reed of sound.

Pansy smiled sweetly, exchanging a glance with Michael. 'Well then, my dears. He is in good, if . . .' she glanced at Luke, only just suppressing a shudder, '. . . unconventional hands. So, you will not need me. I will be at the Gaunt Hotel.' She let her glance linger around the simple room. 'That is a respectable place.'

Tommy slammed the door behind them. 'Good riddance to bad rubbish,' he grunted.

'So say all of us,' said Mara fervently. She glanced at Luke, but he seemed asleep, his lids like grey tissue over his full round eyes.

After ten minutes, Kitty came downstairs, her face still and intent. She was focused inside herself, thinking towards the past and her long relationship with William: on the way their identities had become intermingled after so many years of complete sharing. Looking at her mother's rapt face Mara's heart chilled as she realised that Kitty too thought William was dying.

'Luke,' Kitty was saying, 'I have placed a chair for you in the bedroom. You can sit with him if you wish.' There was tenderness in her tone; Luke's identity too was intermingled with that of his beloved friend.

The old man opened his eyes. He shook his head. 'No, Kitty. You must stay with him, and Mara and Tommy must stay with him. You must hold him, hold him every minute of the day and night. Lend him your life, your blood, which I know is his life-blood. I will be here and pray towards the sacred centre, the golden thread that stretches back to the beginning of time and loops forward to be before us, lying there for us to reach. And then . . .'

There was a moment of pure stillness in the room.

'And then . . .' Mara breathed.

'Perhaps it is not his time to die.' Luke's eyes closed again and he seemed once more to be asleep.

In the following days they did exactly as Luke had suggested. Kitty cooled her husband with flannels, forcing dribbles of food into his mouth. While she did this, Mara or Tommy would hold both his hands, rubbing them and talking, whispering how much they all loved him and needed him. In the night one or other of them climbed into the bed beside him, and held him, warming him where he lay.

Luke moved little from his place downstairs. He drank water but ate nothing. In the early hours of the morning they heard, but did not see, him going about his rigorous ablutions. Occasionally he would hum a wordless tune, repeating a single sound over and over again.

Michael came each day, looked helplessly at the motionless figure of his father, and went away. On the second day he called in at the Post Office to send an urgent wire to his brother Samuel.

The doctor came, examined his unconscious patient and when his suggestion of the Infirmary was rejected, shrugged his shoulders and left. When Miss Aunger turned up at the cottage to report on shop affairs to Kitty, she was politely and firmly sent away to use her own initiative.

Jean-Paul called and Mara talked to him at the door, explaining about her father's illness in a soft voice. He squeezed her hand tightly. 'I will pray for him,' he said. 'I will ask for a Mass.' Mara remembered the insult of 'Papist!' often shouted after Jean-Paul and Hélène in the street.

The vicar came huffing and puffing at Michael's request, said some conventional prayers over William, looked askance at Luke, and left.

Then, at noon on the fourth day, William started to mutter away at Tommy, who was holding his hand. Mara was sitting beside William on the bed, her arm around him. The words were mumbled but the meaning was clear. 'Decided to stay on, old boy? Glad you didn't go. Time enough.' His eyes were open and there was something of their old light in them.

'Time enough for what, Pa?' Tommy grinned up at Mara.

'Army, old boy. Killing . . . all those shells made so neat for death. Time enough for that.'

Mara squeezed her father's hand and he turned to smile weakly at her.

'Mother! Mother!' shouted Tommy urgently, clinging on still to the other hand, tears in his eyes. '*Mother!*'

Kitty came bounding up the stairs and burst through the door. William's face turned to her, luminous as a spring sky. He struggled up onto an elbow, away from Mara's clasp. 'Now, Kitty dear girl, how are you?'

Kitty flew to his side. Tommy and Mara stood up, away from the bed, allowing their mother to take their father's hand. Kitty smiled at William. 'Well apart from missing about sixty hours' sleep, I am very fit, dear boy.'

William lifted his gaze to Luke, who was now standing in the narrow doorway. 'Ah! Old friend.' His voice was strengthening by the minute. 'I see you have taken care of me very well.'

Luke bowed his head slightly. 'You are recovered now,' he said.

'It was not my time?'

'It was not your time.' The old man turned and walked stiffly down the steep stairs. Mara and Tommy followed him, but when they got to the kitchen he had gone.

'Back to Waterman's Cottage, I shouldn't wonder,' said Mara, yawning.

'D'you think old Luke's a wizard?' asked Tommy, only half-joking.

Mara put on the kettle. 'He certainly knows something we don't know.'

Then Tommy clapped his hand on his head. 'Father does too. Do you know what he was saying, about me waiting? What day is it? Thursday. I was eighteen on Tuesday. And you were sixteen. We've missed our birthdays.' He rubbed his hands. 'Here we go! Now, with Pa on the mend, you won't see me for dust. Remember the report about that flier bringing down the Zeppelin? That'll be me next year.'

177

Michael, when he called, was surprised to find his father sitting up in bed, well enough to talk with him. He found himself both pleased and relieved at his father's recovery. He had felt slightly guilty about the long talks he and Pansy had had, about him taking over as head of the family, and the need to think seriously about what they should do with Kitty, as after all, the poor thing had no legal rights at all, had she? They would be very kind, of course. Pansy had such a good heart, thought Michael fondly. Always thinking of others.

He coughed. 'Well, Father, now you appear to be out of danger, so I can tell you my news. Pansy and I are to be married very soon. We will travel to York and be married by special licence from the Bishop. We want no fuss – we are far too old for that. We'll go to York and come back man and wife. Pansy is staying at present at the Gaunt Valley Hotel. Poor thing complains very little, but I know she is very uncomfortable there. Being married immediately will solve that problem, of course.'

'So it will.' William reached out and shook his son's hand enthusiastically. 'Well done, my boy. I wish you every happiness. If only I could get Kitty to consent to marry me. But she still holds out after all these years.'

Michael spread his hands and looked at them. Pansy's words about it being very convenient, really, that his father and Kit weren't married were ringing in his ears. 'Oh, Pa, it has all worked very well so far. There is no need to disturb things, is there?'

William eyed him. 'It is up to Kitty, as it always has been. That has never stopped me pressing my suit and never will.'

Michael stood up. 'Anyway, it is good to see you on the mend, Father. Perhaps you'll inform Kit and the others of my intentions? Pansy and I are off to York on Monday.'

William smiled easily at his son. 'Certainly I will. I am sure Kitty will be delighted. Well done, old boy. Well done.'

The marriage between Michael and Pansy, achieved quietly

on a two-day sojourn in York, was a cause of low-key celebration in the family. The recovering William and Kitty were enthusiastic, pleased that two isolated people had found some happiness. Mara and Tommy were resigned that, if Pansy were to be around them for ever, as seemed to be the case, then it were better that she should be in Michael's tall house in Priorton than cheek-by-jowl with them.

With his father improving by the day, Tommy was finally to be allowed to volunteer for the Army. Kitty decided to have a family feast, to celebrate William's recovery, her oldest stepson's wedding, Tommy and Mara's birthdays, and as a farewell to Tommy.

The feast was held in the long workroom at the Waterman's Cottage. Refusing any help from Pansy, Kitty cooked the meal herself, assisted by Miss Aunger who, like Luke, would sit at table with them. Luke as usual made some of his Middle Eastern delicacies to add to the feast. And as usual Kitty extended the party, this time with Mr Clelland, who had taught Tommy as an infant. She did not invite Michael's cronies from Priorton, aware that they would feel driven to refuse an invitation to the unconventional Scorton ménâge, where it was known that Kitty Rainbow had the servants sit at table.

To her great delight, Mara was encouraged to invite Jean-Paul and Hélène, a concession which Kitty made with a rather mischievous twinkle in her eye. Michael and Pansy, arriving to see the strange collection of people, exchanged helpless looks and took their places of honour beside William and Kitty.

William made a little speech welcoming Pansy to his family, ending by mentioning that he had so enjoyed his two daughters that it was a delight to welcome the third, though he hoped she didn't choose to go off to Africa or America or even Russia, like one daughter he could name. He sat back in his seat to laughter and the patter of applause.

Mara could hear Pansy, under cover of the clatter as they got on with their meal, whisper to Michael that, in fact, Leonora was not William's daughter, was she? Mara opened her mouth to protest but stopped as Michael scowled rather darkly at his new wife, growling, 'Nonsense, m'dear. Utter nonsense.'

During the meal William quietly enquired of Mr Clelland's work in the Pacifist movement. The schoolteacher put down his napkin and glanced around the table. 'Sir, it is difficult here at your table. Young Tommy is off . . .'

Michael cleared his throat, indicating agreement that this was not the place.

'It is my table, sir,' said William coolly. 'Words are not swords, they are ploughshares, fashioned so that we can reap the benefits of greater understanding, even if we do not agree.' He glanced at Tommy, who was leaning forward in his seat. 'I am sure that Tommy is not afraid of a few ideas.'

Mr Clelland took a breath. 'Well, sir, in the first place, I do not believe in the taking of human life. We are told *Thou shalt not kill*, and that is the essence of what I feel about all this. We feel also that the war is being fought – on both sides – to satisfy territorial greed, imperialistic possession. It is promoted by the manufacturers of arms who see fathomless profit in the exercise—'

'Sir!' Michael interrupted hotly.

'The call to war engages the natural virtuous patriotism of young men, their energy and search for adventure, their desire to prove themselves on any field of battle, their imagined memory of mythic battles of yore. It engenders the sacrifice by womankind of their brothers and fathers, sometimes themselves. It engages all this, and distils it into some kind of death-wish which will destroy a generation.'

You could hear a pin drop in the room.

'These young men are like lead soldiers on the playing boards of the generals, who care no more for the individual life than for an inanimate toy. For them the lead can be melted down again and again to recreate the sacrifice. For them it is just a game. For each man and boy, for each family, it is their continuity. Their immortality.' He sat back then, and glanced around the table.

Jean-Paul looked at him quietly. 'Sir, my country is overrun. If your country were overrun, would you still not fight?' He glanced at his sister, who was placing her knife and fork and spoon in an odd pattern on her plate. 'Were I not prevented by my obligations here, I would fight, enthusiastically and with a good heart.'

Mr Clelland shook his head. 'That, I agree, would be the greatest test. The enemy in our streets, in our parlours. And I understand that that is your experience. But I say to you – *no!* I would not fight. I'd work my soul out to make sure the ordinary men on the other side would not fight. I would appeal to their consciences, for they are Christians, all.'

'I see what you say about wanting to have the adventure, wanting to prove yourself,' said Tommy slowly. 'But what about patriotism? If what you say worked out, there would be no countries, no flags . . .'

Mr Clelland looked at him thoughtfully. 'Would that be a bad thing? What about brotherhood? What about an international brotherhood where there were no national borders to fight over? Where ordinary people, not nabobs, had charge of things, respected each other's rights?'

Michael stood up. 'I'm not sitting here listening to this. This is treason.'

William glanced sharply at him. 'You will sit down, Michael. These are merely notions, ideas. We need not be afraid of ideas, just their consequences. The war now being fought in the trenches, which your brother is about to join, is the consequence of one set of ideas. As is the mire and carnage in which your beloved sister Leonora now struggles.' He looked pointedly at Pansy, whose mouth had closed, tight as a purse. Mara hid a smile. Pa didn't miss much, didn't miss much at all.

There was a tense silence, then Kitty stood up and held out her wine glass. 'I have two toasts which I would like to make.

The first one is to France . . .' She smiled at Jean-Paul, who was looking at her with shining eyes, and Hélène, who was picking away distractedly at the hem of the tablecloth, oblivious to all around her. 'France, who has to endure these awful battles on her own ground day by day, day by day.'

All of them, including Mr Clelland, drank the toast.

Kitty raised her glass again. 'And I give you my son, who, whatever you or I say, Mr Clelland, will join the battle tomorrow. Yes, because he feels brave and wants to prove himself. But also, like many of us, because he is a patriot.'

'Hear, hear!' said Michael and Pansy in unison, gulping back their wine.

Mr Clelland raised his glass to Tommy. 'I wish you safe journey, son, and pray that God will look over you, Tommy. With all my heart I pray it.'

Mara blinked tears from her eyes and went to hug Tommy. He hugged her back cheerfully, saying, 'What's all this? It's no funeral, I promise you that.'

'Then how about some music, Tommy? Where's your squeezebox? You haven't packed that yet, have you?'

The air was hot and sultry. The horses, their sides heaving, nostrils dilating, were caked with grit and sweat. A film of dust made the drivers' faces into grey masks. Their eyes were red-rimmed, and expressionless.

Fires danced along the horizon, here and there casting a cupola or a church spire into black relief. Behind them the countryside was being systematically destroyed. It seemed as if all the world were in retreat. Gun carriages and baggage wagons pitched and rolled like ships in a dust storm. The nurses and orderlies sat wooden-faced in their bumping cart, numbly conscious of hopping, hurrying refugees dodging between the disordered chaos of infantry and artillery. In retreat.

Two cows mooed discontentedly, driven steadily through the mêlée by a fierce-faced, very old man who was poking them determinedly with a stick. A young woman with a baby strapped to her chest also carried a brace of squawking ducks tied by their legs and slung round her neck. A girl of no more than nine, head down, led a thickset donkey with two smaller children on its back.

These robust souls were lucky. Less ambulant people – mothers with clusters of tiny children, old men and women – were stuck by the roadside. The nurses stirred uneasily as their ears were assailed by women's voices, crying, beseeching, pleading, cursing, to a chorus of cackling geese and barking dogs.

Leonora started up at the shrill despairing cry of a child. Pavel grasped her arm and roughly pulled her back down. 'Steady, sister. Nothing can be done.' That was when she pulled her apron up over her face and head to shut it all out, trying to make herself into stone so she would endure and survive.

And stone she stayed during the long bone-shaking trek back to Moscow. The journey took weeks; first by wagon, then by train. At the first of many railway stations they waited for two days to get on a crowded train. Waiting patiently alongside them were peasants in rough white linen tunics, their wives in coloured head scarves. Less patient were the small groups of Polish gentry, the men in dark clothes and women in hats and veils, surrounded by their elaborate trunks, boxes, bundles and bags. The train was too full of people to take their luggage, so it had to be left behind. Then it was their turn to wail.

At one half-day stop, in a simple ceremony, the nurses were presented with little silver crosses of St John, hung from black and gold ribbon. In her bunk that night Leonora held the cross close to her eyes, looking at it and trying to feel pleased at this recognition for all the work they had done. But no feeling would come.

She still felt cold and hard as stone as she rumbled through Moscow in a carriage and had herself deposited at the door of the Poliakovs'. She put down her canvas bag and tried to pull the iron knob which set the great bell clanging. It would not move. She tried three more times. At the fourth attempt when she still did not succeed, she closed her eyes and let blackness seep in, sliding to the ground and lying down. Her last thought was that all she wanted really was to sleep. A nice long sleep. Then she would be better.

12

A Departure and a Return

Tommy called at the shop to say goodbye to Mara and Kitty. He would allow neither of them to come with him to the station. 'Can't have women weeping all over me,' he said.

'Huh!' said Mara. 'We'd have the flags out, cheering you on to go there and win the day for us.'

But when he shook their hands manfully she was gulping back tears. 'You be careful, you great galumphing boy. Don't really try to be the hero. We need you here.'

Kitty kissed him on the cheek. 'You're my brave lad,' she said steadily. 'Now you take care.'

He went to the factory to say goodbye to Michael, avoiding Pansy. 'I know I've been a bit of a clot, Michael, but I'm off to do what's right.'

Michael put a hand on his shoulder. 'You do the family credit, Tommy. Go and do your best.'

'You'll keep your eye on Mother and Father?'

'Naturally. You've no worries about them.'

'And no hard feeling between us?'

'No hard feelings.'

They shook hands again and Tommy made his way down to the shop floor to shake hands with the foreman and the other men he had worked with, and to steal a kiss from Maisie and the other girls on the pretext of never seeing them again.

'Gerraway with yeh!' Maisie kissed him on the other cheek.

'Yeh'll have the Kaiser beat an' be back here plaguin' us again in no time.'

The next morning Mara sat in her bedroom, giving her hair its hundred strokes, disentangling the curls, imposing some order. Tommy had looked so very young, standing there in the shop doorway. Too young to be going off to kill people. He should still be here. He would be such a very big miss.

The two of them had played and lived together most of their lives. Being so different, they had never lived in each other's pockets. But now to Mara, Purley Lodge seemed as hollow as a drum without Tommy. Her mother and father were such a bonded pair. Mara and Tommy had always been outside that intimate circle, but they had each other, and that created some kind of balance. Of course, there had been Leonora to mother them both a bit, up till a few years ago. With Leonora gone, Mara and Tommy had seen themselves, and were seen as, a pair. Tommy had perpetrated his many scrapes, while she'd had her own recent adventures – going away to Hartlepool to work, picnicking with Alexander and Dewi in Livesay Woods, kissing Jean-Paul in the street.

Of course their parents, secure in their own affections, and essentially unconventional themselves, were open-minded towards such departures from accepted behaviour. Mara wondered now whether the indulgence shown towards these childish actions by the tolerant Kitty had kept them both in the world of childhood longer than the more sophisticated trio of Leonora, Michael and Samuel. Perhaps that was why Tommy was really too young to go to war. And she herself was too young to take the risk of kissing someone in the street.

She stopped brushing and looked at herself keenly in the mirror. Perhaps Kitty keeping them in what Michael called a 'half-savage' state would now bring disaster in its wake, as he always predicted.

Soon Tommy would be marching around, drilling on some draughty parade ground, rehearsing the taking up of arms in anger, preparing to kill as many Germans as he could: young, old, watchmakers, miners, blacksmiths, all.

'And what are you doing, Mara Scorton?' she said to herself in the mirror. 'Helping Miss Aunger sell stockings and the dreadful "open drawers" to an ever-dwindling group of customers. What a waste of time.' She started to pin up her hair. 'And mooning around over Jean-Paul. And spending time with poor old Hélène, who is getting more and more strange with every day that passes.' Hélène had taken a fancy now to that blacksmith at the bottom of Bridge Street, or more properly to the fire in that great hearth of his. She was always hanging round there.

And what about Jean-Paul? Right back in his shell again. He had been really morose ever since Tommy's farewell dinner. Mr Clelland's pacifist talk, far from discouraging Jean-Paul from fighting, seemed to have made him feel guilty for not being in his place at the front line, helping his beleaguered country.

Mara pinched her cheeks to make them red, pulled on her jacket and tripped down the stairs to her mother, who was waiting anxiously with the old pony and trap, ready to set out for work. 'Come on! Come on, daydreamer. We need an earlier start when we're setting out in this contraption.' With Tommy not there to drive they had to fall back on much older transport.

After work that night Mara made her way to Bridge Street, as she did most nights, ostensibly to see Hélène, but always to spend some time with Jean-Paul if he were on the right shift. Even when he was being stiff and polite, she wished to spend time with him.

As she turned a corner she could feel the heat of John Maddison's forge before she saw it. Hélène was leaning on the wall talking to the fire. John Maddison was making iron fire blazers, a useful little task which filled in time between the horseshoeing and the mending of oven parts which were now the staples of his trade.

John Maddison's fire blazers were famous in the district: intricately made, curved cunningly to fit any parlour fire, guaranteed to make the fires roar in no time. The blazers had clever double handles which saved knuckles from being burnt. John worked on his own now, his son having volunteered to be a farrier in the Army.

The blacksmith looked up as Mara approached, pulled a dirty rag off a peg and wiped his dripping brow. 'Yeh gunna tek yer marrer off home, Miss Scorton? The lass must be starvin'. She's been here all day again, like. Standin' there hours on end leaning against the wall, staring at th' coals, jabberin' away at th' flames.'

Mara took Hélène's arm. 'Sorry, Mr Maddison. She shouldn't . . .'

The blacksmith shook his head. 'She's nee bother, like,' he grinned, showing a mouthful of blackened, crowded teeth. He shovelled some fresh nuggets onto his fire. 'Spooks a few of the livery men, like, and the farmers, but that's no bad thing. Impident buggers, some of them. Sorry for swearing, Miss Scorton.' He winked at her then, showing he wasn't sorry at all.

Hélène pulled away from Mara's hand. In the cavernous hearth which housed John Maddison's fire, tongues of flame were reaching up into the great chimney before they settled to the white burning glow which was as much John Maddison's tool as his great hammer. Hélène's body went rigid and she started talking away in French, moaning and gesticulating.

Mara shook her. 'What is it, my love? What's wrong?'

Hélène started to breathe very heavily. 'He is there!'

'Who, Hélène, who?'

'Alex – did you see? Struggling in the centre of the fire. Shouting, calling to me.' She then reverted into incomprehensible, rapid French and Mara, step by step, pulled her away from the forge, and down the street into her own house.

The Derancounts' dwelling was in chaos. The fire was dead, cinders strewn over the narrow enamel hearth. All the cupboards were hanging open and the curtains had been pulled off their poles. 'Oh, Hélène, what have you been doing?' said Mara resignedly.

Hélène looked round with wondering eyes. 'The baby. I was looking for the baby. It's gone, Mara. Gone.' She gripped Mara's face tightly between her hands. 'Did I kill it, did I? I dreamt one night that I did. But that was only a dream, wasn't it? I did not really kill it.' Mara's head jerked back as her face was released.

Hélène set straight an upturned chair and sat on it. 'I wouldn't kill my own baby, would I?' she said sadly.

Mara stroked the other woman's wild hair, pushing it behind her ears. Then she took a brush from the mantelshelf and started to brush the tangled locks. 'Don't worry about the baby, Hélène. The baby is all right. Just fine.' She pinned the hair up into a semblance of tidiness, then poured Hélène a glass of water. 'You drink that. And as soon as I get the fire away I'll make you some tea. You just get your breath and then you can help me to fold all these things and put them away, so it will be nice and tidy for when Jean-Paul comes from the pit.'

Helene looked blankly at her then took the glass and started to sip the water.

Mara rolled up her sleeves and set to work, gaining some satisfaction from imposing order on Hélène's house, where somehow she could impose no order on Hélène and her wandering mind.

When Jean-Paul returned from work two hours later the house was in order, the fire in the range was blazing and steam was rising lazily from the boiler full of hot water. He looked round. 'Where's my sister?'

His voice was brusque. She looked in vain for some softening, some recognition of what she had done for him. 'She's asleep. Jean-Paul, she's been acting so strangely. She spent all day at John Maddison's and is seeing . . . all sorts of things in his fire. The house was upside down, chaos. I've just finished sorting it.'

He threw his cap into a corner and rubbed his face with both hands. Then he looked at her. 'Do you know that I sometimes hate her – my own sister?' Then he stood up straight. 'Now you must go home, Mara. You should not do all this work.'

'I don't want—'

Mara was interrupted by a knock on the door. Jean-Paul opened it. Kitty stood there, a soft beret on her head and a shawl around her shoulders. 'I presume my daughter is here?' she said, her voice remarkably even.

He opened the door more widely. '*Entrez, s'il vous plaît, madame.* As you see, I am just home from work.' He spoke quickly. 'Mara was about to leave. She has been here helping my sister, who—'

Kitty stepped into the little room and looked round.

'Hélène's in bed,' said Mara steadily. 'She ripped this room apart looking for a baby that doesn't exist, and I stayed to put it straight. And to watch her while she went to sleep.'

Kitty nodded. 'Well, now her brother's here . . . I have the trap out on the road, Mara. I thought you should not be walking back up to the Lodge in the dark. Shall we go?'

In embarrassed silence Mara pulled on her jacket then said an awkward goodbye to Jean-Paul. She climbed into the trap and sat quietly as Kitty clicked her tongue for the pony to move forward. She was annoyed with herself for feeling guilty with no cause. In some ways she wished there had been a cause.

It was Kitty who spoke first. 'I must learn to drive that motor car,' she said. 'Don't you find Tommy is such a great miss, Mara?'

It took Leonora many days at the Poliakov house to get back into any normal rhythm of sleeping and waking, of eating meals in more than just single hurried mouthfuls; to get used again to wearing, and sleeping in, clean white linen. It took days before her legs stopped aching and her feet reduced their swelling, before she stopped flinching at the sound of church bells, or the yells and shouts of servants in the nether regions of the sprawling house.

Monsieur and Madame Poliakov treated her like a returning heroine, Madame weeping for her own sons who were now doing service for Mother Russia. Lucette donned her nurse's uniform to play the nurse, sharing a little in Leonora's limelight. The second morning, Leonora, turning over in bed and catching sight of her on the little chair, called her 'Larissa'.

'Larissa, who is she?' Lucette asked sharply.

'A comrade. She nursed with me nearly to the end.'

'She went? She ran away, this Larissa?' said Lucette.

Leonora turned over and stared at the wall. 'She died.'

'That's sad,' said Lucette, injecting the right note of sorrow into her voice. 'But never mind, darling Leo. You are here and safe with us.'

Leonora threw off the blankets and put her bare feet out of the bed. 'I shouldn't be here, Lucette. I should be back with my unit. There is so much work to do, so many wounded boys . . .'

Lucette held Leonora's arm in a vice-like grip. 'No, darling Leonora. You must stay in bed. Get back your strength. You can return when you are strong.'

Leonora looked at her with dull eyes, then heaved her legs back into bed. She took Lucette's apron in her hand. 'Really, Lucette, I know the uniform flatters you and in it you look like a little angel of virtue, but you should not wear it. You have no right.'

Lucette had a bright red patch on each cheek. She pouted. 'I thought it would please you.' A tear appeared very fetchingly at the corner of her eyes. 'I wore it to please you.'

Inevitably, Leonora relented. She touched her friend's hand. 'It's just . . . we wore our aprons, no matter how hard it was out there. We tried to keep them clean. Washed them in rivers, beat them on stones. But in the end we had to wear them ruined, stained . . .'

'That's true, it *is* ruined,' said Lucette cheerfully. 'My

stepmama told Marika to burn it. She tried to wash it but had hysterics when blood ran from it. My stepmama has ordered you a new one.' Lucette stood up. 'You are right. I'm so thoughtless. I will change.'

She vanished, and returned in an entrancing green dress, narrowly cut, showing a remarkable amount of ankle. Leonora sat up and pushed her hair out of her eyes to get a better look. She smiled. 'Some people, Lucette, might call that little outfit indecent.'

Lucette laughed, very satisfied at the impact she had made. 'A little better than that horrible old nun's outfit, anyway.'

They were interrupted by a discreet knock at the door. Lucette's stepmother bustled in, bringing in her faintly spicy aura.

'You have a caller, Leonora – Monsieur Scorton your brother is here. Will you wish to receive him in my boudoir, perhaps? Then you will be saved the journey down the stairs.'

'No, I . . .' Leonora put a hand to her hair again. 'I will come downstairs.'

Lucette leapt from the bed. 'I will attend to Monsieur Samuel while Leonora makes herself . . .' she allowed her gaze to drift over Leonora's unkempt hair, her creased, faintly greasy face, '. . . presentable. A little less *distraite*, perhaps.'

As the door clicked behind her Leonora allowed herself a chuckle. Lucette would never change. Selfish to the last pore, and yet always getting away with it, tossing her flossy head or smiling her winning wise-baby's smile.

She scrubbed her face clean in the bowl which had been laid out for her. Then she pulled her hair back severely from her face and tied it with a ribbon. She completed her ensemble with a plain grey skirt and a ruffled blouse with a grey silk petersham tie. The blouse had come from her mother's store in Priorton, a going-away present from Miss Aunger when she had first left for Russia. How long ago that all seemed.

The family were gathered in the winter sitting room and there were shouts of 'Huzzah!' and boisterous applause from

Clément Poliakov as Leonora made her entrance. He came and kissed her twice on each cheek and held her to him in a great bear hug. 'The heroine recovers!' he beamed.

She fought herself free and looked across at Samuel, now on his feet, framed by the outrageous baroque intricacy of the marble fireplace.

She almost didn't recognise him. He looked ten years younger than he had in the Caucasian forests. Without his greatcoat he looked thinner; his wild hair had been cut short and his beard and moustache shaved off. He came towards her and took both of her hands in his and drew them to within an inch of his lips. 'You're skinnier than ever, Leonie. And younger.'

She laughed. 'I was just thinking that about you.'

'How are you now? Clément says that you returned half-dead.'

'I am well now – I have been sleeping for England. If sleeping could win the war I'd have won it single-handed.' She pushed her hair back. 'Those last stages of the retreat were a nightmare. My dear friend Larissa died. Just another death. I became less than human – a stone – not caring for anything except my own survival. I became a monster.' Her eyes filled with tears.

His hands tightened on hers. 'Many soldiers end up feeling like that, Leonora. In their thousands. You'd given enough, from the very bottom of yourself.'

She shook her head, retrieved her hands and took a step away. 'There can never be enough, Samuel. I'll be going back to work soon. They need every pair of hands.'

'You can't, Leonora. I told you. You must go home. Kit sent a message . . .' He scrabbled in a pocket for the telegram. 'There was yet another message waiting for me when I returned. As you see, my father's gravely ill. This communication is days old. For all we know . . .' His voice trembled.

She blinked. William had always been a quiet chime resounding through her life: closer than a stepfather and perhaps less judgmental, more forgiving than a natural father. 'We'll go directly,' she said.

He shook his head. 'I would like that, but first I have meetings, people to see. A major report to write for London about the meeting in Switzerland. Vladimir Lenin was there, also Leon Trotsky . . .'

'Samuel! You're impossible! You have just said that William may be dying!'

'As I say, the telegram is old now. I've wired Kitty to find out whether he . . . We can get away on Friday for certain. We won't make it overland now. We'll have to go by sea, through Finland. That'll take some fixing.'

'You two must not go and leave me here,' wailed Lucette in English. 'I'll die of frustration with all these wretched *baboushkas*,' glancing at her stepmother, 'and this gloomy talk of the war.'

'Did you not listen? Our father is gravely ill,' said Samuel sharply. 'How can we take a stranger home at such a time?'

Clément Poliakov jumped up, rubbing his hands together. 'Samuel, poor little Nurse Rainbow has not even sat down. Sit here, my dear, beside me. You haven't yet told me half of your stories.'

The next day Samuel brought in another telegram from Kitty. *Father pulling through crisis. Tommy enlisted. Michael married. Writing.*

'Thank God!' said Leonora.

'Michael, the old dog!' grinned Samuel. 'Never knew he had it in him. Born bachelor, always was.' He took Leonora's hand. 'But you must still go home to see them, my love. This seizure of Pa's might not be the last one.'

'It is three years since I was home,' she said slowly.

'There,' he said briskly, 'the decision is made.'

In the end, it took all of Leonora's persuasive powers to stop Lucette from accompanying them on the ship to England. The younger girl was finally quelled by the promise of a visit if things were all right at home, after the war.

Before they left, Samuel took Leonora back to see Valodya at the flat. She followed the fast-flowing conversation with less difficulty this time. And this time it excited her, set her mind racing.

Today, there were fewer comrades around the table. One of the men was missing because he had joined the Army, to do further work for the revolution from the inside. He had gone off with packets of revolutionary leaflets in his knapsack. A man and his wife who distributed pamphlets had been arrested by the Tsar's secret police. However, those left still buzzed with excitement and a sense of significance which was out of kilter with the shabby room and the unprepossessing appearance of its inhabitants.

Leonora's head was still whirling with ideas as they left. 'There really will be another revolution, like the one in 1905, won't there?' she said to Samuel, as he handed her into the carriage. 'Pavel Demchenkov was always hinting at it. And some of the young soldiers – one boy, his father had been a martyr in the 1905 revolt – talked of joining the revolutionaries. Not that the martyr's son will ever do that,' she added sadly. 'He was killed by a shell soon after he talked to me.'

Samuel nodded. 'That was one reason I was down in the Caucasus, to see such men. Demchenkov is a good man. They need good men.'

'So there will be an uprising? Are you for it?'

He shrugged. 'It's not a matter of whether one is for it or against it. Nor is it a matter of if, but of *when*. The British concern is that, whatever the outcome – though naturally we are with the Tsar – this revolt should occur *after* the defeat of the Germans, not before.'

'But they can't win, can they, Valodya and his friends? The Tsar—'

'Nicholas is a fool.'

Leonora glanced at their driver, hoping they had not been overheard, that he did not speak English. She shivered, feeling less at home now than she had at any time in Russia. The cocoon of the Poliakovs' stifling house, with its grateful peasant servants and complaisant master, had first been cracked for her when she had heard the litany of grievance and suffered injustice intoned by Valodya and his friends; it had been completely shattered by her experience among the working soldiers at the Front; it had been crushed to dust by the messages she had been asked to take from dying boys to devastated mothers and fathers in the back streets of Moscow which even now, as she jogged along with Samuel in the fiacre, her hand in his, were rumbling with revolutionary unrest.

Pansy spent the early weeks of her marriage to Michael sorting out his domestic arrangements. 'I will do it now, dearest, for once and for all!' she said, fondly patting Michael's sleeve.

Sadly she had to let Mrs Malloran go. As she said to Michael, the woman was kind and well-meaning but sloppy and careless to a degree. It would be unkind to suspect her of dishonesty, but heaven knew where all Michael's hard-earned cash went to. From now on they would keep a little notebook with every penny down in there. Then there would be no worry about whether anyone had or hadn't been dishonest.

Pansy allowed Michael, who had previously thought Mrs Malloran as honest as the length of the day, to salve his conscience by giving the woman five guineas, a very good reference, and an introduction to Jacob Sleight, from his snooker club, who was in sore need of good cleaning woman for his dusty solicitors' offices in the Market Place.

Pansy replaced Mrs Malloran with two intelligent young girls, country bred, just in from Weardale. They were amenable and easy to train, and between them cost less than Mrs Malloran. The best thing about them was that they lived out, with an aunt in the town. Pansy would not have them cluttering up the house when she wished to be alone with Michael. She and Michael were now, as she said to her mirror reflection every morning, a pair. Each was to be all the other one had, and all the other one could want.

When she had the Royle sisters trained, and had sorted the house to her own satisfaction, she gave two luncheon parties. One for Michael's friends: a select group of businessmen and their wives. The other was for Michael's family: a late celebration of their nuptials, rather more in keeping with Pansy's aspirations than that uncomfortable feast at Purley Lodge. William, despite being much improved, arrived wrapped in rugs, with Mara and Kitty supporting him on either side.

They noted differences straight away. Michael's house was cleaner and bleaker. The rough bachelor's detritus had been swept away by a tremblingly firm Pansy, who had blamed the whole mess on Mrs Malloran, rather than Michael's own habit of hoarding, and insistence to the long-suffering Mrs M. that piles be left where they were. Mara's nose twitched at the familiar smell of lye soap and lavender polish. That smell had haunted the house in Hartlepool and had, till recently, started to creep into the Lodge.

Kitty looked at the table. 'I see we're to be your only guests, Pansy.'

Pansy pulled down the sleeves of her plain grey dress and folded her arms. 'We had a luncheon last Sunday for Michael's . . . town acquaintances.'

Kitty looked at her for a long minute. 'You mean we are not respectable enough to have been invited.'

'Come on, Kit, Mara,' said Michael hurriedly. 'Shall you sit down? This is a time for celebration.' He was sporting a rather richly shaded soft cloth jacket with a matching waistcoat and contrasting yellow paisley cravat.

'I'm sorry, dear Kitty,' said Pansy hesitantly, 'but you and William have chosen to live as you do, after all. I thought,' she sniffed affectingly, 'I thought it would save embarrassment.'

Kitty smiled suddenly. 'Of course you did. And as a respectable married woman and in your own house you must do as you will.' She leaned over and touched one of the tea roses which blowzed over the edge of the heavily carved sideboard. 'And you brought roses in from the garden! That is so nice; bringing the very last of the summer inside. So little of it left.'

Mara relaxed. For a moment she had been angry on her mother's behalf, but Kitty needed no defenders.

Pansy shot Kitty a glance, suspecting irony of some sort. But both Mara and Kitty were smiling blandly, showing a resemblance between them, as transitory as a flash of memory: a resemblance which hardly ever surfaced.

The meal was perfect, served with well-rehearsed efficiency by the Royle sisters. Michael watched with pride and affection as Pansy presided over his table; modest, quiet Pansy who had brought sensibility and unobtrusive warmth into his life; who lifted from him onerous decisions about his household and his person, and allowed him to concentrate on his work which, if he were honest, was his greatest love. He now enjoyed wonderful meals, beautifully wrought, every day of his life. New items of clothing appeared in his wardrobe as part of Pansy's attempts to 'brighten him up'. A cosy fire blazed away in his study in the evenings as he went through the papers he had brought home from the factory.

Pansy did not trouble him with questions, or uncalled-for conversation. And most important, he was pleased to find, in the first week after their York wedding, that she did not persist when he explained that the carnal side of married life held no interest for him whatsoever.

The decision to remain a bachelor had never been a difficult one for him. But now the comforts of married life were folding him in their warm grasp, seducing him with their ease, bringing him to savour Pansy's quiet presence with a relish which surprised him. He had already, with a little gentle prodding from her, begun to look back on his bachelor years as the 'bad old days'.

William was struggling to his feet and Michael's attention snapped back to the present.

'Michael and Pansy, it gives me great happiness to see the

two of you so content. I am delighted to see you settling down to life together. I wish you the happiness that Kitty and I have enjoyed all these years. I could give you no greater wish.' He smiled gently at Pansy. 'Many many times have I asked her to marry me, to no avail. You will be pleased, Pansy, that I persist with my suit. Your health.'

After the perfect lunch they all retired to the parlour, but after some desultory conversation there seemed little to do or say.

Kitty walked to the window and peered out. 'Oh dear, and now it's coming on to rain. I'm afraid we must go. The trap will get damp and with William . . .'

So, to a general air of relief, they returned early. When they reached the Lodge, Mara asked if she could keep the trap to go and visit Hélène and Jean-Paul.

Kitty looked at her closely. 'Are you and that young man still very good friends?' she asked.

Mara shook her head. 'I don't know,' she said. 'I don't know at all.' She knew that she had not stopped thinking of him for many days now. She knew she was puzzled by his coolness.

Jean-Paul seemed quite pleased to see her. She looked round the bare room.

'Hélène has gone for a walk by the river. I told her to meet me at the bridge at . . .' he took out his watch, '. . . four o'clock. She is under strict instructions. Perhaps you could wait and we could walk along to meet her together?'

Mara sat down. For several long minutes the ticking clock seemed the only living thing in the room. Then she stood up. 'This is no good, Jean-Paul. No good at all.'

He looked at her, frowning. 'What's no good?'

'Can you remember? Can you remember when you kissed me?'

He veiled his eyes. 'I remember it.'

'Then you'll also remember that in the last few weeks, after you kissed me, you've been treating me as though I were some leprous naughty child, who, quite inconveniently, has made friends with your sister.'

He threw up his hands. 'I should never have done that – touched you. You are so young . . .'

She took hold of him then and kissed him. After the weakest of struggles he kissed her in return. She disentangled herself and took a step back. 'There – does that feel young?'

He shook his head. 'You are very direct.'

'I am my mother's daughter. No proper Priorton girl, probably no proper French girl either, thank heavens. Those girls would let you blow hot and cold, come and go as you please, and swoon with unrequited love. Then you could kiss them and leave them just as you fancy.'

'That is unjust, Mara. I have battled with myself, fought to keep away from you. You are so young, and I've nothing to offer you. I have a sister who is insane and whom I will kill one day. And even though I love you, my greatest wish at this time is to be in my own country and kill those cursed *Boches*.'

'You'll get killed yourself.'

He shrugged. 'That is not important. When enough of us, enough of them, are dead, they will have to go home. If I survive I will come back here and tell you I love you and want nothing more in life than to be with you. Be with you here, in France, anywhere.'

'But you want this other thing more? Like Tommy to go and fight, and perhaps get killed?'

He rubbed his head. 'These are the times we are in, Mara.'

Mara sat down on the bench and held out her hand. 'Come and sit beside me, Jean-Paul.'

He took her hand and sat beside her. She moved until she could feel the warmth of his shoulder against her. Then she pulled down his head to hers and kissed him again: a very light and a very soft kiss. 'You volunteer for your war,' she said. 'I will take care of Hélène.'

'She needs watching day and night.'

'She can come and live with me at the Lodge.' Mara glanced

round the room. 'Or I can come here. There's no problem in that.'

She wondered briefly what Kitty would think of the idea. Or William. Well, she would have to deal with that problem when she came to it.

Later, as they went to fetch Hélène from the bridge, their arms swung together, the backs of their hands touching. Mara turned her hand and caught his, and they walked down to the bridge, hand in hand.

13

Homecoming

Leonora and Samuel were seen off at the station by the Poliakovs, father and daughter: Lucette amid fountains of tears and Clément patting his dry eye with a large silk handkerchief. The platform swarmed with soldiers and they had to fight their way onto the train. They had climbed into their carriage and the train was pumping up steam, when Valodya came bounding onto the platform like a great bear and thrust a packet through the open window into Samuel's hands, talking to him at high speed in his thick southern accent. He kissed Leonora on both her hands, then stood back.

Slowly the train started to pull away and he waved his straw hat, melting from sight for a second in a cloud of steam. Leonora leaned out of the window to wave, and noted how Lucette moved closer to the big man, apparently unconscious of her hand on his arm as she balanced the wild waving of the other hand towards the train.

'The minx,' Leonora said, sitting down. 'Now she's setting her cap at Valodya.'

Samuel shook his head and laughed. 'You mean instead of me? It's just a habit of hers, like a bee heading for a flower.'

Leonora drew off her gloves and laid them on the warm seat beside her. 'You must have been tempted,' she said carefully. 'So young. So beautiful.'

He took her bare hand and kissed it on the palm in a way which made the hair on the back of her neck stand on end.

'How could I be tempted,' he asked, 'when I have a sister who is as brave as she is beautiful, spirited rather than flirtatious? A sister who—'

Leonora snatched her hand away. 'Don't say "sister". It feels so bad.'

He grabbed her hand again. 'Don't feel bad. We have different mothers and fathers so there's nothing wrong with it, not before God. And anyway, being brother and sister for so many years is good. Do you think other lovers will have known each other inside out, as we do, before they fall in love?'

She relaxed. 'When you say it like that, it doesn't seem wrong, I will grant you that.' She stretched out her legs in front of her, relaxing suddenly. 'Oh, Sam, it's so nice to be here, just the two of us . . .'

Then she realised what she had just said. The carriage was indeed empty. 'How can that be? The station was crowded, bursting with people.'

'Shsh. I bought the other two tickets as well. Unfortunately, our friends seem to have missed the train.' He touched the structure above his head. 'So you can have two bunks and I can have two bunks. It's a long journey.' He smiled mischievously. 'And perhaps at some point I can share your bunk and you can share mine.'

The train stopped for a moment and then lurched on. She looked at him for a moment, tingling again with the voluptuous momentum of their first meeting in Moscow. 'Only if you're a very, very good boy.'

Sam stood up, shot the shining brass bolt on the door, then pulled down the ornate blinds, inside to the corridor and outside to the passing world, shutting out the view of the boulevards which were racing by, wreathed in steam. Then he removed his lightweight coat, and put it onto the hanger provided. He drew Leonora to her feet and helped her out of her coat and hung it over his. He reached out towards her again. She put away his hand and removed her own jacket, took off her own hat, took out her own pins and shook down her hair. 'Now what, dear brother?'

It was after they had made love for the first of many times on their journey home that she leaned back against her bunk and asked Samuel about the packet which Valodya had given him. She savoured his naked, lean strength as he stretched across her to take the packet from his coat pocket. He turned up the oil lantern and held it to the light. 'It contains letters to people – comrades – in England. And two articles to be submitted to English newspapers.'

'Will you send them?'

'Oh yes. Our people will take a peek at them first, no doubt. But they'll be passed on.'

She glanced around the compartment. 'The police – they sometimes come onto trains. They boarded ours on the way to the Front, checking papers and such. And they took two men off. Pavel says there are informers about.'

'So there are. Always where there are oppressive police there are informers, saving their own skins at the expense of others.'

'Will you hide it, the package?'

He nodded, then leapt to his feet to check the blinds at both sets of windows. He took out a screwdriver from an inside pocket of his coat, moved over to his own bunk opposite, then unscrewed the back support and placed the package very carefully behind it. After replacing the panel, he stood back to examine his handiwork. 'You'd never know it was there, would you?'

She shook her head and held open the bedclothes. 'Now, are you coming back? There are bits of you which are suddenly getting rather pink.'

As it turned out, the train was searched at two stations. The tumult on each occasion gave the pair time to put on their night attire and arrange themselves on their own bunks before the hammering came on their carriage. Samuel, tousled in his dressing-gown, opened the door and what ensued was very brief and polite. The officers, in a strange uniform which Leonora didn't recognise, looked at their papers, searched the carriage very briefly, politely saluted them both and left.

'And that's it?' said Leonora.

'That's it,' said Samuel. 'Now, where were we . . . ?'

The train journey seemed to Leonora to be a racing, continuous dream punctuated by short periods of sleep, and by meals with wine and iced tea brought to the door by the interested but discreet steward.

If the train journey was a jolting, voluptuous dream, the voyage from Helsingfors to Hull was a nightmare. Their vessel was a cargo ship which had been pressed into military service and was run by brisk Royal Navy personnel.

'I didn't realise it was a Navy ship,' muttered Leonora.

'Only kind there is on this stretch now. This one will have been requisitioned,' said Samuel, 'and I had to pull strings for us to get on it. I couldn't find what it was transporting, but I think we'll be safe enough.'

They were separated, then directed to two crowded cabins, one designated for men, the other for women. The sea was rough and the little ship bucked and turned like a panicking horse. Samuel endured this well, as was his stoical custom. On her original voyage out to Russia, Leonora had proved to be a good sailor. This time she had to learn what it was to fall victim to seasickness.

In all the time she had worked at the Front, she had never felt so bad. One morning, when she did not turn up at their prearranged meeting place beside the lifeboats, Samuel came in search of her. She was kneeling by her bunk with her head in her hands.

He lifted her bodily out of the mass of moaning women in the cabin, put her over his shoulder and carried her up the ladders. Then he propped her up under the lifeboat and vanished. Five minutes later he came back with another man whom she recognised as the First Mate. He led them to a tiny capsule of a cabin which turned out to be his own.

There Samuel laid her tenderly on the bunk, covered her with a blanket, and knelt beside her. 'It won't be long now, sweetheart. It won't be long.'

But she knew there were many hours to go. Samuel stayed with her for the rest of the voyage, forcing brandy through her lips at intervals, holding the bowl for her when she tried in vain, yet again, to be sick. He wiped her face with flannels and changed her like a child when she was sick on her blouse. Once she came to long enough to smile weakly. 'I'm sorry,' she said. 'I must look like a witch.'

'Absolutely,' he grinned cheerfully. 'Never seen you look such a sight in all the time I've known you. Whoah!' He reached out to grasp her shoulders as she began to shudder again. 'And, though I don't want to sound like one of your Auntie Esme's music-hall songs, I have never loved you more.'

Kitty frowned slightly at the sight of a very thin and tired Leonora as Samuel helped her off the train. Then she kissed her eldest daughter on the cheek. 'My dearest, dearest child.'

Leonora looked around and put her hand out to Mara. 'Mara! You're a giant! You must have grown another foot at least!'

'And how is my wandering boy?' Kitty turned to hug Samuel, wondering at the fact that this very middle-aged man was her stepson.

'You've been in the wars, Leonie,' Mara said, hugging her sister very tight. 'It's you who've shrunk.' Her body was aching with a relief she hardly recognised. Missing Leonora had come to be a well-tuned habit. Their relationship, half-filial, half-sibling, was complicated.

The motor car was waiting at the station gate. Samuel looked around for a driver. 'I'm driving,' Mara told him firmly. 'I tried this morning, and it's not as hard as it looks.'

'Wouldn't it be better if I—' he began.

'No,' said Kitty firmly. 'She can manage, although you can crank the handle if you like. I did it before and it kicks like a donkey. I'll put the luggage into the trunk. Leonora can sit with me in the back and you can sit beside Mara, and tell her what she's doing wrong.'

Mara pulled on her gloves, took a breath and settled down to the intricate task of driving a car through Priorton, where people bobbed about in the road like rabbits. Driving had not seemed so hard yesterday afternoon when she had practised in the lane.

Kitty settled herself beside her oldest daughter and held her arm all the way, finally allowing the relief she felt at the safe arrival home of her first-born to flow through her.

'Whoa, Mara.' Samuel put a hand on the steering wheel and straightened it, as the car swerved again. On one corner it lurched forward and pushed a delivery bicycle into the hedge. Mara pulled on the brake but the rider, a dark child with a broad grin, pulled his bicycle from the hedge and stood to one side as she cautiously started again. The engine drowned out the boy's piercing whistle and his yell, 'Yuh wanta watch out, missis!'

In the Market Place other people shook their heads at the lurching car, recognising its fawn and brown livery belonging to Miss Rainbow, who had the shop. Funny family, those Rainbows. Everyone thought so. At Michael Scorton's house the lace curtain twitched as Pansy Scorton, née Clarence, clicked her tongue and called Michael to see what a *show* his family was making in broad daylight. Even so, Mara did manage to get them safely back to Purley Lodge, and Samuel said that was very good, considering.

William, sitting in the kitchen on the hard-backed settle, beamed his greeting and stood up, opening his arms wide to incorporate his adored stepdaughter and his much-loved son. Luke was at his side, smiling his faint delight at the favourites' return but tolerating only the briefest of handshakes.

When the hugs and handshakes were over, Mara introduced Leonora and Samuel to Hélène, who was crouched on a stool by the fire. The French girl refused to shake hands and returned her gaze to the fire, muttering under her breath.

Leonora raised her eyebrows. Mara shook her head. 'Hélène's been poorly. She's had a bad time in France before they came here, she and her brother Jean-Paul. And now he's just gone off to travel to France to join the French Army.' She blushed. Jean-Paul had been keen to go. She had cut his hair for him before he went, mourning the loss of those silky dark curls. Without them he looked younger, more fragile. She had seen him off at the crowded station and he had given her a resounding kiss, much to the delighted disgust of the gathered crowd, some of whom muttered on about her membership of the scandalous Rainbow family who, as everyone knew, did not know how to behave.

Mara glanced at her mother. 'I'm staying with Hélène, Leonie, keeping her company, in their house down in Priorton.'

Leonora frowned. 'You're not here? I so looked forward to . . .' She had been anticipating some lovely close times with Mara, keeping her little sister enthralled with her traveller's tales. The thought of being with Mara had kept her going through the last bumping stage of the journey, when she and Samuel had sat apart in the train, cautious again about who might see them.

Kitty was bringing in the last of the bags from the car. 'It's quite convenient, really, Leonora, for Mara to stay there. There's so little space here. If Mara's down at Bridge Street there's more room here for you.' She looked at Samuel. 'Michael sends his good wishes, Sam, and invites you to stay with him while you're here.'

'There isn't room here to swing a cat,' said William gruffly. 'Sorry, old boy. Different if we were up at the Hall, of course.'

That invitation from Michael had taken a bit of wangling; Pansy had been so set against it. 'Our maids are so new,

209

untrained for visitors, Michael.' She had wrung her hands appealingly.

Michael, genuinely looking forward to seeing his younger brother again, had, unusually, overruled his wife. 'The house is perfect, dear. You have done a wonderful job. Never has it been more ready for guests.'

Now, at Purley Lodge, Luke moved quietly towards the scullery and Samuel took his place beside William on the long settle. 'That'll be fine, Kit. Seems Father here is well, so I don't mind where I'll lay my weary head. I've slept in many queerer places in the last six months.'

'I thought we'd have some tea, and you could make your way down to Priorton afterwards,' said Kitty. 'You can take the motor car.'

Leonora was sitting on a chair holding Mara's hand in hers. 'And how have you been, Tuppence? Getting yourself bombed on the coast, I hear? Couldn't you bear to leave the heroics to me, then?'

'Doesn't compare to what you've been up to, Leonie,' said Mara gruffly, tears clogging her throat. 'Not a bit.'

'Yes,' said Samuel cheerfully. 'Quite the heroine, our Leonora. She has a medal from the Russians.'

Leonora glanced at him. He sounded hearty and distant, altogether too brotherly. Very different from the man who had been holding her with passion, and with compassion, in the last two weeks.

'A medal! Show me! Show me!' said Mara.

'First tea,' said Kitty firmly. 'Luke's been making your favourites, Leonora, and they need to be served hot.'

Later that evening Samuel gave Mara and Hélène a lift back into Priorton. In the car, Samuel questioned Mara about Pansy. 'She must be quite something, to bowl old Michael over.'

'You'll be surprised,' said Mara. 'Quiet as a mouse. Wouldn't say boo to a goose. But there's something . . .'

'What?'

'She's like a very quiet, very slithery snake.'

'Ugh! But wasn't it you who brought her here in the first place?' He slowed down to accommodate two traps wending their weary way up Prior's Chare. He had to stop and let them get to the top and the engine faded away altogether. Mara got out to crank start it again.

She climbed back beside Samuel. 'I was lodging with Pansy and her sister. When Pansy was bombed out, and her sister was killed, it seemed the only thing to do. Ma insisted. And like I said, then she just seemed quiet and whispery, as if the elder sister had bossed her around. Now I realise it was the other way on. Really, she must have held her fat sister in the palm of her hand. Cut everyone else out of their lives . . . She's doing the same thing to Michael. Fattening him up like a spring sow, and dressing him up in fancy clobber like a peacock. Once she got her eye on him he didn't have a chance.'

Samuel laughed. 'Now you have me dying to see her.'

He dropped the two girls off at the top of Bridge Street and watched as Mara dragged Hélène past the glowing fire of John Maddison's forge, past the houses where men were sitting on their haunches, smoking a pipe in the last rays of the sun, to a narrow house halfway down.

He chugged away, wondering how his smallest stepsister had got involved with that strange young woman. But, like Kitty, she had always been one for waifs and strays, had little Mara. Dogs, cats – once even a fox lamed in a tussle with a rather inefficient hunting dog. Then there were the gypsy children whom she gathered into a little woodland schoolroom so that she could play teacher. Now, here was the rather beautiful, fey scrap of a Frenchwoman. It seemed the more things changed, the more they remained the same. Events in life going round like a fairground carousel. He wondered if that would eventually prove the case in this Russian business.

He pulled up outside Michael's tall house in the Market Place. His knock was answered instantly by a maid who curtsied very demurely, took his coat and led him into the drawing room. Michael leapt up from his seat and shook his hand very heartily, then introduced him to Pansy. The thin wisp of a woman looked up at him, smiling shyly.

'Very pleased to meet you, Pansy. Seems Michael's been a lucky dog. Lucky indeed.' He said the words, wondering what on earth Mara had been talking about. This certainly was a very pleasant woman. No snake at all, as far as he could tell.

At the Lodge, Leonora snuggled down into Mara's bed, finally pleased to be back in the sounds, sights and smells of home, even if the Lodge was cramped compared with the wide, high rooms of the Hall. Kitty had promised to take her down there tomorrow, to meet the Hospital Commandant. She would offer to work there while she was home. That would keep her occupied until she felt strong enough to go back and join another unit in Russia, and start again. Already, seeing William just about recovered, Mara newly grown-up and Kitty as bubbly as ever, she felt guilty about being here, instead of *back there*, doing her proper work.

She tossed and turned restlessly in her bed, missing Samuel, who had only been inches away from her, if not in bed with her, for the last fortnight. She was used to him now, the weight, the sense, the feel of him. Now, as never before, she ached for the touch of his hand on her breast, her inner thigh.

She stared at the ceiling. Samuel had been hearty and brotherly ever since they arrived in the north, nothing more. She sat up in bed and hugged herself. It would be so hard, being here in Priorton, and not acknowledging what there was between them. So hard.

Mara, in the house in Bridge Street, put out the lamp and climbed into the bed of the absent Jean-Paul. She wondered what it was between Leonora and Samuel. You would think they would be jollier, closer to each other, after spending the long journey together. In fact, they acted like polite strangers. They must have fallen out or something. They had always been such good friends before, such jolly companions. Yes – that was it. They had fallen out over something. She would ask

Leonora about it tomorrow. She snuggled down. It would be so good to spend time with her sister. She had so many questions, so much to tell her.

In the event Mara didn't get the chance to ask Leonora anything, and Leonora did not get to visit the hospital the next day. Instead she succumbed to influenza, finally allowed to rage through her body as she relaxed on her home ground. Samuel came, once, to visit her. She could barely lift her head to see him, and it was only later that her puzzled mind reconstructed the conversation, in which she finally recalled that he had talked about leaving; he had people to see in London.

Mara and Kitty took turns in sitting with her. One day Mara was leaning on the windowsill, writing letters, long delayed, to Dewi and Tommy.

'You were always so important to me, d'you know that?'

She turned at the sound of Leonora's voice, which was regaining something of its old strength.

'Important?' she said, putting down her pen.

'I had this baby, did you know?'

Mara blushed and shook her head. 'A baby? Where . . .'

'Oh, it's not anywhere. I did not exactly have it. It was . . . it kind of, came away, just before you were born. I've been thinking about it a lot in Russia. It was the blood which reminded me. All the blood.' Leonora closed her eyes. What was she doing? She had promised herself she would not mention the terror.

Mara's head was spinning. She had heard of these things. Miss Aunger's married sister had had a miscarriage and not much later, according to Miss Aunger, had died herself, of a broken heart. But to think of such a thing in relation to Leonora who was so funny, so perfect, so much in control of her own life . . .

'You lost it?' she whispered. She wanted to go across and take Leonora's hand, but couldn't.

213

Leonora struggled to sit up. Her hand trailed across the counterpane. She nodded. 'I was only young. Not that much older than you are now. Nobody knew. Living up there at the Hall we might have been on another planet. There was only us, and Luke and Matthew and John, who was alive then. Then you were born.' She laughed briefly. 'You looked like a skinned rabbit.'

'You must . . .' Mara was prickling with the confidence she had been offered. 'It must have been so terrible,' she ended lamely.

Leonora nodded. 'Kitty came and put you in my arms. You were such a tiny scrap.' She smiled faintly. 'How you've grown up into such a giant I'll never know.'

Mara moved at last. She came over to the bed and sat beside Leonora. 'Oh, Leonie.'

'You made all the difference, do you know? You clung to my finger and all my raging insides locked together and seemed to fit again. Kitty and I shared you.' She laughed, then took Mara's hand. 'I thought about you so much out there in Russia, Mara, in all that mud and blood. I kept thinking of you being the life out of all that death, all that blood. That it would be all right in the end because you were there.'

'Oh, Leonie, I'm only a . . . person. It's too hard for me to take all that on.'

'Sorry, Tuppence, I'm getting carried away.' Leonora swung her legs out of bed. 'Now I'm going to stop being the invalid and get on with things. Can you help me get my clothes on? There's work to be done.'

'Are you sure?'

Leonora grinned. 'Sure as shot. We'll not win any war lying on our backs, will we? We need to get back to work – me to my nursing and you to your teaching, teaching the next generation how *not* to fight wars. Now that's a good idea!'

'Teaching?' A shadow fell across Mara's face. 'Not teaching, Leonie. I can't. It was awful – Hartlepool. I'm working in the shop now.'

Hopping on one leg, trying to get a stocking on, Leonora frowned. 'Shop? But you were so good at that teaching lark, love. You enjoyed it – I remember from your letters! And Kitty said you'd had such good reports.'

Mara shook her head. 'I have nightmares, Leonora, of children in shrouds. And my headmaster . . .' She shuddered. 'He was killed, you remember. I can't go back.'

Leonora, busy pulling on her petticoat and shift, didn't answer for a moment. Then she put a thin arm round Mara. 'One day you will, pet, one day. I feel it in my bones. Now, pass me my blouse. I'm sick of nightdresses and bedsocks. Sick of them.'

Mara relaxed, and selected a blouse with a grey silk peter-sham tie. She held it out for Leonora to slip her arms in. 'Leonora, what's wrong between you and Samuel?'

Leonora dropped her chin to her chest to button her blouse. 'Me and Samuel?' she echoed blandly.

'You seem such bad friends, barely saying anything. And now he's gone off in such a heck of a hurry. Did you quarrel?'

'Quarrel? Never.' Leonora sat before her mirror and started to put up her hair. 'We're the best of friends, me and Samuel.'

'But—' Mara was interrupted by the door opening. Hélène came in, and without looking at them, began to open cupboards and drawers.

Mara caught her hand. 'Stop, Hélène.'

'What on earth is she doing?' said Leonora crossly.

'My baby, I'm looking for my baby.' Hélène clutched hard at Leonora's arm. 'We have a baby, Alex and me, Mademoiselle. He fights in the war, you see? He had to go. But the baby was stolen, *hélas*. And Alex talks to me. I see him in the flames – he tells me I must find the baby. If I find the baby he will come home to me. I must find the baby or he will die. Don't you understand?' She shook Leonora's arm hard and peered too closely into her face. 'You do see, don't you?'

Leonora pulled away her arm and sat down hard on her bed.

215

'Get her out of here, Mara, before I kick her out, will you? She's mad as a hatter. Do you hear me? Get her out!'

Leonora's recovery was rapid, but Kitty managed to keep her away from the military hospital another week, urging her to get fresh air. So she walked up to Livesay Woods. She went over to the workshop with William to look at his latest project. She was invited to tea with Pansy and came back nonplussed. She strolled down to the shop with Kitty and met all her old workmates – men and women she had grown up with in the drapery trade.

Mara took her to a meeting of Priorton Socialists and she reacquainted herself with Mr Clelland, who had just been sacked by the vicar for preaching anti-war ideas to his pupils in the church school where he taught. Leonora loved the meeting, was engaged by the rhetoric, the flow of words which reminded her of Valodya and his friends, of Pavel Demchenkov and his prickly idealism.

Mr Clelland drew her into the discussion. 'And we have here someone who has been close to events in Russia. Miss Rainbow has news of the meeting in Switzerland where Mr Vladimir Lenin and Mr Leon Trotsky called for the workers to lay down their arms, to join in the natural brotherhood of man.'

'I have no direct news of that,' said Leonora hurriedly. 'I knew someone who was there at the time of the meeting, that's all.' Still the faces were turned keenly towards her.

'Is it true there are strikes and bread riots in spite of the war?' said a man at the back of the hall.

She nodded her head. 'But it is not as simple as it seems, sir. There is talk of revolution, but still so many of these same people love their country, and to talk of revolution while hundreds of thousands of ordinary Russians are fighting for their country feels like a very personal betrayal. But now the Tsar has suspended the *Duma* – the parliament, that is. And this has caused great offence, not just with the

216

workers but with those who used to have some power and influence. Bread is so scarce now that the people fight over supplies. Convalescent, recovering soldiers are rioting to save themselves from going back to the Front.'

'And is it true you worked right there at the Front, nursing the soldiers?' asked a woman in the front row.

'Yes, madam. Well . . . very near. I, and many other Russian brothers and sisters.'

Mara sat beside her, aching with pride in her sister, interested anew in the details of her experiences which these strangers were drawing out of Leonora: details which so far, her sister had not mentioned at home. The two of them were still buzzing with excitement at the meeting when they got back to the Lodge, where Hélène was waiting with Kitty.

Kitty looked up from a letter she was reading. 'It's from Tommy,' she said. 'He's still playing at soldiers out there on the coast. God forgive me, but I find myself praying the war will end before they send him.'

William looked up from his paper. 'There is no chance of that, my dear. If you read the papers, the Army's digging in now, prepared for a long fight.'

Kitty pointed with her glasses. 'A letter there for you, Leonora. From Samuel, looking at the writing.'

Leonora snatched it up. *Leonora. They are sending me East directly. Had not thought it would be so soon. There is so much to do there. Good to know you are safely home and not still out there in the mire. In haste, Samuel.* She turned the letter over, looking in vain for a word of endearment, a reassurance that what had gone on between them had not been a dream, a figment of her imagination.

The flush, the excitement of the Labour meeting had faded from her cheeks. She looked bereft. 'What's the matter, Leonie?' said Mara sharply. 'What's wrong?'

Leonora shook her head. 'Nothing, just that Samuel's off back to Russia without so much as a by-your-leave.' She threw the letter on the table and stalked out, slamming the door behind her.

Kitty glanced at the letter, then placed it carefully in its envelope. Mara chivvied Hélène to put on her jacket and as they walked back to Bridge Street, wondered just what it was with Leonora and Samuel. There had seemed such tension between them. Her mind leapt to herself and Jean-Paul. There had been just such a tension between them, when Jean-Paul was pulling back from showing his affection. She frowned. That couldn't be. Samuel and Leonora were brother and sister, weren't they? But then of course they weren't, not by blood. And, seeing as Kitty and William had never married, they were no real relation at all.

She looked round. Hélène was nowhere in sight. Wearily she made her way back up the street to John Maddison's forge. She heard the shouts before she saw the scene. A horse was tethered to John's shoeing rail, and in the corner was Hélène, fending off John and a farmer's lad. In her hand she had John's coal rake, still glowing red at the tips.

John mopped his brow when he saw Mara approaching. 'Yeh'll have ter get that thing off her, Miss Scorton. She was off down the street with it a minute ago.'

'Stand away,' she said quietly. 'Stand away.'

The two men backed off and stood slightly to one side of Hélène.

'Now what is it? What's the matter?'

'Alexander was in the flames. I saw him again. He was dying. He's the one! It's him!' Hélène thrust the rake towards the farmer's boy. 'He killed Alexander and took my baby.'

Mara shook her head. 'No, no, Hélène. Put that down, put it down now!' She paused. 'He can't have the baby. The baby's in the house. I think I heard it cry.'

Hélène's hand lowered. 'You're sure?'

'I think so. Put that on the ground.' She waited while Helene did so, then held out her hand. 'Come on, Hélène, let's go home.'

When they got to the house, Hélène started her usual frantic search, raking out cupboards and clearing off shelves. When she finally ran out of steam, Mara put her arms round her and rocked her to and fro, wondering just how long they could go on like this before Hélène did someone or something serious damage.

14

Hélène

The Rainbow assistants, removing the dustcloths, rearranging gowns and gloves for the day, nodded at Mara as she walked by, casting curious eyes on her striking but dishevelled companion. Mara clutched Hélène's arm, glumly aware of the harm her friend could do in the immaculate mahogany-lined domain of Rainbow and Daughter.

Kitty was just opening a ledger as Mara entered her office. She glanced at Hélène and brought out an extra chair for her. Mara made her sit down, which she did reluctantly, stared at the window and started to mutter in French.

'She's upset again?'

'I can't leave her, Mother. She's wandering all over the place now, doing strange things. Even in the house she's raging around, demolishing everything in sight. This morning she was raking the fire out and spreading the cinders over the mat. I can't see how I can come to the shop to work, and watch her as well.'

Kitty looked at her thoughtfully. 'I'm as sorry as anyone about Hélène, dear, and I know how attached you are to her brother – but how long can this go on? What's going to happen to your apprenticeship if this situation is allowed to continue? Perhaps she should . . . You know, there are places where people who . . . people with her difficulty can go.'

'You mean the asylum? Would you put *me* in an asylum? Hélène's not a lunatic! Anyway, I promised Jean-Paul I'd take

221

care of her.' Mara removed Hélène's hand from the inkwell on Kitty's desk. 'He's fighting now with the French Army at Champagne. I wrote to him again, telling him that she was all right.'

'Champagne – where the wine comes from?' Kitty paused. 'But how can you cope with her, Mara? You have no experience.'

'I'm taking care of her. I just need to stay at home with her, watch her.'

Kitty ran her hand over the ledgers in front of her. 'It's true we're not too busy here, more's the pity. Turnover's right down, what with the shortages, and the so-called breadwinners away winning the war, instead of winning the bread. It's been obvious for some time now.'

'So can I stay at home with her, Mama, watch her? Take care of her?'

Kitty sat back in her chair and sighed. 'There's another solution – it's been on the cards for a while. I need to talk to both you and Leonora. Now you coming to me with this request makes it even more necessary.'

Mara looked mystified.

'Perhaps you could bring Hélène to the Lodge for tea tonight?' Kitty suggested. 'About four. Leonora's on what they call a split-shift at the hospital, but she doesn't have to be back up there till five.'

'Are you saying I can stay at home with Hélène?'

Kitty stood up. 'We'll see. Go home with her now. And bring her to tea. I've work to do here.'

The Commandant at Purley Hall had been pleased to welcome Leonora onto his staff. As he told her, Purley Hall had been her home, after all, before it was transformed into a rather improvised, but modestly efficient, military hospital for recovering soldiers.

The senior nurse, Sister Hunter, a stout lady with very starched ribbons who was surprisingly light on her feet, was not so enthusiastic about Leonora. She'd had her fill of do-gooding ladies who wanted the romance of a uniform without besmirching their hands with bedpans, scrubbing brushes and soiled dressings. Her way of expressing her censure was to give such women an avalanche of loathsome tasks when they first arrived. Those who faced the avalanche without complaint survived to do more interesting and romantic things, like laying out the trays, or dealing directly with patients, who did need a calm hand on a fevered brow, a restless hand held still, from time to time. The less hardy souls left the Hall to indulge themselves with a more genteel contribution to the war effort.

Full of guilt for not returning to what she saw as her real task in Russia, Leonora welcomed the hardship. She passed Sister Hunter's various tests with flying colours, doing the loathsome jobs efficiently, her experience showing with her every action. At the end of a week Sister Hunter could not hold back her curiosity and asked her where she had trained.

'At the Princess Golitzin Hospital in Moscow, Sister. But that was just the barest Red Cross training. You would have laughed. To be honest, the best training I had was on the spot among the soldiers. We had a surgeon called Pavel Demchenkov, who was a wonderful surgeon and a great teacher. There in the field he would show you the benefit of one dressing over another; how to improvise when there *were* no dressings, even no drugs, left. Lots of things.' For a second she felt bereft that she would never see Pavel again, never smell the rotten-sweet smell of his cigar, or hear the rough, hard timbre that his voice assumed in the most despairing of circumstances.

The romance of her foreign adventure and the rigorous efficiency of her actions finally won over the dour Sister. Leonora was adopted as Sister Hunter's mascot, her experience in the field trotted out at every opportunity to demonstrate the high quality of care at Purley Hall Military Hospital.

Leonora was occasionally irritated but mostly amused by

this. She counted it a small price to pay to be back at work, at least for the time being. It was good to see these young and not-so-young men recovering from their injuries. They made her think of the Russian boys she had last seen broken by savage wounds, whom she had patched together with her makeshift dressings. She prayed that some of them might now be in Russian hospitals, also improving day by day.

She relished the hard work too, because it kept her mind away from thoughts of Samuel; she had not heard from him since that last, abrupt message. When, in rare quiet moments, her mind strayed back to him, she was covered with embarrassment. Perhaps it had been all too easy for him. Had she, bowled over by this glamorous man, half-stranger, half-brother, been too eager to demonstrate her passion? Had she been too easy a conquest for him? And once he had brought her down from her forbidden-sister pedestal, had he lost interest in her?

She warded off these disconcerting thoughts by going to Sister Hunter and asking if there was anything really difficult she wanted doing. Sister laughed a rare laugh and said, if she was that serious, she had a room which needed clearing and scouring for a patient who was arriving with, of all things, malaria.

The only part of hospital routine that Leonora did hate was the obligatory split-shift – from five-thirty in the morning till one-thirty, then from five in the afternoon till eleven. There seemed no time for a proper sleep, no time to do anything else. She regretted the fact that she had seen so little of Mara since her return, what with her job and Mara's everlasting obsession with this mad French girl.

That afternoon, Kitty and Mara and Hélène all turned up at the Lodge at the same time when Leonora was helping Luke to lay the tea-table. Soon afterwards William arrived, taking off his cloak to reveal the soft, many-pocketed jacket in which he did his watchmaking.

Mara grinned at Leonora and said she was pleased to see

her sister looking like a proper nurse at last, and Leonora threatened to throw a tea-cake at her. Hélène ignored them, sat down obediently and ate steadily, deaf to the continuing banter about the 'lady of the great house' doing good works among the poor soldiers.

Kitty waited until they had all finished, put down her knife and glanced at William. 'William and I have been talking about the shop. Today, and for some time before today, it has occurred to me that the time for the shop is over. It has made my little family a good living in its time. As you know, we've always only lived on the proceeds of the shop.'

'Never let me contribute a thing,' said William lightly. 'It seems I was always destined to be a kept man.'

'Unfortunately the shop's only barely breaking even just now,' said Kitty.

'But you're not in penury,' put in William.

She chuckled. 'We're saved from penury of course, because William will step into the breach. You know I've always made a great thing of paying my own way, taking care of us myself. But somehow, with this war, the shop seems suddenly reduced to a toy that I play with, and that makes me uncomfortable because I've worked hard and loved it all my life.'

Hélène got up from her place, went to the window, and leaned her head on the glass and started to sing.

Kitty glanced at her and went on: 'I can see you have more important things to do than be with me in the shop, Leonora. Much more important things. And Mara's a conscript rather than an enlisted man to the "shop of war". You've had a brave stab at it, but taking care of waifs and strays seems more in your line, Tuppence.' At this she glanced again at Hélène, then put up a hand as Leonora and Mara began to speak together. 'So, my dears, I have decided to sell the shop. Its time is over.'

'No more Rainbow and Daughter?' said Leonora. 'Inconceivable.'

'No more Rainbow and Daughter. The shop itself will not raise much. No properties on the High Street are bringing anything at all – I'll be lucky to sell it. But the shop owes me nothing. We've had a good living from it, haven't we? I might just give it to Miss Aunger, lock, stock and barrel. Then at least she can keep it ticking over, keep herself and the others in work.'

Mara frowned. 'What will you do, Mama?' The idea of Kitty without her shop, Kitty not bustling around working harder than anyone else, was almost unthinkable.

Kitty put her hand on William's. 'William and I have much to think and talk about. I want him to teach me how to make watches. I can't think it's any more difficult than fine embroidery, and, though I say it myself, I'm very good at that.'

William cleared his throat and *harrumphed* at this insult to his lifelong craft. 'Thank you, my dear. I think it will not be quite the same kettle of fish, not quite. More parts to deal with in watchmaking for a start.'

Kitty ignored him. 'And there may be something I can do for the Commandant down at the Hall. Not nursing like you, Leonie, but counting towels or rolling bandages. If my son is out there risking his life, which he will be before long, I'll feel better doing something directly for the war.'

'He's dead,' said Hélène.

They all jumped.

'Tommy?' said Kitty, frowning.

'I saw him running against the guns.'

'It's Alexander. Take no notice,' said Mara. 'She keeps talking about him. She sees scenes all the time in John Maddison's fires. It's her fancy, because she misses him.'

Leonora looked crossly at Hélène. 'You silly woman,' she said fiercely. 'You silly, crazy woman, frightening us like that. We have enough to worry about without—'

'Leave her alone,' said Mara. 'She doesn't know what she's saying.'

'Really, Mara,' said Leonora, still upset. 'The woman needs some help. There's the hospital at Sedgefield, they—'

226

'I tell you, she's not a lunatic. She's just upset. That thing which happened in France . . .'

'What thing?' Leonora was jealous of Mara championing this stranger. 'We've all seen bad things and we're not crazy. She couldn't have seen, or experienced, worse sights than me.'

Mara glanced at her father. 'No? Her mother was violated by soldiers, Leonora, and then she was too. Her mother died shortly afterwards.'

William stared at his hands. Leonora flushed, remembering her own helplessness, as she watched the Cossacks entering homes, and heard the screams of the women. 'That's war,' she said stubbornly, fending off her own guilt.

Mara stood up. 'How can you say that? If war means accepting *that*, then I'm against it. What has *that* to do with frontiers and territories, with crowns and sceptres? What has *that* to do even with being human, being civilised? I'd have thought you'd have known better, Leonie.' She looked at her sister with a stranger's eyes.

Kitty pulled Mara down beside her. 'Shsh, shsh,' she said. 'We've all been so distracted, but we must not go to war with each other. We must never do that.'

William nodded from one to the other. 'So, Mara, you can keep your watch on Hélène, if that's what you want to do. We're content with that. We will make sure you get a little allowance. And you, Leonie, can go on nursing . . .'

'I'm only there for the time being,' Leonora put in. 'I'm going back to Russia as soon as I can.'

'. . . And your mother and I can spend more time together. You never know, she just might learn how to make a decent watch.'

As her parents smiled at each other Mara thought once more of how self-sufficient they were in their mutual devotion, and how William's recent illness had threatened that golden circle. That might be Kitty's real reason for selling the shop – the couple's determination to spend the rest of their time together, before one or other of them would be absent forever. Nothing else would have made Kitty give up the shop. She loved her business nearly as much as she loved them all. It would be a great sacrifice for her.

Leonora started to clear the table. 'I'm happy about that if you are, Mother. I do think it would be a good idea, though, if Mara went to college or something, and didn't dally around quite so much. She could be working towards eventually teaching again.'

'Don't!' said Mara. 'Don't talk about me as though I were a shoe. I'll make up my own mind about teaching and college, thank you very much. At present I'm taking care of Hélène.'

'Perhaps we could get Mr Clelland to make up a parcel of books for you, so you can keep up your studies, as well as you writing all those letters,' said Kitty thoughtfully. 'Would you like that?'

'I might like it, but I can ask Mr Clelland myself, thank you,' said Mara crossly. Then she dragged Hélène to her feet. 'Now we can go home, so that you can talk about us to your hearts' content when we're gone. How Hélène's a lunatic with no asylum, and I'm a teacher who can't teach.'

'You really should—' began Leonora.

'Stop, stop,' said Mara, making for the door. 'Will you *stop* telling me what to do? You're not my mother, you know. What's happened to you, Leonie? You used to be funny, my friend. It must be Russia. All of a sudden, you've got very, very old.'

The door slammed behind her and Leonora lifted her eyes to Kitty. 'I wasn't . . . I didn't . . . oh, Mother.' She started to sniff.

'Mara didn't mean anything.' Kitty put an arm round her daughter and waited till the crying had died down. Then she dabbed Leonora's wet face with her own embroidered handkerchief. 'You needed to cry, love. You've never cried since you got back. Those terrible things you wrote about. How could you bear it?'

Leonora pulled away, plucked out her own snowy handkerchief and blew her nose. 'Sorry, Ma.' She dabbed her eyes. 'But I'm not really that old, am I?'

Kitty laughed. 'Well, I'm just a spring chicken and you're my daughter. So you can't be old, can you?'

But later, as she was feeding supper to a man who had one arm missing and one arm healing, Leonora remembered Mara's words. Perhaps somehow she had become old without noticing. Perhaps that was why it was so ridiculous that she gambolled and played with Samuel like some seventeen-year-old. Perhaps he was laughing at her now, somewhere out in the East. Perhaps he was thinking that she was far too old to have these thoughts, to feel these passions.

The next night, in her absence, Mara's future was again the topic of conversation at Kitty's tea-table. This time Pansy and Michael were having tea with them, invited so that they too could hear Kitty's news of the shop. Michael thought that giving it up was a sensible move. Not worth the effort nowadays. No real profits in drapery. 'Time you retired anyway, Kit.'

Pansy nodded her head sagely. 'So wise. It's really all been getting too much for you, Kitty.'

'Nonsense,' said Leonora. 'She's been running it as smoothly as ever.'

'She's going into clockmaking,' William told them. 'Into competition with me.'

Kitty smiled at his joke. 'It's purely a commercial decision, Pansy. The shop has been my prop and mainstay all my life, it has been my delight and my independence. But now I find myself bored with the routine, the low turnover, the low profits. Working with William, I'll be making profits in *that* business, and in no time at all I'll be sufficient unto myself again. You watch.' She chuckled. 'Now that's a good thing to say, isn't it? I'll make a living out of making watches.'

'So she will,' said William ruefully. 'She'll take all my trade from me, nothing so certain.'

'And what happens to Mara in all this?' asked Pansy. 'She loses her apprenticeship, I suppose? She so needed to buckle down to something.'

'She has her hands full with the madwoman,' said Leonora briefly.

Pansy shook her head. 'I can't understand that you take all that so lightly.' She shuddered. 'I see the pair of them in the High Street sometimes. Such a bizarre sight. To be honest, I walk in another direction. You should hear what people say . . .'

'I've told you before, Pansy,' said Kitty evenly. 'We do not trouble ourselves, in this family, with what people say.'

'Pansy's right,' said Michael abruptly. 'The woman's dangerous. To herself, certainly, but to Mara also. She'll end up injuring the child, that's for certain.'

'Well,' said Kitty, the merest thread of uncertainty in her voice, 'I know Hélène is a bit strange, but Mara watches over her well, and she did promise the brother.'

'If the woman gets worse,' said Leonora authoritatively, 'there's no saying what she might do.'

'Surely, Leonora,' said Pansy, happy for the opportunity to press her point, 'you know of a doctor who could advise us?'

Leonora shook her head. 'I don't.' She frowned, thinking that Sister Hunter, who seemed to know many doctors, might be the one to approach. 'I might be able to find out . . .'

'Perhaps someone just to look at her,' said Kitty doubtfully. 'We wouldn't want Mara in danger.'

Pansy drew in her breath. 'You're so wise to do this, Kitty. So very wise.'

Michael listened with pleasure to this interchange, proud of the contribution Pansy was making to the well-being of his family. Then he turned to his father to talk about a continuity problem on one of his production lines, which was baffling the ingenuity of the factory engineer. 'Wondered if you'd take a look down there at it, Pa? Needs your inventive eye, I think.'

*　　*　　*

The next day, Mara was trying to get Hélène, who had no interest whatsoever in food, to eat her tea. It was a painstaking process; sometimes she had to hold Hélène's face still so that she could spoon the food in.

'Come on,' Mara said finally, stuffing a piece of bread into Hélène's hand. 'Eat, will you. Eat!'

Hélène pulled Mara's hand towards her, and very deliberately bit it hard. Mara winced, drew the injured hand back and slapped her. Hélène let out a bloodcurdling scream, leapt up and pushed Mara so forcefully that she fell off her stool, then raced from the house.

'Witch!' shouted Mara. 'Mad French witch!' She sat on the floor for a minute then pulled herself wearily to her feet and started after Hélène. By the time she got to John Maddison's, the blacksmith was struggling with Hélène in his doorway. 'Yeh'll have to stop her for good, miss. She tried to jump right in me fire this time. It's gettin' so I canna turn me back.'

He let Hélène go and before Mara had time to grasp her, she was off again, down the bank towards the river, fleet as a greyhound, with Mara pounding after her. They were followed by curious glances, catcalls and even whistles as they careered down the bank.

At first Mara thought Hélène was going to jump into the river, but she veered off along the footpath, then back up the bank, scrabbling across fields and up towards the ridge which reared over Killock Quarry. When she reached it she turned and started to throw loose stones at Mara, forcing her to take cover behind some whinbushes.

When Mara finally caught up with her she was standing right at the edge of the dry cliff; in the distance Mara could see the ragged seams of stone, raw as wounds.

Cautiously Mara drew closer. Hélène looked her in the eye. She began to say something in French and then she said very slowly, in English: 'Little Mara, you are my friend. They took my baby, and Alex ran before the guns and was consumed in the fire. There is nothing left. Tell Jean-Paul that it was right.'

231

Then, quite undramatically, she took two steps backwards and vanished.

'*No!*' Mara raced to the edge of the precipice and peered over. 'Hélène!' she screamed. Her friend was lying, one leg at an awkward angle, on a ledge twenty feet below. Her face was even whiter than usual, and she looked quite dead.

Mara looked around. Hélène's meandering path had led them in an arc, back towards Purley Hall. She leapt to her feet and ran and ran, right into the hospital, barging past protesting orderlies and cheering, bedridden patients, not stopping until she found Leonora. 'It's Hélène,' she panted. 'She's dead.' She grabbed her sister's arm. 'You must come. Come on!'

15

Distinguished Conduct

Mara, Leonora, and Sister Hunter, directed by a blustering, purple-faced Commandant, took twenty minutes to get back to the quarry. The Colonel confined himself to commanding, shouting orders and encouragement which the rest politely ignored. Leonora picked up an old rope-ladder from the stable as she passed. Sister Hunter, having eavesdropped on Mara's gasping account, brought sheets and ropes.

Peering over the cliff edge, Leonora assessed the situation. She turned to the Colonel. 'Look at that leg. We'll need splints. We'll have to haul her up somehow.'

'A few more pairs of hands would be useful,' he said. 'And a stretcher.'

Mara climbed down the rope-ladder onto the narrow ledge. She knelt beside Hélène, reaching out to take her into her arms.

'Don't touch her!' ordered Leonora, climbing close behind her. Leonora touched Hélène's neck, her head and then her pulse. 'Steady as a rock,' she said. 'Your friend's not dead, Mara. She's knocked out, and looking at it, she appears to have broken her leg. But she'll live.'

Mara sighed with relief.

'Now if we move her in from the edge, I can get at her to splint the leg. Then we can put her on the stretcher.'

After a long ten minutes there was a hubbub of noise above, as the Colonel returned with a gaggle of recovering soldiers and two orderlies carrying the stretcher and the splints.

Sister Hunter lowered the splints and a roll of cloth. Leonora set about her work. Hélène moaned as her leg was moved, then dropped back into unconsciousness as Leonora strapped on the splint with quiet efficiency.

Mara watched her sister with admiration. 'You must have done that a thousand times,' she said.

'I feel as though I've done it a thousand times,' said Leonora grimly, tying the last knot. She looked Mara in the eye. 'This will really have to stop, Mara.'

'What?' said Mara, knowing what was coming.

'The woman's not safe to be out. Or to be out *with*. She needs proper care, in an asylum.'

'I told you—'

There was a clatter and a wood and chain ladder clanked onto the stone beside them. Two rope-ends came snaking down. The Colonel's bulbous face appeared above them. 'We'll hoist the stretcher up with her on it,' he bawled. 'You two come up on the ladders and guide it, one at each end. See that it doesn't tip the creature out.'

They did as they were told, clambering up the ladders with one hand and guiding the stretcher away from out-jutting rocks with the other. It took some time. Once, the stretcher slipped and swung out of Mara's hand, and she had to lean over perilously far to grasp it again. She was relieved to be hauled over the rim by a corpulent orderly with very tired eyes. 'Well done, young woman,' he said. 'And you, Nurse, very well done.'

They made a strange procession across the fields. The Colonel led the way, striking out at the nettles with his stick, followed by a straggling line of soldiers burdened by ropes and ladders, two beefy orderlies carrying a body on a stretcher and two nurses. Mara brought up the rear, trailing behind, stumbling with an exhaustion intensified by her relief that Hélène was not seriously hurt.

At one point, when the orderlies were hoisting her over a stile, Hélène came to life and screamed at the sight of the uniforms, almost making the men drop their burden. Mara moved forward beside her, calmed her down and then held her hand the rest of the way, making the whole progress even more awkward.

Mara was aching with exhaustion when they finally arrived at the circular gravel drive before the great portico. The orderlies started to lift Hélène into a waiting Army ambulance.

'Stop! She can go into this hospital, can't she?'

The Colonel shook his head. 'No, my dear. Nurse Rainbow has done admirable first aid and the patient must go to the Infirmary. This hospital is for the casualties of war. She must go to Priorton Infirmary.'

She grasped his sleeve. 'But you don't understand, sir, Colonel. Hélène here, she's a casualty of war. She's here in England because of the war. She runs away in fear because of her experiences of war in France. That's why she had the accident.' She looked earnestly into his eyes.

The Colonel was a tyrant to his men, and belligerently efficient with his medical staff, but he had a well-known weakness for a pretty girl. And this one, with her tall figure, her tumble of hair and her clear, direct gaze, would take some beating. He hesitated, but to his relief, Leonora put her arm round Mara and pulled her away. 'Hélène will be better off in the Infirmary. Trust me, Mara.'

Mara broke away and strode towards the ambulance. 'Then I'll go with her.'

Leonora caught her arm again. 'Wait. She'll be fine. You need to clean yourself up, and pull yourself together.' She glanced at Sister Hunter, who nodded. 'I'll take you home. Then you can make your way to the Infirmary later.'

A soldier cranked the engine, and they watched as the ambulance roared away across the gravel. The two orderlies followed the Colonel back up the steps, and Sister Hunter turned to Leonora. 'I wouldn't have taken you for sisters, Nurse. Your sister is very unlike you.'

Leonora grinned. 'Chalk and cheese, Sister. Chalk and

cheese. Anyway, thank you for letting me go with her. I'll be back in less than half an hour.'

The two sisters were silent as they walked down the long drive and along the pathway to Purley Lodge. Before Mara could open the door Leonora stopped her. 'Was it deliberate, Mara? Did she do that deliberately? Try to kill herself?'

Mara shrugged. 'I don't know.'

'That means you think she did.'

Mara opened the door. 'Don't twist my words, Leonora. I know you want rid of her. You'll take care of those soldiers with their broken heads and their broken bodies, but you've no interest in Hélène, who's as much broken by the war as any of those. Don't worry about me. I'll have a cup of tea and then ride down to Bridge Street on one of the bicycles.' She opened the door and stepped inside without a backward glance.

'Mara, I—' But Leonora found herself staring at the peeling green door, still trembling from being slammed.

The following day Mara went straight to the Infirmary, but was not allowed to see Hélène. She was informed by an officious sister that Miss Derancourt was fast asleep.

Miserably she trudged back to Bridge Street. Kitty had called the previous night to commiserate over Hélène, but also to try and persuade her to come home for a few days. Mara refused, saying very firmly that she must be at the house when Hélène returned home.

After her third fruitless visit to the Infirmary she sought out Leonora to go with her, to support her insistence on seeing Hélène. Leonora, still in uniform from her morning shift, instantly secured more attention than Mara. She was shown into the matron's narrow office which had a window overlooking the railway yards.

The matron gave a nod of recognition. 'Good morning, Miss Rainbow,' she said to Leonora.

'This is my sister Mara Scorton, Matron.'

The matron shook Mara's hand cordially.

'I want to see my friend, Miss Hélène Derancourt,' said Mara.

The matron shook her head. 'I regret to say that is not possible, Miss Scorton. Miss Derancourt was moved just an hour ago to Sedgefield. One of their doctors visited her here.'

'Sedgefield?' burst out Mara. 'You've let her go to the lunatic asylum?'

The matron looked at her calmly. 'The young lady was beside herself. Raving. She had to be restrained. She attacked one of my nurses, who was trying to keep her away from the fire in the ward. She seemed determined to throw herself onto it.' She glanced at Leonora. 'She's properly committed now.'

Mara launched herself at Leonora, starting to pummel her. 'It's you! *You've* done it. *You've* been here. The matron knows you. You started this. You'll be satisfied now, I suppose?'

Leonora backed against the wall and put her hands up to protect herself. The matron yanked Mara away. 'Calm yourself, miss!' she said grimly. 'Calm yourself!'

Mara ran out of the room. Leonora hurriedly thanked the matron for her time and followed, catching her sister at the Infirmary gates. 'Stop, Mara, stop! Don't you see, she's best there, at the proper hospital. They'll help her, if help is possible. Perhaps she'll return to her old self. Come home. Come home now.'

'Home?' Mara stood stock still. 'I'm going home – back to Bridge Street. And remember this one thing, Leonora Rainbow. I'll never forgive you. Never. That matron had talked to you before. She knew you.'

'There were papers to sign.'

'But I'm in charge of her. I wouldn't have signed any papers.'

'You wouldn't have been able to – you are not of age. I only—'

'I'll never, ever forgive you,' Mara repeated distinctly, then turned and walked away down the narrow cobbled street.

*　　*　　*

'Leonora tells me they've put that Frenchwoman in the asylum,' said Michael to Pansy, the next night after dinner. 'Apparently she fell down Killock Quarry and broke her leg and then she went on to cause mayhem in the Infirmary.'

Pansy poured cream on his trifle. 'Well, Michael, I am the last to criticise dear Kitty, but anyone can see that this is a consequence of the sheer anarchy which goes for normal behaviour in that family. Not you, dearest. I do not count you among them. You are entirely different.'

Michael nodded, his mouth full of trifle. 'No decent schooling, no discipline . . .'

'Well, perhaps things are different now. Perhaps now one would hope Kitty will toe a more respectable line?'

Michael cocked his head. 'Now why would you think that, my dear?'

'You once said that Kitty never ever took money from your father. Well, now she's sold . . . given away the shop. She has Mara to deal with, living in that very rough area of the town and refusing to come home. How can Kitty let her daughter live there? She must rescue her from that. Surely now William is paying the bills, he can bring them all into line. Surely now he can impose more respectable obligations on them all?'

Michael finished his trifle and touched his chin with his napkin. He shook his head. 'I know it's hard to understand, dearest Pansy, but it has never been a matter of money. Not really. Kit has always done exactly what she wished and it looks as though Mara's cut from the same cloth. Money will make neither of them feel obliged, not one jot. Now, my dear, is there a spot more of your delicious trifle on the sideboard?'

Pansy was just about to ring the bell for the maid Peggy Royle to clear the table, when the doorbell clanged through the house. Peggy came in to say that Miss Scorton had called, and she had shown her into the drawing room. Was that all right, Mrs Scorton?

Pansy's dress whispered as she glided into the drawing

room. 'Mara dear!' Pansy smiled thinly. 'How good to see you. Won't you sit down?'

Michael followed Pansy in and sat heavily on the chair by the fire. He rubbed his hands and held them to the flames. 'Well, Mara, to what do we owe this rare pleasure?' He was quite serious; there was not an ounce of irony in his tone.

'I've a favour to ask, Michael.'

'Ask away.'

'You know they've committed Hélène to the asylum?'

'If I may say so, Mara dear—' began Pansy.

Michael put up a finger to pre-empt the well-meant torrent. 'We do know. Leonora discussed it with me.'

She looked at him for a long minute, then said, 'Anyway, I'm at Bridge Street on my own now. Father will let me have a small allowance but I don't wish to take it. I wish to make my own way.'

Pansy and Michael exchanged glances at this assertion which so nearly reflected their earlier conversation.

'Like mother, like daughter,' murmured Pansy.

'Thank you, Pansy,' said Mara. 'I'll take that as a compliment.'

'Commendable, a person taking responsibility for themselves,' said Michael briefly.

'Well, I do want to keep myself. As well as that, with Tommy and Jean-Paul away, and my friend Dewi out there on the Front, and Samuel fighting with the Russians, or whatever he's doing there, and Leonora doing her nursing . . . I think it's time I helped with the war, if only to help it finish.'

'Commendable,' repeated Michael.

'So I want you to give me a job at the factory. That way I can keep myself, stay in the Bridge Street house and keep it for Hélène when she gets out of that asylum. And for Jean-Paul when he comes back from the war.'

Pansy clicked her tongue in disapproval.

'What will you do? Fill shells?' said Michael.

'They turn you yellow,' said Pansy, shuddering.

Mara put up her head. 'Anything.'

'There's some clerical stuff . . .'

'Yes, yes, I have a good hand at writing. Even Mr Clonmel my headmaster used to say that,' she said. It was the first time she had mentioned Mr Clonmel, in ordinary conversation, since the events in Hartlepool. 'Anything like that. To be honest I'd be grateful not to have to fill shells, although I would do even that. I'd not like to get yellow skin.'

'You'd have to turn up every day, mind! No shilly-shallying in the streets.'

Mara's cheeks flared. 'No. None of that.'

'Very well. Eight o'clock sharp, Monday morning.'

Mara stood up. 'Thank you, Michael.'

'I don't suppose you want tea?' said Pansy, less than graciously.

'No, thank you.'

When she had gone, Michael started to wonder whether he had done the right thing.

'Nonsense, Michael,' said Pansy firmly. 'It will allow you to keep an eye on her. And it will impose some discipline on her life. She was born to indiscipline. It is not the child's fault that she is illegitimate.'

Michael frowned slightly. 'That wasn't in my mind, Pansy. Not at all.'

She touched his sleeve. 'Of course not, Michael. You are such an innocent, dear. Now, would you like me to fetch your cigar before you settle down to your papers?'

Mara, walking back down Bridge Street, reflected that Michael, puffing and overweight now, was getting more and more like Heliotrope. When she reached the top of the bank she saw her mother's motor car beside her door with a crowd of children gathered around it, like inquisitive crows. Leonora was leaning on the low bonnet, laughing with them. For a second Mara's heart ached for the child inside herself, that child who had worshipped her funny, lively big sister, and had encouraged her to take the plunge and go to Russia.

Mara greeted Leonora coolly. She could not, would not, forgive the betrayal.

'Mother sent me with post for you.' Leonora smiled at her. 'She had to give me a driving lesson first, of course.'

How could Leonora smile? How could she, knowing how very offended Mara was with her? Mara marched into the house.

Leonora followed her and then scrabbled in her bag. 'One from Dewi, one from Jean-Paul, and one from Tommy, who says he is on his way, just setting out for France. Don't look like that! I haven't been opening your letters. The names are on the outside, and Ma had one from Tommy and let me read it. He's on embarkation leave in Plymouth.'

Mara sat down at the table to open them. The one from Jean-Paul, as usual, was simply a picture card of a view of France, inscribed, also as usual, *From your friend Jean-Paul Derancourt.* He never wrote a letter in the real sense of the word.

Tommy was more expressive: *Looking forward to it, though I know it will be no picnic. There is nothing worse than all this drill, all these war games with no enemy to get your teeth into. But at bottom, Mara, I'm the smallest bit scared, but from what I sense, so is everyone else. Pray for me, sis.*

She opened Dewi's letter, scanned it, then dropped it on the table.

'What is it?' said Leonora sharply. She picked up the letter and read in a whisper: '*I have sad news, bad news, Mara. That scamp and scoundrel, that friend of mine, Alexander Hacket-Barrington, has shot his bolt. He loved to play the risk, always after a gong. But this time he has not pulled it off, poor chap. Daring sortie in the night ended up in Fritz's pillbox going up in a blue light and poor Alex with it. He was burned very badly. They say he is to be recommended a medal. Distinguished Conduct, no less. Do you know, he never felt fear? Strange thing that. Fear runs around here like the rats in the trenches. One side of you is revolted by them; the other side ignores them . . .*'

Leonora looked at her sister. 'Will you tell her? – the Frenchwoman?'

'Her name is Hélène. Why should you care whether I tell her?'

'Mara! Of course I care.'

'And of course I'll have to tell her. It turns out now that Alex *was* burned, you see? She saw the truth. A strange world, isn't it, where seeing the truth makes people call you mad, and makes them lock you away like a lunatic.' Tears were standing in her eyes.

'But what about the baby, love? This baby she thinks she had? That was not true. That was her mad fantasy.'

Mara shook her head. 'She had to have something to remember him by, so she invented the baby, don't you see? He just left her with no goodbyes, so she had to make it different. Make it proper in some way. Or it would have been just another version of what those soldiers did to her in France.' She shrugged and picked up the letter again. 'Of course Alex was much more polite about it. Quite the gentleman. "Distinguished Conduct"! Poor Alex. Poor Hélène. His conduct was anything but distinguished to her.'

'That's hardly the same,' said Leonora wearily. 'In war . . .'

'Of course,' Mara said with as much sarcasm as she could muster, 'I forget that it's you who have the definitive experience of war. I'm obliged to bow to your knowledge in all that. But why is it hardly the same? Why not?'

'Come home,' said Leonora. 'Come home.'

'I can't, can I? I am so angry with you, I can't bear the sight of you. That'll make us both uncomfortable.'

'Mara, please. I did what I thought best. For her and you.'

'It was not your business.'

'You *are* my business. All through that time in Russia I was thinking of you. How, when I came back, I would tell you how much you had always meant to me. How the thought of you kept me going.'

'Like I said before, Leonora, you're not my mother. That's

242

the mistake you keep making, interfering like this. Kitty wouldn't have done it, she has more sense. You know that. You are not my mother,' she said distinctly.

Leonora found herself clutching her bag too tight. 'Mara, I—'

'I don't want to live with you,' said Mara distinctly. She opened the door and held it wide. 'I don't want to see you. If you can leave me to myself I'll have to work out a way to go to that place, get hold of Hélène, in whatever state she's in, and tell her that she saw the truth about Alex. That he did burn in flames.'

She stood back as Leonora passed her, and peered through the window as Leonora got one of the bigger boys to crank the car engine for her. Then the motor roared into life and the boys chased the car down the street.

Mara went to the table and sat down, fingering the letters again, feeling more alone than she had ever been in her life, even in those first days at Hartlepool in the cold upper room of the house of Pansy Clarence and her sister Heliotrope. In those days she had been a child, full of a child's optimism, a child's resilience. Now, less than a year later, she was an adult. In this grown-up universe Leonora, her heroine, had become her adversary. Tommy, the mischievous little boy, was in a world of men, on his way to war. Dewi was growing up a second time in the heat of battle at a place called Loos.

And Alex, brave Alex, was dead. Beautiful fragile Hélène was locked up in a lunatic asylum. Jean-Paul, whom she thought she had loved but whose face was now so hard to conjure up, he was fighting in his own country, avenging his sister and his mother, and sending Mara cold stranger's greetings, once a month.

She had no room, or time now, to be a child. From Monday she would be in a job at Scorton's Works, where the means of death for boys like Alex, Dewi and Tommy was precisely manufactured. Childhood had no place there.

She squared her shoulders. So what? Now at last she would

be the grown-up. There was one way forward and that was on her own, here in Bridge Street.

Strangely enough, there was a degree of pleasure, of relish, in that.

PART TWO

The Scent of Battle

1917

Still may Time hold some golden space
Where I'll unpack that scented store
Of song and flower and sky and face,
And count, and touch, and turn them o'er.

Rupert Brooke, *The Treasure*

16

'Service?'

'So what do you think his Nibs wants us for? If he says this leave's cancelled I'm bunking it,' said Tom Scorton fiercely to his bosom pal, Duggie O'Hare.

Duggie shook his head, wary of his friend's belligerence. He thought briefly of the optimistic, bright-eyed lad he'd met in the training camp. 'Some fancy scheme it'll be, me old fruit!' he said. 'Some little treat. I think the feller loves us like sons. Could only do that, couldn't he, after our good showing on the exercises, Tom?'

'If he loves us, man, he has a bloody funny way of showing it,' said Tom bitterly. 'They're bad buggers, the lot of 'em. One of them tells you you're the best man he's had since Mafeking and gives you Sergeant's stripes. Then he cops it, doesn't he?' That had happened to Tommy's first Colonel, whom he had worshipped. 'And the next feller comes out, barely out of short trousers, and he's busting you down to Private for conduct unbecoming. Twice in two years it's happened to me. Must be a record.'

'In this war?' Duggie's red hair glittered in the lamplight as he shook his head with great vigour. 'You make quite a jest, my boy. Now then, your Uncle Duggie feels it in his waters that there's something up here, and he has only one piece of advice for you, son. If the sainted Colonel asks you to be his servant, you turn it down, turn the bugger down.'

He pronounced it *bagger*. Tom smiled. Duggie's plummy

tones, acquired in ten years as butler to some London banker, could still not drown out the sharp cockney edge of his voice. Neither had his genteel experience wiped out his love of crude words where they could be fitted in.

The two men's boots clattered companionably on the stone flags of the shallow corridor which ran along the back of their temporary headquarters: a modest straggling building rather flatteringly called 'le Château' in the local village. This dusty, many-windowed mansion had been requisitioned from its reluctant owner, who had ridden off furious-faced in his De Dion Bouton. He had returned a day later, mollified, when he learned of the promised compensation and took up rather noisy residence in his own attics.

Of the many hard things Tom had learned in France, one of the hardest was to recognise that he and his comrades, who had come to this land as heroes, rescuers, white knights, were not always welcomed by its people. In one place the villagers had even removed the tops from their water pumps to stop the soldiers using them.

Another disenchanting aspect of Army life he had come up against was this thing about servants. Officers had soldier-servants who, like their servants at home, took care of them like babies. 'Taking care' in this context might be scrounging within the regiment for better food for one's officer, or requisitioning fruit or vegetables from the locality, or even stealing a bottle of brandy or wine to relieve the poor chap's boredom at having to eat under wartime conditions in between hampers from Simpson's or Harrods in London.

In addition the servant was certainly there to clean his officer's boots and to brush thickened French mud off greatcoats bought in Savile Row. It was not as if being a servant was an easy, safe billet either. In the main, officers were bred to be, trained and educated to be, flamboyantly courageous. And often, they expected their servant, their shadow and surrogate, to echo this quality in the field. It was not unknown for officers to volunteer their servant for field duties of one kind or another. Then, back from the firing line, the servant would revert to laundering and catering like a demented housewife under very adverse conditions. Sometimes he had to do all this for a man who had only just learned to do up his own buttons and who had been fed with a spoon by his nanny till he was nine. And often the quality of love they had for their officer was that of a fond nanny: understanding, indulgent and subservient.

'And all for the occasional tip, and a pat on the head like some arse-licking dog!' Duggie, an expert on these matters, had said, relishing Tommy's disgust. Officers had been after Duggie as soon as he came: with his experience of deference he would have been an asset. Duggie had turned them down flat. He warned Tom that he should not be seduced by some beguiling officer into being his servant. 'And I should know, mate, 'cos ain't I bleedin' well done it for years? Too bleedin' ignorant to get out until General Kitchener pointed his *farkin'* finger at me from a poster in Waterloo Station!'

Duggie and Tommy had just returned from three days' bruising behind-the-lines training instigated by their Colonel, newly promoted and very keen. They had listened with seasoned cynicism to the Colonel saying to his gathered men that they were to take full advantage of this opportunity, to sharpen them up after four days' slacking . . . *er, rest* . . . behind the lines. The men must be ready, sharp as knives, for their return to the front line. Their lives and their country's honour depended on it.

Two items of interest were doing the rounds among the men. One, that there was 'something big' in the wind, if not now, then very soon. The second was that the Colonel was on the look-out for a servant, having lost his last one to a sniper's bullet. Tommy and Duggie had overheard him on the practice field, talking to another officer. 'Offered Parker to the MO as a stretcher-bearer after that last sortie, and some blasted German took a potshot at him. Unsporting, what?'

'Meat!' Duggie had whispered fiercely in Tom's ear when he heard. 'Bleedin' *meat*! That's all we are.'

At the final gun-drill, Duggie and Tom had handled the guns well and the Colonel had been fractionally kinder to them, making rather a fuss of Tom. This had led Duggie to start harping on about this servant thing yet again.

Marching back to camp, Tom had dwelled on the prospect of being a soldier-servant. It had its advantages. You had first go at resources, even if they were crumbs from the officer's table. You were near the centre of information: you could earwig on conversations. You did have fractionally less front-line action. And Tommy was wearier than he dare admit of the unique blend of sheer boredom, sheer terror and numb despair which were the ingredients of life at the French Front.

Anyway, this Colonel seemed congenial enough.

Duggie was worried that a direct offer might tempt him. 'Don't do it, Tommy boy. He'll have your soul first, heart next and then your trousers if you ain't careful. Take it from one who knows.'

'That happen to you, then?'

Duggie had been very cagey about his life before he enlisted. 'It happens to anyone, mate, who, for a measly weekly wage, offers to wipe someone else's arse for them. Nannies, nurses, footmen, butlers. All of them get shagged one way or another.'

'My father has servants.' Tommy had offered this cautiously. 'He doesn't sh—'

'Doesn't he now? Surprise surprise. Servants, eh? Couldn't 'ave told you were a toff, mate.'

'I'm no such thing. But my father did have three servants that he loved. Certainly didn't shag them, one way or any other. Egyptian brothers they were. He brought them back from some archaeological trip in the year dot. They did everything, the house, the garden, the food.'

'Toffs, like I said,' Duggie grunted.

'But these three men, Duggie, they didn't in the least feel

250

like servants to me – although I don't really know what that means.'

'So how was that any different, then?' the other man persisted.

'It was as though we were guests in their lives, in their house. They kindly conceded that we might share their space. But there was no subservience. Not so much as the Colonel shows the Brigadier. None at all, although they loved my father like a brother, and my mother like a daughter. They kind of brought me and my sister up, like three old wizards about the place.'

'Well maybe, just maybe, son, that's different. Or maybe you just *think* it's different but it's the same bladdy thing, from their side. Dead now, are they?'

'Two of them are. There's only Luke left now. He must be ancient – older than my father. Still does most things for him, though. Helps him with his clock-making, takes care of his workshop.'

'So what's that but subservience, arse-licking?' began Duggie aggressively.

Tom came to a halt. 'Seventh door down, the Sergeant said. Here we are.' He knocked on the door.

A short bark invited their entry. They marched in, saluted, and stood to attention before the Colonel, who was lounging behind his desk fiddling with a very long Meerschaum pipe. He finally got his pipe lit, and gestured with it in a shadow of a salute. 'At ease,' he growled.

They stood easy.

The Colonel's cheeks collapsed inwards and he took a long draw on his pipe, for a second allowing its bliss to flow into him. 'Briefly, Scorton . . . O'Hare,' he said, 'I'd like you to act as ghillies and beaters for a shoot this weekend. We need a couple of fellers who know the ropes, who speak English. Fly the flag, what? Show'm what we can do.'

'A shoot, sir?' said Duggie politely. His aggression had seeped away from him, as it always did when he was actually face to face with the gentry, as opposed to castigating them behind their backs.

'The gentleman who has kindly lent us his château has now decided we are friends, not enemies, and has invited us to hunt boar with him.' The Colonel frowned. 'I had a good man, who would have done splendidly. But, alas, the feller's no longer with us.'

Tommy shuffled his feet. 'We're due leave on Saturday, Colonel. Missed out on the last lot.' He started to sweat, desperate that these precious few days would be cancelled. The thought of this leave had kept him going for three months.

The Colonel shook his head as though trying to release a buzzing bee. 'The sacrifice applies to myself as well as you, Scorton. I, too, look forward to a home leave, but duty calls! Courtesy to the natives and all that. Two days delayed, that's all, chaps.'

'Will we get those days tacked on the end, sir? Extra days' leave?' pursued Tommy, grimly determined. 'My home's in the North of England and it is impossible to—'

The Colonel shook his head again. 'Regretfully, no, Scorton. We're due back in the trenches as soon as we return. There's to be a show . . .' He paused, his eyes bland, neutral. 'As I said, Scorton, I as well as you will be making this sacrifice.'

Tommy glanced furiously at Duggie, who was staring at his boots. How many times had he noticed that Duggie's bravado, his revolutionary zeal, was confined to situations out of officers' sight and hearing? He could not rely on any support from his pal in this situation.

The Colonel also looked at Duggie. 'Well, what d'you say, man?'

'Well, I suppose . . .' Duggie was actually sweating.

'Good man. And you, Scorton?'

Tommy scowled, but reluctantly nodded his head. 'If Private O'Hare . . .'

'Good man. Knew I could depend on you.' The Colonel drew on his pipe and closed his eyes. 'And when we get back from leave, Scorton, perhaps we could talk about a further matter. I really need a good servant.' He stood up, placing his Meerschaum pipe carefully on the desk. 'Well, then. Tomorrow morning, four sharp! Here at the house for kitting up. There will, of course, be appropriate emoluments and that should not come amiss on leave, what?'

Outside the door Tommy turned a hostile face to his friend. 'Well thanks, Duggie, for your great help in saving our leave.'

Duggie stood and beat the plaster wall with his fist, making the dust rise in the air. 'There – d'you see? That's what they do to you. When they're with you, they still your tongue and numb your head. They grab your common sense, your dignity and crumble it between their fingers. Don't you see? They shag you without even putting a finger on you.'

Mara had a major battle with Michael to get away from the factory to see Tommy in London.

She enjoyed her job at Scorton's Works and had never missed a day before. In her two years there, three clerks had left to enlist and two were early and unwilling conscripts, it being deemed that their jobs could easily be done by women. So within six months Mara had found herself running the office as chief clerk in charge of five other purchasing and invoice clerks, all women, and responsible for their training and welfare.

As Michael was forced to admit to Pansy, Mara was quick and efficient, and had a natural bent for teaching these wooden-headed females. He'd never had such immaculate paperwork, never been so well-informed as he went about the business of procurement. The purchasing records made a good impression on the government and Army personnel who came from time to time to check on them.

There was no pulling the wool over the eyes of these grim, bustling men, who came to urge Michael to greater and greater efforts, telling dire tales of the shortage of shells. We couldn't, after all, leave our boys with so little protection, could we?

Mara, privy to these conversations, agreed. Now that 'our

boys' included Tommy as well as Dewi and Jean-Paul, she was eager that they should not be let down by what was happening here in Priorton. Like many Priorton women, she scanned the growing casualty list every day in the newspapers for familiar names. Like many Priorton women also, she was somewhat confused by the reports of Allied Army successes, which seemed to be accompanied by a bewildering list of wounded and dead.

Her life was now full to overflowing. She studied Saturday mornings and two nights a week with Miss Corbell from the High School. Miss Corbell, introduced to her by Mr Clelland, was taking her through the syllabus so that in a year or so she should be able to take her matriculation exams. Then one day she might – just might – be able to go on to train to be a proper teacher.

She had a regular unpaid sideline now in letter-writing; first a trickle, then a stream of girls from the factory approached her outside the office or even at the house in Bridge Street, to ask her to write letters to their brothers and sweethearts in the Army. This led to requests from some women that she should teach them to write for themselves.

Some of the women had never completed their schooling, having been kept home by harassed mothers to help cope with a houseful of demanding pitmen. Some unfortunates had toiled on at school, sitting at the back of classes of fifty or sixty, their only attention from the teacher being the administration of the dreaded stick for dumb insolence, for blotted copybooks, for black nails and snotty noses, or for their alleged stubborn stupidity.

Some of the women, who could actually write quite efficiently, enjoyed Mara's style, and 'borrowed' affecting phrases which were passed from one to the other. These were used time and time again in letters to France or Mesopotamia, letters to gladden some Durham lad's heart before, with a stoical pitman's resignation, he went over the top into the face of the guns yet again.

Many of the girls confided to her that they revelled in factory life. They'd never been away from home before, and despite the long hours and the risks with the sulphur, they enjoyed their friendships with other women, and the magic significance of their pay packet inside the family.

Mara herself also enjoyed the magic significance of her own pay packet, her own independence. She loved the Bridge Street house. It was clean and cosy, its bare essentials supplemented now by odd items bought by her from her wages, or brought for her from Purley Lodge by her mother and father.

William regularly offered Mara modest sums of money to supplement her wage. When, each time, she refused to take it he would clap his hands and tell her she was getting more like her mother every day.

Mara's mantelshelf was now graced by a clock made by Kitty herself, a gift on Mara's seventeenth birthday. For Tommy's nineteenth birthday, on the same day, Kitty made a pocket-watch. She had sent it to him in France, carefully wrapped in a woollen scarf which also carried, tucked into its folds, some bags of raisins and almonds.

Mara frequently bumped into Leonora on her regular Sunday-dinner visit at the Lodge. It had taken the sisters many months to slowly return to civil, even friendly terms since the furore over Hélène going to the asylum, two years ago now. Even so, the intimacy of their earlier years was gone, the presence of the Frenchwoman in Sedgefield lying like an unsheathed sword between them.

Leonora, working sixty hours a week at the hospital, had regular twinges of regret that she still had not returned to Russia. Her work at the hospital was so much appreciated, and each time she was on the point of making enquiries about a possible journey in these impossible times, some crisis would come up and her obligation seemed to be here in Priorton.

She still found time to serve on various committees to do with the war effort, or the Independent Labour Party which was spreading its wings in the town. She became friends with the teacher Mr Clelland before he was banished to keep pigs on some farm in the wilds of Northumberland as penance for his betrayal of his country in resisting conscription.

At the ILP meetings across the county, Leonora's views and insights into the volatile Russian situation were sought, as it was known that she had lived there and worked among Russian soldiers. It was also known that her brother, serving somewhere in Russia, kept her posted on the situation that was boiling up there.

This casual assumption caused some heartache to Leonora. Samuel's occasional letters were indeed full of information: journalistic accounts exhibiting coolness and objectivity. But they were entirely lacking in presence, passion and feeling.

She wrote back to him in kind, telling him of developments here in Priorton, the work of the Party, of the rising unrest filtering through from the soldiers in the hospital, regarding the war; of her certainty at last that women, working in factories and shipyards, offices and warehouses, were demonstrating their right to vote without needing the bustling middle-class suffragettes to show them the way.

With every calmly expressed paragraph Leonora felt as though she were moving away from the intoxicating certainties of the brief affair she had enjoyed with Samuel. To dull her pain she searched out more and more work, more commitments, more committees, deaf to Kitty's pleas that she should take some time to relax, to enjoy herself.

One Saturday in June, Leonora drove to Mara's house with the news that Tommy was to be in London on leave. 'It seems the leave has now been cut short. He only has five days to get from some far-flung spot near Belgium, and if he comes up here, he'll only be in time to turn round and go back again. Says can we get down to London to see him for a couple of days?'

'Oh, we must see him. Must,' she repeated. As the long months and years stretched out since he had embarked, Tommy's letters had become less and less frequent, more and more abbreviated; the ones which arrived were brief, scrawled in an unsteady hand. The real Tommy, the Tommy they knew, was nowhere to be found in those cursory lines. He even signed himself 'Tom' now. Although his words were cheery, misery radiated from the page.

'I won't be able to get there myself,' said Leonora. 'They're shorthanded at the hospital and I'm chairing two ILP meetings bang in the middle of next week. Anyway, it's you and the parents he'll want to see.'

'When's he coming?' said Mara.

'He'll be there by Wednesday next and Ma proposes travelling on Tuesday. William's not so well. Feels he can't make it.'

'Michael might not let me off.'

'Of course he will.'

Mara frowned. 'He'll have to consult Pansy, of course.'

'What? The octopus?'

They both laughed at this. Two years into their marriage, Pansy was in control of every aspect of Michael's life, apart from the running of the factory. And she would even turn up there some lunchtimes, with a delicacy in a covered basket, to refresh him in a hard-pressed day.

Michael loved it. He had given up his bridge club and his gentleman's snooker club; he had stopped playing cricket and tennis; he never visited his father and stepmother without Pansy on hand, purring his praises or putting words into his mouth.

'Well, Mara, if Pansy tries to prevent you, I'll take her on.'

'I can fight my own battles,' said Mara briefly.

'Ouch! So you can, Mara, so you can,' said Leonora. 'So, shall I tell Ma to get the train tickets?'

'Tell her to get one – I'll pay for my own. But you can tell her I'll go. I wouldn't miss seeing Tommy, Pansy or no Pansy.'

Leonora pulled on her gloves and stood to go. She looked her sister up and down. 'All dressed up! Are you going somewhere?'

Mara looked her in the eye. 'I'm going to see Hélène at the hospital. I go once every fortnight,' she said evenly. 'I have to catch the train.'

'Can I take you there? I can hang onto the motor, for sure.'

Mara stared at her thoughtfully. 'Would you like to see Hélène?' she said. 'Could you bear it?'

Leonora felt herself challenged and answered in kind. 'Because I'm the reason she's there – is that what you're saying?'

Mara shrugged. 'Water under the bridge now, Leonie.'

'I'd rather it hadn't happened, none of it, Mara. Older and wiser, isn't that what we all are? Come on then, we'll drive there. And yes, I'd like to see Hélène. My conscience has pricked me for years, getting her committed like that, without telling you. I should have kept my hands off, been more like Kitty. You hit a chord there.'

'You're right to feel bad about it,' Mara agreed, 'although she might have ended up at the asylum anyway. But that was up to me. You should have know that.'

'I've thought, since, that it was envy. I think I envied her. There I was, just back from my heroic efforts in the wastes of Russia, dying to see you, wanting to get back to where we'd been, the two of us, comrades, best friends, playmates. And there you were, wrapped around this Frenchwoman, more concerned about her than you were about me.' She put an arm through Mara's. 'Aren't I foolish? Jealous of a poor homeless French girl.' She laughed ruefully. 'Poor woman. How could I? My sympathy muscle must have been entirely wasted when I was abroad. I never felt the least bit sorry for her.'

Mara breathed out with a long sigh and hugged her sister's arm. 'Like I said, Leonie. Water under the bridge.'

Leonora drove them to Sedgefield, the motor car and its two lady occupants swathed in veils drawing attention in the villages through which they passed.

'And have you heard lately from Jean-Paul?' Leonora called above the noise of the engine.

Mara shook her head. 'Not for more than a year now. It's strange, you know, but I can't bring his face to mind. I can imagine Tommy's face, all right. And Dewi's face. Even brave, bad Alex. But not Jean-Paul's, even though I . . . he . . .'

'Though you loved him?' prompted Leonora. Etched clearly in her own mind was an image of Sam's face, complete with every line, every wrinkle, every freckle, every crease. Whatever happened now, it would be etched on the inside of her skull until the day she died.

'I thought I did. But now I feel nothing, to be honest.'

'But you still keep your eye on Hélène?'

'I couldn't desert her, could I?'

'No, I suppose you couldn't.' Leonora pressed hard on the pedal to make the car go faster.

At the hospital the nurse showed them to a room with a long window which overlooked green parkland. Mara watched the door click behind the nurse. 'Hélène must be all right today,' she said thoughtfully.

'All right?' said Leonora, peering through the window at the figures trailing across the lawn with their heavy uncoordinated gait and occasionally wild gesture, so savagely out of tune with the real world. She wondered if she could have nursed people like this. She shook her head. People with bullet-holes in them, even with no arms or eyes, were much easier to deal with. They die or they survive. They do not wander around like their own ghost.

'Sometimes I come all the way here to see her and they won't let me. They'll say she's been "very upset" and they've given her something to calm her, or had to put her under restraint or something.'

The door creaked open and they got to their feet. Hélène stood in the dusty light, clinging to the nurse's arm, her face white, deeply scored with fresh scratches or older scars, her hair in two tight childish plaits.

'Mara! Dear child.' She struggled free and raced across to embrace Mara, kissing her repeatedly, one cheek after the other. 'Jean-Paul, he was just saying, "The girl Mara, you must take care of the girl".' She turned to Leonora. 'And this is your mother? Ah Madame, your daughter is a treasure. I was just saying to Jean-Paul . . .' She grasped Leonora's hand and shook it with a powerful grip.

'Just saying?' Mara disengaged Hélène from Leonora, sat her in a chair and knelt beside her. 'Hélène, I keep telling you. Jean-Paul is back in France, fighting the Germans.'

Hélène rubbed her forehead with the heel of her hand. 'Yes. Yes. You say this. Jean-Paul says I must agree when you say this.' She turned to Leonora. 'Mara knows. She came to tell me. Alex was burned, you see. I saw it. But it's such a long time since we have seen this man, my brother. In my dreams he has no face.' She grabbed Mara's arm. 'Do you forget his face, little Mara?'

Mara struggled for a moment, then left her arm in Hélène's grasp. She thought wildly that she might actually tell the truth. That she could *not* remember his face. Then she shook her head. 'No, Hélène. How could we forget him, his face? Do you remember the box he made me? The beautiful box? Don't I keep his letters there?'

Hélène grabbed Mara's shoulders and shook her violently. The nurse by the door moved uneasily from foot to foot then relaxed as Hélène took Mara's face in her hand and stroked it. 'You have a letter for me?'

Mara struggled free and pushed Hélène back into her chair. 'Just wait a minute, Hélène. Yes, I do have a letter.'

'Read it to me. You know I cannot read English.'

Mara fiddled with her bag and pulled out an envelope which, Leonora noted, was not the characteristic Army green. It looked suspiciously like the common or garden stationery available at Reaveley's, on the corner of the Market Place.

Mara opened the letter and started to read. '*Dearest Mara and Hélène, I think of you both every day . . .*'

Leonora, watching her, recognised the fiction. She was suddenly full of admiration for the steady, generous, caring regard with which Mara treated her friend. Then she jumped as the French girl leapt towards Mara, grabbed the letter and stuffed it in her mouth and started to chew it. 'I will have it, I will have him,' she mumbled through a very full mouth.

The nurse walked across. 'Come on, flower, let's not be a naughty girl.'

Hélène started to fight and struggle, swearing and screaming in French. Her loose dress fell open, revealing long knife scars stretching down her uncorseted breast. The nurse pulled her away through the door and it swung closed behind them. Her screams came back towards them through the thickness of the door.

Mara breathed more easily. She glanced at Leonora. 'She's not like that every time, you know,' she said faintly. 'Sometimes she's her old self. Sometimes she even sings. She tells me stories of when she and Jean-Paul were young.'

'What a dreadful state she's in,' said Leonora with feeling.

'Just like France,' said Mara tersely. 'Mauled over and spoiled.'

'Those scars. Those horrible scars.'

'She does it to herself. She's always trying to . . . end it all. For me she's a heroine. A casualty of the war no less than those boys you spend your time sewing up and spoiling.'

Leonora glanced at her but failed to find vanity or melodrama in the face and tense figure of her sister standing beside her. Mara was speaking her thoughts, her version of the raw truth.

They walked to the motor car. Mara cranked the handle, then jumped in beside Leonora as the engine fired into life. They were a mile down the road when Leonora turned to Mara. 'I'm proud of you, you know. Really proud of you, Mara.'

'Don't be daft. I'm doing nothing. Nothing. Look what you

did in Russia. And what you're doing now, in the hospital. Now *that's* some cause for pride.' She paused. 'I wonder, Leonie . . . would you come with me to see Michael, so we can persuade him to let me have some time off?'

17

The Innocents

The château was set on a shelf of land, in the middle of a shallow basin fringed by trees and woodland. The cottages sheltered beneath the lip of the basin, their rooms, barns and pigsties overflowing with soldiers, billeted according to their rank. In the far distance, the Somme snaked its way downwards between steep wooded banks, catching the late summer light.

The guns and the beaters were marshalled by a portly man who sported curling moustaches and wore a balding green velvet jacket. The Colonel 'lent' Duggie O'Hare to a Lieutenant from another regiment and kept Tom to load for him.

Duggie made off after the Lieutenant, spitting the word 'Meat!' out of the side of his mouth as he ran.

'What did the feller say?' demanded the Colonel, glaring after him. 'What was that?'

'He said "Wait!" – to wait for him, sir. After it's all over.' As Tom shouldered the Colonel's guns, he smiled to himself, applauding the bravery of his friend at spluttering anything at all, considering how petrified he was of these people, who were cut out of the same mould as his former masters.

The day's attraction for all these men in khaki was the opportunity to hunt boar, a quarry long missing for the English sportsman. The hunters padded along, across a meadow, and paused at the edge of a wood.

'*Silence!*' The man with the velvet jacket put his fingers to his lips. He gestured to his feet, where there was a distinct footprint in the dry clay. The guns moved off on tiptoe. Tom stepped on a twig and it went off like a rifle shot. 'Quiet!' growled the Colonel.

'*Silence!*' whispered the man with the velvet jacket again.

'*Silence!*' came urgently from the other end of the line.

'Silence!' This time in clear English. Tom distinguished Duggie's plummy tones, and grinned. His pal would enjoy being the spoilsport here. No sensible boar would stay within half a mile of these clod-hopping jokers with him around, that was for sure.

There was a loud report to the right, followed by a high-pitched scream. The whole line tensed with the joy of the kill. They waited while a French beater plodded across, then held up the remains of a bloody rabbit. '*Un lapin. Monsieur a tué un lapin!*'

The ensuing 'halloos' and applause made quite certain that any boar would get well away. Once the flurry of excitement had died down, they continued on their way. After thirty yards they stopped again, and the Colonel, not to be out-done, bagged a squirrel. There were more cheers, and his host shook his hand heartily. 'Well done, Monsieur, very well done.'

After another hour's vain search for the boar, they called it a day. The French beater tied the rabbit and the squirrel to a long walking stick, and carried them, dangling and dripping blood, back to the château.

Duggie, walking along with Tom, ten paces behind the Colonel and the Lieutenant, muttered, 'There, see, my boy? It's all about meat. Bleedin' stinkin' meat! That's what this war is about. Didn't I tell you?'

'Whoops!' Mara clutched Kitty's arm as yet another motor car swerved by, throwing up spray from the recently fallen rain. 'Have you ever seen so many vehicles? It's busier than

Hartlepool, and that used to make me blink,' she shouted into Kitty's ear.

It was not just the motor cars. Two-wheel carriages, four-wheel carriages, bicycles, men and women, even children, pushing and pulling carts of various sizes, and people on horses, ponies, donkeys, mules. And then there were the people on foot, running, walking, striding, stalking, stumbling, tumbling about a city's business. Mara wrinkled her nose at the air, which reeked of vinegar and dust laced with old cheese, rotten fruit and the occasional drift of very fine perfume. Beside all this, the very idea of Priorton, even on a market day, was like a dream of peace.

Their hotel, a small establishment off Jermyn Street, was only a short walk from Regent Street. However, as they made their way there, the press of people and traffic made such an onslaught on Mara's senses that she felt as though she was burrowing into the heart of this great city just as the moles burrowed through the ground under the lawns of Purley Hall.

At last they reached the café. They stood for a moment just inside the door, scanning the faces of the many uniformed men sitting in various kinds of company. Tommy was nowhere to be seen.

'Madam?' A doddery old man waved a spotless cloth at them and showed them to an empty table. They sat down to wait. They had drunk a whole silver teapot of tea, and watched several dozen people move to and fro through the etched glass doors, when Mara stood up. 'No. Oh dear me!'

A thickset man in a battered, barely clean uniform approached them; his hair was thin and he had dark rings under his eyes. It was a long ten seconds before Kitty recognised him and leapt to her feet. 'Tommy!'

Their hearty embrace drew glances in the crowded tea room.

'Well, Mara. No kiss for your favourite brother?'

She kissed him, and held onto his hands. 'For goodness'

sake, Tommy, what have they done to you? You look all . . .'
She paused, smelling the whisky on his breath.

'Proper shook-up?' He put her hands away from him and
took a step back. 'We're all of us shook-up in this war, Mara.
I should be grateful, of course. At least I'm alive. Over there
in France there's lives being thrown away like potato peelings
into the pig swill.' He did not lower his voice.

A flutter of outraged sensibility rippled across the tables
around them; several middle-aged men in immaculate uniforms cleared their throats almost in unison.

'Sit down, Tommy!' said Mara grimly. 'Come on, sit
down!'

'Tommy. Tommy? Wrong name, love. You have to call me
Tom now. Too many Tommies out there, all of 'em mown
down like sheaves of corn. Some officer'll say "My Tommies"
– d'you know that? Like he was saying "My foxhounds" or
"My ponies". So I can't be one of them, can I? Expendable,
like somebody's dog, or their horse.' He paused. 'D'you know,
they docked our leave, me and Duggie, cause they wanted to
hunt some bloody boar with a Frenchman. Bastards.'

An elderly Brigadier raised his hand and the doddery waiter
scuttled across to him. A slight red-haired man, who had been
standing at the door clutching his military cap, made his way
through the tables towards them. He grasped Tommy's arm.
'Tom, old boy, get a hold of yourself.'

Tommy beamed. 'Duggie! Here's the boy. Mother, Mara, I
want you to meet my comrade in arms, Duggie O'Hare.' Then
he slumped down in the chair, quite unconscious.

Duggie glanced at them. 'Sorry about this, ma'am, miss.
Poor Tom's been on the juice, more'n he can take. Shock of
getting to where you don't have to duck and swerve seems to
have got to him. Lost the will to pretend, he has. Seems these
desk wallahs in here ain't too pleased at him.' He, too, made
no effort to keep his voice down. 'Can't stand the sight of a bit
of trench mud, can they? Too untidy by half.'

Kitty, normally never worried about appearances, still saw

266

the need to get out of this place; the air all round them was heavy with disapproval. 'Can you carry him, Mr . . . O'Hare? We should leave before we're escorted out by that rather frosty-looking man who's coming towards us, don't you think?'

Duggie frowned down at his friend. 'Blighter looks skinny enough, ma'am, but he's very solid. I know of old. Tried to drag him out of a shell-hole once and nearly broke me back in the attempt.' He was relishing the drama, seeing it as a poke in the eye for the shirkers and warmongers he thought he saw around him.

'For goodness' sake! I'll take his legs and you take the arms,' instructed Mara. 'Hurry, will you?'

Helping Duggie manoeuvre the comatose body of her brother round the tables, past the wrathful clientèle of the café, Mara had a flash of memory, an image of her struggle to move the body of Mr Clonmel; she saw herself bossing Joe Bly around, desperate to get the head teacher outside, away from the collapsing school.

Out on the pavement, they leaned Tommy up against a wall and caught their breath. Very slowly, he crumpled in a little heap on the ground. Kitty thrust her bag and her umbrella into Mara's hands, knelt down on the dirt and tapped his face. 'Tommy, come on, love. We've come all the way down to see you, and you've come all the way back from France to see us. Wake up, you idiot. Wake up.'

Behind them Duggie put his fingers to his mouth and whistled up an old-fashioned hackney carriage pulled by a very tired horse which had obviously only missed war service by a whisk of his mane. They propped Tommy against the steps and heaved him in.

As the carriage rumbled over the cobbles Duggie explained to them that Tom had been very put out at being unable to come all the way home because of the short leave. 'Normally, old Tom's very solid. Taking everything Fritz could throw, head down, no nonsense. You know how it is.' Then, after this blasted hunt, he had been 'kind of frightened, ma'am, in a funny way, of meeting you and your daughter here.'

He went on: 'The lad won money last night, ma'am, at cards and so got his hands on a bottle of whisky – appropriated by some nefarious means, I shouldn't wonder. It's whisky caused this, otherwise he'd 'ave known to keep his trap shut,' he concluded, virtue exuding from every pore.

Mara was irritated at the unctuous confidence of this man, his possessive attitude towards her brother. There was something false about him. His voice was too grand for the words he used, his manner both cocky and obsequious. 'Have you known my brother long, Mr . . . ?'

'Just call me Duggie, miss. Yes, we been together now a long time, your brother and me, neither of us to be whittled off when those around us is being blown away like sawdust.'

Tommy was stirring.

'Now, my boy,' said Duggie. 'You apologise to your Ma here for causing a ruction there in the caff.'

Tommy started to cry and Kitty took his hand and drew his head onto her shoulder. 'No need to say sorry to me, son,' she whispered through tears of her own. 'I've been in a few ructions in my life, I can tell you, and am none the worse for it.'

'So where are we going, Duggie?' said Mara, deciding that a neutral, pleasant manner was the only way to deal with this creature.

'A little place I know, where me and Tom has been staying.'

Duggie's 'little place' was an inn in an alleyway running up from the river. Dark outside, neat inside, it was called 'The Princess Louise'. The landlady was a Mrs Marmion, who had been a housekeeper in the same household as Duggie, and she had bought the inn with the pay-off from a grateful master whom she had saved from drowning in his own bath.

Mrs Marmion was brisk and cheery, very much mistress of herself and her surroundings. She produced thick slices of bread for Tommy, and some peppery soup. He ate the lot. In half an hour he was very, very sick. After that he was sufficiently improved to join them for tea, set by Mrs Marmion on a snowy cloth at a table from which they could view a slice of the Thames with its tangle of masts.

Duggie gave Tommy his chair and tactfully retired to the kitchen regions for a jaw with his old friend Mrs Marmion.

Skilfully Kitty guided the talk towards Priorton and affairs at home. She told funny stories about Michael and Pansy; about the great strides she was making with the clocks. Tommy got out his own watch and showed it to her, saying that really, it did keep perfect time. Kitty went on to tell how William was working on a splendid new idea; about the factory and Mara's good work there. 'She's practically running the purchasing side of the office.'

'Don't know how you can take that place, Mara. Hated it myself,' Tommy interrupted Kitty, slurping his tea from a large cup. 'With old Michael looming all over you all the time.'

'It's not the place, which is a bit black and stinky for me,' said Mara. 'It's the people I like. The days go over very quickly. And Michael's all right if you get the job right.'

'So what about the teaching? What happened to that? I know you had a fright, but you were good at it. Good at it.'

'She'll go back to it,' asserted Kitty. 'But she must go to college and do it properly this time.'

'I'm studying to get my matriculation,' said Mara. 'So I'll go to college next year, or the year after that.'

'Good show! Make things rather than break them, that's the ticket.' Tears were standing in his eyes. Mara put a hand on his arm and he shook it off. 'And how's Pa? How's the old rascal?'

'Quite well really, considering the turn he had,' said Kitty. 'Much more his old self now. He's enjoyed playing master-and-apprentice with me and now he's set me on in charge of the clocks and left me to it. He and old Luke have got all his books and archaeological stuff out of the storage boxes and they've spread them out in one of the barns. They're creating some kind of catalogue or index, I believe.' She laughed, and Mara thought how young, how alive she looked. 'And he's on at me yet again to marry him, the dear thing.'

Tommy grabbed her hand. 'Marry him, Ma. Why don't you marry him?'

'After all this time? Dearest boy, I—'

He took her shoulder and shook it. 'Do it for me, for Mara, will you!'

Kitty looked troubled.

'Makes no difference to me,' said Mara.

Kitty wriggled her shoulder free and took Tommy's other hand in hers. 'Why, Tommy?'

'Call me Tom,' he growled.

'Why, Tom, after all this time? You never troubled yourself about it before.'

He laid his forehead on her shoulder. 'Things are different now, Ma. Once, it seemed as if everything would go on for ever, and none of that mattered a jot. Now, though, it seems like we're all made of the finest tissue paper and the slightest wind can blow us right away. D'you know, sometimes I can't even remember your face? Or Pa's, or Mara's? It seems as though there's a world of "before" which has gone for ever. I can't even write to you because it's as though I'm writing into a void.' His head was down. She could not see his eyes. His voice was wretched, desperate.

'Marry Pa, Mother,' said Mara suddenly. 'If Tom feels like that you have to.'

Kitty took his face between her hands and looked him in the eyes. 'Well, dearest boy, if you and your sister say so, I suppose I must.'

There was a great crashing at the door and Duggie burst in. Tommy shook off Kitty's hands, and Duggie's eyes veiled themselves as he took in the situation. 'Well, my boy, guess what the delightful Mrs Marmion has come up with? Two tickets for the Old Phoenix Music Hall. Ain't that the thing?

Like gold they are. So why don't you take your beautiful sister there, Tom? And I'll escort Mrs . . . Miss Rainbow back to Jermyn Street. No use sitting here moping, is there?'

Mara stood up. 'What a wonderful idea! I've not been to the music hall since we were little. Can you remember, we went to see Aunt Esme and Uncle Thomas do their piece at the Sunderland Empire?'

'Ha! You've relatives on the Hall, have you?' Duggie chuckled. 'Now I see where you get your talent with the old squeezebox.'

'She's not a real aunt,' said Kitty, putting her teacup and saucer neatly in alignment with her plate. 'She's my oldest and best friend, the friend of my childhood. Calls herself Esther Rainbow on the stage.'

'Esther Rainbow? Seen her many a time. Wonderful talent. And, if I may say so, a wee bit naughty from time to time.'

Kitty smiled. 'You may say so, Mr O'Hare. As I said, she is my dearest and oldest friend.'

Duggie put his hand on his heart. 'Tom, dear boy, I think I'm in love with your mother!'

'Idiot!' Tommy was rebuckling his tunic. He ran his fingers through his hair, smoothing it back before he put on his cap. 'But the music hall's a very sound idea.'

Mara put on her jacket and coat, relieved at the total reversal of atmosphere wrought by the strange Duggie O'Hare.

'That's better, old fruit,' beamed Duggie. 'Now you young ones go off and enjoy yourselves.'

The door clicked behind them and Kitty looked up at Duggie. 'Those tickets weren't for them, were they, Mr O'Hare? They were for you. You and Mrs Marmion, probably.'

'Those bright eyes miss nothing, do they, Miss Rainbow? You ain't wrong. Mrs Marmion got them for me and her. She'll play old Harry when she realises they've gone off with them.'

'Why did you do it?'

''Cause me and that galoot of a son of yours look out for each other, ma'am. And I ain't never seen him so down. He's got me out of scrapes an' I've got him out of scrapes. He keeps his pecker up normally. But them shortening our leave seems to have got to him. And half a bottle of whisky didn't help. *In vino veritas* – ain't that what they say? Well, there's no room for bleedin' *veritas* in this war, I can tell you. 'Scuse my language, ma'am.' He paused. 'I ain't never had a brother, not that I know of, coming from the orphanage. But I dare to say, just between you and me, of course, that I love old Tom like a brother, an' I'll look after him like one.'

'Thank you, Mr O'Hare,' said Kitty. 'Thank you from the bottom of my heart.' And she reached up and kissed him on the cheek.

At that moment Mrs Marmion barged in through the door with a tray in her hand, which she dropped with a clatter. 'Excuse me,' she said. 'Excuse *me*!' And she turned and stumped off.

Duggie raised his straggly ginger eyebrows. 'Oh dear,' he said. 'I think our reputations ain't what they were, Miss Rainbow.'

She was pulling on her long gloves. 'Don't be silly, Mr O'Hare. I think Mrs Marmion is quite the woman of the world. Just you take her tray to her and explain what happened. Then you can walk back West with me. I could go on my own, but I haven't been in London since I was quite young, and I might just lose my way.'

He clapped his hands together. 'I'll give you the grand tour, Miss Rainbow. Show you Piccadilly, the Mall, and James Street, where I worked before the war.'

'Worked, Mr O'Hare? What did you do, then?'

'I was a butler, ma'am. Butler to Sir James Writherd.'

Kitty laughed and turned to adjust her hat in the mirror over the fireplace. 'No wonder you're so very good at taking care of people.'

With her back to him she did not see the shadow which

272

passed over his face, before he went to placate Mrs Marmion with promises of a cosy evening in, afterwards.

At the theatre, Tommy laughed along with the delighted crowd at all the jokes about the Kaiser; he sang along with the patriotic songs about being proud to be British, and the enumeration of the colourful virtues of the various British Regiments. He beat his knee as the band played rousing military music, and stood, ramrod rigid, when the National Anthem was played at the end.

Mara took his arm as they made their way through the crowd down Drury Lane towards the Strand. She was desperate to ask him about the war, and his views on it, to report back to Leonora and William, but she dared not risk it. Instead she talked about the girls at work and some of their funnier sayings, and went on to descriptions of how Pansy was babying Michael so that he was just about eating out of her hand, getting fatter day by day.

'He looks years older than Kitty now,' she confided. 'You'd never guess she was his stepmother. Of course, Pansy can't stand the sight or sound of Kitty, although she's such a mincer she never actually comes out with it, just tries slyly to sour everyone's view. She actually told me once that dear Kitty couldn't help her background.'

'What a favour you did us all when you brought that little monster out of Hartlepool,' said Tommy.

Mara groaned. 'Don't remind me!'

They stopped by a café. Tommy peered into the window. 'This looks all right. Why don't we go in for a cup of tea?'

A fat man in a grey apron served them with tea in a thick brown pot, and a plate of ginger biscuits. Tommy removed his cap and placed it carefully on the empty seat beside him. 'I want you to do me a favour, Mara.'

'Anything, Tommy – sorry, Tom. I just can't get used to it.'

'Will you listen to what I tell you? Don't cry or try to stop

273

me. Just listen. We're not supposed to talk about any of it. And to be honest, I was soldiering on like you're supposed to, taking it all. Perhaps having to stay for that pantomime of a boar hunt and losing two days so I couldn't get home, that was the last straw for this camel's back. Now I want someone to hear it before I die. And it's not just about me, it's about tens of thousands, hundreds of thousands of others.' He shook his head at her protest. 'And when you've heard this, you're not to tell anyone, not Ma or Pa or anyone, at least till the war is all over. Promise?'

She nodded, feeling her hair stand on end in anticipation of she knew not what.

Then, in a cold angry voice, he told her the substantial truth about his experiences in the last two years. About the danger, the boredom and drudgery of the days, the nightmares and fears of the sleepless nights; about the vulnerability of the human body, where rotting remains – a stray arm or leg, or skull – becomes commonplace, a matter of no importance; about the execution of a comrade who had become disoriented and had turned back in the middle of an action to ask someone what to do; of the rage of an officer as he dressed down a gibbering soldier, accusing him of cowardice. Of officers and men brave to the point of insanity, who made an ordinary terrified infantryman feel half a man. Of swallowing and swallowing your own terror, and going on and on until that terror filled you to the base of your skull and urged your brain to stop, *stop the madness*.

He turned to Mara, his eyes blank, unseeing. 'And you're not supposed to say this, not to your comrades. I can't say it even to Duggie. Instead you say, "Bit of a bad one, that!" or "I see old Robson bought it. Pity, that!" At the same time your inside is screaming with fear and disbelief, with mountainous sorrow for a lost friend and no time to grieve. Grieving's bad for morale, see? And do you know what? You start to think, let the bloody Kaiser have the lot – the Empire, France, Belgium, whatever. Just let it all stop.' He was sweating.

It's only when you get back here you even allow your brain to think it.'

She squeezed his hand. 'You can't go back like this. You're in no fit state.'

His eyes cleared and he stared at her. 'Can't? *Can't?*' He looked round at the empty café and started to bellow: 'Listen to the innocent. Listen to her! Spouting treason with her nursery rhymes. Tempting a poor fellow. Tempting . . .' He grabbed his cap, leapt to his feet and raced out of the café.

Mara followed him, hesitating at the counter. The owner waved her away with his cloth. 'Go and see to the boy. A cup of tea is poor recompense for what he's gone through. Follow him.'

Tommy was fifty yards away, leaning quietly against a wall. 'Sorry about that, sis. Got carried away a bit.'

She took her cue from him. 'That's all right Tommy . . . Tom. Come on, you can take me back to the hotel. Mama'll be thinking I got onto the stage and gave them a turn.'

He was quiet as they walked through the still-busy streets, but when they were within sight of the hotel, he clutched her arm for a second. 'You must keep all that to yourself, Mara. Promise? Not a word.'

She nodded. 'But I won't forget.'

'That was why I told you. There's one more promise.'

She nodded again.

'When you get married, as you no doubt will, and when you have children, as you no doubt will, will you call your son Tom? Not Thomas, nor Tommy, but Tom?'

'Of course I will. And you can be his godfather.'

He shook his head. 'I'll not be there, sis. There's no question of that.'

'Don't be silly,' she began.

'No. Please. I thought that at least tonight, with you, I could tell the truth.'

275

18
Detonations

Mara spread out the pages of her midnight notes on the kitchen table in the house in Bridge Street. She shuffled the pages about in different orders, but no matter how she did it, they did not seem to make any better sense. The story was formless: page after page of heartbreaking detail of a soldier's view of the Battle of the Somme; they expressed chaos, like a long scream delivered by a thousand voices.

Running her fingers down the pages, she could hardly believe that Tommy had said so much in such a short time. Yet this was what she had written through the long night hours at the hotel, after her mother finally got to sleep. And as she read through them again she could hear Tommy's voice, cold with suppressed frenzy, saying the words distinctly and clearly.

The following day Tommy had been smiling and cocky as they waved him and Duggie off at the crowded railway station. She and Kitty had kissed and hugged their soldiers, just like the hundreds of other mothers, sisters and sweethearts around them. Like them they had waved until their men were out of sight.

Kitty blew her nose. 'Why, oh why do we have children, to do this to them?'

'You didn't do it,' said Mara soberly. 'He volunteered to be a soldier. The Kaiser invaded France. Nothing to do with you.'

'But I saw the reason for it, didn't I? In my heart I applauded him for taking the plunge. He was to be a hero. The war is right, surely? We thought that. We think that.'

'What about me? I was jealous of him. I wanted to go myself, to fight. But now I'm glad I'm not a man.'

The train journey home was unbearably long, with neither of them inspired to talk about lighter things; both of their minds were filled with thoughts of Tommy, bitter and aged, ruined by the war and unlikely to come home. In the back of Mara's mind, too, lurked Jean-Paul and Dewi, whose experiences would be similar to her brother's. Worst of all was the thought that there was nothing unique about Tommy's suffering.

They were both relieved to see the slender, erect figure of William at Priorton Station. When he saw them he swept off his hat and held his arms open wide. They both dropped their bags and ran to him and the three of them clasped each other as though to save themselves from drowning.

William stood back a little. 'It was bad?' he said simply.

'Oh, William, he was so terribly changed, so changed,' said Kitty, allowing herself to cry at last. 'My little lad is like some bitter old man. There's no glory in that.'

It was in the car on the way home that Kitty told William of her plans. 'We're to have our photographs taken, William, every last one of us, and send them to him directly. And, as soon as it's humanly possible, we will be married and have a photograph taken of that and sent on to him.'

William coughed. 'That will be the occasion for great satisfaction, my dear, but I do wish its inspiration had not been so very sad,' he said soberly.

Now, in her own house, Mara surveyed the poignant scraps of paper before her and knew with an extraordinary certainty that the jaunty wave, the shaking cap, was the last they would see of Tommy. These pages were all they had left of him – pages whose horror was too great to show those others around her, who loved him so much.

At a loss to know what to think, what to do, she moved to

the window and watched two boys playing hopscotch. They laughed and shouted, as first one, then the other gained the upper hand. She leaned her hot head against the cold windowpane to see more clearly. How many times had she played hilarious games of hopscotch with Tommy on the stone flags of the stableyard at Purley Hall? Their mother Kitty had shown them the game, learned on the street when she was a child. She had hitched up her long, elegant skirts and hopped with them. How they had laughed at her antics! Mara could hear again Tommy crying, 'It's me! Me! I won. I won, didn't I, Mama? Didn't I? Aren't I the best?'

'That's it!' Mara leapt across to the cupboard and scrabbled in the drawer where she kept the work she was doing with Miss Corbell. She found an empty exercise book, pushed the papers aside and began to write about the hopscotch game. And then other games she and Tommy had played together as children. About the treehouse and going fishing with old Luke . . .

That was what she could do! She would write down everything she could remember about Tommy. She would go to her mother and her father and ask about him – even Michael. What had he been like that first day of work? She would write everything down. And then she would put those pages together with these others that told his terrible story of war. And then perhaps it might all fall into place, like the pieces of a jigsaw. But even if it didn't, Tommy would not merely be accounted for as a horrified witness of the terrible way in which men treated men. There would be other things to know him by: things which made him special, a unique person, so easy to love. Things as simple as a child playing hopscotch as his mother had taught him. In this he was both unique and universal.

Clément Poliakov had an essentially practical, even pragmatic nature. In the 1905 uprising he knew it was safe to spit on the revolutionaries, mock them in public. He had kept faith with his contacts on the outer fringes of the aristocracy, people who could ensure favours where necessary for the promotion of his business. And he knew that then, they were not under threat.

But the cataclysm had come in March this year, when the Tsar, finally conceding that the Army could not keep him in power, and for the sake of his 'beloved Russia', had abdicated. Clément Poliakov had loved the Tsar next to God, but he was a businessman, and in business you had to flow with the tide of history. So, he transferred his allegiance to the Duma, the new provisional government. In fact, he told himself, he had always felt much in sympathy with the despised middle classes who had struggled under the heel of the decadent aristocrats.

This government would bring the country together again, salvage the loyalty of the soldiers and prosecute the war with renewed vigour. The members of the Duma were, after all, like himself, men of intelligence and energy, natural leaders of their communities. And as he said to Samuel many times, a proper democracy, led by the middle classes, had been the engine driving England's greatness, had it not?

Poliakov's characteristic mistake was to proclaim his support too loudly, because, to his chagrin, the business of revolution was not yet over. The powerful Menshevik Soviet opposed the Duma, whose days were numbered.

The revolution, incredibly, knocked on Poliakov's own door. Workers in his manufactories were electing their own workers' committees, demanding some say in their hours of work and more equitable rewards for their hard labour. He protested to all and sundry that the profit margins must be sustained to ensure the survival of the business. These people were like children, he said, who wished to eat all their food on the first day of the week.

He longed for things to settle back to where they had been. If that was to be without the benefit of a Tsar, so be it. He stayed awake at night brooding over it. If only he knew which way to turn, the most profitable place to lay his proper allegiance.

There was always the Englishman. He felt that he had some kind of inside knowledge, with Samuel Scorton visiting his house now on his frequent visits to Moscow from Petrograd and Zürich. Clément worked hard to wheedle information out of Scorton, who seemed to know many people at the centre of events.

However, when pressed, Samuel would laugh and say he was just a simple businessman, trying to keep his transactions on line, even in these confused times. The new régime, whatever it turned out to be, would be as dependent on trade and commerce as had the old. And, with Russia withdrawing from the war, and the barriers of neglect and bribery torn away, perhaps trade and commerce would gain their proper focus in the life of a great nation.

Clément, not deceived by this, just fingered his nose and nodded wisely. 'I wait, I just wait, my dear Samuel. You would say my powder is dry. It's true these workers at my Moscow works are spoiling for a fight – I can feel it in my bones. But even that will blow over. We have had flurries like this before.'

Samuel drank his wine and kept his peace. He wasn't here to argue and convince; there were highly paid politicians and diplomats rushing around doing that. It was his job to listen, note and report. And keep communications going with whoever would come out on top of this mess. Clément Poliakov's ostrich-like attitude was not unique, in this or any other revolution. There were many who felt that if they held on long enough, it would all go away. This time, Samuel felt certain, they were wrong.

He was visiting the Poliakov house when a dishevelled manager, sporting two black eyes, came to inform Clément that the workers had ransacked the plant, taken everything they could lift, and destroyed that which they could not move.

From the hallway, Samuel could hear Clément slap his hand on his desk. 'The fools. *Imbéciles!* They will never—' He was interrupted by an almighty bang which threw him across the room with a crash, and brought a section of the ceiling down on top of him.

Samuel, Lucette behind him, rushed in from the hallway. They tore away at a heavy French armoire, lifted plate-like lumps of plaster and uncovered an ashen Clément, who held his arms out to his daughter. 'Lucette, my dear . . .' Then he slumped backwards, his eyes rolling to the back of his head.

Lucette let out a penetrating continuous scream which lasted until Samuel slapped her, and told her to go and see if her stepmother and the others were safe. He thrust her out of the door, poked around the wrecked room and finally pulled the foreman from underneath Clément's desk. The man dusted himself down and looked around unsteadily. 'Monsieur Poliakov?' he said.

'Dead,' said Samuel briefly. 'But that's what you intended, isn't it? You must have signalled to them – or did you bring the bomb yourself? You would need time to get under that desk.'

The man continued to dust himself down without looking at Samuel. 'I don't know why you should say that, sir. I have always been a faithful servant to Monsieur Poliakov.'

'But these are very unusual times?'

At last the man looked at him. He shrugged. 'Yes, these are very unusual times, Monsieur. *They* obliged me to do this. It seems that our masters now wear very different clothes.' He looked wearily at Samuel. 'So what do you propose to do about this?'

Samuel walked to the window and peered out into the crowded street. 'What can a foreigner do? These are very unusual times.' When he turned round, the room was empty save for the slumped corpse of Clément Poliakov. He turned back to the window and saw the foreman fighting his way through the crowd, running across the square as though a thousand devils were after him.

Then his ears were pierced by the sound of wailing and he was obliged to stand and witness the battle between wife and stepdaughter over the corpse of his erstwhile host.

He went across and pulled them apart. 'Stop! Stop! You're hardly better than assassins yourselves.' He took a breath and

282

broke his rule of not interfering with events. 'Now, where can you go? There'll be looters here by tonight. You must get away.'

'But Clément . . .' said Madame Poliakova, wringing her hands.

'You can take him with you. Have him transported to some church and they will give him a decent burial. That's more than he'll get if you stay here. They'll set fire to the house when they finish.'

Madame Poliakova sniffed. 'We could go to the country, perhaps right away, to Kiev. My family . . .'

He knew that in Kiev, too, there would be houses burned, and more detonations, but he said, 'Yes, that's a good idea. Now go and put some things together.' Madame bustled away, wailing afresh.

Lucette stayed in the study. 'I am not going with those country clods to Kiev, Samuel,' she said. 'Without dear Papa,' she glanced affectingly at the shrouded corpse, 'to protect me, they will turn me into one of their servants, or marry me off to some clodhopping cousin with cross eyes and a limp.'

'You'll have to go with her, Lucette. Look out of the window, you foolish girl. It's not safe for you here any more. You must go away.'

She wiped her eyes on her sleeve and sniffed. 'Then I will go to England.'

'England? There's nothing for you there.' He leaned down and picked up a fragment of the grenade and turned it over in his hand. He had seen grenades just like this on his last leave to England. In his brother's factory.

'There is safety for me in England, Samuel. And my beloved Leonora is there. She wants me to come. She writes so in her letters.'

He glanced at her sharply. 'Leonora – letters? You didn't mention . . .' His own letters from Leonora were terrifyingly cold and distant; in tune with his own, he supposed. He had been so sure she would understand that he could not write to her as her lover, not to the house of his father and her mother. He had risked a single love letter, explaining his dilemma, asking her to bear with him. When the work was over they would surely be together. She had not responded. 'You had letters from Leonora?' he persisted.

Lucette pouted. 'I do not tell you everything. But I *do* tell you now, Samuel – either you use one of those rabblerousers you drink vodka with to get me to England, or I sit here in this room and let those vipers kill me . . . or do what they will. They are men, after all, are they not?'

He looked at her through narrowed eyes. He had more to think about today than this spoiled chit of a child. He had had intelligence that Vladimir Ilyich Lenin, surprised by the forward thrust of the revolution at home, was worried that he would miss it, and was negotiating with the Germans safe passage through Germany to Petrograd. *Now*, as Samuel had written in his report, *the crucial stage will begin.*

Mara looked up as the looming figure of her eldest stepbrother cast a shadow over her ledger. 'Morning, Michael.'

'Good morning, Mara. Glad to see you're here so very early. Making up for lost time, no doubt?'

She looked at him steadily and his florid cheeks reddened further. He coughed. 'So how did you find our little brother?'

'Do you want me to tell you the truth, or do you want me to say he was hearty and heroic, full of the joys of spring?'

'There's no cause for mockery, Mara. My enquiry was genuine. I asked how you found him?'

'If you want to know, he was jumpy, haunted. He's lost some hair and some weight. He had black rings round his eyes and he looks at least thirty years old. That was how we found him.' She took a trembling breath.

Michael blinked at her through his new spectacles. 'Don't cry, dear girl.' He put an arm around her shoulder and drew her to her feet. 'Come into my office, and tell me how it was.'

In his office, drinking a glass of water poured from his

own jug, Mara found herself spilling out many of the things which Tommy had told her, confiding much more than she had at home. She only just stopped herself telling him of the exercise book in her drawer at home, where it was all written down.

Michael, standing beside the glass partition which gave him an overview of the whole shop floor, frowned. 'This is too great a burden for you to take on, Mara. Tommy should never have—'

'But who should he have said it to? You weren't there, and he would never tell my mother all this.'

'But he shouldn't have told you.'

'Are you saying he should have kept it to himself, painted a picture of the brave infantry fighting clean battles where no blood flows from the bodies of the dead?'

'That would have been better than leaving you with a nightmare view.'

She started to cry again, and he gave her a starched white handkerchief that smelled faintly of Pansy. She blew her nose. 'Michael, once, at the very beginning, I wanted to go and fight the heroic fight with him. Did you know that? Isn't it the least I can do, to have his nightmares for him? To show sympathy for what he's really going through?'

With some difficulty, he knelt beside her and put his arms round her. 'My dear, that is so brave.'

'Well!'

They both turned round guiltily at the sound of Pansy's voice. Michael hauled himself to his feet. 'My dear,' he mumbled, 'Mara has had such a difficult time down in London. Tommy . . .'

'So it seems.' Pansy smiled sweetly at Mara. 'Perhaps you need some time on your own to collect yourself, my dear? I was just bringing Michael his mid-morning snack, so I have the trap here. I could take you home.'

Mara pushed her hair back and sniffed. 'No, I have work to catch up with. Thank you, Pansy.'

Pansy put a possessive hand on her husband's arm. 'You must insist, Michael dear. The poor child is distraught.'

Michael glanced uneasily from Pansy to Mara and back again. 'Perhaps if she wishes it, dear, Mara should work it off. I myself have found that work is the panacea for most things.'

For a split second, a rare shadow of anger passed across Pansy's mild countenance. Then she smiled and nodded. 'You are always so wise, dearest Michael.' She turned to Mara. 'There, dear, you may go back to work. No doubt you'll feel better in no time.'

Mara found herself dismissed. Sitting back at her ledger she thought wryly that perhaps Pansy should volunteer for the General Staff in France. Certainly the old girl wasn't bad at strategy. Not bad at all.

As she picked up her pen she wondered what had made her blurt all that out to stodgy old Michael, when she had been much more circumspect with her mother and father, even Leonora. The only thing she had shared with her sister was her absolute certainty that Tommy would not come back, and that they had all better start preparing themselves for it now.

The following Sunday, Leonora showed Mara a letter from Lucette Poliakova, the girl she had taught in Moscow. 'Her father has been killed by a bomb, and she says that Samuel has advised her to escape from the dangers in Russia; he apparently insisted that she come here to me, saying I would take care of her. Take care of her!' exploded Leonora. 'How can I do that? There is no extra bedroom at the Lodge, I'm away from the house from dawn till bedtime, and you couldn't thrust her on our lovebirds, could you? It looks as though Kitty and William are doing their courting all over again, don't you think?'

Since her decision to marry him at long last, Kitty and William seemed closer than ever. They spent half the day with Luke in the barn cataloguing William's collection, the other half in the workshop on some new project – something to do with signalling mechanisms for trains. They were never more than six feet from each other. Mara wondered whether it would be different, after the knot was tied at the end of the month. She wondered too whether, in her life, she would ever meet anyone whom she could love that much.

'She could stay with me, I suppose,' said Mara hesitantly. 'Of course I'm out at work myself and the place is not grand. But it is in the town . . . there is more life down there.'

Leonora frowned. 'It'd be too much for you, what with your work and visiting Hélène, and your studies.'

Mara thought about her other self-imposed midnight task of writing about Tommy's life. Then she shook her head. 'It will be all right. There's a spare bedroom, although it has little in it.'

'There are boxes of stuff from the Hall in the barn. We can fake something up from some of that. Lucette's a charmer, mind, but such a spoiled wretch; never lifts a finger for herself.'

Mara grinned at her. 'Well, she'll just have to learn, won't she?'

That evening Leonora brought boxes down from the Lodge and the pair of them set about making Mara's spare bedroom habitable, even pretty. When they had finished, Mara stood there, very still for a moment.

'What is it, Mara?' said Leonora sharply. 'Is there something wrong?'

'I'd give anything, anything, for us to be doing this up for Hélène. That she was coming home whole and well, ready for Jean-Paul. She seemed much better the last two or three times I've seen her.'

'Would you like me to come with you, perhaps to see if she could come home?'

Mara shook her head. 'I'm not sure. I couldn't take care of her like I should.'

Leonora paused, then ventured, 'So you think Jean-Paul will come, eventually?'

'Yes.'

'But not Tommy?'

'No.'

There was a long silence before Leonora said, 'And what will you do when Jean-Paul comes back?'

'I'll probably be in college by then, so the house will be empty.'

'No, I mean something else. About Jean-Paul – about you and him.'

'I told you, there's nothing left. I'll have to tell him.'

'Do you know, you've become a very cool customer, Mara.'

'Have I? No, I didn't know. Must be the war.'

The next night Mara stayed back at work after all the others had gone, to make up for work lost on her trip. She was aware of Michael moving about behind his glass panel, and the odd echo from the factory floor told her the night shift had taken over. With no other women in the office to interrupt, she got on quickly with her work. She had just checked the second lot of orders when the door opened and her father entered with a bulky package under his arm. 'Well, Tuppence, are you joining the night shift?'

She stood up behind her desk. 'What are you doing here, Pa?' She looked behind him. 'Where's Mother?'

'I persuaded her to stay at home just this once. She and Luke are making a party supper to celebrate the completion of this project.' He heaved his package on to her desk.

'Is that the wonderful signalling thing?'

'Yes. I thought I might catch Michael and show it to him. It's a project for after the war, when those ghastly things he's making now are not needed.'

'Well, he's in there.' She nodded towards the door. 'You're lucky to have caught him.'

He went through, and she heard the rumble of their exchange and some laughter. She put her head down and got on. Five minutes later they came out, obviously in very good humour with each other. Michael looked across at her. 'I'll say one thing for you, Mara Scorton, you have a very clever father.'

'And mother,' said William.

Michael laughed. 'If you say so. Now, Mara, we're going down to the far end of the bottom section. There is another problem with the continuity belt down there, and I thought this genius of a father of ours might take a look at it, as he has graced the Works with his presence.'

She smiled after them, thinking that it was a bit more like the old days, seeing the two of them together again. Pansy Clarence had a lot to answer for.

She was entering and checking her third batch of advice notes when she felt the explosion, was catapulted from her chair and showered with glass from the partition. In seconds she had hauled herself to her feet. She put her stool upright, sat on it and peered at her hands in the semi-darkness. They were pouring with blood from glass cuts; she felt her face and knew she was bleeding there too. She looked around for Joe Bly, for Mr Clonmel. No! No! This was not Hartlepool. That was before. This was Priorton. There was no bombardment here. Surely the guns could not reach here from the North Sea?

Then she leapt up and started to run. 'Michael! Father! Oh my God, Father!' There were others running beside her, but they all had to stop at the entrance to the bottom section, which had collapsed in on itself and was belching smoke and dust as though it were alive. Her ears tuned into the shrieks and shouts and she started to pull at the planks and girders closest to her. 'Papa! Michael! Oh dear God, where are you in all this?'

'Watch out here, dear boy,' said Duggie out of the side of his mouth. 'Soggy bit coming up. Just about digests you, this mud.'

Snow floated down, settling delicately on their shoulders. 'Snow in April,' grunted Tommy. 'Would you credit it?'

They were seventh and eighth in a single line of soldiers cautiously making their way towards a destination which, they were assured by their Sergeant, was always over the next rise. Tommy jumped to a tufted bit of ground which looked solid enough. To their left, half a dozen tanks had sunk in the mud and were stuck at strange angles, like floundering beasts. Scattered in their wake were Lewis-gun magazines and rifle-grenades discarded by their carriers as they fled.

'Down!' Tommy slammed his hand on Duggie's shoulder at the thump of a barrage from their left and the crackle of gunfire. The man in front of Duggie fell, his head torn away. They hauled themselves to their feet and walked over the fallen man, stumbling and slithering, throwing out their arms to keep their balance. The line scattered now and then as a shell burst near them, then doggedly set off again on their ordained route.

They walked for another sodden five minutes, then the Sergeant called a halt again to get his bearings.

Tommy and Duggie stood, the ground sheets over their shoulders dripping onto the heels of their boots. Duggie cupped his shaking hands to create some shelter to light his cigarette. Tommy looked around, his coldness and weariness making his interest merely clinical, as though all this were happening to quite another person. The contours of the roads and the shell-holes were softened by the rippling mud. As far as the eye could see, the land was muddy plateau, bare of any flower or grass, pockmarked by stubby trees and short stretches of hedge which lent an eerily domestic presence to this inhuman landscape.

A shell dropped to his left and mud sloshed onto Tommy's face like rain. He sat down, put his rifle on the ground in front of him and kicked it away. 'That's it. I'm not going any further.'

His action caused a wave of concern right down the file which needed no words to set the Sergeant moving in their direction. 'Get up, will you?' Duggie kicked his gun back by his hand. 'Get up, you silly bugger. Men have been shot for less.'

'I'm going nowhere.'

Duggie leaned down and hauled him to his feet.

'What's this? said the Sergeant close behind him.

'Private Scorton slipped in this bleedin' mud. 'Scuse the language, Sergeant.' Duggie thrust Tommy's rifle back into his hand. 'Ain't that so, son?'

'Yeah,' said Tommy wearily, hoisting the rifle back over his shoulder. 'That's so, Sergeant.' The snow had transformed itself to delicate dew drops clinging to the Sergeant's luxurious moustache. 'Just slipped in the mud.'

The Sergeant took Tommy's shoulder and shook it. 'You watch it, son. We all need you here. Don't forget that.' He looked along the line and raised his voice. 'Just sixty more yards, lads, by those pillboxes, see? We're to dig in there.'

'Dig?' Duggie's voice came from behind Tommy now. 'The man jests.'

They plodded on.

'Here, lads.' The bellow of the Sergeant in front drew them to a halt. 'We 'ave been 'ere before. You may or may not recognise it, but we 'ave.'

This was to be their jumping-off ground: a staggered line of battered dugouts occupied in turn twice by the Germans and once before by themselves. Now it was to be their turn again. The one they were assigned to, with two others, was not bad. It was well boarded and deeply supported in the German manner. Before squatting on his haunches in the driest corner Duggie poked beneath the duckboard and lifted out a German belt complete with buckle. He left it on his bayonet and passed it to Tommy. 'There y'are, son. You can have that. Bring you luck, that will. There now, can you hear? The shelling's stopped.'

Tommy forced a smile onto his face and tucked the belt into his backpack. 'Good thing too, Duggie.'

They got out their dry-pack rations and cold tea, and those who had them lit their cigarettes. Soon the firefly glow of cigarettes was all they could see in a sea of blackness. They all jumped as the Sergeant dropped into their dugout. 'Clean forgot, lads. Post.' He called names and handed the letters round. Tommy was last. They lit a shaded lamp so they could read them.

Tommy read his, then slumped back, his hand over his eyes. 'It's from Mara,' he whispered.

'From your little sister, Tom?' Duggie frowned.

Tommy nodded and handed over the fragile sheet. Duggie peered at it: the neat flowing writing talked of a terrible accident, of their father and their eldest brother being killed in an explosion at the Works. He was not to worry, she wrote. They did not suffer. Remember before, when William had been so ill? It was nothing like that. Clean and quick.

Duggie whistled. 'Explosion? Ye gods! Talk about coals to Newcastle! That's the kind of letter the Colonel writes to the Mums and Dads.' He put a hand on Tommy's shoulder. 'Are you all right, son?'

'All right?' said Tommy. 'Yes, I'm all right.' Then he turned his face to the mud wall of the dugout and appeared to go to sleep.

The next morning, when Duggie woke up from a cramped and freezing sleep, Tommy was gone. Duggie crawled around to look for him in the vicinity of the dugout, dodging the sporadic dawn chorus of the German snipers. He bumped into the Sergeant on his travels and had to explain his purpose.

The Sergeant shook his head. 'Trouble, there. I knew it with that lad.'

'He's a good boy, Sergeant. A good lad. I promise you.'

'Private O'Hare,' the Sergeant ducked as another sniper's bullet cracked overhead, 'they're all good lads, every last mother's son of 'em. Now get back in the bloody dugout, or I'll be *two* men down.'

19

Bequests

There was nothing to put in the coffins.

At first Mara and Leonora did not reveal to Kitty that not a hair, not a scrap of her beloved husband remained. They merely said that she must not see William; she must remember him as he had been, fit and well. It was Pansy who let the cat out of the bag. She arrived in Michael's motor car, dressed in deepest black, to discuss, in her timid, worried way, the problem of the weight of the coffins. 'It will be odd, there being nothing in them, of course.'

Mara came into the room just as she was saying it. 'Mama . . .' she began.

Kitty put out a hand to quieten her. 'What about the weight in the coffins, Pansy?' She frowned. Unlike Pansy, whose face had its usual bland smoothness, Kitty's face was white and strained, her eyes red and swollen with weeping.

Pansy adjusted the bag on her knee. 'We must get the undertakers to weigh them down somehow. It will look so undignified if the bearers race down the aisle as though it were a mere plank they carried on their shoulders.'

'A plank?' Kitty raised wondering eyes to Mara.

'Mama.' Mara sat beside her mother and took her hand. 'There was nothing. No scrap, no sign, not of either of them. In all that devastation . . .'

Kitty pulled her hand away. 'But why? Why didn't you tell me? Do you think I am to be pandered to like some imbecile?'

'I'm sure the child meant nothing by it,' said Pansy sooth-ingly. 'I—'

Kitty turned on her. 'Oh, will you shut up, woman, with your simpering vulgarities, your blind mask of virtue.'

Pansy stood up, clutching her bag to her meagre bosom. 'Well! Well! I understand you are distraught, Kitty. But I too have lost my hus—'

'And all you're concerned about is what people think!'

Pansy looked at her for a second, her normally soft face hardening. 'How do we know ourselves, Kitty, except by our standing in the community? My dear sister Heliotrope was adamant about this. And my dear husband Michael had great standing in this community. It is my duty to protect and promote this. I had great respect for him and will insist on respect for his memory.' She looked Kitty up and down. 'And Michael's father William had respect in this community, too – even if you do not. And you have so little feeling for him that you will not even wear black.'

Kitty leapt up at that and took Pansy by the neck of her black crêpe dress, shaking her like a black kitten which has made a mess on the carpet.

Mara stood back.

'I will have you know,' said Kitty grimly, giving the scrawny neck another shake, 'I loved William from the top of his head to the back of his heels. We were one when we worked together shoulder to shoulder in the daytime, and when we made love at night.'

Mara wondered whether Pansy's purple hue was caused by her embarrassment or by the fact that she was probably choking.

'. . . I have loved him to the core of my being for twenty-five years. And I will *not* wear black, which he hated. Nor will I put on a show to pretend a body is there when it is not!'

Mara put her hands on her mother's shoulders, and Kitty

stopped throttling Pansy, who staggered away, aghast. Breathing heavily, she smoothed down her dress and picked up her bag.

Kitty took a breath. 'I will love and honour William all the rest of my days, and I will ensure that he is remembered in this town, and that Michael, a dear boy whom I loved from a child, many many more years than you have known him, will be remembered as his son.'

Unsteadily Pansy made her way to the door. When she turned her face had paled to the colour of ice. 'You will be sorry for this, you . . . harlot. I will make you sorry.'

The door slammed behind her and Kitty turned to Mara. 'Oh dear, I was very unkind, wasn't I?'

'She deserved it,' said Mara fiercely.

Kitty was silent for a moment. 'I'm pleased she came to stir her trouble, though. Otherwise, because of your kindness, I would have done something which is a nonsense.'

'But there has to be a funeral, Mama.'

'We can't bury . . . nothing. It's a nonsense. William would have laughed at it.' Strangely, the encounter with Pansy had lit something inside Kitty which had begun to melt her frozen despair. 'We will do something else. We will have a service remembering him, how modest, how clever, how quiet, how funny he could be.' Then she jumped up and caught Mara's hands. 'And we'll build something. We'll build a library for his books and his collection, where everyone can come. A workshop for inventors! That's better than the mockery of an empty coffin.'

Mara hugged her mother. 'Wonderful, Mama. What a wonderful idea.'

Kitty frowned. 'Mara, where's the machine, our signalling mechanism? William took it that day . . .'

'It's in Michael's office. They left it there when they went down.'

Kitty was already at the door. 'Come on. We'll go and get it. I don't trust that Pansy an inch. Not one inch.'

*　　*　　*

Tommy ducked behind an out-jutting wall as three men in a strange officer's uniform – Australian, perhaps – came into the *estaminet* and took a table under a narrow window. An elderly woman approached them, carrying a tray with a bottle of wine and three glasses; she had to endure an argument to insist that yes, *messieurs*, this was absolutely the only wine which they had and no, *messieurs*, there was no brandy. A little coffee, perhaps, and some bread and meat – but no brandy.

Tommy bit into his own bread, and was just taking a mouthful of wine when a tall thin man with a dark beard slid along the bench to sit opposite him. The man addressed him loudly in rapid French which he did not understand. Tommy took a mouthful of bread and grunted as he chewed, a noise which could be interpreted as assent or dissent, depending on what was expected.

The man murmured to him then, almost under his breath. 'It is Tommy Scorton, Mara's brother?'

'Jean-Paul?' His sense of shock must have penetrated the room because one of the Australians shot a glance in their direction.

Then the bearded man started to talk again in rapid French using two voices, taking the two parts in the conversation. The Australian shouted for another bottle of wine and more bread, and the moment passed.

Tommy finished his bread and wine with slow deliberation, cocking his head at Jean-Paul's cues, nodding now and then. At last he finished and wiped his mouth on his sleeve. Jean-Paul threw an arm round his shoulders, drew him to his feet and guided him through to the back of the café, still chattering. Once outside they leaned against the wall and breathed more easily.

'What are you doing here?' whispered Tommy.

'Same as you, I think. I lost track of my unit and just had enough of it. I'm going back to England, through Boulogne.'

'You can't do that. They arrested a feller there the other

296

week. Swanning around with medals, silly blighter. Shot at dawn.'

Jean-Paul looked Tommy up and down. 'You got rid of your uniform.'

'I buried it. Walked for hours through the night, then I found this stuff on a washing line, changed into it and buried my uniform. The farmhouse the clothes came from had been blown to smithereens. Funny, the washing still there.'

'You wish to go home?'

Tommy slid down the wall until he was crouched on his haunches. 'I have to. My father died. He was blown up in my brother's factory. With my brother's explosives, I assume.'

'Mr Scorton? That is a terrible thing, Tommy. I am so sorry. He was a fine man. A very gentle man.' Jean-Paul looked distressed.

Tommy stared at him for a long minute. 'There is a God.'

Jean-Paul gazed along the wrecked village street, at the pall of destruction on the horizon. 'You can say that here?' he wondered.

'What I needed today, above all, was to hear someone say that thing about my father. To speak to someone who knew him. To remind me of what a good man he was.' Tommy stood away from the wall.

'Now where are you going?'

'Now that I've met you, and now that we've talked, I'm going to disinter my uniform and go back to try and find my unit.'

'Will you not come with me, to Boulogne?'

Tommy shifted his weary head. 'It wasn't meant to be. I am not meant to go from here. I can see that now.' He shook hands heartily with Jean-Paul. 'You will tell them I love them, won't you?' he said gruffly. 'And that I'm sorry about Pa. And, wherever I am, I'll watch out for them, in Heaven or on Earth. I'll dream of them. Will you say that?'

Jean-Paul put his arms round Tommy and hugged his resisting body. 'I will tell them, you can be very sure of that.'

Tommy watched Jean-Paul mount a battered bicycle and shoot off down the road, then he turned and started to walk back the way he had come. He had walked a mile when he whipped round at a shout behind him. 'Hey, tommy!'

It was the Australians, on horseback and full of the bad wine of the *estaminet*. One turned to the other two. 'There, told you it was one of those English shirkers. Spotted him in the bar.' He toed Tommy with his muddy boot. 'And where might you be going, tommy?'

Tommy looked at him for a minute, then shrugged. 'I'm on my way back to my unit,' he said.

They giggled at that. 'Isn't that what they all say, these shirkers?' the same Australian continued. 'I tell you what, tommy, you hop up behind and we'll give you a lift.'

'I have to collect my uniform.'

'Don't worry about that, tommy. There'll be no need for that where you're going. Now hop on.'

The second Australian was fingering his pistol.

Tommy took the proffered arm and leapt up behind his interrogator. He felt calm about his fate. With no uniform or weapons, and being discovered in the wrong place, there was no question, no question at all that he would be up for desertion.

Michael's coffin was buried with full honours and a packed church, with two priests and all the leading citizens of Priorton in close attendance. Kitty, Mara, Leonora and old Luke found a place at the back of the church and listened to a closely scripted eulogy which placed Michael instantly in the league of the angels. Kitty thought tenderly about the sturdy, serious boy whom she, not much older than him, had taken on when she joined forces with William.

Leonora thought of the instant older stepbrother who, in

league with Samuel, had transformed her, a little intruder in their masculine abode, into their Guinevere. She wondered if Samuel had received his telegram telling of the double tragedy. Mara thought of Michael's last brief kindness to her, cut short by the bustling Pansy. She thought of Tommy, out God knew where, unable to say his last farewell to his father. Luke sat impassively, his fine lids down over his eyes, looking older than the church itself.

The later service, with no coffin, and purely in remembrance of William, intended to be small and intimate, drew even greater crowds. As well as the notables from the town, there were generations of men who had worked with, and for, Mr William Scorton at the factory. Miss Aunger and all the staff of the shop came; even the cleaner Mrs Grayling paid her respects. The Commandant and the senior staff from the military hospital attended, in full uniform.

Listening to the rolling spate of words Mara, sitting beside Luke, was filled with a sense of Tommy's pain as he told her of his time in France, and she allowed herself to mourn the boy she once knew. She found herself composing in her head a letter to him, saying how dense the feeling was in the church, how filled with their father's sheer kindness, how that very kindness seemed to be flowing outwards and onwards, not ceasing with these holy words, which talked of the ending of a life and a rising in the world to come. She found herself closing her eyes tight and praying that William, now free of his body, would be with Tommy to give him strength in the hard days to come.

When the time came for the eulogy there was a stir as Kitty, dressed in a high-necked coat of darkest green velvet, stood up and turned towards the congregation to speak. She spoke of the man she knew who, she was certain, was still by her side. She told the story of their almost-lifelong partnership and finished with the simple sentence: 'Here was a good man.'

Mara put her hand on Luke's and he allowed it to lie there.

The following day Kitty, Leonora, Mara and Pansy were summoned to a solicitor's office, next door to Michael's tall house in the Market Square.

Mr Sleight's face was grave as he looked from Pansy to Kitty, then to Leonora and Mara. 'There is a problem here, Miss Rainbow. For many years I have been harassing Mr Scorton to make a proper will. He has demurred and demurred.' The solicitor looked round. 'I meet this sometimes. Those who think the making of a will is the beginning of the end. They do not wish to leave this life. Even if one understands the reasons,' he turned very deliberately and bowed formally to Kitty, who nodded gravely, acknowledging the implied compliment, 'one has to say it is most ill-advised. I feel that Mr William Scorton, good man that he was, was somewhat unworldly.' He shuffled his papers about and fished one out. 'There is one document, signed and properly sealed just a month ago. I can't imagine what drove him to this, but we have this at least to be thankful for. It is a properly drawn up deed of gift to you, Miss Rainbow, according you absolute and unassailable ownership of all his books and implements; and the whole of his collection of antiquities . . .'

Kitty clasped her hands, a smile of pleasure on her face.

'. . . with a request – but not, I must aver, a condition – a *request* to keep them together as a whole entity. It was, he was kind enough to inform me, intended to be a wedding gift to you. Hence the document. Would that the documents of the marriage which were to be drawn up had existed at that time, then my news for you today would not be quite so disturbing.'

He fished out another document from the heap on his desk and turned it over, looking at it very carefully. 'Mr Michael Scorton, however, did leave a will. Effectively he leaves everything . . .' He put on his glasses and read '. . . without hold or let, to my dearest wife Pansy Clarence Scorton.'

Pansy stroked the black suede gloves which lay across her knee. Mara stifled a great desire to lean across and smack her face. Leonora frowned and put the tips of her fingers on Mr Sleight's desk. 'You are trying to tell us something, Mr Sleight.'

He nodded gravely. 'In the absence of any will, the whole of Mr William Scorton's estate would have gone to Mr Michael Scorton, as his eldest son. As, unfortunately, father and son met their demise . . . er . . . simultaneously, the whole of Mr William's estate will go to Mrs Pansy Clarence Scorton, as Mr Michael Scorton's heir. Everything, everything, goes to Mrs Pansy Clarence Scorton.'

'What?' Mara leapt to her feet. 'But that's not fair! Papa would never have wished that. You're his lawyer. You should—' She felt her mother's hand on her arm.

'Calm down, Mara,' Kitty said, drawing herself to her feet. 'There's nothing Mr Sleight can do about this. There are many "shoulds". I *should* have married your father years ago. He *should* have made a will. But this is not the case. Mr Sleight can do nothing about it.'

Leonora was at her shoulder. 'Come on, Kitty. Mara! We have no more business here.'

Pansy stood up. 'Oh, this is all so very awkward. Dear Kitty! You know I would never see you in difficulty.' She put a hand on Kitty's arm. 'You can see I have private business here now with Mr Sleight. But if you just wait outside we'll have a little chat. I am sure there is something I may do for you and your poor girls.'

Kitty looked at Pansy's small hand, impelling her to remove it from her green velvet sleeve. 'I've always worked for a living, Pansy, and I always will. My daughters too. We will need nothing from you.'

Pansy smiled faintly. 'Always so independent, dear Kitty! Now I hope you won't attack me for this, but wasn't that very independence, in the end, your downfall? And as for Mara's job, well, we shall see. Perhaps it would not be appropriate now . . . Anyway, we will talk about that at the Works on Monday morning, Mara. There is the motor car to collect, of course. That must be part of the estate, I imagine, Mr Sleight?'

'We should have left you to rot in Hartlepool,' said Mara contemptuously.

'Mara!' said Kitty. She turned to shake the lawyer by the hand. 'Thank you, Mr Sleight. I'm certain that you did all you could for me and for my children.' She laughed. 'Anyway, who knows? This may be a wonderful new beginning. I never did want William's money, unlike some.' Her eyes flickered sideways towards Pansy. 'Perhaps it is right that he leaves me as he found me. Independent and my own woman.'

Leonora chuckled too and winked at Mara, willing her to do the same. 'Right as always, Kitty. No one, till now, in our family could be described as a sycophant or a parasite.' She nodded with open malice at Pansy.

Mara laughed with her and they all swept out, arm in arm, past Pansy, whose cheeks were bright red with anger. In the Square outside it was market day, and the streets and the stalls were so busy humming with life that it was hard to think that there was a war on.

'Phew!' said Mara. 'Mama, you were brilliant. What an act. That showed her, the little worm.'

Kitty pulled down her coat and fastened her belt a bit tighter. 'Act? Who said it was an act? I meant every word of it. You can't go back to the Works, Mara, but aren't you nearly ready to sit your matriculation exam? It will be college for you soon. And Leonora can go to a big hospital and train to be a proper nurse, not just one wearing a red cross who lays trays and empties bedpans.'

'I wanted to go back to Russia,' said Leonora. 'But . . .'

'How can you go?' said Kitty. 'There's a full-scale revolution going on there.'

'Even so there's no money for college, or for nurse's training. We could—'

'There's no good being second best, is there?' said Kitty. 'I have things – jewels your father gave me, watches he

302

made for me through the years. I can sell those to pay for all that.'

'And you?' said Mara. 'What about you?'

'Well, I can go back to the shop and work for Miss Aunger, if need be. And there's the signalling mechanism that I worked on with your father. William may not have left a will, but the device is patented in my name. Who needs factories and manor houses and motor cars, when we've all got our heads and our hands?'

'Unlike Pansy Clarence,' said Mara.

'Unlike Pansy Clarence,' said Leonora.

'The house?' yelped Mara. 'Won't Pansy even own the Lodge, the roof over your head?'

'She'll have us out on our ear for sure. Did you see that look in her eye?' said Leonora.

'You can live in Bridge Street with me,' Mara offered.

'No need,' said Kitty. 'There's Waterman's Cottage – William's workshop. It always was and always will be mine. I paid for it with my own money. I insisted.' She put her hand to the door of the motor car, then pulled it back as though it burnt her. 'Ouch. I forgot. The car belongs to that woman now.'

'That's all right, Mama,' said Mara. 'We can walk.'

It took them nearly an hour to walk to the Lodge, and they were foot-weary when they arrived. In the distance they could see a figure on the doorstep.

'Who on earth is that?' said Mara. The person was sitting on a trunk and holding a small case in one hand and a fur muff in another. The figure leapt up and flung itself into Leonora's arms. '*Darrling* Leonora. *Sesistra!* Here I am, and here are you to *safe* me from that devilish place.'

'Good grief,' groaned Kitty to Mara. 'Please God, not another waif or stray.'

Leonora was laughing with Lucette, as always amused at her excess. 'Kitty, Mara, may I present Miss Lucette Poliakova, late of Moscow. And yes, she *is* a waif or stray. And don't

303

worry, Kit. Mara has a room all prepared for her.' She smiled demurely at Mara. 'It's the least she can do, seeing that she was the one who lumbered us with the delectable Pansy Clarence!'

'Are you all right, my boy?' Duggie had loped up to Tommy and was facing the other way, lighting a cigarette.

Tommy held up his handcuffs, and pulled away in vain at the wheel of the field gun to which he was shackled. 'I'm fine. Can't you see?'

'How long did you get?'

'Twenty-one days' field punishment number one: two hours chained to this and sixteen hours running around at the double. Hero's work.'

'You're a fool to yourself, my boy. Running off like that was insane. Then for Gossake! Trying to come back!'

'I met a Frenchman who knows my family. Said kind words about my father. It was worth it.'

'Worth all this? You won't survive twenty-one days of this caper.'

'I won't have to. One time when they're keeping me on the hop, I'll hop off again.' He giggled.

Duggie threw his precious half-smoked cigarette down in the mud. 'You're bleedin' mad, boy. You should be in *horspital*, not chained to that friggin' wheel.'

Tommy laughed shrilly. 'Language, Duggie, language! Do you know you've lost all the marks of the gentleman's gentleman while you've been down here? No class at all, *dear boy*.'

'I'm bleedin' tellin' yer, do it once more an' they'll top yer, sure as God made little apples,' Duggie growled, looking round in the gloom uneasily.

'Ah. God! Now you mention Him I have to tell you He's here. I know it, Duggie. He sent Jean-Paul to say that good thing about my Pa, so He'll take care of me when I hop off again. He'll take care of me if they top me. They can't do anything to me now, Duggie! Them or Fritz . . .'

304

'You're mad, me boy, mad as May butter.'

Tommy chortled. 'Mad? Have you looked round here lately, Duggie?' He clutched at the other man with his chained hand. 'Promise me, Duggie, promise me that if I do hop it, and they do top me, you'll be there when it happens? You'll see, and then you'll go and tell my mother and my sister what really happened? Don't let it be blanked out.' His hand dropped, and he looked closely at the other hand which was red raw beneath its constraining chain. 'Hop and top, hop and top – see, Duggie, I'm a poet and I don't know it.' He giggled again. 'Hop-and-top. Hop-and-top.'

'Private O'Hare!' The Sergeant's bellow made Duggie jump. 'What are you doing, talking to that scum? Didn't I tell you he was beyond the pale? Beyond the bloody pale.'

20

Retrenchment

In the first few days of their acquaintance, Lucette fascinated Mara. The Russian woman's manner and her richly curling version of English, her elaborately decorated clothes and her fluttering hands – all these had an exotic appeal.

These days, it was true, Mara had a fair amount of time to observe her guest. The day after the reading of Michael's will, she had received, by messenger, a package with all the odd personal things she had left in her office at the Works, and a warmly hypocritical letter from Pansy, saying *given the situation etc etc* . . . There was also a crisp five-pound note. She thrust the letter and the money back into the envelope and gave it to the man. 'Will you kindly return this to Mrs Pansy Scorton, and say I have no need of any of it?'

Refusing to allow herself to be distracted by her sister-in-law, she got out her books and started to spend half the day studying for her examinations, and the other half continuing her memoir of Tommy and writing a letter to Dewi Wilson, which was a month overdue. And she never missed her visits to Hélène.

Now, of course, there was Lucette to keep her entertained. Warned by Leonora, she carefully showed her guest the household tasks she was expected to do and left her to do them. 'Two pins and she'll have you waiting on her hand and foot!' Leonora had said.

When Lucette realised she wasn't going to be waited on

hand and foot, she shrugged and got on with her tasks quite efficiently, chattering gaily as she did so. She had decided from the outset that she and Mara would have a romantic friendship. After all, they were both beautiful, even if Mara was somewhat tall. They were of an age, and had they not both lost their darling fathers cruelly, in almost identical events? Such tragedy bound people closer, did it not?

In the evenings she painted Mara colourful pictures of her life in Moscow, and told ghoulish tales of the depredations of the revolutionaries. 'Without Samuel I would not have survived,' she declared on the second evening, her hand pressed to her bosom. 'He was determined to save me from those fiends.'

Mara smiled. 'He's quite the adventurer, our Samuel.'

'And he loves me!' declared Lucette.

'Loves you?'

'Passionately.'

'But he's old, Lucette. Anyway, much older than you.'

'The same age as my dear father,' said Lucette complacently. 'And he too loved me passionately.'

'Passionately?'

'Did not your Papa love you passionately?'

Mara found herself blushing. There was something in the air which she could not fathom. 'He loved me. I know that, though he didn't say much about it.'

Lucette looked at her through narrowed eyes then changed tack. 'And Samuel, he loves me like a father and like a lover.'

'Perhaps you've got it wrong,' said Mara desperately.

'Wrong? Wrong?' Lucette scrabbled in her bag and pulled out a small wallet from which she took a letter. She thrust it under Mara's nose. 'Look at it. Does he not love me? See what he says.'

Unwillingly, Mara read: *My Darling, I tremble at the risk of writing to you in these terms, but just once, I must say what I feel. My own one, how long will it be until there is just you and*

I? Never have I loved anyone as I love you. The hours we have spent together are jewels in my heart. I have so much to do in this place but thoughts of you distract me. I have to put those thoughts away in a steel box at the centre of my heart and get on as though nothing has happened. Bear with me, my darling. This is the last time I can write to you in these terms until the world rights itself and we can be together in the blazing light of day. Till then we must be careful. Ever your Sam.

Mara thrust the letter back at her. 'I mustn't read this, Lucette. You must let no one read it. It's private. Personal.'

Lucette put it carefully back in her folder, and her eyes glittered at Mara in the lamplight. 'But it shows,' she insisted, 'it shows that he loves me, doesn't it?'

'Oh yes,' admitted Mara. 'It shows that.'

She was troubled at the confidence, and wondered whether it might be wise to speak to Leonora about it.

In the week after the funeral Kitty and her daughters were confronted with a whole new set of circumstances. Mara lost her job. Kitty quitted the Lodge before Pansy had time to throw her out. She and Leonora moved in with Luke at the Waterman's Cottage. They adapted one end of William's workshop as bedroom space for themselves, concealed discreetly behind Chinese screens filched from the Purley House stores.

Kitty did visit Miss Aunger and ask for a job, but had to withdraw very quickly as the sales lady made a great fuss about giving the shop back to her wholesale. Instead, Kitty put cards in shop-windows in Priorton, saying she would mend watches and clocks at any reasonable price. She was relishing the challenge of not to be put down by Pansy; the battle was keeping her mind from the loss of William, at least in her waking hours.

Mara and Lucette spent part of every day at the Waterman's Cottage. One afternoon, when Leonora was between shifts, Kitty and her daughters gathered together in the workroom to sort out what they could sell.

Luke helped them to make three substantial piles of goods. One – by far the smallest of the three – consisted of objects from Kitty's life with William with which they would not part under any circumstances. The second pile consisted of items of which they were quite fond, but which they would sell if it were necessary. The third group, a veritable heap of clothes and jewellery, boxes and knick-knacks, was to be sold immediately.

They surveyed their three piles. 'There now,' said Kitty. 'This will provide our start-up fund. There'll be money here to make sure you get to teaching college, Mara, and for you to get your proper nursing training, Leonie – if that's what you both decide. There'll be enough here for me to do further work on the signalling mechanism – even perhaps to manufacture it, after the war. No matter what else we do, we'll all take a share in this. We'll be equal partners – and this time, I'll get Mr Sleight to draw up the proper papers.'

Mara nodded. 'All drawn up, good and proper. Start as we mean to go on.' The door at the end of the workroom opened and they all swung round, half-expecting William to come through. It was Luke, puffing and blowing under the weight of a substantial box. Mara rushed over and took it from him. 'Where do you want it, Luke?'

'If you put it there, Mara, I would be very grateful.' He pointed to the 'definitely for sale' pile. She placed it on the floor beside the pile.

'Open it,' he said.

Mara opened it. 'Heavens!' Nestling there in neat lines were row upon row of sovereigns glittering in the autumn sunshine filtering down from the great skylights.

'What's this, Luke?' said Kitty quietly.

'It is all the money my brothers and I earned from Mr Scorton in these past years. Except some sums for a journey we made once, back to Egypt. And there is gold there, from our father's house in Alexandria.' He paused a second, remembering. 'It is all there, except for the small sums I have paid at the hospital, for my brothers Matthew and John before they died.'

Kitty was perplexed. 'What do you want us to do with it?'

'It is to go on the pile,' he said. 'It is for Mara to go to her teaching college. It is for Leonora to do her nursing. And it is to start a factory to make those little machines. And perhaps, afterwards, it will be something for Tommy to come home to after the war. And then perhaps some money for the building we will make for the books and all Mr Scorton's old things.'

It was the longest speech they had ever heard Luke make.

'Luke, we can't. We could never . . .' blurted out Leonora.

The old man folded his arms. 'Do you say that this box with its contents does not have the currency of the other items on that pile? Things gathered there so that this family, which my brothers and I have loved for forty years, may prosper?'

'No . . . no.' Leonora was confused.

Mara shook her head. 'You have us all bewildered with your kindness, Luke. You and your brothers have been our family too. You really want this?'

'I do.' He was being very patient, treating them all as children.

'Right,' said Kitty thoughtfully. 'You shall be a full quarter partner in all our enterprises, Luke. The workshop for the machine will be the Rainbow Works; the building for the books will be the Scorton Institute. What we have here now on this mat will be the foundation for all that. I'll get Mr Sleight to draw up the papers straight away. We will all be legal partners.'

'You may do what you wish, Kitty,' said Luke. 'Mr Sleight already has my papers, which say that this is yours when I die.'

Each of the women stifled the instinct to hug the old man, knowing his abhorrence of effusive gestures. Only as children had they been allowed to touch him naturally, to hold his hand and hug him when they felt like it.

Luke turned away towards the stairs. 'Will there be five for supper, Kitty? The young Russian woman waited awhile, and has gone off to walk in the woods.'

'Lucette?' Mara put her head in her hands. 'Uh oh. I forgot her, with all this happening.'

Leonora grinned. 'She'll be on the prowl, after the walking wounded from the hospital. She hungers for male company, does our Lucette.'

The day after the setting up of the partnership, Mara left Lucette with Kitty, and went to visit Hélène. Without the use of the car, she now had a train journey and a long walk to get to the hospital. Leonora gave up her afternoon sleep in the middle of her split-shift and came with her, as had been her custom lately. Mara never quite knew whether this was a kind of penance for having been instrumental in Hélène being in the asylum, or whether the hospital itself interested her.

Leonora often talked with the nurses and sisters while Mara sat with Hélène and turned the pages of a picture book or brushed the woman's hair out of its tight plaits and into something like its former glory. Hélène had lost much of her English now; the words she retained she spoke with a strong Durham accent, picked up from other patients and some of the nurses. At the end of the visit Hélène's hair always had to be returned to its tight plaits, but on good days, the process seemed to soothe her.

In the train on the way back, Mara told Leonora about Lucette's tale. 'She says Samuel is in love with her.'

'In love?' Leonora laughed. 'Lucette flirts with everyone, you and me included. And she thinks everyone is in love with her.'

'No. No. She showed me this love letter he had sent her. I know she shouldn't, but she did. I've never seen such passion, Leonie. It sizzled off the page. It was certainly his writing, his name at the end. He must love her very dearly.'

Leonora was silent.

'What do you think, Leonie?'

312

'If that's what you saw, you must be right.'

'But what do you think? Don't you think it must be wonderful to have someone love you like that?'

'I'm sure it must. Now, Mara, would you mind if I dropped my head on your shoulder and tried to get some shut-eye? I'm back on duty at five and how I'll keep awake till eleven I just don't know.'

That night a weary Leonora changed the last four dressings and made the last lot of patients comfortable, read a letter and a Rudyard Kipling story to the boy in the end bed who still had bandages on his eyes, cleared the sluice for the last time, and finally settled down at her table at the end of the ward to write up reports, glad to be off her feet for ten minutes.

She could hear Sister Hunter moving down the ward, looking closely at each patient, whispering a word or two to those who were still awake. Leonora looked up as she reached her. 'All quiet?' she asked.

'Not a stir, not a whimper,' whispered Sister. 'There was a messenger from your mother, Nurse. The Commandant says you may go the second your duties are done. There is some matter at home. I'll take over here.'

Leonora stood up, frowning. 'Thank you, Sister.'

She took up her bag, and her heavy cape from the hook by the door and fled. She came through the side door, still fastening her cape, and hurried down the path. There was a crashing behind her and someone caught up with her, grabbed her shoulder, and turned her round, gasping, 'What a swizz, coming out of the side door, when I was waiting patiently at the front.'

'Samuel!' He was standing before her in the solid flesh, his Russian fur cap pulled down hard on his brows. 'What on earth—'

He hugged her hard, and kissed her all over her face. 'Darling, beloved sweetheart girl. I thought Kitty would insist on coming for you herself. I had quite a battle.' And he kissed her again.

She pulled away. 'Sam, what about Lucette?'

'What about her? Kit says she's safe enough down in the town with young Mara. Making a nuisance of herself, no doubt.'

'Will you go down and see her?'

He shrugged. 'No time. Raced here from London to see Kit, about Pa and Michael . . . Can't tell you what it felt like when I heard about that.' He paused. 'And to see you, of course, my darling. I'm back on the seven o'clock train, and then onto Zürich tomorrow.'

'But Lucette!'

'What about Lucette?' he said, trying without success to take her again in his arms.

She wrestled away from him. 'She showed Mara a love letter from you. Mara said it sizzled off the page.'

'Love letter? I've written Lucette no love letter. No letters at all, in fact. You are the only person I ever write to. I did write a letter which might be called a love letter, when you first came home. Just one, saying how hard it would be in future to write to you, in those particular loving terms, with Kit and Pa here.' He paused. When he spoke again his voice was very grim. 'In fact, I gave it to Lucette to post.'

This time when he reached for her she stayed in his arms. 'Poor Leonie. What a frozen mutt you must have thought me.' He kissed her. 'Uncaring . . .'

'Unloving . . .' She kissed him.

'Forgetful . . .' He pulled her into the shadow of the trees. 'Sweetheart, this is impossible. We must be together. I can't survive this if we can't be together. But if we go down to the cottage, Kit will be there. I love the woman, but—'

Leonora laughed. 'The stable loft,' she whispered. 'The stable loft.'

They crept past the ambulances and the Commandant's motor car. The horses whinnied as they felt their way, with confidence, along the edge of the stalls to the narrow loft ladder. This was the place of adventurous trysts going back

314

to childhood. Here she had been Guinevere to his Lancelot and Michael's King Arthur. Here, a long time ago, they had slain dragons and fought demons.

Now they lifted the hay bales to one side and pulled off wisps to make a soft nest for themselves. Then Leonora removed her cloak and laid it on the fallen hay. She took off her starched collar and put up her hands to loosen her hair. Watching her with his great eyes, Samuel took off his cap and smoothed back his own thick hair. Then he undid his greatcoat and placed it on top of the cape, knelt down and opened his arms. 'Well, my darling Guinevere,' he said hungrily.

'Children's games,' she said. And she knelt beside him.

They got back to the Waterman's Cottage as the cockerel was crowing. Weary with spent exultation they kissed in the little porch. He breathed into her ear: 'Whatever happens, Leonie, now we have each other.' He watched her climb the steps to the workroom and then went and threw himself, fully dressed, onto the makeshift palliasse which Luke had constructed on the kitchen floor.

Upstairs Leonora undressed by the big worktable and crept behind the screens into her bed. She stifled a yawn. One hour's sleep before she had to start another shift. She would never manage.

Kitty's sleepy voice emerged from the other bed. 'I didn't realise about you and Samuel, Leonora. You should have told me.'

Leonora lay very still for a moment. 'How did you know?'

'Well, brotherly love is one thing. But the look on his face when he came here for you, and found you gone – and the joy with which he went leaping off to get you.' She yawned. 'And then the fact that both of you vanished for the rest of the night. Do you know, finally I worked it out. Aren't I clever?'

'Do you mind?'

'Mind? I love the boy. And you sat in church and heard

how much I loved his father. He's so like William, is Samuel. Not in looks, but he too has a great heart. How can you not love him?'

The chaplain talked about God to Tommy. About forgiveness and repentance. Tommy nodded wisely at this. 'Yes. That is all right, sir. You can tell them I forgive them. For they know not what they do.'

The chaplain flushed. 'That is not an apt quotation, Private Scorton. In less extreme circumstances I would consider that blasphemous. I was referring to your own repentance. Your own sins.'

'Sins?' Tommy smiled dreamily. 'Oh yes, I've sinned, sir. I think I might have sinned twice. But I've never even been with a woman, do you know that? Not once. Not enough time for it yet.' He laughed wildly. 'No time for it at all, eh? Anyway, these two sins. I got drunk once at home before I enlisted. And then I got drunk in London because I was terrified of seeing my mother, and not being able to tell her the truth. You see, sir, she was always able to make things better for me when I was little. But this time she couldn't. Not even you . . . not even your God could—'

'Private Scorton, I must remind you—'

'Anyway, I couldn't tell her so I told my little sister. Perhaps that's another sin. Unfair to burden these evils on such an innocent head. But that's all. I can't remember another sin. Not at all, sir.'

'What about deserting your comrades on the field of battle? Not once, but twice. That is the reason you are here and that is what you may wish to repent.' The chaplain resisted the urge to take out his watch and check the swiftly passing time.

'But don't you see, sir? I have explained it over and over again.' Tommy's voice drove on. 'The first time was about my father, d'you see? He was blown to bits in my brother's factory. D'you know what that factory made? Munitions. Munitions for France. I had a letter which told me this. And then' – here his voice dropped into a monotonous sing-song: '*I-had-to-go-and-see-about-it, then-I-met-a-man-who-knew-him-and-it-was-all-right-so-I-started-back-but-those-Australians-got-hold-of-me-and—*'

The chaplain cleared his throat. 'I have heard all that, Private Scorton, but what of the other time?'

A secret smile settled on the boy's face. 'Well, sir, I knew this would happen, that they would top me anyway. So, sir, I thought I'd just hop off again and make it happen quick, so you can get on with your war.'

The chaplain frowned. 'It is not my war, sir. Er . . . the medical officer has looked at you, Private Scorton?'

'Yes, sir!' Tommy stood up and saluted. 'And he said I was fit as a flea. Absolutely combat-ready.' His eyes moved to the area just behind the chaplain's shoulder and he started beaming. 'And now my father has come for me.'

The faintest sliver of dawn light was creeping through the narrow window. The chaplain nodded, relieved. 'Your Father will gather you up to His bosom, my son, as He does the halt and the lame, the poor and benighted—'

'No, no, sir. Don't you see him? Just behind you there . . .'

The escort had moved into the room, and the chaplain had to squeeze back while they tied the boy's hands.

Tommy started to shout. 'My father, Mr William Scorton of Priorton in County Durham, sir. He has come to gather me up to his bosom, all right.'

'Come on, son!' The Sergeant's voice was urgent, pleading with the boy to make his task easy. 'Come on now.'

The chaplain raised his voice. 'Is there anything further I can do for you, my son?'

'Private Duggie O'Hare has to be there, sir. They promised that. He didn't want to at first, but he said he would do it for me.' They were moving him out of the room now, and he was calling over his shoulder.

The chaplain glanced at the Sergeant, who nodded. 'Your friend will be there, Private.' Then the chaplain's voice dropped into a low melodic chant of prescribed words, which were a comfort to him and the soldiers who, wooden-faced, were walking this boy to his death. But the words had no meaning for Tommy, who was chattering now to his own father about Mara and the games they played in the woods above Purley.

His chatter slowed as they started to walk to the single post and pinned a whitened tin lid above his heart. Then he caught sight of Duggie, tense-faced at the very edge of the clearing, and he smiled. 'Tell them, Duggie. Tell Mara and my mother. Tell them when you see them that my father was with me and it was all right. Tell them it was all right. My father was with me.' He continued the words even when they blindfolded him. 'Tell them my father was with me. Mr William Scorton, of Priorton, County Durham. Tell them it was all right. Father? Father . . .'

The words were still coming when the shots rang out, and for a whole minute there was a silence like no other silence in the world.

Lucette smiled prettily as Leonora came through the door. 'Ah, Mara, we have a visitor. You wish me to be the maid? Shall I make tea and biscuits?'

Lucette had been wandering round the little house all afternoon, the personification of boredom. She had wandered around the town all morning and come in complaining that Priorton was a dark and dingy place, full of grubby, boring people. When Samuel came back he would take her to London. He knew she was a person of the city; she needed light and stimulation.

Now Mara, catching Leonora's intent look, closed her books. 'Have you been shopping, Leonie? Would you like some tea?'

Leonora smiled coolly. 'No. I just wish a word with Lucette here.'

'Ah.' Lucette sat herself on a hard-backed chair and spread her skirts out gracefully. 'You have some time for me? I thought the great nurse would, perhaps, be too busy. You

318

look so pretty in your uniform. Perhaps I could help at the hospital also? Those poor soldiers.'

'You wouldn't last a day,' said Leonora casually. 'Not an hour.' She cast her eye round the room. 'Now then – is this your bag, Lucette?'

'But yes. Poor dear Papa brought it back from Paris for me three – no, four – years ago.'

Leonora picked it up and poured the contents onto the table. Lucette caught her arm. '*Hein! Mais qu'est-ce-que tu fais?* That is an impertinence.' Before she could stop her Leonora had picked up the wallet. Lucette stretched to snatch it back but Leonora jumped onto a chair and held it high. From that position she opened it and teased out Samuel's letter.

Lucette stamped her foot. 'This is too much, Leonora. They are private affairs.'

'They may be someone's private affairs, but they are not yours. I think you have stolen someone's private affair. Ah, I recognise this writing. It is Samuel's. And the letter, when it was in its missing envelope, was addressed to me.'

Lucette laughed shrilly. 'You! It cannot be so. Samuel loves me. When he comes here, he—'

'He has been, and gone back to London on the seven o'clock train this morning. If he loves you so, why did he not come to see you?'

Lucette sent a glance of limpid appeal to Mara. 'It is unnatural, is it not, Mara? A brother and sister?'

Mara frowned. 'Leonie?' she said.

Leonora jumped down from the chair and reassembled the contents of Lucette's bag. 'The fact that Samuel and I love each other is not unnatural, Mara, because Samuel and I are not, in any emotional way or in law, brother and sister.'

'You mean,' said Mara, 'the letter I read the other day was from Samuel to *you*?'

'That's right,' said Leonora. 'Strange as it seems, that is the case.'

'Perhaps I was wrong,' said Lucette, conciliating now,

'keeping the letter, trying to save you, dearest Leonora. Protecting you from yourself.'

Mara and Leonora exchanged a glance and they burst into laughter. 'There's no stopping her, is there?' spluttered Leonora. 'Now, Lucette, we should have some tea and make a toast to passion spent.'

They were halfway through the tea, still confusing Lucette with their giggles, when the roar of an engine outside caught their attention. Lucette peered through the lace curtain. 'Ah, a very grand motor car. A chauffeur! Now perhaps . . .'

Their second visitor was Pansy, in conciliating mood, who had come to offer Mara her job back. Apparently the office was in chaos: she was now being harassed by those military inspectors and none of the girls on the line were up to the work. She needed a good manager and one could not get a man to work for you these days for love or money. The fact that there was a war on seemed to cut no ice with some people. They'd rather be off playing heroes than seeing the bullets were made in the first place.

Mara stopped her in mid-flow and introduced her to Lucette. Pansy peered at the Russian woman with interest, noting the fine jewels and the elaborately dressed hair. Lucette, in her turn, impressed by the car and the chauffeur, was at her most charming.

Pansy nodded wisely. 'I read in the newspapers that aristocrats are fleeing those dreadful events by the day.'

Lucette shook her head sadly. 'There is nothing left for us there now, nothing at all.' She did not deny the assumed aristocratic status. Perhaps she should call herself Countess.

'I'm afraid, Pansy,' said Mara, 'it would be impossible for me to return to the Works. My mother wouldn't hear of it and I am busy with my studies, and some other writing I'm doing, for Tommy.'

'How is he, Tommy?' Pansy's question was perfunctory, a polite reflex. She was not really interested.

Mara frowned. 'We've not had a letter in ages. I'm trying to get Mama to write to the Army and ask about him.'

But Pansy was here to pursue her own goals. 'I would have thought, my dear, that the salary would be welcome.'

Mara shook her head. 'Money is not a problem, Pansy. My mother's busy looking round for premises to manufacture this mechanism she's invented. There's a great deal of interest in it. She has a partner,' Mara wondered what Pansy's reaction would be if she knew the partner was the despised Luke, 'and she's looking for premises in the middle of the town, where she may establish the memorial library for my father. So, you see, our hands are very full!'

'Oh dear, I had hoped you would help. Let bygones be bygones. There is so much to do.'

That was when Mara was struck by her inspiration. 'Perhaps Lucette could help you? Not with the Works, of course, but with your day-to-day pressures in the town, and at home. Lucette is so bored here; she is used to some social life.'

Pansy nodded sagely. 'It must be a great comedown for such a person, living in a house like this.' She turned to Lucette, a kind, sweet expression on her face. 'Would you like to help me, my dear?'

Lucette smiled appealingly. 'If I can help you in any way, Madame . . .'

Pansy fished out a black-edged, heavily embossed card from her bag. 'Come and talk to me tomorrow. I must hurry away now as I have an important meeting with Mr Sleight regarding some matter of the estate.' She sighed. 'It is all such a responsibility.' She fluttered away and into her car.

Lucette shut the door behind her. 'What a charming lady,' she said. 'Is she very rich?'

Mara and Leonora exchanged a glance. 'Very, very rich,' said Mara.

Later, as Mara was showing her out, Leonora whispered, 'Do you think it will happen?'

'Sure to. That will be a marriage made in heaven. They're made for each other. An aristocrat to look after? Pansy'll be transported. You watch. Within a month she'll be fattening Lucette up, dressing and prinking her like a prize Pekinese.'

21

Jean-Paul

Lucette returned from her first visit to the tall house in the square in a state of badly suppressed excitement. Pansy's large house with its fine furnishings was more what she had expected to find in Leonora's family. Her erstwhile friend's apparent poverty had been quite a shock when she first arrived in Priorton.

She made a barely dignified scramble to assemble her things, chattering to Mara as she did so. 'Poor Madame Pansy, she is so lonely since the tragedy of her husband. More than anything she must have company. Do you know, she has such a pretty bedroom, a guest room which she says will be mine?' She fingered a heavy pearl necklet which Pansy had given her, but did not mention the gift to Mara. She had also confided to Madame Pansy her 'countess' status, wondering whether it was indelicate to use it here in England. Pansy had assured her that it was quite all right to use it; in England they knew about countesses, although they didn't actually have one in Priorton.

Now Lucette beamed at Mara. 'And I am to help her with her shopping, and to talk to her of Moscow and St Petersburg. I will read the newspaper to her, for she says she is no great reader and that will help me with my English. And I am to have a salary – is that not fun? The only money I have ever had, I was given by my darling Papa. And now I will earn my own.' She was pink with excitement. 'And she has sent the motor car to carry my boxes. Is that not very kind?'

She was just dancing out with the last of her bags when she bumped into a bearded man on the doorstep. '*Je m'excuse, Mademoiselle!*' he said automatically.

Lucette blinked. '*Vous êtes français, Monsieur?*'

Mara flew to him. 'Jean-Paul, Jean-Paul!' They embraced very tightly for a moment then stood back and surveyed each other.

'You have changed,' she said. Her eyes ranged across the face that had so frustratingly eluded her memory. Jean-Paul was thinner now, his beard almost engulfing his face. His skin was white, free from the ingrained coal dust which she had been used to. His eyes, if anything, were brighter and more luminous, and now they were shining into hers. How could she have forgotten this face, which once again was making her heart pound?

'You also. Such an old lady now.' He hugged her again and she could feel his ribs against her breast, his bristly cheek against hers. 'Such a beautiful old lady. You must be nineteen years now.'

Lucette was waiting expectantly.

'Have you all your boxes, Lucette?' said Mara stubbornly.

Lucette scowled and stumped off towards the car, which had its usual circle of admiring children. She looked out of the car window at Mara, who was standing in the door, and smiled suddenly. '*Il est très beau, ma p'tite!*'

Mara slammed the door behind her.

Jean-Paul was looking around. 'Hélène . . .'

'She is still at the hospital, Jean-Paul. I wrote and told you. Sometimes she is well, and quite happy, but sometimes she is troubled and wild.'

He sat down. 'My poor sister. They will let me see her?'

'I can take you today. I visit her most weeks. You've come such a long way.' She blushed and looked around the room,

324

so very much her own now. 'Where will you stay? Will you stay here? It was your house, after all.'

He laughed. She had forgotten what a rich foreign sound that was, just as she had almost forgotten his face. Suddenly her body remembered the prickling tension of their last embrace.

He touched her shoulder. 'I cannot stay here, Mara. It would not be proper. You are the old lady now. There is the Commercial Hotel. I will stay there. It is just for a few days.'

She battled with her disappointment.

'I come to see Hélène, and you, and to collect the package.'

Mara frowned. 'Package?'

'The package from my father. The one which brought you here into our lives.'

She raked in the cupboard and brought out the box. 'You need it now?' she said.

'It is probably a vain thought, as the war still coughs and barks and sputters on, over there. But I thought, when I return, I will take it to a notary in the village to make sure the land and the farm are mine after the war, if they do not belong to some cursed *Boche* by then. Then I will go back and farm like my father. I will take Hélène there, and—' He did not finish the sentence.

'Are you on leave?' asked Mara.

He laughed shortly. 'No – I give myself leave. Many French soldiers give themselves leave. It takes me a very long time to get here. I will rejoin when I return.'

'Will they let you? Don't they shoot deserters?'

He shrugged. 'There is some flexibility in the French Army. It has been a long war. But the English? Perhaps a little different.' He paused, then braced himself. 'Mara, I must tell you something about Tommy.'

He told her of his encounter with Tommy at the *estaminet*. 'He had discarded his uniform, and his weapons. That was very dangerous.'

Mara froze. 'My mother's written to the Regiment as we've

325

not heard from him since we saw him in London. He was in a terrible state then. Terrible. We have to tell Mama this, now. This minute.'

They walked silently together through the town to the empty premises which Kitty and Luke, with the help of John Maddison the blacksmith, were converting for the manufacture of the signalling device. Kitty was still there, moving old lumber. She had a kerchief on her head and wore a long black apron and black sleeves to protect her dress. Her face was smudged with old dust, and for once she looked her age. She stared blankly when she saw Jean-Paul, then smiled when she realised who he was. 'You have changed, Jean-Paul.'

'He has something to tell you, Mama,' said Mara.

'Will you sit down, Madame?' said Jean-Paul rather nervously.

'No, thank you,' said Kitty. 'I'm used to standing up for things.'

Jean-Paul repeated the story of his encounter with Tommy. Kitty's lips tightened and she fished under her apron into a pocket in her dress. She handed a piece of paper to Mara. 'I had a letter from the Regiment saying he is missing, believed killed in action.' Her face was stony. 'I was going to bring it to the house to show you, but there's so much to do here.' Kitty's habit of self-sufficiency, of absorbing trouble and then dealing with it in her own way, had forced her to continue with her routine, to protect Mara for a few more hours from this black news.

'We'll never know what happened to him,' whispered Mara.

'He must have got away somehow,' said Jean-Paul, forcing optimism into his voice.

'If he escaped, he would make his way back here. He *will* make his way back here.' Kitty's voice was cold as winter rain, deliberately drained of the powerful pain that was tearing at her. 'Now then, I have to get on with things here. Will you be taking Jean-Paul to see Hélène, Mara?'

*   *   *

Hélène was delighted to see Jean-Paul, whom she took to be her father. She flew into his arms, chattering away in French, drawing forth comments and laughter from him, taking him across into the corner, telling Mara and the nurse to go away, go away!

The nurse folded her beefy arms across her chest and watched her, not without affection. 'Do the bairn a bit of good to talk in her own language. Talks and chatters like that in her sleep, she does. And there's no understanding her. But Ah canna understand some of the others and they claim to speak English!'

Jean-Paul said very little on the way home in the train, except that he would come for Hélène, after the war. He would only ask that Mara watched her till then. Mara nodded without speaking and followed his gaze out of the window to the landscape, that familiar combination of green woodland and low moors, pockmarked by villages blackened with coal dust exhaled by the ever-present mines, or rancid clouds from the attendant, belching ironworks.

They walked back to the house in Bridge Street, where Jean-Paul had left his pack. On an impulse Mara said, 'There's no need to stay at the hotel, Jean-Paul. Lucette's room's empty if you can bear a flounce or two. This is your house, after all.'

He looked at her carefully. 'Are you sure?'

'The people around here, they're used to the comings and goings at this house. They think we're very eccentric. They'll hardly notice you.'

This wasn't true, but she was suddenly desperate for him to stay. She wanted to ask him more about Tommy, and about himself. She wanted to tell him more about herself – how she had changed, about her studies and her growing desire to study more and to teach, of the memoir she was writing of Tommy – of how kind Michael had been to her the day before he died. The revelation about Samuel and Leonora had stirred her very deeply; it had made her realise just what was missing from her life. The thought had struck her forcibly, just today,

that when her mother Kitty was her own age, she had alread'
had Leonora and was running her first shop.

Now Mara felt hungry to be really close to someone, as clos'
as Leonora was to Samuel. And now she was realising, for onc'
and for all, that that someone was Jean-Paul Derancourt.

'Are you sure?' Jean-Paul let out a great breath and pu'
down his pack. 'That is so good. It has been a long journey
Anyway, they would probably arrest me as a *Boche* spy, in th'
Commercial Hotel.'

'First, would you come up to Waterman's Cottage to se'
my mother again with me? If we hurry you can meet my siste'
Leonora before she does her second shift at the hospital. She''
want to hear about Tommy from your own mouth.'

In the end they took Mara's bicycle and walked it to the edg'
of the town, then rode it together through the lanes and th'
pathways to the Waterman's Cottage. Sitting on the crossba'
with her feet up, she leaned back against his chest, his chir'
tucked into her shoulder, his moustache tickling her cheek
She made herself relax and enjoy the ride. She was quit'
disappointed at the bottom of the last hill, when Jean-Pau'
wobbled to a stop and begged that they should walk before h'
expired altogether.

Kitty was not back from the town, so Mara introduce'
Jean-Paul to Leonora, who shook him heartily by the hand an'
said she hoped he had found Hélène well. Then she listened
troubled, to the story about Tommy. 'It sounds bad, doesn't it
But why have they written to Mama about him being missin'
in action?'

'Perhaps that's what they always say.'

'I don't think Mama'll rest until she knows.'

'At least she has this new project, the library. She's hopeles'
when she's got nothing to do.'

Leonora was pulling on her cape. 'Well, I must leave you
young things to it. Goodness knows when she'll get home
She and Luke weren't back till after my late shift last night
Came wobbling through the trees in that old trap of William's.

pulled by an ancient nag they must have saved from the knacker's yard.'

She hugged Mara. 'Now don't you worry about Tommy. Things will be all right.' She shook hands briskly with Jean-Paul. 'I would tell you to take care of her, Mr Derancourt, but she'd probably hit me with her bicycle pump.' Then she raced away herself.

'We should probably go too,' said Mara, 'if my mother is going to be that late.'

They met Kitty and Luke in the trap just outside Priorton. Luke pulled the horse to a stop. 'Is there some more news?' called Kitty anxiously.

Mara shook her head. 'We just went up so that Jean-Paul could meet Leonora, and tell her directly about Tommy.'

Kitty sat back in the trap. Luke's gaze met Mara's. 'You must not worry, Mara. It will be in order.' His voice was like dry paper.

It was awkward, going back together into the house at Bridge Street. Mara busied herself pulling curtains, poking the fire and turning up lamps. Jean-Paul vanished upstairs with his pack and she went through to the scullery to fill the kettle.

In five minutes Jean-Paul reappeared without his jacket, his collar off and his shirt loosened at the neck. In his hand was a slim-necked bottle of wine, which he put on the table. 'I have carried this for you from France, to say thank you, from the bottom of my heart.'

She took the wine and looked at him. 'What shall I do with it?'

'We shall drink it, you goose! But first I must shave this forest from my chin. Suddenly I feel like an old man. Here – let me.' He took the bottle from her and pulled out the cork with his white teeth. Then he took two china cups from her dresser and filled them with wine. 'We will drink to the good health of your Tommy and my poor Hélène. But first the removal of this beard. I do indeed look like my father, as Hélène thought.' He took the steaming kettle from the fire and carried it into the scullery. She could hear him crashing around and whistling a tune she did not recognise.

Calmly she took a sip of her wine, enjoying the thick, sharp, peppery taste. She glanced into the flames as they leapt up, having been liberated from the dead weight of the kettle. She would drink to Tommy's health and wish for tonight that it were possible for him to be alive. Just for tonight.

Jean-Paul came through the door, his face shining, blood beading slightly where he had nicked his cheek. She could see the shadowy hollow at the base of his neck. He had lost ten years in age in ten minutes.

'Ah!' he said. 'You cheat! You drink before the toast.'

She shrugged, smiling slightly. 'I was thirsty. I've had a hard day.' She stood up and put his cup in his hand. 'Here is your toast. To all the innocents. To all the people like Hélène and Tommy who've been turned inside out, perhaps destroyed by this stupid war.' She took a great gulp.

He took a sip. 'To those innocents, and to the other innocents, like you, who have not been turned inside out by the war. The innocents who will make the future.'

She put her cup carefully on the table. 'Will you do something for me, Jean-Paul?'

He looked at her gravely. 'Anything.'

'Will you make love to me properly, here tonight?' She shook her head as he tried to protest. 'Not for anything in the future. For now. Just now. You will go off in the morning and I will probably not see you again, just as I will not see Tommy again. But I want this. I may go on and be a teacher and have a life, but I don't want that, without knowing what it is like to make love with someone you love. There will be a whole tribe of women like that, and I don't want to be one of them.'

He put down his cup, took hers and held her hands closely to his chest. 'You feel this, Mara? It beats for you. It has every day since you rattled on my door as a child clutching the package from my father. I did not honour my father, but I thank him with my heart that he sent you to me.' He leaned forward and kissed her brow below her falling hair. 'I am astonished at your proposal but I am so very moved that you ask.'

Mara reached up and kissed his newly shining cheek. 'Remember, this is not about after the war, Jean-Paul. There are no promises offered and none taken.'

He drew her very close then, and kissed her assiduously, his mouth moving over her lips very lightly at first, then pressing harder and harder until she was sure he would come through to her teeth. Then his touch softened and his mouth opened slightly so the tip of his tongue could trace the outline of her lips. Her own lips opened and her face and neck started to burn; her breasts started to tingle.

He moved away from her and his hands went to pull out her hairpins and smooth her tumbling hair away from her face. 'I will try to make it right for you, little one,' he whispered. 'To make you feel delight. And there will be no baby, I know the way.'

Then he stood back, picked up the wine and their china cups and said in a louder, more everyday voice, 'I should carry you upstairs in true romantic style, my darling, but after my adventure with the bicycle, I will beg you from my heart, will you go up first?'

Kitty was in bed when Leonora came home from work. She crept around, taking off her clothes and folding them and hanging then on the hooks they had rigged up. There was a stirring and a weary voice came from the other bed. 'Clump around if you want to, dear. I couldn't be more wide awake.' Kitty sat up.

'Sorry, Kit, did I wake you?' Leonora turned up the lamp slightly and sat on her mother's bed.

'No, love. I'm bone weary, but all these thoughts are flying back and forth in my head.'

'About Tommy?'

'About Tommy and Michael and William. It seems so trite and selfish in the middle of this great war but I keep wondering what it's all for. All the work, all the living, all the eating and the sleeping. I thought I had come to terms with William's . . . passing quite well. Because he is always with me. We're kind of baked into each other's souls. But this thing with Tommy, and not knowing what has really happened to him. My little boy. I'm defeated by this. Defeated.'

Leonora took her hand and held it tight. They were both silent for a moment. Then Leonora took a breath. 'Well, dear Mama, I was going to wait until I was really sure, to tell you about this. But in my heart I am sure. I looked at my face in the mirror at the hospital, and I said that is the face of a woman . . . Perhaps I should know better at my age, but I think I'm expecting a baby . . .'

Kitty sat bolt upright. 'A baby? Sam's baby? Are you sure?'

'Well, I have only "missed" once. But in my heart I am so sure.'

'Oh my dearest girl, what wonderful news.'

Leonora laughed. 'You are the strangest woman, Kitty Rainbow. Only you would react like this. Here am I, older even than you were when you had Tommy, with no husband, and no money, in this condition, and you are delighted!'

'A life in the midst of all this death. We can only rejoice. Anyway, it's a family tradition to have our children with no husband and no money. Didn't I have you like that, before I met William? My own mother had me like that, though she was not so lucky. At least Ishmael found me and was the best father a person could wish for.' The tightness and stress had vanished from her voice. She yawned.

Leonora turned down the lamp and climbed into bed. 'If it's a boy,' she said into the darkness, 'I will call him Thomas William Rainbow Scorton; if it is a girl she will be Catherine Maria, like you.'

Kitty put a hand across and touched Leonora's shoulder. 'Thank you, dear girl. Now I can sleep.'

Leonora rolled over in bed. What an insane family. News which would have been greeted as the greatest disaster in many families was here welcomed with relief and a sense of resolution.

What-a-way-to-get-leave. *What-a-way-to-get*-leave. The click-ing of the train on the rails drove the words into his brain like rivets into steel. To get ten days' leave at this stage in the middle of the June offensive was extraordinary, but none of his fellow soldiers objected. Promotion too. The circumstances were, without doubt, extraordinary.

He had spent five days at Mrs Marmion's in London, eating, drinking, building up courage for this visit North which he was dreading. Beside him in the carriage, three men in their thirties were playing pontoon for pennies, on an upturned suitcase. They were in civilian clothes and had not the mark of soldiers.

'Fancy a game, Corporal?' said one. 'Penny a spot, winner takes all?'

'Don't mind if I do.'

'Feelin' lucky?'

'Must be lucky, old chap,' said Duggie. 'I'm alive, don't you know?'

'You've changed,' Mara said to her sister.

They were striding through the town to meet their mother in Back Market Street. In her pocket Leonora had a letter from Samuel. *Dearest Darling. There! I will be open now, open for ever. Tell the truth and shame the devil. I miss you every second as I breathe, but have to put that on one side because of the drive of events here. Kerensky has now been made Minister of War in the Provisional Government. Fellow's only 36! Even younger than you! And he has the fate of this country in his hand. He's already set about democratising the Army, to the dismay of the officers. But he goes round talking to the men and he sways them, sometimes to wild applause and hurrahs. He is very much for the war and advocates it wherever he goes, so we must support him and hope that he prevails. The Government have, thank God, turned down a German offer of a separate peace, but the Bolsheviks rumble on about peace, and plot to get the soldiers to lay down their arms and embrace their German and Austrian comrades. God help us if that happens. Lenin is declaring now that the Bolsheviks will take power and rule alone. No chance of that. Still it is very odd here, not knowing who is your friend and who your enemy. Take care of yourself, my darling, and always remember your Samuel. PS: The London postmark means that I have given this to a comrade who is travelling West, to post for me.*

'Me changed?' said Leonora. 'That's nothing – so have you.' She had noted it when Mara had opened the door to her. Her sister's face had looked both extraordinarily bright and strangely smug. 'Did you have a nice evening with Jean-Paul?'

'Yes.' Still that smug smile.

'Where did he stay?'

'At Bridge Street.'

'Aha, I see!'

'Do you now? Well then, now we've sorted out why *I've* changed, what is it that's changed *you*?'

'I'm expecting Samuel's baby.'

Mara stopped. 'What? Leonie, that is . . . amazing,' she said helplessly.

Leonora grabbed her arm. 'Keep walking. Kitty will be waiting. We're late already.'

Kitty had sent Leonora to collect Mara; she thought she had found somewhere for William's Memorial Library – a disused Wesleyan chapel which they could buy for a song. The building was small, not much bigger than a large house. The door set in a Gothic arch was ajar when they arrived. Inside the light flooded in from narrow, high arched plain glass windows, creating a crisscross pattern on the dusty wooden floor and casting shadows from the substantial oak beams onto the ceiling.

'What do you think?' Kitty was standing in a pulpit, set to the right, halfway up one dusty wall on which hung a dusty picture of Bethlehem with its flat roofs and its wide blue sky.

'They say John Wesley himself preached from this spot.' She climbed down the steps. 'What do you think? Don't you think it will be splendid? All that back section for William's books, and cabinets all down the sides with his objects and tools arranged in them. And tables down the centre for people to sit at and read and write. We can have newspapers available. And there are rooms out the back for offices, perhaps workshops for craftsmen.' She looked from one to the other. 'Don't you think this is just the ticket?'

'It's ideal,' said Mara. 'I can see Pa's collection here.'

'It's a good space,' said Leonora. 'You could keep one end clear for meetings. Talks, lectures – that kind of thing.'

'You're meeting daft,' said Mara. 'Think everything can be solved with meetings.'

Leonora's current passion was the No-Conscription Fellowship, for which she was raising funds in her meagre spare time. 'It's not meetings, it's politics. And everything can be solved with political action, given the public will,' she said.

'That's all very well in the broad scheme of things, but here we're involved with turning this chapel into a library. A simple, practical act,' said Mara.

'Practical politics!' said Leonora triumphantly. 'A practical act which makes permanent changes in people's lives.'

Mara laughed. 'You're beginning to sound as though you're addressing a meeting, Leonie!' She turned to her mother. 'But what about the money, Mama? Surely you'll need any money we have for the Rainbow Works – tools, the development funds. You said that.'

Kitty shrugged. 'Mr Sleight's offered to buy Waterman's Cottage from me on Pansy's behalf.'

'What?' said Mara angrily.

'Apparently she thinks the estate is blighted by my presence. So we'll need somewhere to store William's collection anyway. We can buy this chapel and there'll still be a bit of money over to get shelves and cabinets made, and rent a house in the town. To be honest it is a bit of a long pull, trailing back and forward to the estate. Neither Luke nor I are getting any younger. And Waterman's Cottage has little meaning for me without William. It is the past. We must look to the future. And we'll need a bigger place now that—' She cocked an eyebrow at her eldest daughter.

'I've told Mara,' said Leonora happily.

'Well, Mara, you can see we'll need a bigger house.'

'You won't get a joiner to do that kind of work just now,' said Mara. 'They're all working in factories, or in the Army.'

'Then we'll store William's things here, keep them dry, and fit it out after the war. Surely to God that won't be long now.'

'From the papers, it looks as though it'll go on for ever,' said Mara gloomily.

The door creaked open and they all turned to see Luke, insubstantial as a ghost, slide through, followed by a red-haired man in uniform.

'Duggie!' said Kitty, her face lighting up. Then her eyes strayed to the empty space behind him and her pleasure stilled. 'You have bad news,' she said dully.

He took her hands and held them both between his, then guided her to sit beside him on an old pew. He looked up. 'Will you sit down too, Mara, and . . .'

'This is my elder sister Leonora. Leonora, this is Duggie O'Hare.'

'I'd have known you, miss. You have a look of him.'

Then he told them, as simply as he could, what had happened, leaving out his own, very last act. 'He was no coward, Miss Rainbow. He was just in a spin. There's more of that than people here will see. He had seen the Frenchman and talked of his Pa, and was returning to the Regiment.'

'Poor Tommy,' said Kitty very quietly. 'Poor little boy.'

'But he was very clear, ma'am, very clear. He kept saying he could see his father – that his father was with him. That I was to tell you that. The priest said he meant God, but he said no. "My father Mr William Scorton," he said. He said it was all right because he was with him. You were not to worry.'

'God?' said Kitty. All their eyes were drawn to the dusty picture of Bethlehem above the pulpit.

'No, he said it was his father, William Scorton.'

The air seemed to crack and groan in the silence which followed.

'Thank you for coming, Mr O'Hare,' said Mara. 'I'm writing a . . . kind of memoir about Tommy. It would have been so difficult to finish, without knowing the end.'

With the greatest effort of his whole life Duggie clamped his mouth together over the final truth. The truth that the volley of shots had not completely killed Tommy, and that the young Lieutenant, whose job it was then to complete the task, was too revolted, and had handed Duggie his pistol. 'Do this for your friend, O'Hare,' he had said, his young voice threaded through with that steely authority which had made Duggie 'jump to' since they had plucked him out of the orphanage to be a pantry-boy at the age of eleven.

'They gave me this leave so I could come and tell you.'

'Nice of them,' said Leonora bitterly.

'Do you have a long leave, Duggie?' asked Kitty with strained politeness. 'Will you return to the Front?'

'Oh yes, ma'am,' said Duggie. 'There's still a job for us to do, and to be true, the Army is the only family I've known. Except for young Tom. I loved the boy like a brother.'

The tears started to roll down Kitty's cheeks then, and Leonora sat beside her in the pew and put an arm round her. 'Oh, Mama!' said Mara, throwing herself on her knees on the dusty floor before her mother. She put her head on Kitty's lap and wept.

'He said you weren't to worry,' said Duggie, dismayed but determined, unsurprised by the weight of sadness around him. 'He said to say he was all right. His father, Mr William Scorton, was there.'

Leonora looked at Duggie, her eyes dull with pain, her mind

337

on Samuel out in Russia, now crumbling into total revolution, not knowing who was his friend or who his enemy. 'There can't be much more of this, can there, Mr O'Hare? Not in this life?'

PART THREE

The Kindness of Years

1921

These hearts were woven of human joys and cares,
Washed marvellously with sorrow, swift to mirth.
The years have given them kindness. Dawn was theirs,
And sunset, and the colours of the earth.

Rupert Brooke, *The Dead*

22

Being Gulliver

The dinner-bell clanged and the clatter of feet on stone echoed through the college. Mara walked behind the rest, clutching her copy of *The Church in Rome in the First Century*, a series of lectures by George Edmundson, MA. She had spent the afternoon in her room, making notes on St Peter's martyrdom in Rome.

As she walked in the wake of the swishing skirts of the other chattering girls, she wondered again at the hoops she had had to go through to achieve full teacher rank. Two years to matriculate; one more year's pupil-teaching; and a rather hypocritical attendance at St Luke's Church to get a reference from the vicar in support of her application to St Brenda's Church of England College for Women.

And when she arrived at the College she had found herself obliged to revert to the status and outlook of 'schoolgirl' in order to conform. As she had only briefly experienced school in any conventional sense, this institution with its bells and registers, its formal meals, its signings-in and its signings-out, had come as a considerable shock. The requirement to sit still, writing notes at lectures, on religion and literature, or the philosophy of education, brought back the fidgets which were the last residue of her childhood illness. Her apparent inattention had brought glares and even steely reproof from offended tutors.

Her fellow students, all three years younger than she was,

seemed so young. To her, their giggling night-time confidences over cocoa sounded like the babbling of children. Sustained by thoughts of Jean-Paul (and three passionate letters sent since she had arrived), she was nonplussed by the girls' crushes on some of the more vital and attractive women tutors. And she was contemptuous of their swooning over the young clergyman who lectured them on The Early Church, and limped from a wartime injury.

Mara would have run from this alien place in a week, had it not been for her year as a pupil-teacher, where the sheer drudgery of the days had been perpetually eased by the light in the children's faces as they began to understand something: the communal dreaming as she read poetry to them, or enacted some stirring story. For her those bright faces were the future, the only hope after the stormy days of the war.

To teach children as a full professional was now her firmly set aim, and she would grit her teeth and endure anything to achieve it. Despite her delight in his survival, and her own hunger for his presence, she had steadfastly refused Jean-Paul's passionate plea for her to marry him, and live with him at the farm in France which he had gradually retrieved from its wartime wilderness.

Then, after a year in France, he had rented his farm to a neighbour and returned, he said, to be near her and near Hélène, who was still enduring her strange dream of life at Sedgefield Asylum. He had got work again as a joiner at Black Owl Pit, and was renting the same house in Bridge Street. In her college vacations, she and Jean-Paul met every day. They walked the streets and woods of Priorton, and made love at his home.

She loved him no less, but her desire to teach grew by the day.

Tonight, the students ahead of Mara swished their way through heavy oak doors, took their places at the long tables, and continued their chatter until the delicate tinkling of a bell tolled them to silence.

The academic staff marched in, led by the Principal, Miss Bullock, an extremely clever woman who had performed brilliantly at Oxford in the years in which it was not considered proper to award women degrees. Miss Bullock lived up to her name, being short-necked and built rather like a comprehensively padded box. She was a fearsome creature: to be called to her room on a disciplinary matter had made many a strong woman weep, be she staff or student.

Now, the Principal took her place before her chair, a high carved edifice more suited to a Bishop. Beside her stood Miss White, who was a much younger woman, perhaps only thirty-five: a tall, slender creature, with sharp features and bobbed hair, she was the object of much romantic speculation by the girls. The fact that she was also very brilliant and actually in possession of one of the earliest Oxford degrees paled beside the rumours that she had lost her father, her two brothers and her fiancé in the Great War and had had poems written in her honour. Miss White lectured on the Principles of Education: here, her combination of practical ideas and idealistic fervour went down very well with all her students.

The assembly was complete; Miss Bullock uttered a rather attenuated Latin grace and they all sat down, the discreet chatter mixing with the clatter of plates and serving dishes.

The maids, trim in black and white, began to serve, with practised efficiency, a meal which would not have disgraced a major hotel. It was a legend in the College that students put on a stone in weight in their first term. This did not happen to Mara, who ate only a fraction of what was served and, in her two hours of afternoon freedom, walked away any extra pounds as she strolled through the parkland and along the river. She needed that time away from the College, to clear herself of the sheer press of people, which seemed to her to be the major and confounding characteristic of communal life.

At this particular evening meal she picked at her food, chatting in a desultory fashion with the girls either side of her. In general her fellow students were kind enough towards her, but wary of her. Her extra years, and widely different experience, set her apart from these daughters of ministers and doctors, making her feel, as she said in a letter to her sister Leonora . . . *like Gulliver*.

She once made the mistake of championing the miners in their current dispute with the pit-owners, referring to her friend who was a joiner at a pit, and who now refused to take the wage reduction proposed by the owners. For men such as he, she told these girls, the strike was the only possibility, the very last resort. That discussion in the students' sitting room had petered out into polite and silent disbelief. The rumblings of post-war discontent and disillusion in the country threatened these girls, rather than concerned them. And the fact that someone would refer to their *friend* the pit joiner was, to put it mildly, bewildering.

This evening the meal, as always, seemed unendurably long, but at last the bell tinkled again and they all stood. It was Miss White's turn to say Grace. '*Thank You, Lord, for the food with which You have graced our table, the joy with which You fill our hearts. May we think tonight of those who are not so fortunate, whose table is empty, whose hearts are troubled.*'

Miss Bullock's 'Harrumph!' could be heard right through the dining hall. Miss White looked around at the company, smiling slightly, before referring to a small piece of paper and giving out notices about a changed lecture-time the following day and the cancelling of hockey *pro tem* because the games-pitch was waterlogged by a stream which had been diverted by some *very* naughty children who had built a dam. She waited for a few seconds for the appreciative buzz to die down.

'Lastly,' she said, 'I would be grateful if Miss Scorton would come to speak with me in my room after dinner.'

The girls waited for the staff to leave, before they made their own way out. The girl beside Mara smiled sympathetically at her, obviously thinking there was something wrong with her work – the usual reason for being called to Miss White's study. 'You have to watch White, Miss Scorton. She'll feed you tea and biscuits and then strike with that steely mind of hers and make you feel like a lazy worm.'

Mara was puzzled. All her work was up to date and, she knew, of very high quality. Her years of struggle to qualify herself were paying off handsomely in terms of the academic work here. They had not prepared her for hockey and lacrosse, of course, but that she survived by playing with more strength and speed than skill.

'Good job it isn't Bullock,' went on the girl on the other side of her. 'She'd be sharpening her silver knives to pin you up against her wall.'

Miss White's study had tall windows on two sides, which looked towards the river. Underneath each window was a broad table: one was set up as a desk and was very cluttered, the other had two piles of paper, one written on, the other blank. Beside them stood an ink-stand.

Miss White was sitting on a low couch beside the fire, a silver tea tray on a small table in front of her. She smiled her dazzling smile. 'Come and sit down, Miss Scorton. Would you like some coffee, my dear? My cousin sends this from America. It is very good.'

Mara refused a biscuit, sipped the coffee and waited.

Miss White put down her own cup. 'Well, Miss Scorton, I was wondering. How have you found College?'

'The work is very interesting.'

'You work to a good standard, my dear. You're undoubtedly clever and you write very vividly. Did you not consider University? More and more women are taking that step now.'

Mara shook her head. 'It's taken the greatest of upheavals for me to get here for these two years, Miss White. University would have been out of the question.'

'Mm.' Miss White took a sip of her coffee. 'Have you been happy here? Do you have friends?'

Mara hesitated. 'The girls here are nice. They're good souls . . .'

'But . . .' prompted Miss White.

'They are just out of the egg, these girls,' Mara burst out, 'from some manse, some lawyer's cosy villa, or some village schoolhouse.'

Miss White smiled thinly. 'Where they come from is not their fault, any more than where you come from is your fault.'

Mara threw up her hands. 'I know, I know. I say that to myself but it doesn't make it any easier. I get so annoyed with them. Their universe is bounded by some little High Street or some country parish . . .'

'And yours isn't?'

'Well, I think now that I grew up on a kind of mental island away from most things people would recognise. My father travelled when he was young, and we still have an old Egyptian friend from that time. He has lived with us always. My brother and my sister lived in Russia. My brother is there now. I myself stood in a school in Hartlepool with the German shells falling all round, the bloody head of my Headmaster a foot away. My mother . . . well, I think it's just that I feel part of a much wider world.'

'So what is it that you particularly get annoyed about?'

'Well, for instance, in Russia at this minute, according to my sister, there's a famine so great that millions are starving. It seems from the papers that British war tanks are trundling the streets of Dublin. Nearer home, there's a miners' strike here in this county and the counties alongside. In local villages, men who fought in the war are being labelled traitors; their families are going without food. And these girls here eating their three-course lunch and their three-course dinner, hardly know about any of this, still less do they care.'

'But you know – you have miners in your family?' Miss White glanced at a small folder on the couch beside her. 'I thought your family were manufacturers. Rainbow Works, it says here.'

'We are. That's my mother's factory. My sister, mother and our old Egyptian friend are partners in that. But all around us in our part of the world are miners and ironworkers. My . . . best friend is a joiner at a pit who is on strike now.'

Miss White raised her finely plucked brows. 'Best friend?' she said.

Mara drove on. 'My mother and sister work for the relief of this situation, collecting clothes, food and stuff. I've letters each week from them, full of anger at the way the miners are being portrayed in the papers – as though they're criminals.' Mara put her head up. 'Many times, I wish, instead of trudging to morning chapel here, or sitting down again for another interminable meal, I could be helping them. My family are practical people, who have more in common with those people on strike than with priests or lawyers. We should all be involved.'

'Bravo!' said Miss White.

Mara blinked.

'I applaud your concern, Miss Scorton. You make me feel guilty: we should all feel guilty. But all we can do here in this College is work to be great teachers. Then we can go out into that hard world as educators and make a difference. That is our revolution – the life of children. It may not make a difference now, but it will in five or ten years.' She laughed. 'You may think it's too slow a revolution.'

Mara looked at her with new interest. 'What you say makes sense,' she said slowly.

'Well, thank you.' The mannered voice was very slightly tinged with irony. 'You are very kind, Miss Scorton. However, now we must came to the nub of my wish to see you this evening, which concerns your membership of this College. It seems to me that, well into your second year, you're isolated, you appear to have few or no friends—'

'I have many friends at home,' Mara interrupted warmly. 'To be honest I didn't realise that becoming bosom pals with

347

fellow students was part of the requirements to train to be a teacher. To surround oneself with a bevy of friends?'

Miss White contemplated her for a second or two. 'What do you do here, my dear, when you're not writing those excellent essays, or striding angrily across the park?'

It was a secret Mara had told no one here, but this intimate tête-à-tête, the deep gaze of this intense woman seemed to tease the secret to the surface. She blushed as though it were a very guilty thing. 'I write . . . I write.'

'Ah, I see.' Miss White glanced across at her own table with its neat piles of paper. 'Well, Miss Scorton, writer to writer, would it be too intrusive to ask what it is you are writing?'

'I am writing a kind of memoir of my brother.' She hesitated. 'I have called it "A Boy's Story". My brother was called Tommy. He enlisted in the Army at eighteen near the beginning of the war. The war changed him from a sunny boy to a haunted man. Then he was killed. In fact, he was executed for cowardice. He is dead.' Her voice was as dry as parched leaves.

'A sad story.'

Mara leaned forward in her seat. 'But it isn't! It is a kind of evocation of Tommy in our family. This family of mine are unusual and we were nurtured, brought up in an unusual way by our mother. Without constraint, not broken to the harness, you might say. I see now that this was a wonderful thing, a thing we took for granted.' Mara took a breath. 'Schools seem to me to be about breaking people rather than making people. No school I have ever been into even tries anything different. What a wonderful school it would be, which could do *this*. But . . .' She took herself in hand. 'Anyway, this book is about the making and breaking of a free creature. I have imagined the things I did not know, but . . .'

'. . . but what you say is still an indictment of what we have done, what society has done . . .' said Miss White.

Mara frowned at her. 'I'd not thought of it in those terms,

348

to be honest. It's a very personal story. You make it sound like an article in *The Times*.'

'No matter. Your "Boy's Story" sounds fascinating.' Miss White hesitated. 'Would it be an imposition to ask if, at some point, one could read it?'

Mara shook her head. 'It's not completed. I thought I had the ending, but it is eluding me. I have tried and tried to invent an ending, but it always feels wrong. It doesn't fit with the rest.'

'When it is completed, would you let me see it?'

'Yes,' said Mara, 'I suppose I will. Yes, I will.' There was a silence and Mara wondered whether she should make a move to go.

'I am attempting to write something myself,' offered Miss White.

Mara glanced at the laden writing table. 'Is it a textbook, Miss White?'

The other woman laughed. 'Goodness me, no – there are too many of those already. No, strangely enough, in some ways it is like yours. However, it is my own direct experience I am trying to write about, just before and during the Great War. You might call it "A Girl's Story". I was in College, then nursing in France . . .'

'My sister was a nurse during the war,' volunteered Mara, 'on the Russian Front. Right near the front line.'

'Good gracious!' said Miss White, leaning forward. 'How—'

But she was disturbed by a knock on the door which was immediately opened. Miss Bullock bowled in. 'Miss White, I—'

Mara leapt to her feet, gasped, 'Thank you, Miss White,' and fled. But even as her feet carried her swiftly along the stone corridors to her own little room, she knew that for the first time in eighteen months, she had made a friend in College.

'You have children, comrade?' The man spoke Russian with a Polish accent.

Samuel eyed his new companion warily. 'You, comrade, do you have children?' he countered.

The man had been pushed into the cramped cell to join him the day before. He had seemed exhausted and had slept on the narrow shelf which counted as a bunk for four hours before he rose, shook himself like a dog and introduced himself to Samuel as 'Paul'.

Now, Paul was peering at Samuel with tired eyes. 'I had sons – three of them. All fought in the West against the Germans. Two were wounded, then sent back again to perish. The third was in one of the first soldiers' soviets. We always supported the people.' He raised his eyes to the slit-like window of the cell, which opened onto the corridor outside. 'But he was shot by his comrades in a misunderstanding about a woman.'

Samuel grasped an opening. 'My sister, perhaps, would have nursed your sons. She worked with the Russian Red Cross close behind the front line.'

'Your sister? An Englishwoman?' His hands were shaking, the man called Paul. He put one hand over the other to stop the tremor.

'She had a vocation.'

'Ah. It is not unusual. My country is riddled with foreigners, meddling, pursuing their vocations. Spies, infiltrators, agitators, thieves, so-called bankers and businessmen.'

Samuel sat up straighter, his back hard against the wall. 'If you refer to me, I am – I was – a simple businessman.'

Suddenly Paul's face was thrust into his. 'That, sir, is what everyone says,' he said in a loud voice. Then his voice dropped to a hoarse whisper. 'Give me something, sir, some small thing that I can tell them. A name. A traitorous contact. Just that one thing. Save my life and that of my daughter.' A soiled, claw-like hand grasped his. As close as this, the man reeked of fear.

'They promised you this? That you and your daughter would be safe?' murmured Samuel, his mouth barely moving.

'Yes, yes. Anything, sir.'

Samuel sighed and pushed him away. 'My dear man, they will kill you anyway. And they will kill me anyway. Don't humble yourself.'

Watching Paul cowering in the corner, Samuel reflected that it should be him. They had kept him here for weeks, with barely enough food and water to stay alive. He was as thin as a rake and his skin was breaking out in red patches. As the soldiers pushed the lump of dry bread and water towards him they told him he was privileged to share in the plight of millions of starving Russian people, in this devastation brought about by the iniquities of the Allied Governments who were playing cat and mouse with the Bolshevik Government, which was the true voice of the people.

He had waited tensely for worse than this, but it did not happen. The senior investigating officer, a small man with a beard, had questioned him closely, pushing his face into his, and yelling in his ear. But no one had laid a hand on him. He had heard shouts and screams in the night, some no doubt coming from Paul here. But he had been left alone.

The next morning, a protesting Paul was dragged from his cell, and then ten minutes later the same guards came back for Samuel. He was not taken to the interrogation room as he had expected, but was hustled along three sour-smelling corridors into a narrow office with filing cabinets and a bunch of spring flowers stuck into an elegant vase on the scratched desk. He blinked. The colour of the flowers almost blinded him. They made him think, in a way he had not allowed himself here, of Leonora and Michael and himself as children, leaping through the Priorton meadows gathering armfuls of flowers for Kitty. As would his own children.

The soldiers lounged against the wall, watching him.

His nose itched and he blinked tears from his eyes. He wasn't sure whether the tears were for him or for the sheer unexpected vision of the flowers. He fought back a smile at the ludicrous thought of flowers as a form of torture.

The door opened behind him and the soldiers stood up in a slack form of attention. Two figures moved into his line of vision. One was the small bearded officer who regularly questioned him. The other man was tall, blocking the light in the small room.

Samuel raised his eyes and looked blankly into those of his old friend, Valodya.

'Will you sit down, sir,' said the bearded one, bowing and scraping to the big man.

Valodya blinked hard at Samuel. 'So, there is a suspicion you have been plotting against the people, *Mistaire Scorton*.' Then he started to speak very quickly in English, spitting the words out like bullets. 'Don't worry, Samuel, this donkey does not understand English. It seems you are a plotter and a spy. But then we were all doing that, weren't we – plotting to our advantage? Now we have the bookkeepers and termites in charge and we warriors will have to hold the candle till it extinguishes and burns our fingers. Then there will be the long dark.'

Samuel shook his head, trying to make sense of all this, suspecting that it was yet another ploy to get him to spill the names of people he had known . . .

Valodya's voice raced on. 'Keep faith, Samuel. Keep faith. I had to leave you here some time so they would not suspect. They will not hurt you, not yet. You will have a visitor – a prominent English writer. Between you and me, the fellow's a peacock, a preening bird. He will visit you and secure your release, and you will both go back to Britain and say what a civilised lot we are. Have I not invented a good scene? Propaganda, propaganda. There is so much of this splintered truth, my dear, that we don't know the truth ourselves. It is easier to believe the propaganda.' He paused, then said softly, 'I remember always your lovely sister, comrade.'

Valodya stood up and pulled on his long leather gloves. He

turned to his colleague. 'These English are bunglers, playing children's games in men's affairs,' he said contemptuously in Russian. 'Harmless cockroaches.'

He swept out, leaving Samuel with a hunger to touch him, to embrace him in the bear-hug of former days.

The bearded one wearily signalled to the soldiers, who took Samuel back to a different cell. This one was on an outside wall with a window. Here there was a table, with a bowl of water and a towel. And on the bed, which actually had a blanket, were laid his own clothes: the outfit he had been wearing two long months ago when he had first entered this filthy place.

Leonora lifted Kathy onto a high sideboard and left her feet dangling. 'Now stay there and don't move until I say so.' Then she set about hauling Thomas out from behind the tall sofa. 'Right. Now your turn.' She wedged him between her knees while she brushed his thick springing hair to some semblance of order. Then she pulled his coat on and buttoned it to the neck. After that she lifted him up and placed him beside his sister, so that he too would be prevented from running off.

'Stay!' she admonished them both while she turned to the overmantel mirror to tidy up her own hair and pin on her hat. Through the mirror, she could see them both, alike in size but resembling each other in so little else. Thomas, graceful and curly-haired, was the image of Mara at the same age. This wasn't surprising, considering he, like Mara, had both Scorton and Rainbow blood.

Kathy, his twin, resembled her father; she had Samuel's large eyes, and his slightly large head. She was not a pretty child but she would be beautiful when she grew to adulthood, when her large features would finally be balanced by a much larger body. As it was, she had a kind of *gravitas* which was somewhat disconcerting in a three-year-old.

'There!' Leonora turned round. 'Now we're all very smart.'

'Auntie Mara'll say we're the best of all,' said Kathy.

'The smartest,' agreed Thomas as he flipped out his legs and took a great leap to the floor before Leonora could get to him. He rocked on his toes, but did not fall.

Leonora lifted Kathy to the ground.

'Is Kitty coming?' asked Thomas. He was obsessed with his grandmother, always at her heels when she was around.

'No, she is at the Building.'

'I can go and help her,' he said. 'I always help Kitty at the Building. And the *factwy*.'

'Sorry, sweetheart, Kitty will be too far busy. We're going to visit Auntie Mara on our own.' She smiled at his disappointment. The conversion of the 'Building', destined to be the Scorton Institute in memory of William, was just about complete. Kathy and Thomas had played in it as it was being renovated for the whole of the last year. Kitty herself, with the help of John Maddison and Miss Aunger on leave from her shop, was busy installing the last of the books and objects, and taking delivery of the glass cabinet in which would be placed William's watchmaking tools and some examples of his watches and clocks, his mechanical artifacts.

'Can I sit in front in the motor car, Mama?' said Kathy.

Leonora looked from one expectant face to the other, and decided against it. They would fight even if she mentioned taking turns. 'No. You can both sit in the back and you may take two toys each. And I have apples. It is quite a long way.'

She drove carefully, ignoring the chatter and the occasional wail of animosity from the back. Usually she got away to see Mara on her own. Today, because Kitty was busy with the Building, she had her hands full.

In fact, the twins were mostly with Leonora. She was used, now, to carting them around with her wherever she went. They came to the factory with her in the mornings when she went to do some invoice ledger work in the little cubby-hole of an office; they accompanied her to the Co-operative store and the market when she did her shopping. If she went to an open

Labour Party meeting she took them, complete with toy-box, to play at her feet.

For the occasional meeting where she was actually a speaker, she left them with Kitty, either at the Rainbow Works, or at their shared house on End Gate, the road which led from the Market Place down to the river.

She and Kitty had bought the house between them when their little factory had been up and running very successfully for a year. It was a relief to get out of the confinement of the Waterman's Cottage. Luke, though still active, was more fragile by the day, and needed space in which to retreat, and be about his own meditations in his own little room.

Leonora's contribution to the house came from her modest savings from her nursing, and one substantial cheque which arrived out of the blue from Samuel, to be drawn in a very complicated fashion, on a Swiss bank.

Samuel had never seen the twins. His Russian adventure seemed to have swallowed him completely, the revolution having come and gone, and with famine raging in Russia, a civil war was being pursued with the Bolsheviks wobbling around a bit in the saddle. For fifteen months she had received hurried notes, parcels with toys, or wrongly sized clothes for the children; a silk scarf for herself. Then nothing for a year, by which time she thought Samuel was dead. The kaleidoscope of emotions which she endured during these months left her numb. She buried herself in the insistently mundane daily demands of the two babies, forbidding Samuel to enter her tortured thoughts.

Then she had had a visit from the surgeon, Pavel Demchenkov, on his way to America. Her hopes were raised again. Pavel, a skeletal shadow of his former large self, was a refugee now, despite his good revolutionary credentials. His support of the Mensheviks was seen as treason. He told her that Samuel was alive and in prison in some place far to the east of Moscow. Pavel said the message from Samuel was 'to wait', and to keep her pecker up.

So, allowing her spirit to lighten in a guarded fashion, she had settled down to wait, inventing stories for the twins about their father, who was saving people from wolves deep in the Russian forest.

'Is this a castle, Mammy?' a voice piped up from the back of the motor car. Not Kathy's growl, so it must be Thomas. 'Is Auntie Mara locked in a cell?'

She slowed down, changed gear, and pulled hard on the brake. 'No. This is St Brenda's College, not a prison. But perhaps Auntie Mara sometimes feels as though she's locked up there.' She had often wondered how Mara, with her odd, free spirit, managed in what must be a boarding-school atmosphere. But Mara never mentioned that. She just talked about the lectures, the children she taught, the ideas and the books. And now her looming final exams.

'There she is!'

Mara was standing out of the wind in the shadow of the gateway, a neat cloche hat jammed onto her short curls, her collar fastened tight up to her neck. Leonora viewed her sister with a rush of affection. Mara was thinner now, and she seemed taller, more elegant by the day. Leonora leaned across and opened the door, shivering at the draught of cold air. 'Quick, love. Jump in!'

As Leonora expertly manoeuvred the car and turned it back again down the street, Mara fended off questions from the twins. Leonora parked outside the only substantial property in the little main street, the White Swan. Here, as usual, they would enjoy their monthly afternoon tea in warmth and unlooked-for elegance.

Unbuttoning the children and settling them into their chairs, Mara asked about those at home.

'Well, Jean-Paul sends his love,' said Leonora. 'He's fed up with the strike but busy doing some joinery at the Building for Kit. She thinks he's wonderful. I drove him to see Hélène last week.'

'And how's she?'

'Do you know, she seems much better? Calmer, less haunted.'

'And what about the Building?'

'Just about finished. It is looking very good. I've set up a little group to run a voluntary lending library from there. Kitty's keen for it to be used, not for it to be some kind of mausoleum. And she says you must be sure to get out for the dedication in July. You're to take a train to Durham and we'll collect you there.'

Mara rolled her eyes. 'Easier said than done. You should have heard The Bullock, on about this girl who'd got special dispensation to get out for her brother's wedding, and was late back off the train. All about weak vocations, self-indulgence and mendacity. The poor girl was trying to sink through the floor.'

'You must come. Kitty would cancel it, I think, if you didn't. Surely you can handle some old woman, even if she is called Bullock.'

'You might as well say you can handle General Kitchener. She puts the fear of God in me.'

'You? I can't imagine anyone terrifying you.'

'You should be here.' It had taken Mara just a month to realise that under the brilliant rhetoric and the almost ready charm which she could lay on when she chose, Miss Bullock was indeed a bully. The Principal's powerful aura was a strange mixture, composed of her undoubted brilliance and a colossal ability to crush, with word or look, anyone who crossed her. Regularly she had the domestic staff and the academic staff in tears. Girls, too, would escape her presence reaching for handkerchiefs. It was an open secret in College that she was locked in battle at present with Miss White, who was trying to bring new ideas into her teaching of Education.

Miss White, of course, never cried.

'Good afternoon, Miss Scorton.'

Mara scrambled to her feet. 'Miss White!' The object of

her recent thoughts was there before her in the White Swan, looking divine in a short dove-grey dress and a velour cloche hat on her cropped hair.

Miss White's gaze wandered to Leonora and the children. 'This is my sister, Miss Leonora Rainbow. And my nephew and niece, Thomas and Kathy Scorton.' Sticking to the family custom of not going into elaborate explanations, she left Miss White the task of unscrambling the probable relationships. The fact that Leonora was old enough to be Mara's mother, and the children who were sitting watching with wide eyes carried their father's, not their mother's name (as did Mara herself), took some working out.

Leonora was standing now. She shook Miss White's hand heartily. 'Good afternoon. My sister tells me you're the best teacher at the College, Miss White.'

'Does she now?' The brilliant smile flashed. 'And are these your children, Miss Rainbow?'

'Yes, they are.' Leonora and Mara waited for the challenge. It often came. Not so much because people objected to the Rainbow way of going on, but the fact that they did not hide it, or dissemble about it, caused great irritation.

The challenge failed to arrive. 'Aren't you lucky? It's the regret of my life that I have no children of my own.' The tone was sober, measured. Leonora and Mara exchanged a glance. Miss White went on, 'And you must be the one who was a Red Cross nurse in Russia? How fascinating.'

Leonora nodded towards the twins. 'Their father is still in Russia. In prison, as it happens.'

'Fascinating,' repeated Miss White. 'Oh dear, that sounds heartless. I mean, I knew Miss Scorton was somewhat different but it is only now I am realising just how different.'

Mara took a breath. 'Would you join us for tea, Miss White?'

'I would love to, my dear, but alas, I am here as someone's guest.' She waved her hand into the dark corner of the café and they all looked across.

Mara stared, looked harder, then broke into a peal of laughter as, under a neat moustache and behind a prematurely lined skin, she recognised a very familiar face. 'Good grief!' she said.

The man in the corner stood up. 'Mara?' he said.

They raced towards each other and a hearty handshake developed instantly into a great hug and kisses, which caused a restive fluttering among the White Swan's more select customers.

Miss White looked on quizzically. 'You seem to know my student, Dewi?'

'Know Mara Scorton, Amy? Why, this was the girl who taught me all I know about climbing trees and having picnics, now still to be a child in the middle of a so-called Great War.'

The rocking of the little tug upset the dyspeptic stomach of Bertram Langley, rendering his normally pale face a luminous shade of green and his even paler eyes red-ringed. Nevertheless, with a writer's assiduity, he continued to question Samuel closely about his adventures in and out of Russia during the last ten years.

To keep his own mind off the relentless surge of the sea as it slapped the little boat, Samuel answered willingly enough, prefacing it all with his love and affection for Mother Russia and her people. But even with Bertram Langley he divulged no names, apart from that of Lenin whom he had met once in Zürich, Bruce Lockhart, the English agent safely back in England, to whom he had fed information now and then, and the spy Reilly, who had paid him handsomely for useful insights. These names were known to Langley, so this was no betrayal.

Samuel never mentioned Valodya; as far as Langley knew his 'coming upon' this English prisoner, whom he subsequently rescued by forceful representations to the authorities, was an accident. Langley was to be the hero in his own story and no betrayal would drift back by literary accident.

The writer returned again from being sick over the side.

'And have you a family, Mr Scorton?'

'Oh yes, Langley, I have a family. After those London wallahs have had their bite at me, I'm going straight home. And I may tell you, this time I will stay.'

23

Back from the Dead

The day after their encounter in the White Swan, Miss White sought out Mara in the library. 'I thought you'd either be working in here or walking the pastures, Miss Scorton. I drew the line at walking the pastures, but considered the library a fair option. Can you spare me a minute?'

Mara gathered up her books and followed her, aware of the quizzical looks of other girls in the library. Walking along the wide corridor Miss White cocked her head up to speak to her. 'You would wonder how I knew your friend Dewi Wilson, Miss Scorton?'

'It's really not my business, Miss White.' After their first ecstatic greeting in the White Swan, things had been a bit awkward between Mara and Dewi. In the end they had retired to their respective tables with some relief. Mara was more relieved a few minutes later, when Miss White and her guest left the café arm-in-arm. She had waved politely towards them and they smiled back.

'I suppose not,' Miss White was saying thoughtfully, 'but still, I will tell you. Dewi was a soldier in my brother's Regiment when my brother died. He came to talk about him after the war. So, he's a very slender connection with a brother I loved. We have similar ideals about life. I think Dewi will be a Labour Member of Parliament before the decade is out. Since our first meeting we have become very close friends. I think I can confide that to you.'

They were at the door of Miss White's sitting room. She pushed open the door. 'You go in,' she said. 'I have a supervision in C11. Don't answer the door, whoever knocks.'

The door clicked shut behind Mara. Dewi was standing on the carpet before a blazing fire. He strode across and took her hands. 'My dear Mara,' he said.

She was uncertain of how to handle this. It seemed so long ago since their childish games in Purley Woods. And their wartime letters had finally faded, as her concerns were more and more focused on Tommy, and on events at home. And on Jean-Paul. 'What do you want?' she said.

'Seeing you . . . you are so beautiful now. The war that destroyed so much has made you blossom. Do you know that, Mara? Seeing you again has made me think about things. I was sad when you stopped writing. Now I think we might be friends again, even something . . .' He took a breath. 'I loved you, you know. I loved you then and I think I love you now.'

'What about Miss White?'

He shuffled his feet. 'Amy and I are old friends – loving friends, if you like. But seeing you . . . I want to marry you, Mara.'

'*What?*' She put a hand on his arm. 'You can stop that, right now. I'll always be friends, Dewi. But I'm buried now in this desire to be a teacher, and a good one that'll change the world – a bit of the world anyway. They make you stop teaching when you marry, didn't you know that?'

'But you could still—'

'I said stop it, Dewi! If I were to get married, and I'm not, it would not be to you. I love someone else.'

'Who? Who is it?'

'You met him at my mother's Christmas party – Jean-Paul Derancourt.'

'The Frenchman? But he's years older than you!'

'Miss White is years older than you.'

'It's not the same.'

'Why not?'

He was silent for a second, then he started on another tack. 'But isn't this Jean-Paul a miner, Mara?'

'He's a joiner who works at the pit – when they let him, that is. He's on strike at present.'

'On strike? Don't you think that's a bit . . . odd? How could you consider a man who works in a mine? Could you wash his pit clothes? Could you live—'

She started to smile. 'Well, well, Dewi Wilson, stalwart of the Labour Party! So much for the equality of man, so much for—'

She was interrupted by a thundering knock on the door. She put her finger to her lips and stood stock still.

Miss Bullock's voice came through the wood. 'Miss White? Miss White? I wish . . .' The door handle started to turn. Then Dewi coughed a very loud and a very male cough. The turning stopped and they could hear heavy steps stumping back down the corridor.

They relaxed.

'There, now we've got Miss White in trouble.'

'She's a big girl – she can cope with it. Mara, are you sure?'

'Sure.'

Dewi let out an enormous sigh. 'Well then,' he held out a hand, 'pax? We'll still be friends, won't we? We haven't found each other again just to lose each other, surely.'

Mara kissed his cheek. 'Just you try to lose me now.'

They were sitting talking in a friendly fashion when Miss White returned twenty minutes later. She glanced from one to the other and smiled her satisfaction. 'All sorted?' she said.

Mara stood up. 'All sorted,' she grinned. 'Now if you don't mind, I'll get back to my books.'

As she walked back to the library she reflected that Miss White had courage as well as wisdom. The woman was a saint.

*　　*　　*

Duggie O'Hare surveyed the bulky, flint-faced woman before him with interest. Getting into this place had been as bad as getting into a German bunker. He had been told at first by the gatekeeper that the young ladies could not, absolutely not, receive visitors during the week. 'Only two till five Saturday and Sunday and then with notice. The Principal is set on it, believe me.'

He mentioned the war, then, and matters of life and death, and the gatekeeper sent his wife scampering across to the castellated main building with a message. Then the gatekeeper shut the door firmly on him and Duggie had to kick his heels for a good half an hour before the wife returned with a boot-faced woman in a maid's uniform. Boot Face in turn led him grimly across the courtyard, up a sweeping mahogany staircase and kept him standing while she entered some tall double doors.

After a minute she came out. 'Principal'll see you now,' she said sourly. The unsaid 'sir' hung briefly in the air between them.

He ventured in. A large woman sat behind a small desk beneath a Gothic window. She looked so square that he wondered briefly if she operated on castors rather than legs.

Miss Bullock glanced down at the blotter before her. 'Mr O'Hare? I assume the gatekeeper said we do not allow mid-week visitors.'

Duggie turned his cap in his hand and met her gaze with that combination of innocent appeal and deference that years of service had taught him. 'Excuse me, ma'am, for being just an ignorant soldier, but I have a message for Miss Scorton from her brother.'

'Could he not bring it himself?'

'Alas, ma'am, that will not be possible. The poor boy's dead. Died a hero's death in the war, ma'am. Gave me a message for his sister which I would now deliver.'

She tapped a square finger on the blotter. 'The war? The war? My dear man, the war has been over nearly three years now. I warn you, I am used to ploys and deceptions from perfidious intruders.' Her colour was high, her lips clamped like a vice. Her mission to protect her young ladies was stamped on her countenance like the Imperial Seal.

Duggie blinked. He had been called many things in his thirty-five years, but never a *perfidious intruder*. He took a breath and proceeded to follow his rule that telling ninety-five per cent of the truth was the most effective way to succeed in deception. 'It's like this, ma'am. Didn't I have a dog's luck and get caught by them Huns? And didn't they ship me back to their prison? And didn't I escape and, for survival, and no other thing being available, ma'am, take some chickens for food? And didn't they put me in one of their danged – excuse me, ma'am – own prisons, me pretending to be dumb and them thinking I was German? And didn't they forget all about me at the end of the war? I couldn't let on to be English. They'd have torn me limb from limb, what with the reparations and them all starving and that. So I served my sentence.' The five per cent untruth was that it was a French prison where he served his time. And they were not going to let out a thief, Englishman or no Englishman.

Miss Bullock pursed her lips. 'You served your sentence?'

'That's correct, ma'am. Then I came home and have just collected my back pay.'

'Well, you could have arranged to see Miss Scorton on Saturday or Sunday.'

'Sadly not, ma'am. D'you see, I've re-enlisted in the Army and embark for India at the weekend.' This was another lie. He leaned forward. 'I particularly wanted to tell her with my own lips, ma'am, just what her brother said.'

She stared at him for a full minute then lumbered to her feet and moved to the door. Duggie was rather disappointed that she moved on little dumpy feet, rather than castors. When the room was empty he surveyed his surroundings with an expert eye. Good silver, inferior pictures of simpering

Victorian childhood idylls, heavy Victorian furniture . . . The door opened behind him and he swung round.

Mara ventured towards him, frowning. She was just recovering from being hauled out of a lecture by Miss Bullock and marched along the corridor to the Principal's own study. Miss Bullock was in the doorway. Duggie winked at Mara, shaking his head slightly. She kept her face blank.

'Well, old Tom never said you were a looker.'

Mara could feel Miss Bullock's eyes boring into her back. Mara eyed Duggie coldly. 'Mr . . . ?'

He moved to shake her hand heartily. 'Duggie O'Hare, Miss Scorton. Me and your brother was the best of mates.'

'You were?'

He looked round. 'Would you like to sit down, miss? I've something to talk to you about. About your brother.' He looked into her eyes.

The door clicked behind her and she could hear Bullock stumping along the corridor. 'What is it, Duggie? What is it? You already told me about Tommy.'

'There was one more thing. I missed one thing and it's been haunting me ever since. I wake up in the night and it goes through my head. *What a way to get leave. What a way to get leave.*'

'What is it, Duggie?'

'I couldn't say it that time while your dear mother was there. But Tom wanted—'

She interrupted him, looking around the plush, overstuffed room with its neat piles of books and papers. 'I can't listen to this here, Duggie. We'll talk in the town. There's an hotel called the White Swan – with a little tea room. I'll meet you there in half an hour.'

He looked round the room. 'And will they actually let you out of this maidens' citadel on a *Wednesday*?'

She smiled slightly then, relieving the tension building up between them. 'Well, no. But I'll be there anyway.'

They propped Miss Bullock's door open to show they had

left the room, and Mara walked him to the great door, ignoring the curious glances of girls whom they passed. Then she raced up to her room to get her warm coat and hat and walked sedately through the building and out of the gates, ignoring the gatekeeper who whispered knowingly to his wife, but did nothing to bar her way.

When she arrived at the café, Duggie was sitting at a corner table, presiding over a large silver teapot before a plate of muffins smothered in melting butter. He poured her tea and placed it carefully before her. 'It feels funny this. It should be me standing behind you, Mara, in me butler's gear, pouring it out for you.'

She sipped the tea and looked at him over the rim of her cup. 'Old habits die hard, eh?'

'Well, Mara, I was in service all my life – before I escaped into the Army, that is. And truth to tell, I've never sat at a table alongside someone like you. I'd be more likely to be standing at your elbow—'

Mara laughed. 'Bowing and scraping?'

'That's it. Ain't it awful?' He was comfortable now. 'Funny, innit? Things so changed now.'

'The war's changed everything. None of us will ever be the same.' Mara stirred her cup, avoiding the moment of talking about Tommy. 'We're all children of the storm. My mother said that once.'

'But then we're lucky, ain't we? There's the millions eaten up by the storm.'

Mara stopped stirring and looked at him. 'You've come to tell me about Tommy,' she said bravely. 'So you might as well say what you came to say.'

So he told her. He told her everything again, starting from when he first got together with Tommy in the training camp. He spoke of the gaiety and attraction of Tommy's character, of his exuberant innocence; he described the good times and the bad. Then he poured himself another cup of tea and very quietly spoke of the final event. 'That was what I couldn't say,

367

last time – about what they had me do. He wasn't finished, see? And it was the officer's duty to do that . . . Well, he couldn't. So he orders me to do it, doesn't he? The coward.' He let out a great sigh. 'There. It's out. Now you can tell me to get myself away.'

Mara sat very quiet for a second, then: 'Did you ever tell my mother this?'

'I bin there again. But I couldn't tell her.'

'How was she?'

'As always she was extraordinary. She asked me to tell her about him again. Cool, calm. And really proud of young Tom. Showed me that memorial place, for Tom and his pa. What a woman!'

'She's very special.'

'Must all be cut from the same cloth, in your family.'

'Was Leonora there? She's very special too.' Mara's tone was distracted. Her brain was racing with all that Duggie had just told her. She wanted to be alone in her room to think about it, to understand the true tragedy of Tommy's last moments. 'And are you still in the Army, Duggie?'

'This?' He fingered the cap on the table. 'No, not really. It's convenient to get around in, a uniform. People stand aside for you.'

'What will you do? There's little enough work around.'

'Well, your ma offered me a job at the Rainbow Works but I ain't sure. Not used to the country, you know. I like London meself.'

'Country?' Mara laughed. 'With the colliery wheels and the gas works and the factories?'

'It's country to me,' said Duggie solemnly.

Mara stood up and put out her hand. 'I'd love to stay, to talk more. But I'll have to rush away now. I've skipped two lectures already and there'll be old Harry to pay.'

His chair scraped back. 'I'll walk round with you.'

'No, you sit down and enjoy your muffins; finish the tea.'

'Will it be very bad up there?' Duggie asked. 'That woman would scare the shirts off a brigade of Huns, no question.'

'She might be bad, Duggie. But you've experienced worse and so have I. You have to keep things in proportion.'

Later as she stood outside Miss Bullock's study, her heart in her boots, waiting to be summoned, she pondered her own brave words. While she waited, the maid went in with a tea tray and fifteen minutes later came back to collect it. She endured another long five minutes before the door opened slightly, and Miss Bullock's voice told her to enter.

By the time she got into the room Miss Bullock was back behind her desk, her head down over a paper. She took several long seconds to complete her sentence, then she looked up. 'How great is your desire to be a teacher, Miss Scorton?'

'I've always wanted it, Miss Bullock. Always.'

'Do you think you're fit to be a teacher?'

Mara's lips hardened. 'As a matter of fact, I do, Miss Bullock. I am top of my year in my subjects and got distinctions on my practice.'

'Ah. You make the common mistake of thinking that teaching is only a matter of aptitude and intelligence.' She leaned forward, her eyes bulging slightly. 'How much more it is a matter of *attitude*.'

'Do you say that my attitude is at fault, Miss Bullock?'

'Do you think it demonstrates a worthy attitude, flouting the rules here and going off to meet a man . . . *a man* . . . in the middle of the week?'

Mara was suddenly reminded of Michael's outrage at finding her '*in the arms of that man* in the middle of the road' – the day he caught her kissing Jean-Paul. She shuffled her feet to relieve her legs, which were aching now with standing so long. She realised that, with her finals only weeks away, she was being threatened with expulsion. 'We need to keep this in proportion, Miss Bullock,' she said reasonably.

The pink of Miss Bullock's face deepened to a delicate

shade of damson. 'How dare you, Miss Scorton, how dare you suggest . . . ?'

Wearily Mara pushed back her hair which had flopped over her brow in the run back to college. 'I dare, because I am no a little girl from some genteel girls' school. Miss Bullock, have pulled the body of my headmaster from a building tha was being shelled. I achieved my matriculation by studying on my own, not in any school. I have run an office full o women in an armaments factory where the deadlines ebbed and flowed with the battle failures on the Western Front. have sat in a café in London while my brother recounted, in exquisite detail, the horror of fighting and living under fire If you are saying all these things have affected my attitude I would say you're right. But they can only affect it for th good. Don't you see that?'

Miss Bullock was visibly discomfited. 'It was not that, Mis Scorton, that I was challenging. It was today's escapade. You must understand—'

'Miss Bullock, I am twenty-one years old. For nearly two years I have gone along with all these rules because I can see that, with these girls who are virtually just out of the egg, they may be necessary. Today I decided to behave a an adult.'

Miss Bullock's jaw was dropping.

'If, for that, you wish to keep me waiting, to bully me and reduce me to tears, you have not succeeded. If, for that, you wish to expel me, then that is your prerogative.' Mara turned on her heels and stalked out, ignoring the voice behind her calling, 'Miss Scorton! Miss Scorton!'

She walked with slow deliberation to her room, put a match to the prepared fire and watched the flames lick up the little chimney. Then she went to her desk and started to write, almost word for word, what Duggie had just told her. She had almost finished when there was a knock on her door. Miss White poked her head round. 'Am I disturbing you?'

'No. No.' Mara took her coat from the back of a chair. Come in, sit down.'

Miss White sat down, her elegant ankles neatly together. You weren't at dinner, Miss Scorton.'

Mara covered her eyes with her hand. 'Blast it. Is it that me?' Her empty place would trumpet her absence. 'Oh, I'll ave really shot my bolt with Miss Bullock now. She'll sack ae, sure as shot.'

Miss White raised her eyebrows. 'I heard that there had een . . . an exchange of views.'

'Did she tell you I was a reprobate, that I wasn't worthy o teach?'

'Actually not. She did ask me to put an item down for the ext staff meeting, about College policy regarding conditions or more mature students.' Miss White glanced around the oom. 'So what kept you?'

Mara picked up the sheaf of papers. 'A man came, who new my brother. Saw him die. He was forced to . . .' She opped. The words wouldn't come. 'I came straight up here o write it. It just about finishes the story. A great act of iendship.' She straightened all the papers up on the desk nd put them in a cardboard folder. 'You said you would ead it. Will you?'

Miss White stood up and took the folder from her. 'Cerainly. It will be a privilege, Miss Scorton.'

'There's no hurry. I can't do anything more to it now, till fter the exams.' She paused. 'That is, if Miss Bullock lets ae sit them.'

'Have no fear, you will sit your exams. Just make sure you now your stuff.'

The door closed behind Miss White, then it opened again, nd her head reappeared round it. 'Oh, by the way, they're eeping your dinner warm for you, in the little kitchen. I told aem you'd reported in with a migraine.'

That night, huddled in bed, Mara's mind wandered from ae notes she was reading, back to Tommy and those terrible, ridiculous, final moments. Then from Tommy to Jean-Paul. Suddenly she wanted Jean-Paul with her, close and loving as she knew he could be. Making love. Making life.

Their agreement was that they should wait until she had qualified. Wait the five years she must teach to fulfil her obligation for her bursary. Well, now Miss Bullock might subvert that agreement by telling her to leave. Then the decision was taken out of her hands. One part of Mara wished for that. Perhaps the wait would be too long. A lot could happen in five years. Just look at Tommy.

24

A Splendid Offer

Leonora lifted the curtain at the dusty factory window and peered outside. 'It looks like we're in for a visitation.'

Kitty came across to take a look. 'So we are,' she said. The long-nosed shining car had stopped and the liveried chauffeur was handing out an elegant, if rather heavily built young woman in a coat rather longer than was now the fashion. She was followed by a slight woman dressed in plain grey who looked like a governess or a lady's maid. Lucette had changed a great deal in her time with Pansy, who still wore her mousy plainness as a disguise.

'Now what does Pansy want with us?' said Kitty thoughtfully.

Duggie O'Hare, now happily working in the forward dispatch area of the Works, brought them up the stairs. 'Miss Clarence and the Countess Poliakova,' he said, for all the world as though this dusty working office were a London drawing room. Kitty's lips twitched as she met his bland gaze. He scooped up the children's toy-box, and the twins followed him out as though he were the Pied Piper.

Kitty removed a pile of ledgers from a stool and her own work-overall from another. 'Well, Pansy, won't you take a seat? And you, Lucette?'

Leonora had stayed by the window. 'How are you, Lucette?' she said politely. The person before her was nothing like the sylph-like creature whom she had known in Moscow. Lucette's face was bloated and her hands were dimpled. Her clothes and hat, though expensive, were over-decorated and old-fashioned, reflecting the taste of Pansy rather than Lucette herself.

Lucette sniffed. 'How kind of you to ask, dearest Leonora. Unfortunately I am in the throes of the most dreadful cold. The climate in this country is so enervating. You have no real heat and no real cold.' She coughed affectingly and dabbed her lips with a lace handkerchief. 'And—'

'Yes, poor Lucette,' interrupted Pansy. 'We have had Dr McHugh three times this week, haven't we, dear? And you told him how you had suffered. And he mixed a special linctus for you, didn't he?'

'I—'

'Yes, and you told him you were only ever helped by that linctus you had from Paris.'

'Yes, my Papa—'

'Dr McHugh went scampering off to check in his medical textbooks, didn't he, dear?'

Kitty exchanged glances with Leonora. 'What can I do for you, Pansy? To be frank we have a good deal to get on with here.'

'So I see. The workshop down there looks very busy.'

Kitty nodded. 'Business is very good,' she said with an uncharacteristic flare of pride.

'Very good indeed, when you think we started entirely from scratch,' added Leonora dryly.

'Yes, my dear.' Pansy sailed on. 'All credit to you. Both of you. And with children under your feet as well!'

She had sold the Scorton Works as soon as the lucrative military contracts dried up at the end of the war, contributing considerably to the growing unemployment in Priorton.

'And you came . . . ?' prompted Kitty.

'Well, yesterday I was talking over my affairs with Mr Sleight. I have made a new will.' She smiled faintly towards Lucette who dimpled into an obliging smile. 'He is putting things in order for me to sell Purley Hall.'

The Hall had been empty and neglected since the military hospital had closed there in 1919. Pansy never went near the place.

'It always rather surprised me that you didn't live there, Pansy.'

'Well, Lucette did try to persuade me, didn't you, dear?'

'I thought it would be such—'

'Oh no. It is something of a mausoleum, Kitty. To be honest, it makes me shiver. The house in the town is quite enough for me.'

'William and I and the children had some fine times there.'

Pansy looked her full in the eyes. 'Ah yes, dear. But that is very much in the past, isn't it?'

'Well,' said Leonora abruptly. 'What is it you want?'

'The one untidy thing in all these properties is the house in Hartlepool. I had it made good again, refurbished, but Mr Sleight tells me it will get nothing on the open market. So I had an inspiration. I got Mr Sleight to draw up a proper deed of gift, for me to give it to our dear little Mara. Because I thought, without her rescuing me, all those years ago, I wouldn't be here now, would I, with a lovely house in Priorton, and my dear Lucette to keep me company always.'

Lucette had a fit of coughing then and Leonora took her to the washroom. She gave her a cup of water, making her sip it slowly.

As Lucette sipped from the cup, Leonora looked down on her. 'How can you stand it, Lucette? She keeps you, in high style admittedly, but in return you have to give her everything. Your looks. Your youth. Even the words from your mouth.'

Lucette looked at her blankly for a moment. Then there emerged from her a weird, wheezing version of her old tinkling laugh. 'Everything has its price, Leonora. Even for you. Loving Samuel has left you here in this dirty factory with two brats clinging to your skirts. We are indeed a long way from the Princess Golitzin's Hospital.'

Leonora laughed heartily. 'I tell you what, Lucette. I'd rather be where I am, in my dirty factory, than where you are, up that peculiar little woman's jumper like a little Russian bear.'

When they got back, Pansy was placing a parchment lawyer's envelope on the high standing-desk at which Kitty did her paperwork. 'You will make sure dear little Mara gets this? The keys are inside the envelope. Tell her the house is kept aired. I did so want it to be nice for her.'

'I can't accept it on Mara's behalf,' said Kitty firmly. 'I'll let her know. She's doing her final examinations at the moment.'

'Such a clever girl. So like my dear Michael. So like their father.'

Kitty shook her head at Leonora, who looked about to explode. 'If that is all, Pansy? We have so much to do.'

'Well, no, Kitty dear. I was wondering also about this memorial to my dear Michael and to William. If I could contribute to the plaque, there is the wonderful stonemason who carved Michael's headstone. I could—'

'No,' said Kitty firmly. 'That is arranged.'

'At least can I see what you will say?' said Pansy meekly. 'It will be so nice to see how Michael's name will be commemorated.'

Kitty scrabbled on the desk and found a sheet of paper, on which was scrawled:

In appreciation of
the lives, work and courage
of William, Michael and Tommy Scorton
and Luke, Matthew and John Kohn

'What?' Pansy squeaked. 'I can't have Michael's name up there with those Egyptians.'

There was a silence in the room, and they could hear the roar of machinery from the factory floor.

'Luke and his brothers were lifelong friends of William and Michael and of this family,' said Kitty carefully. 'Anyway, it's not you who is having it put on the plaque, it's me.'

Pansy stood up. 'Come along, Lucette,' she quavered.

Then she looked at Kitty, her mouth thin. 'Mr Sleight has been urging me to have something done for Michael. He has suggested a fountain in the Jubilee Park. Properly signified, of course, with Michael's name. I shall do that. And enquire with Mr Sleight regarding legal means whereby we may ensure that Michael's name should not appear on that ridiculous plaque.'

'Oh, for goodness' sake, Pansy,' said Leonora briskly. 'You took the poor man from his family in life. At least leave a shred of him there in death.'

'Well! I—'

Lucette took Pansy's arm. 'Come away, my dear. Come away. You can't blame them for wishing Michael's name to be here. And you will have your lovely fountain . . .' She was steering Pansy towards the door.

Pansy looked over her shoulder. 'This fountain will be remarkable, I have looked at designs,' she muttered.

Leonora closed the door behind them and looked at her mother. 'I think you've coped very well with Pansy, Kit, considering all she's done to you.'

Kitty shrugged. 'I suppose giving Mara the house is a way of rubbing all this in. Showing she can make a kind of difference to us, still. But think of it! All she's done is take the money. Didn't I spend twenty-five years telling William I wanted none of it? Just think how bad it would have been, since we lost William and Tommy, if we'd had the money, but hadn't had the factory and the Building to work on. We'd have been very rich and very sad.'

'Yes,' said Leonora. 'And very fat. Just like poor Lucette.'

Mara put down her pen and flexed her fingers, rubbing them briskly to bring them back to life. The cold was seeping up from the stone floor of the exam hall, through her feet and her legs, up though the trunk of her body and now into her hands. She picked up her paper and re-read her answers, altering and adding words here and there. She knew she had done well:

the questions had been predictable, she 'knew her stuff', and she enjoyed using examples from her actual experience to illustrate the theoretical points she was making.

She put her papers together, set her pens in their shallow channel, and sat back. She supposed she was lucky to have taken these examinations at all. She'd had a nervous few days waiting for a summons which did not come. Miss Bullock had, in the event, ignored her revolt. Mara had sat down in trepidation for each of the examinations, expecting to be hauled out at the last minute. Now she had finished the final one, she felt that somehow it must be all right.

Then the buzzer went, all pens were put down and the supervising tutor took an interminable time in collecting the papers. When they were finally free to go, an almost palpable ripple of relaxation went round the room. The chatter started and rose to a high crescendo as the students swept through the double doors, saying what a stinking paper it had been. Each girl gauged the exact amount of despair to express, to indicate that, really, there had been no problems.

There was a note for Mara on the crisscross board: Miss White requested Miss Scorton's presence in her study at her very earliest convenience. 'Uh-oh,' thought Mara. 'This is it. "We thought it prudent to let you sit your examinations, but . . ."'

Miss White smiled at her as she entered, and came out from behind her desk to take a low seat beside the gas-fire. 'Won't you sit down, Miss Scorton?'

Mara stayed standing. 'Are you going to sack me?'

Miss White frowned. 'Sack?' Then she smiled. 'Don't talk such rot. Now sit down.'

Mara sat down and waited.

Miss White patted the cardboard file on the low table beside her. 'It is very good, you know.'

Mara smiled at last. 'Tommy's story – you read it?' The final spurt of work for the exams, and the constant worry over the looming threat of Miss Bullock had pushed *A Boy's Story* to the edge of her mind. She waited.

'Of course I read it. I thought it admirably written, full of life and love. Heroism of a very special kind, too.' She touched some extra sheets clipped to the file. 'I have taken the liberty of making some notes, with suggestions for smoothing it out a bit here and there. Given that smoothing, it will make a first-class piece of work. So what shall you do with it?'

Mara shrugged. 'Make a neat copy. Show my family.'

'Perhaps someone would publish it.'

Mara laughed. 'When pigs fly. It will be taken as treason, even now, to regret the waste of a single life in their Great War. And to suggest that we wasted our own so cruelly.'

'I have friends in the Peace Pledge Union.'

Mara shook her head. 'First I will show my family,' she said, the finality in her tone brooking no further discussion.

There was a silence. Then Mara ventured, 'I've been waiting for days to be told to go, not to darken these doorsteps again.'

'Go? Oh no, Miss Scorton. How could we let our best student go? Miss Bullock just wished you to – if you'll excuse the vulgarity – sweat a little.'

'Well, I might have to sweat a bit more now. I want to go home for a few days.'

'What! But there are the end-of-term plays, the presentations to the First Years, the—'

'I have to go home. My mother has built a museum and library to be dedicated to my father and brothers. I must be there for the shindig. And I have to go to Hartlepool. My mother writes to tell me I have been given a house. I need to look at it; to think about it.'

Miss White frowned. 'Hartlepool?'

'It's the house where I was living in 1914, during the bombardment. And there is another thing.'

'Another thing . . . ?' prompted Miss White, the neutrality of her tone encouraging confidence.

'I have this friend, Jean-Paul – I told you about him. He's just back at work after the strike. They've had to take this huge cut in pay. I need a long talk with him which can't wait.' In fact she just needed to hold him, to touch him.

There was a long silence. Then Miss White leaned towards her. 'Right, dear girl, I will make representations to the Principal. She would never concede this to you face to face. You shall go tomorrow, but be back in a week, in time for the final revels and the end-of-term dinner.' She addressed her neat gold wristwatch and stood up. 'Now I must go to deal with a *contretemps* between the housekeeper and the Principal's maid.' She handed Mara the folder which contained Tommy's story. And on top of it, she placed two books.

Mara turned the books, peered at their titles. *Married Love* and *The Rainbow*. She looked up at Miss White in astonishment.

'They're foreign editions,' said Miss White. 'The first, by a very sensible woman, will ensure that in or out of wedlock, there'll be no . . . er . . . impediments to that fine career in teaching about which we've spoken. And the second, unbelievably by a man, is a novel so . . . sympathetic to the heart and the senses of a woman. So beautifully written. It's a fine book for any other writer to read. An inspiration. I urge you not to believe the scurrilous reports about these titles.'

Mara turned them over: both had been banned in their time. She wasn't sure whether they were now.

Miss White smiled openly. 'Now you do know that my life is in your hands. One breath of this gift to anyone and it will be me who will be what you call "getting the sack", not you.'

Carefully Mara enclosed the books in the cardboard folder and stood up. 'Then we're bound in confidence, Miss White, you and I. Are you sure I can go tomorrow?'

Miss White put a hand on her arm. 'Quite sure, my dear. Quite sure.'

'And you say your sister was in Russia with you, Mr Scorton?'

'As I said to you yesterday and your colleague the day before, my sister was not really "with me". We happened to be there at the same time. She had been a governess before the war in Moscow, and became a Red Cross nurse on the Russian Front.'

After the black and threatening months in Russian prisons, Samuel had found all this boring: coming to this grey building morning and afternoon, and going over in detail the whole of his time in Russia. He knew why they did it: cross-checking sources and the building up of records was good practice in Intelligence. And they were getting so much better at it now. But the repetitions were boring and insulting in their implication that he might be telling lies. These men were particularly interested in his contacts, of course. They were very interested in Pavel Demchenkov, whom they had vainly seen as one of the minor voices of post-Tsarist moderation. Pavel was now in America. 'Your sister knew the fellow, didn't she?'

'He was a surgeon on her unit. He was a good man.'

'They were all good men. But it's still hard to know who's on our side and who ain't, don't you know? Our American friends have got their eye on old Demchenkov.'

The officer, whom he only knew as Simpson, closed the file with a slap. 'Well, Scorton, I think that'll do for now. No point in pursuing the obvious. No doubt you'll need a breather.' Simpson's eyes narrowed slightly as he called up in his mind the photographic image of the page on Samuel's file. 'County Durham, isn't it? Get yourself up there, Scorton. Breathe a little fresh coal dust. You'll feel at home there. A Bolshevik under every bed, so they tell me.' He chuckled a little at his own joke, stood up and treated Samuel to a very limp handshake. 'Keep in touch. We know where you are.'

'So you do,' said Samuel. 'To be perfectly honest, I'm thinking of settling a bit. I've been wandering too long.' He thought then of Leonora, against whom no woman could hold a candle. And the two strange creatures who, somehow,

Leonora and he had made between them. At the thought of the twins, a frisson of delight and fear was exquisitely fused.

As he came out of Simpson's room he bumped into Bertram Langley, who was loitering in the corridor. 'Ah, Scorton!' Langley put away his copy of *The Times*. 'Thought I'd find you here, old boy. I bet you wouldn't say no to a slap-up lunch at the Savoy? I understand you're going home today.'

How would he know that? Samuel eyed him morosely. 'Well, you know more than I did when I went into that room.' The last thing Samuel wanted was to hear that braying voice right through lunch, and to be obliged to answer questions which he knew would be turned about by Langley, and put into one of those spy novels of his. Even so, it was not Simpson, but Langley who had inveigled him out of his cold cell, and got him safely home. Lunch it would be, then onto the station to check the first train home. To Leonora, who, he hoped, would forget the long times in between and remember the nights in Moscow. Perhaps, just perhaps, she would not beat him over the head and send him packing.

Jean-Paul met Mara at the station and shouldered her case as they walked through the streets of Priorton. 'I could quite easily carry it myself,' she objected.

'I know you could, but today I wish to do something for you, to show that I love you. If carrying the case is the only thing, this is what I do.'

She took his arm as they strolled. 'So you're back at work, Jean-Paul?' she said, loving the familiarity of the warm arm under hers: the sense of ownership, belonging. 'They say the wages are down.'

She could feel his shrug. 'Reduced by two shillings a shift in July, two and six in August, and three shillings in September. I cannot see how a man with a family can manage. It's food out of the children's mouths.'

'You should come out of the pit, Jean-Paul. Couldn't Kitty

take you on?' Leonora had written that Tommy's friend Duggie was now on the strength at the Rainbow Works, working as a general fixer and factotum for their mother. *I think Kit likes it because it is a connection with Tommy, Mara. I think Duggie likes it because he has fallen for Kitty hook, line and sinker. Whether it's because he never had a mother of his own, or he yearns to be the disciple of an older woman, I can't say.*

Now Jean-Paul was telling Mara, 'I did some work for Kitty during the strike. She was good to ask me. I 'ave also done some carpentry at the Building, but I would not stay on.'

Mara frowned. 'Why not?'

'Can't you see?' He stopped and faced her. 'I am not sure of you. I have never been sure of you. You grow up and you meet more educated, younger men. It would be an embarrasment if I work for your mother.'

Mara laughed and reached up to kiss him hard on the cheek. 'Look, dearest goose, I'm not interested in *men*. Other than you, that is. And you're a problem enough.'

'Me? You don't want me?'

He sounded so doleful that she made him put the case down in the deserted street, enfolded her arms round him and kissed him properly. He kissed her back. And she kissed him again. 'There, do you see? That's how much I want you. Aren't we linked together for ever? But, for now, I have to start teaching, find myself a school. There is so much. And you . . .'

'And I will patiently wait.' He touched his lips with his fingers, then touched hers. Then he picked up her case again.

They were nearing Kitty's house. 'How is Hélène?' Mara said suddenly.

'Hélène? Well. It's surprising. These days when I go to see her she is helping the staff with the sewing, and the dusting. Helping to dress patients. There is no wild shouting, nothing. Less and less since the end of the war.'

'Could she come home?'

He shook his head. 'How can she be at home? I am at work

all day now. People know she has been in the asylum. They will throw stones again.'

'It would be different if you lived somewhere else. There is the house in Hartlepool now. You, me and Hélène, we could live there.'

He shrugged. 'Perhaps you should see her before you make any plans.'

The next day, Leonora lent Mara the motor car to go and see Hélène. When she collected Jean-Paul, although his face and hands were scrubbed clean, he had still the coal dust from the morning's shift on the inside of his eyelids. As they rode along she told him of her battle with Miss Bullock, and the kindness of Miss White. She stopped mid-sentence. 'But here I am going on. You must be bored by all this yammer.'

He put his hand on hers as it lay on the wheel. 'I am proud of you, Mara. You are strange and clever like your mother and sister. You will be a good teacher.'

When they arrived at the asylum, Hélène was sitting in a deep bay-window in the great entrance hall. She was sewing, wearing the asylum dress and apron. But her hair now was dressed smartly back into a chignon, and the scars, bleached and silver, were almost invisible on her neck and lower arms. She put down her sewing as they came towards her and held out her hands. 'Mara, dearest girl.'

Mara took Hélène's hands in hers and sat down beside her. 'How are you?'

'I am well.' She glanced round. 'They are kind enough here. And it is easier for me, now the voices are gone.'

'No voices?' said Mara.

Hélène looked at her steadily. 'Nothing. I am at peace.'

'Would you like to come home?'

'Home?'

'Somewhere with Jean-Paul and me.'

Hélène looked from one to the other. 'You will marry?'

Mara shook her head. 'No, not for a long time. But still we can all be together.'

Hélène picked up her sewing again. 'That would be very nice,' she said composedly.

Mara and Jean-Paul went to see Hélène's doctor to ask about the possibility of her coming home. He put his neatly scrubbed hands together. 'It's true Hélène has been much improved lately.'

'How can that happen?' asked Mara.

He shrugged. 'I would like to say that it is a result of our treatment here. In the Middle Ages we might have claimed to have cast out her devils, since they certainly seem to have departed. However, I suspect the real reason is something to do with time. It is seven years since the traumatic events which so destroyed her. In seven years our bodies reconstitute themselves. Perhaps our minds do also.'

'Can we take her home, then?'

He shook his head slowly. 'Not all at once. She is used to this place. You could bring her own clothes and take her out for the day – see how she takes that. Then perhaps . . .' He stood up and came round his desk to shake their hands. Mara was surprised at how small he was, to be the emperor of this strange kingdom.

From Sedgefield they drove on to Hartlepool. The streets here were bustling and busy and they had to weave through heavy port traffic as they made their way down to the docks. Mara stopped at the spot where she had stumbled over Jean-Paul's father, and repeated for him what had happened.

He shook his head. 'My father was a weak man, and a coward, but he left me a great legacy – you. You stumbled over him, you came to me. It is a great gift, for which I thank my father every day of my life.' He picked up her hand from the steering wheel, kissed it, then dropped it hurriedly at the sound of an appreciative whistle from two passing dockyard workers.

They drove to the house on the cliff road where Mara had

lodged all those years ago with the Misses Clarence. The key from the envelope moved easily in the lock. The house was dry and warm as they wandered through the neat, half-furnished rooms. The parlour, which had been demolished by the shell, had been made good again but it was bare and unfurnished the peppery smell of new wood pervaded there.

Mara opened the new shutters and dust danced on the beams of afternoon sun as it streamed across the new floor-boards. 'This is where we would begin,' said Mara. 'This is where we could make it our own.'

Hand-in-hand they wandered around the upstairs rooms. Jean-Paul laughed as she told him tales of the strange sisters who had called this house home. They came to Heliotrope's room, still dominated by her great bed dappled with sunshine from the unshuttered window.

On the next floor Mara's old attic room was spotless; the bed was made up as though to anticipate her occupation. Sun streamed through the tiny roof window.

The springs creaked as Jean-Paul sat down on the bed and he pulled her onto his knee. 'So this is where the little Mara stayed,' he said, kissing her cheeks, then her eyes, tickling her ears with his lips. 'Like a Cinderella in her lair.'

His fine touching made her want him more than ever before. She put her arms round him and started to kiss his cheeks, his lips. He groaned and they slipped downwards on the bed. Holding her with one arm, he freed the other so he could loosen the buttons of her blouse, and slip his hand inside, first on her throat and shoulder then down to cup her breast and pass his palm over her quickening nipple. Then he kissed her in the hollow at the base of her throat and his lips followed the path of his hand. She closed her eyes, the whole of her body quick with feeling. 'We'll get all creased,' she murmured.

His hands went back to her buttons. 'Then we will be each other's servant, Miss Schoolteacher,' he whispered in her ear. 'We will have all of these clothes off, shaken out and hanging on the bedrail. Is it agreed?'

'It is agreed,' she whispered, her hands already busy with his necktie.

It was two hours before they got out of the house, demurely attired in their smooth neat clothes. Almost without thinking, Mara drove down the road and on to the school. The children, just coming out at home-time, crowded round the car. She left Jean-Paul to deal with them and went across the familiar yard and through the familiar battered doors. The first person she bumped into was Joe Bly. He took off his cap and scratched his head. 'Why, yer bloke! Miss Scorton grown-up if I a'n't mistaken.'

She shook hands warmly with him. 'How are you, Joe?'

'Well as ever, Miss Scorton. Well as ever.'

She looked around. 'It all looks the same,' she said.

'Aye. Med good the damage right off. Worked like beavers in those first months after the raid. All over town. Just to show them Germans they couldn't get us down.'

'Good thing too,' she said, feeling that was called for.

'Aye.' He replaced his cap. 'Come on then, I'll tek you to see the Headmaster. Not a patch on Mr Clonmel, mind you. Too soft by half. But he's a fust-class cricketer, I'll give him that.'

The new Head Teacher, Mr Smyth, a lean man with a moustache, was pleased to meet Mara. He listened attentively to Joe Bly's retelling of the tragedy. 'And this girl was a heroine, a heroine I tell you, sir.'

Mara protested.

'And you are still a teacher, Miss Scorton?'

'Not quite. I have just sat my final exams at Teacher Training College.'

'And will you pass?'

'Oh yes, I think I'll pass.'

'Are you good in the classroom?'

She hesitated. 'Well, I am top of my year in practice.'

'Well, Miss Scorton, would you think of returning here? I will have a vacancy in September and this school, this whole area, is in sore need of new blood, new ideas.'

By the time she got back to the car, Mara had promised to come and see Mr Smyth at the end of term to discuss seriously the possibility of teaching there in September.

Jean-Paul had the bonnet up, and was showing the gleaming engine to an admiring group of boys. He pulled it down with a clatter, and rubbed his hands with a cloth. 'Well?' he said.

'What would you think about us coming to live here in September, with Hélène? There'll be a job for me in the school. A few ghosts to be laid. And I'm sure you could get work with one of the shipbuilders. We can make the house on the cliff our own. What do you think?'

'What would the school say to you living here like this with me?'

'Hélène can be our chaperone. And we will be discreet. If I have to wait five years to get married, why can't I wait on my terms, not theirs?'

He turned the handle then jumped in the car as she put it into gear. He laughed. 'Yes – why not? In this also, you are your mother's daughter, Mara Scorton.'

25

All They Want Is Heroes

Very gently, Leonora placed the cardboard folder on the table beside Mara. 'I don't know how you wrote that,' she said quietly.

'Line by line,' said Mara.

Leonora had had to wait until the twins were finally in bed before she could finish the last few pages. She relished these moments of peace every day.

'I kept hearing Tommy's voice, his laughter.' Leonora sat in the seat by the fire and stretched out her legs, yawning. 'I've read others thing about the war. So much of it,' she said. 'This so much better. You've done something very clever, my love. Turned a man people would call a coward into a hero.'

'He *was* a hero. They all were, even Duggie.' Mara was pulling on her outdoor coat.

Leonora looked at her steadily. 'What'll you do with it now, Mara?'

Her sister shrugged. 'It's here. Mama can read it. Anyone can read it.'

'We could bind it, and put it in the Building, with all William's books.'

'Yes,' said Mara uncertainly. 'I suppose that's all right.'

'We could get it printed. Lots of copies.'

'You'd have to ask Mama about that.' Mara checked the angle of her hat in the mirror. 'She might not care for strangers reading it.'

'She's proud of Tommy, whatever happened.'

'Well, it would be up to her. Other people might not like it. All they want is heroes.' She picked up her bag.

'So, where are you going?'

'To Bridge Street. Hélène's come home for a few days. I'm going to collect her at Bridge Street and bring her here to sleep. Jean-Paul's on early turn tomorrow and we mustn't leave her alone.'

A flicker of concern moved across Leonora's face. 'You will be careful, Mara?'

'Now don't start that again! She's better now, just like her old self.'

'But even that was a very fragile self, wasn't it? You get so involved, Mara. And if you're going across to Hartlepool after the summer, to take up the teaching post that you talked about . . .'

'Jean-Paul and Hélène will come with me,' said Mara determinedly.

'What? With you? Do you mean . . . ?'

'I mean that Jean Paul and I will live there. Together. Yes, I mean exactly that.' Mara's tension left her then, and she punched Leonora on the shoulder. 'I can't believe you're acting like a sourpuss prude, Leonie. Who is this woman? The same girl who had a love affair with the bolting vicar? Who went off into the wilds of Russia with a Bolshevik doctor, even if he was just a friend. Who fell in love with her own brother?'

A shadow fell across Leonora's face. 'Samuel is not really my brother.'

Mara laughed. 'All I'm doing is asking you to accept what I do, in the same way that we always accepted Kitty and William's arrangements. In the way Kitty herself accepts our arrangements.'

Leonora nodded slowly and sat back again in the chair. 'You're right, of course, love. Why is it you're always right?' she said gloomily. 'You were right when you told me to go to Russia. And you're right now.'

''Cause I'm the teacher, that's why.' Mara winked and grinned at her sister. She put her hand on the doorknob. 'Would you like to come to see Hélène?' she asked.

Leonora shook her head. 'The children are in bed, and Kitty's down at the Building with Duggie and Luke, putting the final finishing touches to the exhibition.' She sniffed. 'Thick as thieves, Kitty and Duggie, these days.'

'Now don't you get uppity about that. Duggie fixes things for Mama. He makes her laugh. He's her connection with Tommy. And I think being around her helps him a bit as well. What they made him do to Tommy haunts him.'

'You're always so wise, Mara,' said Leonora, irony in her voice. 'It must be that College education.'

Mara stopped. 'Are you all right, Leonie?'

Her sister looked wistful. 'Sometimes I long to run away, Mara,' she confided. 'Get right away, like when I went to Russia. At times I think I must have dreamed all that – all the excitement, even the fear, the sense, now and again, of saving lives, of counting in a bigger pattern. Then, other times, I know it was all very real; I think that out there, doing all that, I was most completely me.' Then she smiled, and pulled herself together. 'Take no notice of me, love. I'm just nithering on.'

But her smile faded as the door clicked behind her sister. She pressed her back against the closed door and gave into the dark feeling which had been nibbling at the edges of her consciousness for days. She could not understand why, suddenly, everything which had been so easy seemed so tiresome.

The twins were their usual perversely pleasurable selves. The factory was thriving. The work on the Building was complete and ready for its grand opening tomorrow, to be properly christened the Scorton Library and Institute. And Kitty was delighted with Leonora's idea of celebrating the opening with a big bunfight for everyone – old friends of William, Tommy and Michael, people who had helped with

the Building, guests from Scorton's Works and their own
factory, staff from Kitty's old shop; the people from the soup
kitchen in the Methodist Sunday School, which Leonora
helped to run in the afternoons.

'And no bigwigs?' Mara had asked on her first night home.

'No bigwigs,' said Kitty firmly.

Now Leonora stood up, shook her head, and opened the
door again and stood outside in the soft night air. Leaning
against the doorjamb she began to realise that her real problem
was that she was bored. *Ennui* – one of Lucette's favourite
words. Boredom.

Leonora knew she loved the twins. And her work at the
factory and the soup kitchen and on the Council was all
absorbing. But sometimes when she touched the smooth
sleeping cheek of Kathy or Thomas, she raged with physical
hunger for just such a tender touch on her own cheek. And
the jogging rhythm of Priorton life seemed to stretch forward
into too distant a future. She was more than forty now, though
just as energetic as ever. But there was a hateful, insidious
difference in the way people treated her. Lucette, in their rare
conversations, took every opportunity to mention her age and
her settled, middle-aged existence.

And now the terrifying thought crept into her consciousness
that Samuel might never return. *Ever*. Perhaps this was all
there was. Could that be true? Perhaps the central adventure
of her life really *was* over.

She raked her hands through her hair hard, making
her hair fall loose from its pins. 'Leonora Rainbow, get
hold of yourself!' she said severely. She went inside again,
slammed the door, and marched over to the fire, poking
it viciously back to life. Then she sat down to make notes
for a speech she would be delivering next week, about
the scandal regarding medical care – or lack of it – for
the poor.

'Mara! Mara! Will you please come here!'

Racing across the Market Place towards Bridge Street, Mara skidded to a stop and looked up at Pansy's tall house. Pansy was leaning out of the window waving her arms like a demented windmill.

Mara ran across. 'What's up? What's the matter, Pansy? Is someone hurt?'

'Hurt? Hurt? Come in, come in here!' Pansy vanished, and Mara approached the door, which was opened by Peggy, the younger Royle sister, who ushered her in.

'What's the matter, Peggy? Is someone hurt?'

Peggy shook her head. 'Can't say. Miss Pansy is like a woman "off", as they say, miss.'

'What's the matter?' Mara looked around. 'Where's Miss Poliakova, Peggy? Where's the Countess?'

'That's the problem. Me and me sister had the afternoon off and when we came back . . .'

'Mara!' Pansy's piteous voice came down to them over the banister. 'Do come here.'

Mara hurried upstairs

Pansy was standing on the landing clasping and unclasping her hands. 'Come!' she said.

Nervously, Mara followed.

Pansy led her to Lucette's room and flung open the door. There was nothing in the room except the stripped bedstead, the mahogany chest with its barren drawers agape, and the huge empty wardrobe.

'What has happened? Has there been a robbery?'

Pansy clung to the bedpost with her thin hands. 'You may well ask that, my dear,' she said brokenly. 'I had a meeting with Mr Sleight, and then a Scorton Works board meeting. I came home and I found this.'

'And where's Lucette?'

'You may well ask "Where's the thief?"'

'You think Lucette stole all this?'

'Yes. She left a note saying she knew she had helped me. Then she took everything. All the clothes, the beautiful outfits

I bought her. The very curtains off the rail. The very sheets of the bed. Irish linen, they were.'

Pansy sat down hard on the mattress, which did not give under her sparrow weight. 'And all the jewels from my bedroom – Heliotrope's pearls and rings, the watches our father gave us on our birthdays, and Heliotrope's little leather attaché case. *And* the trunks which I had as a girl when I went to school.' She raised haggard eyes to Mara. 'I have taken a viper to my bosom, my dear,' she said mournfully, and started to tremble violently.

Mara sat down and put an arm round her sister-in-law, thinking ruefully that vipers came in all shapes and sizes, and that this might just be a case of viper biting viper. 'What do you want to do, Pansy? Shall I go for the Constable?'

The shaking under Mara's arm stopped. She could almost feel the brain in that deceitful and conniving little head ticking over, just as it must have done the day after her sister Heliotrope's death, when she decided that clinging to Mara herself was the best bet.

This time Pansy decided to save her own face. 'The Constable? I think not, dear. What would people say? What on earth would they think of me?' She paused. 'What shall I tell them, those two ninnies downstairs, and the rest of Priorton. They mustn't have tales to tell. I must not look foolish or I won't hold my head up here again.'

Mara thought for a moment. 'You must tell them that the Countess has been called away,' she said. 'Her family has escaped the terror in Russia with just the clothes they stand up in. She has gone to London to join them. And you have been beside yourself with grief because of that. You are so very close, Lucette and you.'

Pansy was relaxing. 'Yes, yes,' she said eagerly.

'And, very generously, you insisted that she must take the wherewithal to make her poor terrorised family comfortable.'

Pansy put her hand over Mara's. 'You are so clever, dear child.' Her voice had regained its idiosyncratic mixture of midity and steely determination. 'Just like my dear Michael. And William.' She squeezed Mara's hand. 'Isn't it the opening of the Scorton Library tomorrow? I had thought perhaps I would not manage to get there. Lucette said it would give her what she called *ennui*. But perhaps I can attend now. It is a family affair, after all, and it is so long since I have seen dear Kitty. What is it, Mara? Why are you laughing?'

Mara was still chuckling as, much later, she made her way to Bridge Street. She had told the concocted story to the disbelieving Royle sisters, who only agreed that it was probably true as she pushed one of Pansy's hoarded sovereigns into each of their apron pockets. Then she settled Pansy in her long dining room to eat her solitary dinner.

Mara had no worries about Pansy. Her sister-in-law was a survivor. It was the rest of them who had to watch out, now Pansy was on the loose again.

Jean-Paul's grave face cleared to a smile when he saw her. 'I had decided you could not come,' he said, pulling her inside. 'I thought you would be working hard at the Building.'

'No, no. It's all done. Believe me.' She followed him through into the house and kissed him, relaxing as she wound her fingers through his hair, relishing the way his long body lined itself up against hers. Reluctantly she pulled away and looked round at the empty room. 'Where's Hélène?' she asked.

He took her hand. 'Come!' He led her upstairs and into the small back bedroom. There, her hand under her cheek like a child, lay Hélène sound asleep.

'She fell asleep in the chair,' he whispered, 'so I lifted her up here. She will sleep for hours.'

'So I can't take her home with me?'

He kissed her ear. 'Not for a long time. In the morning, perhaps?' He pulled her now through to his bedroom. 'And how is it that you're so late, you *monstre*? You leave me brooding here that you are done with me.'

She kissed him on the cheek and sat on the bed. 'Never!'

she said. 'I've made up my mind about you, Jean-Pau
Derancourt.'

'But why are you so late?'

She told him about Pansy, breaking out in laughter onc
again at the thought of her sister-in-law being outflanked

'That woman!' Jean-Paul said crossly, taking Mara's hand
'She deserves a terrible fate, all she has done to you and Kitt
and the rest.'

She lifted his hand and kissed it on the calloused palm
'Don't find fault with Pansy, Jean-Paul. It's because of he
we can get a start in Hartlepool. She gave us the house or
the cliff, remember? Though she would have apoplexy if sh
thought we would be living there together.'

He pulled her round to face him. 'God bless Miss Pansy fo
ever,' he said obediently. Then he kissed Mara's nose and he
eyes, his lips making their way all the way round her hairline
'And God bless Miss Mara Scorton, spinster of this parish. I
that not what they say in this service you deny me?'

'You've been looking it up!' she protested. 'I told you
Jean-Paul, we can't get married for another five years. I mus
do this teaching thing properly.'

He nuzzled her cheek. 'But I will be thirty-five years then
An old man.'

'You will be lovely. And I will only be twenty-six. Plenty
of time for everything then,' she said.

'Very well then,' he sighed, 'but I will always ask you
Every week.'

Mara chuckled. 'My father asked my mother every weel
for twenty-five years. And they were always happy.' She slic
down on the bed and looked up at him in the dim evening
light of the bedroom.

He lay beside her and put his hand just inside the collar
of her blouse. 'With that, and this, darling Mara, I must be
content.'

Samuel saw the woman as he alighted from the London train

The brim of her hat was weighed down by a sprawling red poppy, pierced by a pheasant's tail feather which trembled against her rouged cheek. The soft drape of her velour coat hid her thickening figure. Behind her was a mountain of trunks and boxes; she stood out among the drab workaday crowd of passengers waiting for the overnight train to London. Her fellow passengers gave her a clear space of her own, as though there were some kind of invisible barrier between her and them.

Some of the boxes heaped up beside her were painted with neat initials. *PC*.

Lucette had suffered just the slightest pang of guilt as she packed all the stuff into Pansy's trunks. But really, she had no option, had she? How else could she transport all these things? And how greatly she had supported Pansy all these years! Hadn't she brought joy into that drab little life? Surely Pansy couldn't begrudge her a few boxes? As it was, the boxes would be a bother. They would have to go into storage once she got to London. Her first priority there would be to find a stylish address. Then to begin to live again!

She moved her feet, restive as a horse at the start of a race. The train had been late in. There would be yet more waiting as they turned the thing around and connected the sleeping cars. The engine had already been uncoupled and was steaming backwards. The cleaners were moving onto the train, brandishing brushes, pulling windows down with a clatter.

A tall dark man was sweeping off his hat and striding towards her, a smile breaking out on his tired face. 'Lucette!'

She blinked guiltily, glanced around her, and frowned at the gaunt figure before her. Then her face cleared. 'Samuel!' She held out her hand. 'I thought you were a policeman. What have they done to you? I did not recognise you.'

He took her hand and kissed it. The people around them started to stare with open interest. In a place where linking arms signified engagement if not marriage, hand-kissing was very suspect. 'Well, Lucette,' he said. 'You're not unchanged yourself.'

She tugged at her coat. 'These dreadful clothes? Pansy . . . you know about Pansy? Well, at the start she was so kind, but she is a very strange woman. I was impelled to do what she wanted.' She giggled suddenly. 'Do you know, Leonora once said Pansy kept me up her jumper like a little Russian bear.'

Samuel held her hand tighter. 'Leonora? How is she?'

Lucette looked at him carefully. 'Ah, poor Leonora,' she said. 'You'll find her much changed. Lost her sparkle, perhaps? Obsessed with those children, always round her knees. I say to her about governesses, but . . .'

'She'll have no money,' said Samuel carefully. 'Seems your friend Pansy robbed her of her inheritance. She wrote to me about it.'

Lucette shrugged. 'I do not know about such things. Anyway, Leonie is quite the *Hausfrau* these days, and is no fun.'

He glanced at her luggage. 'So you're leaving Priorton?'

'I have a letter from a cousin of my father who has now reached London. She says everything is so gay there. I burned the letter so that Pansy would not see. She was very cross.' Her lids fluttered over her eyes. 'So I decided to go.'

'And Pansy?' said Samuel.

'She does not know.'

He laughed. 'You're running away, Lucette. Like a little girl from school.'

She shrugged. 'It is the only way. She would not have let me go.'

'That little woman?'

'You don't know her.'

He glanced around. 'It'll be at least ten minutes before the train will be ready. Shall we have some tea? And you can tell me all about the lovely Pansy.'

She smiled and the ghost of the younger Lucette flitted across her plump face. 'What, Samuel? Do you not rush into the arms of Leonora?' She picked up the small attaché case which contained the most precious items. 'After all this time?'

He laughed. 'I am back for good, Lucette. I have all the time in the world now for Leonora.'

But as he followed Lucette towards the station buffet he knew she had put her finger on something. After all this time, and the things that he had endured, there might be nothing left. No feeling. He had dreamed it once, in his prison cell: Leonora seeing his face at last, and screaming.

Kitty and Luke brought the smell of polish and new paint into the kitchen with them, on the draught of night air. Leonora raised her head from her papers. 'All done?' she said.

Kitty shook out her cloak. 'All done,' she said.

'All done,' echoed Luke, still by the door.

Leonora stood up. 'Come by the fire, Luke. You look so cold.'

The old man smiled thinly. 'It is true, Leonora, that there is less and less heat in this country for me.'

'It must have seemed so cold when you first came here from Egypt,' said Kitty, sitting very still with close attention, aware of the honour of talking to Luke about himself at all.

'It turned our blood to ice,' he said simply. 'Our teeth chattered for a whole year when we first came.'

'Then why did you stay?'

'Mr Scorton was our brother, our son, Kitty. You know that.'

In the crystal silence that followed it was as though William was in the room with them. Then Luke coughed: a dry cough, like whispering paper. 'Now Mr Scorton's library is ready, it is time for me to return home.'

Leonora blinked. 'You will go back to Egypt?'

'You can't,' said Kitty, blinking away a tear. 'You can't. You will leave your brothers behind. And William.'

The old man shook his head. 'I will take them all with me in my head, in my heart. And you, Kitty. But the sun will warm me. I will die where I was born.'

'I can't do without you, Luke.'

He smiled his thin smile. 'Mr O'Hare will be at your side, Kitty. He is devoted, as I have always been. He is a fine man.' He turned and left the room and they heard the click of his footsteps as he went along the hall to his room, which had been the front parlour when the house served just one family.

'Well!' said Kitty. 'I thought I was quite past surprises.'

'He seems very determined,' said Leonora doubtfully, 'but he is so frail. So very old. He'll surely not survive the journey to the ship, still less the voyage.'

'He will do it on sheer willpower, Leonie. I know it.' Kitty took off her hat, and moved it round in her hand. 'And I will get on with things. I always have and I always will.' Her words were braver than her tone, which was tired and hollow. Then she looked up at Leonora. 'If he goes, someone must go with him. I can't, as there is so much to do here, but you . . .'

Leonora stood up and took her arm. 'Go to bed, Kit. You look all in. It will be a big day tomorrow.'

'But—'

'Bed! We will talk about all that tomorrow, I promise you.'

Leonora's brain was racing as she sat down again to her papers. Egypt! No doubt the sea voyage would be good for the twins, and there would be so much to see there . . .

A clicking pierced her consciousness and she glanced around. Someone was knocking on the window with a ringed finger. She opened the curtains and peered straight into a dark, haggard face. She drew back in momentary fear, then peered closer, lightning and brilliant sunshine coursing through her veins in equal measure.

She tore across the room to open the door and fell into Samuel's arms. He hugged her with that achingly familiar bear hug, then pushed her into the light of the room to see her properly. He lifted the strands of hair which had fallen from their pins. 'Leonie, Leonie,' he whispered, 'you look just like a girl. Younger even than in Moscow.'

'You . . . They must have . . .'

He laughed shortly. 'They made an old man of me on the outside, sweetheart, but nowhere else.' He kissed her hard then, as though to prove it, and she felt his body quickening against hers. 'I love you, love you, love you!' he said, relieved and delighted that his bad dream of her had been a kind of inner lie, built as a bulwark against his worst fears.

She stroked his face, pushing away the tears with her fingers. Then he stood away from her. 'Stay there!' he said. He fished in his breast pocket and pulled out a ring which glittered in the lamplight. He held it out to her. 'I know that in this family it is a tradition for people to love each other without the benefit of office, my darling. But I wish to break that tradition. I do so want to marry you properly, with a ring, and a preacher feller, and the words "with my body I thee wed" and all that.'

She took the ring from him and placed it on her own finger. 'Consider it done. Tomorrow or the next day. I promise you.'

He roared then and hugged her again, swinging her round and round.

She beat him on the chest. 'Egypt! We can go to Egypt, Samuel!'

'Anywhere! My dearest. Whither thou goest I will go!' he bellowed.

The door opened and Kitty stood there, her hair in fat grizzled pigtails, a big-eyed child on either side of her. She beamed up at Samuel. 'Dearest boy,' she said. 'The last to return.'

'Kit!' he exclaimed. And then it was her turn to be swung round.

Kathy and Thomas scampered to their mother's side. 'Who is it, Mama?' said Kathy, half-scared.

'This is your Papa. Thomas . . . Kathy. Say hello.'

He came across and knelt beside them. 'Hello, my dears,'

he said, much more quietly. 'I can see that you have been taking good care of Mama for me.' His hands were trembling as he pulled their stiff little bodies to him.

'I will go and get Mara,' said Kitty. She was back in two minutes. 'She's not there,' she said. 'Her bed is empty.'

'We-ell. She did go to see Jean-Paul and Hélène,' said Leonora.

They all looked at each other.

'The naughty girl,' said Leonora, her lips twitching. And they all began laughing and hugging each other. The twins, relaxing at last, joined in the celebrations, clinging to their new-found father with growing delight.

Epilogue
Safe Harbour

''Night, miss.'

'Good night, Matthew.'

'Good night, miss.'

''Night, Laura.'

'Good night, Miss Scorton.'

Getting away from the schoolyard was always like running a benevolent gauntlet. Mara was down into the main part of the town before the children stopped pursuing her with their earnest salutations.

Her pupils' fascination with her would be, she knew, short-lived. She was very young and very new. She hadn't, as yet, used the cane. She worked so hard with them that problems of discipline were only rarely raised and easily dealt with.

Her new Head Teacher, unlike Mr Clonmel, did not prowl the school like a sentinel. He spent the first hour of every day in his study reading *The Times*. After that he taught history to each class in turn, so he did know all the children. He was free with the cane and induced a wary respect throughout the school. However, there was less fear in the school than there had been before, and it was no worse for that.

When she first walked in the space where Mr Clonmel had been killed she waited for some tremor, some frisson which might bring the gory detail back to her. There was none. The event was as surely fixed in the past as was Tommy's life, so carefully pinned down in words in her book.

Tommy's story was to be published in London any day now. She already had advance copies. Samuel, in London on his way south to embark for Egypt with Leonora, Luke and the children, had given it to Bertram Langley, an acquaintance of his who was a writer.

Mr Langley had written a very kind letter to Mara, saying he had placed it with a well-known company for her, and that he was certain there would be a very wide audience for *A Boy's Story*. She had refused an offer from someone from the Peace Pledge Union to write a preface, saying the story had to stand on its own, without endorsements, political or otherwise.

And in today's post, miraculously, five copies of *A Boy's Story* had arrived with her own name emblazoned on the cover. One of them was already parcelled up, and addressed to send to Miss White, who had turned up at the opening of the Scorton Library with a devoted Dewi Wilson in tow.

Mara smiled and took a skip as she walked along, thinking of Leonora off on another adventure, this time with Samuel by her side. The children too. Leonora was now officially Mrs Leonora Scorton, and she and Samuel were so happy you could almost warm your hands on them. Without doubt their time apart had made their time together all the more precious. Mara knew she loved Jean-Paul with all her heart, but their love was of a different order. In some ways this was a relief because Mara was not ready just yet for something so all-engulfing.

She strolled past a parade of shops, in which shadowy figures were lighting lamps against the falling autumn dusk, then turned down a small back street and stopped in front of a cabinetmaker's shop.

The closing shipyards had yielded no work for Jean-Paul but a chance meeting had led to work with this cabinetmaker, where he was paid by the item.

She opened the door and peered through. Jean-Paul was standing by one of his pieces – a curved sideboard created from a German pattern book. He stood watching her as she threaded her way through the workshop.

She put her hand on the polished surface. 'That is beautiful, Jean-Paul.'

He bowed his head in acknowledgement. 'It is already sold. And Mr Goldman has three more ordered.' He smiled. 'So, to what is the honour of this visit due, Miss Scorton?'

She started to slide open the drawers, peering into their aromatic depths. 'I just came to tell you I've been thinking about you all day, and not to be late home tonight. Also to tell you that the book about Tommy has arrived and it looks wonderful,' she murmured. She ran a finger across the curved front. 'And finally to tell you I love you, and I like having you in my life.'

He fluttered his polishing cloth at her. 'Away, away, you temptress. You will be losing me my job.'

She smiled sweetly at him. 'Not when you make such beautiful things.' She walked away and he watched her move through the dust and clutter of the workshop until she was out of sight.

She made her way along the dock past the new lighthouse and the ominously silent cranes. The fishing boats clicked together as they rocked against each other in the harbour.

Ahead of her in the house on the cliff was Hélène, quiet and still a little bit fey, but a wonderful housekeeper in the French style. Mara thought the three of them, Jean-Paul, Hélène and herself, survivors of the storm, were a family now. They shared a past and there was no doubt in Mara's mind that, God willing, and barring other storms, they would share a future.

Kitty Rainbow

Wendy Robertson

When the soft-hearted bare-knuckle fighter Ishmael Slaughter rescues an abandoned baby from the swirling River Wear, he knows that if he takes her home his employer will give her short shrift – or worse. So it is to Janine Druce, a draper woman with a dubious reputation but a child of her own, that he takes tiny Kitty Rainbow.

Kitty grows up wild, coping with Janine's bouts of drunkenness and her son's silent strangeness. And she is as fierce in her affections as she is in her hatreds, saving her greatest love for Ishmael, the ageing boxer who provides the only link with her parentage, a scrap of cloth she was wrapped in when he found her. Kitty realises that she cannot live her life wondering who her mother was, and in Ishmael she has father enough. And, when she finds herself pregnant, deprived of the livelihood on which she and the old man depended, she must worry about the future, not the past. But the past has a way of catching the present unawares . . .

'An intense and moving story set against the bitter squalor of the hunger-ridden thirties' *Today*

'A rich fruit cake of well-drawn characters . . .' *Northern Echo*

'Fans of big family stories must read Wendy Robertson' *Peterborough Evening Telegraph*

'A lovely book' *Woman's Realm*

0 7472 5183 5

HEADLINE

A Dark Light Shining

Wendy Robertson

'An intense and moving story set against the bitter squalor of the hunger-ridden thirties' *Today*

'A rich fruit cake of well-drawn characters'
Northern Echo

County Durham's New Morven, blighted by pit closures, is not a place where anyone in their right mind would come to live. And many in New Morven would say the strange pair who have just moved into the big house at the end of Mainstreet *are* out of their minds. But from the moment grocer's daughter Finnoula Montague meets eccentric Jenefer Loumis and her oddly childlike husband, she realises that up to now her life has been only half lived.

Jenefer seems to understand the young girl in a way Finn's tyrannical, bed-bound mother has never done. And when Finn meets unemployed miner Michael O'Toole, who opens her eyes to the shocking poverty – and intoxicating emotional riches – on her own doorstep, it is Jenefer who understands, almost better than Finn herself, what the young girl is experiencing. But when Finn is the victim of a vicious attack and Michael is thrown into prison, even Jenefer cannot arrest Finn's decline into a shadow of the vibrant girl she once was. But then Jenefer has a plan – to transport Finn to the world of gloss and glitter Jenefer herself once knew, a world that returns Finn to New Morven a very different young woman . . .

0 7472 4799 4

HEADLINE